THE BRIDGETOWER SONATA

Original French language edition © Actes Sud, 2017
Original Title: *La Sonate á Bridgetower: (SONATA MULATTICA)*
Translation by: Marjolijn de Jager

This is the first English Language Hardcover Edition
Copyright ©2021, Schaffner Press

License to reprint granted by:
The French Publishers' Agency
30 Vandam Street, Suite 5A
New York NY 10013
Telephone: 212-254-4540

Cover & Interior Design: Jordan Wannemacher

ISBN: 978-1-63964-012-6 (Paper)
ISBN: 978-1-943156-89-4 (EPUB)
ISBN: 978-1-63964-030-0 (E-PDF)

Library of Congress Control Number: 2021936377

Printed in the United States

The *Bridgetower* *Sonata*

SONATA MULATTICA

EMMANUEL DONGALA

TRANSLATED FROM THE FRENCH BY
MARJOLIJN DE JAGER

Schaffner Press

CONTENTS

Sonata mulattica composta per il mulatto Brischdauer
gran pazzo e compositore mulattico.

LUDWIG VAN BEETHOVEN, MAY 1803

PARIS, 1789

I

Borne by the last arpeggio notes of the final rondo, momentarily suspended above the violin—the time of an eighth-note rest—the bow attacked the coda of the last movement, the *allegro spiritoso*, in a dazzling play of shifting and multi-colored cadences whose final very sharp trills were lost in the sound of the full orchestra and the applause of the audience that, having held its breath until then, could no longer restrain itself.

Some people had risen, a more and more frequent infringement on propriety in the boxes of the elegant and worldly, lower aristocrats and upper middle-class. Even more disconcerting were those whose cries of *bravo, bravissimo* accompanied their applause, in emulation of the latest Italian fashion. But the noisy, inappropriate demonstrations did little to distract the young violinist. He was prepared for them.

Long before they'd left the Eisenstadt Chateau in Austria on their long, hazardous, and exhausting journey across Europe, his father had endlessly repeated to him that the customs were different in France, and particularly in Paris. At the palace of Prince Esterhazy where he had grown up and learned his manners, people were silent when they were listening to music: whether it was the music of the *Kapellmeister* Haydn or of an unknown musician just passing through, whether the audience was in a cheerful or a sullen mood, whether they were transported or bored to death, they wouldn't show their feelings until the last note was played and heard.

Such was not the case in Paris. Here music lovers, especially the regulars at the Concert Spirituel, came to be seen as much as to appreciate the music. In full formal dress, they weren't embarrassed to be chatting while a piece was being performed or even to express their opinion loudly and clearly. That was why the violinist was particularly happy because, except for two or three cries when he began the soloist's cadenza toward the end of the first movement, he'd managed to keep this audience of dilettantes spellbound.

Once the final note was played, he moved the violin to his right hand, which already held the bow and perched on the platform where they'd placed him so that, despite his child's size, the audience in the farthest rows could see him. He bowed very deeply, laying it on a little thickly as his father had forced him to rehearse a thousand times. He repeated the motion under the brilliance of the countless chandeliers whose lights came streaming down from their crystal pendants, as sparkles reflected on his honey-colored face. Finally he straightened up, his gaze embracing the immense concert hall with its slightly vaulted ceiling. The three levels were packed: the orchestra with its chairs and benches, the rows of boxes that circled the hall and, still higher up, the gallery that crowned the entire space. How many were they in the large hall of the Tuileries Palace, known as the Hall of the Cent-Suisses—the Hundred Swiss Guards—? Four, five, six hundred? A bit intimidated he turned to the conductor, who signaled the musicians to rise; they stood up and in turn began to applaud. That's when he forgot everything.

He forgot the impossible hours when his father dragged him out of bed to practice his scales, the tedious days doing exercises from the first *Etudes or Capriccios for Violin* by Rodolphe Kreutzer, the moments of paralyzing shyness that would overwhelm him each time the *Kapellmeister* Haydn received him to give him a lesson. He forgot all of it. Now it was only about this platform on which he stood with its gold-enhanced balustrade and its lyre-shaped spindles, the lights, the musicians some of whom played in embroidered attire, sword at the side and plumed hats on the seat, the aristocrats and upper bourgeoisie rivaling in elegance, the ladies with their sophisticated hairdos and hats, clad in frothy dresses with frills and flounces, all of it in a whirlwind of applause, of *bravos* and *bravissimos.*

It was total magic. Dazzled and dazed by the sounds and colors, he once again turned into the nine-year old he was and looked around, searching for his father. It wasn't hard to find him, standing in one of the loges reserved for ambassadors, diplomatic envoys, and other notable foreign visitors, the grand Negro of the Caribbean, more specifically of Barbados, dressed in a sumptuously embroidered woolen kaftan and a turban with gold-thread piping on his head, as a moist pearl flowed down his cheek and a smile full of emotion lit up his face.

II

When, followed by the conductor, the soloist disappeared into the wings and didn't return despite the cries for an encore from the concert hall, the audience finally realized that the concert had truly come to an end. Still, the applause wouldn't stop, it continued *diminu-endo* and did not die out completely until the musicians began to gather up their scores and instruments. Only at that point did the audience start to leave their seats.

People flocked from all sides, scattering around the hall as they headed haphazardly toward the various exit doors. Adding to the disorder, some men would suddenly stop to call out to an acquaintance or direct compliments at some pretty lady whose presence they suddenly pretended to notice, although they'd never stopped eyeing her during the concert. The hall, which only shortly before had quivered with harmonious sounds, was now nothing more than a brouhaha of confused voices amplified by the excellent acoustics of the vast amphitheater.

Following the general movement, the young performer's father decided to leave his seat as well and join his son in the wings. He had reserved a horsehair trimmed chair, in the first row of a balcony loge covered halfway up with wire mesh, one of the most expensive seats in the theater. He could have done no less, considering the way he'd introduced himself to Monsieur Joseph Legros, director of the Concert Spirituel. During the difficult negotiations he'd had with him to persuade him to publicize his child on the poster of one of his important concerts, he had presented himself as 'Frederick de Augustus Bridgetower of Bridgetown, Prince of Abyssinia'. He'd been somewhat irritated, as he felt that the honorable Legros addressed him in a condescending manner. Assuredly, this gentleman only knew Negroes as slaves of Martinique, Santo Domingo, or the island of Bourbon, who'd merely been free since they set foot on French soil. 'No one is a slave in France', so they said, even if most of them continued to be domestic personnel or hold small jobs, which did not apply to him. To have a discussion as equals, it was necessary to dispel any ambiguity right from the start. And he hadn't stopped at simply listing his titles and qualities: 'Envoy Plenipotentiary of Prince Nikolaus Esterhazy at his Eisenstadt Chateau in Austria', then added 'personal friend of Master Joseph Haydn whose symphonies are famous in Paris'. In Mr. Legros' thunderstruck face, he paused briefly before dropping the superb line: 'And my son was his student!'

After such a presentation it was certainly unthinkable for him to reserve a seat on ground floor benches with cushions stuffed with hay costing a mere three pounds.

He opened the door of his box, went down a few steps flanked on both sides by small marble columns and was back on the orchestra level.

Maneuvering through the crush, he tried to find his way to the wings taking care not to jostle anyone, for he wasn't familiar with the Parisians who could be very courteous at times, yet also quite uncouth at others, and who to him at any rate seemed pretty mystifying. His dark features stood out in the sea of pale faces and powdered wigs. As he moved on, eyes and ears open, he took in everything around him without letting it show. To those who courteously moved aside to let him through he reacted with a slight nod of his turbaned head, while from top to toe scrutinizing the boors who brazenly obstructed his passage, and splendidly ignoring those who gave him sidelong glances as they passed by although they were too polite to stare. All of it amused him. He felt as if he were watching a giant theatrical production in which the actors were performing their role under the command of an invisible director. As he was moving along, a woman ahead of him suddenly turned around. Instead of seeing her companion who, she thought, was right behind her, she found herself face to face with a tall Negro. In her surprise, she raised her hands to her face, eyes wide-open, uttering a little cry like that of a frightened guinea hen. Equally surprised, he took a step back. In so doing, he bumped into the backside of a dandy who, reeking of lily-of-the-valley, hat under his arm, had bent in half to kiss the hand of an actress with mincing step, who was nonchalantly waving a paper fan mounted on ivory close to her bosom. Contrite, the musician's father, briefly perturbed by the incident, hastened to ceremoniously offer his apologies to the gentleman and his coquette before continuing his way and restoring the princely attitude he had adopted. He had embraced this style after years as Prince Esterhazy's personal page, present at every court reception and ceremony; during the long walks in the chateau gardens he was his privileged companion, striving to impress the prince as he repeatedly invented his own country with created tales of two-horned rhinoceroses and giraffes with necks so long they'd rise above the tops of gigantic trees.

At last he managed to reach the musicians' platform. On the side was a screen with two painted wooden sections that concealed a short staircase leading to the wings and the boxes. He started to go up but stopped short when he heard loud voices. Curious, he moved closer to the diptych and looked through the split that separated the screen's two sections. He saw two rather agitated people who were still discussing the concert. He quickly figured out what sort they were, most likely a couple of fops who claimed to be setting the tone for all of Paris. The older of the two appeared to be the more upset. Wearing an outdated suit, a flecked garment with wide cuffs embroidered the same way as the edges of the pockets, a shirt with a jabot, a three-cornered hat on top of a wig with curls falling down on his shoulders, he was gesturing wildly as he spoke, raising and lowering a silver-handled cane.

'It's unfortunate for a French musician to be born in his own country. Any music that doesn't come from the other side of the mountains is bad. It's assessed even before it's heard. It's a disgrace!'

He spoke the last words pounding the hardwood floor with his cane.

'Let's not exaggerate, Monsieur Deshayes. You are a composer and you know that it is beauty that counts in music. Didn't you yourself say that "true beauty always resumes its rights"? So, whether that beauty comes from across the mountains or across the Rhine...'

In morning coat and short vest, his interlocutor spoke with a slight Italian accent pleasantly elongating the words he uttered, thereby slowing down the flow of his sentences. It gave his words an almost precious elegance, in contrast to the jerky, precipitous phrases of the man named Deshayes.

'But that's no reason to Italianize France to this extent! For example, take that young Negro we just heard. Why at his first concert on a French stage did they force him to play an Italian concerto? Isn't there a French composer who could have served?'

'Still, it's a Viotti concerto! The sublime Viotti whom every Parisian loves,' the other retorted, a slight sarcasm in his voice.

'So? It's not because French artists have begun to forgive him for not being born in France that we should think there are no other talented musicians in this country.'

'I do not wish to be discourteous, Monsieur Deshayes, but allow me, nevertheless, to tell you that the French audience, all too long imprisoned in Lully's monotony and weary of motets, is eager for something new. And it just so happens that the new is coming from across the mountains. This young man is a violinist. How would he be able to display his art and his talent if he didn't play the sonatas composed for this instrument by the great masters? Geminiani, Corelli, Vivaldi, Cherubini…'

Raising his cane abruptly, Deshayes interrupted him. He pointed it at the man who was contradicting him, careful not to touch him. From the spot where he was watching, the father of the young soloist thought for a moment that the discussion was going to turn into a skirmish. A duel so quickly ensues in Paris. He grew even more attentive when he realized that the object of the disagreement was his son.

'You're one of those half-educated individuals, blindly worshipping anything that's foreign to the national practice. Do you really think there are no other violin masters in France? Such disrespect!'

'Being a talented violinist isn't necessarily the same as a talented composer.'

'I would call you insolent, young man, if I didn't know you as long as I do.'

He emphasized these words by loudly thumping the floor with his cane before he continued in a voice shaking with indignation:

'And that sudden popularity of the violin! A shrill, hard, sharp sounding instrument. It has no delicacy or harmony and, contrary to the viola da gamba, the flute, or the harpsichord, it's exhausting for both performer and listener.'

'I'm sorry, sir,' his young opponent replied, 'the violin's predominance is here to stay. Do you know why? Because it can be an orchestra's principal instrument all by itself! It's no accident that every program of the Concert Spirituel contains a sonata or a concerto for the violin. And, what's more, did you know that a French violin school is in the process of being started right under your eyes, Monsieur Deshayes? Perhaps it doesn't have any great composers, but it already has some brilliant instrumentalists. And it's precisely these Italian masters who allow them to shine. I can cite...'

'I don't want to hear it...'

'In any event, that's not the point of our conversation at all. So let's not get all steamed up! All I asked you was what you thought of the concert we just heard, and you launch into the defense and illustration of the viola da gamba and the spinet and I don't know what other instruments besides. I maintain that this boy's performance was sublime. A fluid, ethereal bow, a phenomenal dexterity, a proud, daring, and precise execution. And that beautiful finish, astonishing for such a young musician! Did you notice the unusual silence during the soloist's cadenza? Did you see how the hall, ecstatic and standing, wouldn't stop calling him back even though they knew he wouldn't return to the platform?'

'No, I didn't see anything but extravagance, peculiarity, and antics on the stage. Certainly no delicacy whatsoever! I can't help it if some of you have a philistine ear. I'd rather put an end to this conversation. I shall make my exit now, sir.'

Out of breath, he seemed on the verge of an apoplectic fit. Loudly striking the floor with his cane once more, he lightly touched his tricorn, turned, and with rapid little steps left the theater through a side door. His young debater, surely not expecting such an abrupt ending, remained momentarily rooted to the spot, his eyes in the direction where Monsieur Deshayes had disappeared. Finally he shrugged his shoulders and moved toward the back of the now mostly empty hall, thereby turning his back to the young musician's father behind the screen. The latter hesitated: should he approach the man and thank him for having defended his son so well? Was he an important personality on the Parisian stage who might be useful to him, from whom he might obtain some help? He only hesitated for a minute. He hadn't come to Paris by chance, he had come because he had decided to follow the example of Leopold, father of the composer whose praises were being sung by every musician he knew and whose fame was approaching that of *Kapellmeister* Haydn: Wolfgang Gottlieb Mozart. The latter now called himself Wolfgang Amadeus, having replaced the extremely Germanic Gottlieb for its Latin equivalent, which he found more practical and more elegant. He was about thirty years old and had now been living in Vienna for quite some time. It was said that at age three he was already picking out notes on his sister's harpsichord, that at four he could remember a piece he'd played only once before, at five he was inventing his own music and at six, in front of the astonished Emperor of Austria, he had played a piece on the harpsichord blindfolded. Leopold knew immediately that his son was a musical prodigy. He had dragged him along, parading him through the great European courts as he financially exploited his talent. Frederick de Augustus had convinced himself that with his son's talent he would certainly earn a great deal more than the two hundred florins Prince Esterhazy paid him annually after five years of fine and loyal service. Following in Leopold's footsteps he, too, had embarked on his grand tour, beginning in Paris. True, he didn't yet know this world very well—he'd only been here about ten days—so he needed to pay very close attention and avoid any blunder that could pass for presumptuousness. But nothing ventured nothing gained and he decided to go and meet the man.

He left his hiding place, quickly caught up with him, and when he reached him bowed slightly:

'My respects, sir.'

The man stopped, surprised but not unfriendly.

'I beg you to forgive this rather unceremonious way of approaching you, but it's the urgency of the situation that forces me to act this way. I am Frederick de Augustus Bridgetower, the father of George, George Augustus Polgreen, the young soloist who was this evening's star.'

The man's face brightened. He held out his hand to Frederick de Augustus who shook it. Seeing him up close, the latter found him to be older than when he was watching him from behind the screen. He must have been about forty, just like himself.

'Delighted to meet you, sir. I am Giovanni Mane Giornovichi. I am a composer and a violinist as well...'

Frederick de Augustus almost fell over when he heard the name. He looked at Giornovichi in disbelief and could only repeat:

'You did say Giornovichi?'

Intrigued, the other stated:

'Yes, Giornovichi!'

What a happy surprise! What luck! Frederick de Augustus couldn't get over it. At first, when he was putting the program together for the concert, his original choice had been to have his son play a violin concerto by Giornovichi before he finally, opportunistically, decided on a concerto by Viotti. In any event, Giornovichi's reputation had crossed borders as much for his virtuosity on the violin as for his antics. He was known to be quarrelsome, a crook around the edges, a cheater especially at billiards and at faro, the gambling card game at which he excelled. He destroyed new friendships as quickly as he squandered money. He used different names depending on his location, an understandable precaution for someone who more than once had to beat a hasty retreat from a town where he was being pursued. And yet, he was warm and quite likeable.

'I am very honored to meet you, Monsieur Giornovichi. Your reputation has already been made, you are one of the best violinists in Paris.'

'What you mean to say is *the* best violinist in Paris.'

Modesty is certainly not his strong point, Frederick de Augustus thought but he didn't pick up on this assertion and continued.

'I happened to be close to the wings and couldn't help overhearing some of your exchange with Monsieur Deshayes…'

'Oh, don't talk to me about that old boor. Stuck in his ariettas, he's one of those people who are afraid of anything new, new instruments and any new form of music, especially violin sonatas and concertos. There are thousands of Deshayes around here, still clinging to their fancy court attire, as he does, who don't realize that once in contact with French soil all music originating elsewhere is transformed into something undeniably French. Is there anything more French than Lully's music or Lully the musician? I congratulate myself on having stayed calm.'

'In any case, I really want to thank you for having defended my son so well…'

'I'm very impressed with your son. In my opinion he's a real prodigy! How old is he?'

Frederick de Augustus hesitated. Should he give him his true age? When his son had begun to conquer Europe, Leopold often claimed that Wolfgang was younger than he actually was. Why shouldn't he do the same?

'He's eight years old,' he said.

'That's incredible! I, too, made my debut at the Concert Spirituel. Still, I had to wait three years before being accepted. And yet I am Italian,' he added with a smile that was supposed to be ironic. 'Your son ought to give another concert. The French audience will come running for such a unique spectacle, a young mulatto violinist. They love anything that comes from the East.'

'I intend to. And should we be so lucky as to have a second concert, we will be sure to play one of your compositions. One of your violin concertos.'

'I would be delighted. It would be a pleasure to help him rehearse.'

'The problem is that finding a hall is not easy. The negotiations with Monsieur Legros were extremely trying.'

'There are other halls besides the one at the Tuileries Palace. There's the one at the Panthéon, at the Opéra, at the Concert des Amateurs... Hold on, I know Gossec the former director of the Concert Spirituel very well. Currently he is with... No, you'd better go see a good friend of mine, the Chevalier de Saint-George. He will undoubtedly recognize himself in your son. I'm sure he'll help you. He has connections. He's the director of the Théâtre des Amateurs. If you like, I'll write you a letter of introduction.'

Frederick de Augustus already had a letter of recommendation from Haydn to the illustrious chevalier but didn't mention it to Giornovichi. Better to let him think that he knew no one yet in the French capital.

'It's Providence that put you on our path, Monsieur Jarnowick. I thank you from the bottom of my heart.'

'Did you say Jarnowick?'

'Oh, forgive me. At the courts of Austria and Hungary where my son was raised, you are known by the name Ivan Jarnowick.'

'I'm glad to hear that. I was born in Italy, my parents come from Croatia, and it's France that discovered my talent. I've just arrived from Dusseldorf and am getting ready to leave for Saint Petersburg. So, Jarnowick, Janiewick, or Giornovichi, Ivan or Giovanni, what difference does a name make for someone who's at home anywhere in Europe! And you, are you Turkish? A Moor? Your name doesn't indicate it. Ah, I know, you're American!'

'Yes, I come from far, very far away and it's a long road that brought me here. But I'll tell you more about that at another time. What's more urgent right now is my son's future. I want his stay in Paris to be a success.'

'Don't hesitate. Come and see me for a letter of recommendation to Saint-George. You can find me at the Palais-Royal. I'm often there in the afternoon, at the Café Le Caveau. If you don't find me there, look for me at the Café de Foy, right next door.'

'Thank you very much. I'm now going to find my son who's waiting for me in the wings. He must be getting impatient.'

'I look forward to seeing you again, Monsieur…?'

'Bridgetower. Frederick de Augustus Bridgetower.'

They parted. By now the hall was practically empty. Giornovichi headed for the back door while Frederick de Augustus turned around and moved toward the wings.

III

Frederick de Augustus didn't find his son in the wings, all he saw were some backstage workers clearing the floor, rearranging chairs and music stands or, perched on stepstools, extinguishing candles with snuffers on handles long enough to reach the chandeliers way up high. The men didn't seem at all surprised to see the oriental prince emerge without warning from the other side of the cluttered set; ignoring him completely, they continued working. Perhaps they thought he was some actor in costume and make-up on his way to the adjoining hall of the Italian Theater, blasé as they were about their universe, the backstage world where everything was merely illusion and trompe-l'oeil. He ignored them as well and, with resolute step to make them think that he knew where he was going, he crossed the full length of the stage exiting through the wings on the other side. He figured that his son could only be in the office of Monsieur Legros, which he knew from having been there several times during the preparations for the concert.

He spotted the staircase he was looking for, went up two landings, turned right down a hallway covered with a thick rug, and stopped in front of a door with a copper sign marked 'Director'. Disregarding the metallic knocker that hung just below the sign, he used his knuckles to knock on the door.

'Come in,' he heard.

Frederick de Augustus entered. Legros was talking with a young man who was simply but elegantly dressed. He was struck by the lengthy sideburns that came down and curved alongside the man's ears, bestowing an extraordinary look upon a face that would otherwise have been totally nondescript.

'Welcome, Monsieur,' Legros said as he came forward and shook his hand, then turning to the man: 'Let me introduce Frederick de Augustus Bridgetower. He is the father of this evening's prodigy.'

'Delighted to meet you, sir,' the man responded without rising from his seat. 'So this is your son,' he exclaimed as he watched George who had stood up from the wing chair where he'd been sitting.

'Monsieur Bridgetower, this is Rodolphe Kreutzer.'

Frederick de Augustus started. Once again, he couldn't get over it. Paris was a city of miracles! Where besides here, he thought, could one meet two of Europe's greatest violinists at one concert? He resolved not to be taken by surprise any more, even if someone were to tell him that Viotti himself was hiding behind the grand armoire in the back of the office. Kreutzer! Kreutzer was even more important to him than Giornovichi.

At first the violin lessons George had been taking didn't follow any rigorous method but depended on the instructors, each of whom had his own method and exercises. So it was hard for him to be aware of his child's progress. As fate would have it, on the very day that he heard about Leopold he also heard that he was not only an educator—his son Wolfgang had never had any other teacher—but was himself a violinist as well and had written a treatise entitled *On the Fundamental Principles of Violin Playing*. Thus he had decided to use the same treatise for George. After an unsuccessful search in Vienna, he'd ended up by obtaining a copy from a printer in Salzburg, and so the work became the handbook that every one of his son's teachers was required to use.

After some time, however, he noticed that none of the violinists at the Esterhazy Palace was using Leopold's book. They were all using the exercises by a certain Kreutzer for their practice. Initially he wasn't too concerned about this but because he noticed countless musicians, month after month, exchanging his son's bow for a new and radically different model, his curiosity gradually changed into preoccupation. No one knew or wanted to explain to him what was going on, not even his son's instructor, who may have been afraid to lose his post, until one evening he couldn't bear questioning it any longer and approached Luigi Tomasini, the first violinist of the prince's orchestra. He liked talking with Tomasini for several reasons: he was the finest violinist in Haydn's orchestra, he loved imparting his fervor for music, for the violin, and Frederick de Augustus thoroughly enjoyed his company despite the irritating remarks about his Moorish origin, which he persisted in laying at his door. When he saw him coming, Tomasini thought that *il Moro*, as he called him, was there to exchange a few pleasantries with him, as was his wont after a concert. But this time such was not the case. Normally so sure of himself, Frederick de Augustus admitted to him with some dismay that, not being a musician, he had a vague feeling there was something wrong in the way his son was learning the violin. He had come for advice.

'Let's begin with the handbook you're using,' Tomasini told him. 'Leopold wrote his method at a time when concerts were given in small aristocratic salons. And, as unbelievable as it may seem today, there were several types of bows, depending on what they were to be used for, and even depending on the country where they were used. For example, there was a "sonata bow"' and an "Italian dance bow".

17

What mattered,' Tomasini went on, 'was the clarity of the sound of the violin, not its power. But today everything is changing: concert halls are becoming larger and larger, the violin is establishing itself increasingly as a soloist's instrument, and the concerto has become the fashionable genre, especially in Italy and France. Consequently, now master of the place, the soloist shows himself to his best advantage by performing his piece with greater speed, sharp registers, shifts, double chords, in short by displaying his dexterity, what am I saying, his virtuosity! A la Vivaldi. So, to provide for these new developments, a new bow is needed that allows the violin to produce a sound that is both powerful and carries, while also offering more possibilities of playing. And that, *mio caro Moro*, is the bow you see now, with a cambered bow-stick cut from wood from Brazil. It's been developed in Paris by François Xavier Tourte with advice from Viotti and Kreutzer. It's lighter, more stable, more responsive, but above all else the range of resonant intensity is broadened and brings out a more powerful sound. Nothing to do with the wooden amourette bow and the convex arch your son is still using!'

Tomasini didn't even realize he was speaking to him in Italian. If he was using his mother tongue it was because he responded to Frederick de Augustus spontaneously. It didn't bother the latter at all, Italian was one of the European languages he spoke. Swept up by his own passion, Tomasini continued: '*The violin is the bow*,' as Viotti said. Buy your son a Tourte bow tomorrow. Forget about old Leopold, turn your son toward Kreutzer and do it soon!'

When he left the conversation Frederick de Augustus felt demoralized and yet enlightened. Thus, despite his worship of father Mozart, he had resigned himself to the fact that the latter's method no longer suited his current approach: if he wanted his son to triumph in Paris like little Wolfgang, he had no choice but to abandon Leopold in favor of Kreutzer.

And there, standing before him, was Kreutzer himself, holding the
flyer that had been handed out at the entrance to the concert hall, which
read:

Mr. Georges Bridgetower - • • *Violon.*
Début de Mr. Georges Bridgetower, né aux colonies
anglaises, âgé de 9 ans.

MR. GEORGES BRIDGETOWER . . . Violin
Debut performance of Mr. Georges Bridgetower,
born in the English colonies, 9 years of age.

The person who had written the flyer was wrong. George wasn't
born in the colonies, but no matter! That touch of exoticism could only
appeal to the public. It had certainly attracted Mr. Kreutzer's attention.

'I am very happy to meet you, Monsieur Kreutzer. You have no idea
how honored we are, my son and I, to make your acquaintance.'

'Monsieur Kreutzer is the solo violinist at the Théâtre-Italien. He is
a teacher as well. Highly appreciated by the queen, he was for a long
time the first violinist of the royal orchestra. Oh, yes, I forgot, he is also
a composer.'

That was a pointless detail. Everyone knew that a great instrumentalist was also a composer or, at least, had composed one work in which
he'd included passages to show off his virtuosity on his own instrument.
This man Legros tended to take him for an ignoramus.

'Most importantly, Monsieur Legros, you forgot to mention that
Monsieur Kreutzer is the author of the brilliant *Etudes* or *Caprices for
violin.*'

Kreutzer who until that moment had seemed indifferent suddenly
showed an interest. He looked at the man in the turban and caftan as if
he were seeing him for the first time.

'You are familiar with my *Etudes* where you come from?'

'There's not a day that goes by without my son working on one of your exercises. Isn't that true, George?'

'Your lessons are very difficult, Monsieur Kreutzer, but I've already mastered a few of them,' the boy stated with a touch of juvenile pride.

'I haven't finished them all. There are only a few in circulation. You were outstanding this evening, young man. More than technical mastery, I think you have a true talent.'

'Thank you, sir,' George replied.

'I didn't hesitate for a moment to book him,' Legros added.

In his heart of hearts, Frederick de Augustus considered him a liar. It had taken several days of discussion and the mention of the name Haydn before he would accept giving George a chance. He was beginning to dislike Legros more and more, but he shouldn't show it. Kreutzer pretended not to have heard any of it and, turning to Frederick de Augustus, he asked:

'Why did you choose a full violin for your son rather than a three-quarter size, which is more appropriate for his age? It would have prevented him from having any momentary loss of bow control.'

'That was because of the sheer size of the hall. We needed a broad enough sound to fill the whole space.'

'It's not that serious; in any event, not many people would have noticed it. How old are you, young man?'

'Nine years old', George was about to say when his father quickly answered for him.

'Eight,' Frederick de Augustus said. 'They made a mistake on the flyer.'

'Eight years old! Three years younger than I was when I gave my first public concert. With time and hard work you will mature. Well, I must go. I hope to see you again.'

He said goodbye to George and his father. 'So, it's all set then, we'll reserve the Machines Hall for this concert,' he said as he took his leave from Legros who saw him to the door, and left.

'Monsieur Bridgetower, the evening was a complete success,' Legros said after closing the door. 'Perhaps we could plan a second concert?'

With his hand on his son's shoulder Frederick de Augustus was looking at him. Legros had certainly changed. Happy, jovial. He was no longer the arrogant man who at their first meeting had said in a disdainful tone: 'Of course I have booked young musicians making their debut in Paris before, but never a totally unknown Negro violinist. I wouldn't have hesitated if he came from Italy. But this, really....'

When Monsieur Legros had finally agreed to book George, the conditions of the contract offered were unfair.

'I'm taking a big risk,' he'd explained. 'I'll lose a lot of money if the hall is only half sold.' In the end Frederick de Augustus had agreed without too much grumbling to accept a fixed fee. He knew very well he was being cheated but for now the important thing was to get his son a booking as soloist in one of Paris's most prestigious halls.

'The hall was packed,' he began again. 'For an unknown who didn't come from Italy that's quite a triumph, isn't it, Monsieur Legros? A second concert, most assuredly. But after this evening's success we will have to take another look at the contract.'

'I am ready to double your fee.'

Frederick de Augustus didn't believe in Legros' offer. The man was too shrewd.

'How much did the concert take in tonight?' he asked.

'I can't tell you yet. The treasurer won't give me the figures until tomorrow.'

'Well then, we will discuss it after I have received my fee,' he replied.

He wasn't going to be duped anymore. This time around he would require at least a percentage of the ticket price.

'Fine. But remember, I'm prepared to double that fee. Let's meet tomorrow afternoon,' Legros proposed.

Frederick de Augustus and his son shook hands with him and left his office.

IV

They left the Tuileries Palace through the large portico of the central pavilion on the side that faced the Louvre. Frederick de Augustus knew it was after eight o'clock when he saw that the streetlights were already lit, because in the month of April the sun didn't set before that time in Paris. Without the halos of light drifting around the lamps, it would already have been dark. It had truly been a long evening since, to be safe, he had presented himself and his son at the Tuileries Palace at four o'clock, even though the concert was not to start until half past six; he wanted to be sure to have enough time, if need be, to deal with any bad surprise Legros might have had in store for him. He'd carefully inquired about the man and was afraid he might play the same dirty trick he'd played on Leopold's son during his third stay in Paris some ten years earlier.

Legros was already the director of the Concert Spirituel then. Wolfgang desperately needed money. The small gallant pieces he himself qualified as 'little nothings' that he played here and there in the salons and the few classes he gave hither and yon didn't earn him very much money. So, with a recommendation, he approached Monsieur Legros who, aware of the musician's reputation, promised to book him for a concert and even reserved a specific date. Happy with the offer, Wolfgang diligently composed a sinfonia concertante for four instruments – oboe, clarinet, horn, and bassoon – for the occasion. However, Paris then just as today, was full of second-class musicians who took themselves for great masters and were flourishing in a milieu of intrigues and jealousy. Wolfgang couldn't resist making fun of them, blithely mimicking them whenever he had the chance. It so happened that one of those musicians was a personal friend of Legros. Incensed, this man, whose name was Cambini, formed a conspiracy against Wolfgang and coerced his friend Legros who, without any hesitation, canceled the concert on the very day it was to take place. It's no surprise that Wolfgang, known as Amadeus Mozart in Paris, despised that city! It's no surprise that he treated the French musicians around him as arrogant, crude, and idiotic. That is why Frederick de Augustus, fearful that such a misadventure might happen to them, arrived at the concert hall two hours early.

※

It was time to go back to the hotel. To hire a carriage at that late hour they had to go to the Place du Palais-Royal where coaches would be parked. Hesitating a moment to decide on the shortest route, Frederick de Augustus took a guess and walked straight ahead in the direction of the Louvre Palace. They emerged from a shady area of the wide central lane they had taken only to end up in another one a few steps later, the pale beam of the streetlamps not being strong enough to fully cover the area between two lamp poles. They passed the Place du Carrousel and then, before reaching the Cour Carré du Louvre, they noticed the Palais-Royal on their left, bathing in the splendor of its countless chandeliers.

'How beautiful!' George said in awe.

Then they were walking beneath the foliage of the chestnut trees, forming a natural rooftop above them. They had never seen anything like it, not in Eisenstadt, not even in Vienna. Rather than returning to the hotel right away, Frederick de Augustus felt like strolling a little longer to make the most of the spectacle without worrying too much about his son who was beginning to yawn.

'You must be hungry, George,' he said, however.

'Oh yes, very hungry.'

'I suggest we have dinner here. We certainly deserve it. You were fantastic tonight, you were touched by grace. I am really very proud of you,' he said as he caressed the boy's head.

George turned to him and smiled. In contrast to his mother, his father didn't pay him compliments very often. Then, without any transition, he asked:

'Papa, why did you lie about my age? I'm nine, not eight.'

Already thinking about the dinner menu, Frederick was caught off-guard.

'I didn't lie,' he said, 'you were born on the 29th of February.'

'But I turned eight on February 29th of last year.'

'Yes, but there's been no other date like that since and there won't be one for another three years. So, you are eight years old.'

'So in two years I'll still be eight?'

'You know, Haydn was born on April 1st but always asserted he was born the day before, on the 31st of March. Why? Because he didn't want some practical joker to take him as an April Fool. Are you going to tell me that what he did makes no sense? Technically you are eight. Don't worry about the rest, just trust me. The younger you are the more you'll amaze the public, and the more you amaze the public, the more famous you will be. Come along now! Let's find a restaurant.'

✄

They couldn't have looked more different. The father, tall and dark-skinned, was dressed in Oriental fashion. Under his caftan he was wearing a ruby red shirt edged in lace around the collar, its tails disappearing in a baggy pair of pants held up by a wide strip of fabric tied around the waist. Barely half the size of his father, the son, whose complexion was more golden than brown, was dressed European style, jacket, vest, silk pants and stockings.

From the start Frederick de Augustus hadn't had any doubt whatsoever about the way his son should be dressed for this performance: his model was Leopold's son! On the same day that he'd settled the date of the concert with Legros, he had begun to study a portrait of Wolfgang at age seven at his first concert in Paris. He was wearing a dark red velvet garment with silver frogs and embroidery on the cuffs of his sleeves. Underneath the suit he wore a vest over a shirt with a lace jabot. His hair rolled up into cadenettes on his temples was tied with a large ribbon into a ponytail. But that portrait was already ten years old. He could use it for inspiration but not exactly reproduce it. Fashion had changed—for example, the jacket had replaced the suit—and he found the dark red color unflattering to his son's complexion. He had him wear a mauve jacket with gold-lamé threads and had also replaced the jabot with a white chiffon scarf tied in the back. On the other hand, his son didn't need to wear his hair in a ponytail, as large natural curls came down to his neck like foamy waves, enhancing the beauty of his face.

※

The thought of dressing exotically hadn't come to Frederick de Augustus right away. He'd started with the principle that if you want to succeed in a foreign country you should be flexible and smooth out any inherited rough patches. This meant you should eat like the locals, dress like them, act like them as much as possible. This was all the more true for a city like Paris, whose population saw itself as the most sophisticated of Europe. So he had no other choice but to dress Parisian style. For that reason he'd put on a satin shirt, its tails slipped into a tight-fitting pair of pants held up by suspenders. Over the shirt, which was adorned with a jabot, he wore a vest encrusted here and there with gold-colored sequins, which he'd buttoned up. Lastly, he'd put on the major part of his attire, a brocade morning coat that he had tailored in Paris itself and that, with its braid-trimmed sleeves, gave him a look he believed to be both solemn and relaxed. It all suited him very well until the moment he looked at himself in the mirror. Something wasn't right. But what was it? His hair! He'd chosen a copiously powdered wig with two rolls just above his ears. The contrast between the wig and his dark face was striking. Suddenly it seemed ludicrous to him, grotesque even. He remembered those rigged out little domestic servants who served as curios for the ladies at the European courts, little piccaninnies whom they would display and whose heads they would sometimes caress while they were being served by them; those ladies who in their naughty confidences would whisper that a little Negro with white teeth, full lips, satiny skin they'd say was burnt by the sun, was sweeter than a spaniel or an angora rabbit.

A raging sense of rebellion coursed through him. He ripped off his wig and threw it on the ground. No, I won't look ludicrous by imitating them.

He opened the large trunk containing their belongings. On their way to Paris they had spent a few weeks in Vienna where they stayed with Angelo Soliman and his wife Magdalena. He had met Soliman years earlier through Joseph Haydn who belonged to the same masonic lodge as he did. He was the best-known African in Viennese high society. The originality of his apparel—an elegant combination of Oriental and European fashions—was particularly appealing to Frederick de Augustus and he wanted something similar for his own wardrobe. Soliman then brought him to one of the innumerable boutiques run by descendants of the Turkish families who had stayed in the city after the Ottoman Empire collapsed. He purchased a fine Oriental-style outfit, complete with a Mameluke saber with a mother-of-pearl and silver knob. Having rid himself of his wig, he submerged his hand in the trunk, pulled out the turban and placed it right on top of his hair.

❦

Father and son finally emerged from beneath the arcades of the Palace and started looking for a restaurant. A streetlight was suspended from every arch of the arcade and there were so many lamps brightening the area that it almost looked like a kind of half-light. The place was teeming with people. They were moving around the galleries, sitting in front of cafés, in front of boutiques to admire the expensive merchandise through the vast glass panes of the shop windows. There were some odd scenes, such as the poet blaring his verses in front of a bookstore, indifferent to the ceaseless racket around him, or the chess players continuing to move their pawns as if the colorful, noisy crowd surrounding them didn't exist, or the small group of men around an orator perched on a stool, loudly calling for freedom of opinion and the abolition of *lettres de cachet*. Turning his gaze toward the central garden, Frederick de Augustus noticed some mostly unaccompanied women in rather gaudy clothes having refreshments at tables set up outside in an area adorned with flower beds. The artificial light from the streetlamps bestowed on them a kind of aura he wouldn't have seen on the famous *Graben-nymphen*, the girls of the houses on the Graben Platz in Vienna. Were it not for his son's presence, he would not only have lingered longer to observe them, but he would certainly have moved more closely toward them. It occurred to him he could come back here another time without his son's inconvenient company. They said that if Paris was the capital of France, the Palais-Royal was the capital of Paris. How very true!

As they wandered around, they passed several cafés and restaurants but, unfamiliar with the area, he didn't know which one to choose. He didn't want a cheap place, some greasy spoon where their different clothes would be out of place. Then he remembered that Giornovichi had mentioned two addresses to him, the Caveau and the Café de Foy. Perhaps he would be at one of them.

They passed by the Caveau first, but they didn't like it, it was too packed, too noisy. They moved on to the Café de Foy, a little farther down. This was a different story, a different atmosphere. They went in. Large and clean, the walls decorated with mirrors and covered with taffeta, it was three-quarters full, with patrons whose elegance was noticeable at first glance. They found a marble table and sat down on a stool covered in red velvet. The menu was à la carte, with more than twenty items from which to choose. It was perfect for them. This way they would avoid the embarrassment of not knowing what to select. Frederick de Augustus had no desire to pass for a country bumpkin just newly arrived in the capital.

⁂

They had finished their dessert when Giovanni Giornovichi literally bumped into them, calling out loud and clear: 'Well now, Frederick de Augustus Bridgetower and his child prodigy! I knew I'd find you here. Such good timing, I have something for you. May I?' Without waiting for an answer, he pulled up a stool and sat down.

'So, you American,' he said, 'may I offer you a round?'

'No, thank you, we're just about to go home. It's been a long day and tomorrow will be a full day as well. George needs his rest.'

'Come, a little liqueur won't hurt. Waiter?'

'Yes, sir, one moment,' the waiter said as he came running with a menu.

With the assurance of a regular customer, Giornovichi pushed the menu aside and ordered three glasses of liqueur, including one for George who refused and asked for a glass of barley water instead. Giornovichi raised his glass and made a toast to the health and success of his two guests.

While they had their drinks, he wouldn't stop talking. His tone of voice changing constantly, he went through a whole range of different sentiments: reverential when he mentioned a patron of the arts who had remunerated him handsomely for a commission, mocking—condescending even—when he spoke about a rival musician whose technique he ridiculed, jovial and shaking with mischievous pleasure when he evoked his not always honest prowess at the game tables, irascible when he carried on against a music reviewer who'd panned him in his newspaper. Everything in his conduct reinforced the legend that followed him everywhere, that of an unpredictable braggart ready for a fight.

Nevertheless, all this boasting didn't bother Frederick de Augustus in the least, quite the contrary, he was delighted and flattered to be sharing his table with Europe's most famous violinist and, in addition, their conversation made him aware of a spirit that had managed to stay free in a society of well-established conventions.

When they got up from the table to say goodbye, Giornovichi stopped him:

'I had time to write the letter of recommendation that will let you introduce your young one to the Chevalier de Saint-George.'

He took the letter out of the pocket of his morning coat.

'Here. I didn't close it so you'll be able to read what I wrote. Believe me when I, who know this city, tell you that it's always good to know what they say about you in a letter, even if it's full of praise. Here you are.'

Frederick didn't need any recommendation from Giornovichi, but how could he say so without offending him? He said nothing: better to have someone of Giornovichi's temperament on his side. He took the letter.

'Thank you.'

'Just be sure that you seal it first. It would be unseemly to hand him an open letter. I hope you'll come back here soon. Without your little boy,' he said with a knowing wink. 'You haven't seen anything of the Palais-Royal yet.'

V

George's fatigue didn't keep Frederick de Augustus from strolling beneath the palace arcades again on their way to the street where the taxis were parked. A few of the streetlights had already run out of oil and gone out but it didn't reduce the illumination or the activity of the place at all. Scattered around in the various galleries, several shops were still open, offering an array of products from the most common to the most unusual, each merchant shouting more loudly than the next, hoping thereby to rouse the curiosity of the passersby. George couldn't get over it. For a boy who'd spent his entire childhood in the restricted atmosphere of the Esterhazy Palace this was a wonderland. The Chateau Esterhazy was magnificent, of course, but its baroque beauty, its opulent salons with their murals depicting mythological scenes, and even the decorum of the celebrations held there, were not of the kind that would set the imagination of a child on fire. Here, on the other hand, everything abounded with life and lightheartedness. Suddenly he stopped, fascinated by an optician-physician who was doing an extraordinary magic trick: he managed to ignite a little wooden twig treated with sulphur simply by rubbing it inside a flask containing phosphorus! It was easier than using a flint to start a fire.

He could have stayed there for hours watching it had his father not forced him away.

A few steps further on it was the father's turn to come to a halt in front of a stand displaying newspapers, novels, and the most recent up-to-the-minute pamphlets, the kind that the countless political or philosophical clubs shaking up the Parisian scene were publishing non-stop. His attention was drawn to a novel *Les Liaisons dangereuses*, not so much because of the book's title as the name of the author, Choderlos de Laclos who, for him, was associated with the fiasco of *Ernestine*, the first opera by Saint-George, a three-act comedy in ariettas for which Laclos had written the libretto. The height of platitudes and bad taste, Laclos' words had been booed from start to finish of the show. They'd dragged Saint-George's music along into the disgrace, having been unfairly assimilated with the inanities of the libretto. Consequently, there had been only one performance. And to think that Marie-Antoinette, the queen, had been present at the opening night! In any event, ever since Frederick de Augustus had known about this he had such a poor opinion of this artillery captain, spur-of-the-moment librettist, that it surprised him to hear the bookstore owner recommend the work with such fervor. According to him, it had enjoyed a phenomenal success from the moment it came out. Everyone had read it and all refined people had to have it in their library. Just words of a smooth talker, Frederick de Augustus thought. No one had spoken to him about this book, not even in Brussels where on Soliman's recommendation he'd spent almost a month to prepare for his arrival in Paris. Still, he stretched out his hand, picked up the item, and started leafing through it. He realized it was an epistolary novel and right away he remembered *Pamela, or Virtue Rewarded*, an English novel he'd read at Eisenstadt when he was the prince's personal page and had access to his library. At the time that epistolary novel, too, had enjoyed an enormous success. Frederick de Augustus had read it in the French translation since the library didn't have a copy in the original language. Although Prince

31

Esterhazy spoke only German and Hungarian, his library also contained works in French, gifts from distinguished visitors to the chateau who wrongfully assumed the prince spoke that language as well, since in Europe it was considered to be the language of distinguished individuals.

Frederick de Augustus skipped the lengthy 'Foreword from the publisher to the reader' as well as the long 'Preface by the editor', and began to read the first lines of the opening chapter:

'You see, my dear friend, I keep my word, & that hats and bobbles do not take up all my time; I'll always have time for you. However, in this one day I've seen more finery than in the four years we have spent together, & I believe that the magnificent Tanville (1) will be more upset at my first visit, when I fully plan to ask what she thought she was doing to us each time she came to...' [1]

He stopped there. He wasn't really taken with any of it. It wasn't his kind of world with its hats and bobbles, no wonder that the libretto of *Ernestine* had seemed so ludicrous.

He closed the book and put it back on the shelf. The disappointed salesman didn't let him go, however. 'Wait, I have something else that is bound to please you, a novel that just came out. It's not well-known yet but I anticipate an even more extraordinary success than that of the Laclos!' Frederick de Augustus had no interest whatsoever in listening to his sales pitch and was beginning to move away when the salesman said: 'The story takes place where you come from, you know.' – 'Where I come from? Where is that?' Frederick de Augustus asked, intrigued. 'Well, your home... the islands where Negroes live.' – 'Because every Negro comes from the islands, is that it?' – 'No sir, of course not. But as I look at you, you certainly don't come from Africa. From America perhaps?' Frederick de Augustus didn't respond. He took the book the

---

1. Translation, MdJ.

salesman handed him. *Paul et Virginie*, he read, by Henri Bernardin de Saint-Pierre, an author he'd never heard of. Did this scoundrel really want to rip him off? 'Never mind,' he told himself, his curiosity aroused. 'I'll take it.'

As he was getting his change, he saw his son next to him who seemed to be growing impatient. He looked truly exhausted.

'You're sleeping standing up, my poor George! Let's go home now.'

They left the arcades and went into the street where the carriages were waiting, some for their masters and others that could be hired by distance or by the hour, reflecting every nuance of the social hierarchy: coaches belonging to people from the court, hired limousines for wealthy foreigners, fiacres and cabriolets. A cabriolet would get them back to the hotel faster since it was the most rapid form of transportation, but with its track being too narrow and its body too tall it could easily roll over. Besides, they didn't have very far to go, just to the Rue Guénégaud, and all they had to do was cross the Seine via the Pont-Neuf, go across the Cité, and slightly up the Quai de la Monnaie. So why run the risk of breaking your bones in a stupid accident only to get back more quickly? Since the cleaner and more comfortable hired cars could only be rented by the half-day, they had no other choice but to take a fiacre. Frederick de Augustus knew that the fiacre coachmen were reputed to be rude to those who allowed themselves to be intimidated. Would they be the same way with foreigners?

Followed by his son, he walked with steady step to where the fiacres were parked. Their appearance caused a stir among the coachmen. They were pushing each other to offer their services as they addressed him as *Monsieur le Marquis* or *Monsieur le Comte*, or else *Monsieur le Duc*. Not to mention *Monseigneur* and *Milord*. It brought Frederick de Augustus abruptly back to his own reality: the entire time he'd been wandering among the cosmopolitan crowd at the Palais-Royal he'd forgotten that he was a black prince wearing a turban and an extravagant kaftan. For a

33

second he wondered if there wasn't a hint of irony or mockery in the way they approached him, but he didn't show it. Quite the contrary, more princely than ever, he chose the best dressed coachman of the lot, who was wearing a bright red livery garnished with silver frog fasteners.

'The Hotel Britannique on Rue Guénégaud,' he instructed.

VI

George fell asleep as soon as he slipped under the feather eider-down and his head hit the pillow. He'd undressed quickly, tossing his clothes in a jumble into the drawer of the dresser in the room he shared with his father. Frederick de Augustus, on the other hand, took his time. After removing his turban, he began to undress, one by one taking off the layers of his attire: the kaftan, the band of fabric that served as a belt, the vest, the shirt, and so on. When he was done, he slipped his feet into his slippers, put on a dressing gown, and put the clothes back in the trunk, neatly folding and arranging them first.

Contrary to his expectations and despite the late hour, he didn't fall asleep right away. Too many things had happened that extraordinary day for his over-excited mind to find the tranquility that leads to sleep. Not wanting to disturb his son, already asleep with closed fists and the serene face of a carefree child, he chose to relax in one of the wing chairs in the corner of the area that served as a living room. Sunk back in the chair, his forearms on the armrests, his heels on a small low table, his mind randomly bounced around the various events of that long day before focusing on the major one, his son's concert. His satisfaction should have been complete, George had captured the highly demanding Parisian audience. And yet, the more he dwelled on the evening's events, the more the importance of the concert itself faded away to to be replaced by his reflections on the ambience around the performance: the immense hall, the public, the musicians, the comportment of the audience. He had a vague sense of having missed something essential, which troubled him, made him uncomfortable. To be accepted into a world structured by the protocol of princes and aristocrats, he had wanted to conform to their ways, expunging anything that in their eyes might have seemed primitive. The foundation on which he'd constructed his public persona seemed to have grown shaky in that concert hall, which he hadn't expected at all since he believed that his stay in Brussels had taught him enough about Paris.

✻

A French-speaking city in the Austrian Netherlands, Brussels was the obligatory pathway for every German-speaking musician who expected to appear on stage in Paris. It was considered to be its cultural backyard, the ideal place for a dress rehearsal before a grand opening on the Parisian stage. On his way to France, Wolfgang himself had stopped there with his father to give two or three concerts. That, at least, is what Soliman had asserted and Frederick de Augustus had no reason not to believe him, with Wolfgang and Soliman, like Haydn, as brothers in the same Masonic Lodge.

Frederick had loved his Brussels stopover. Planning on two weeks, he'd stayed almost twice as long. From the first week on, the French he'd spoken so little during his time in Hungary and Austria had come back to him without any difficulty. In addition, he made his son converse with him in French at least two hours a day so that he, too, would be able to handle it comfortably. He adhered to that ritual as much as he adhered to George not skipping a single day of practice of one of Kreutzer's *Études ou Caprices*.

In Brussels they immersed themselves not only in the music that was fashionable in Paris but in literature and theater as well. Everywhere he went Frederick de Augustus rummaged around to unearth anything that might provide him with information on the French capital. He regularly bought *Le Journal de musique, Le Mercure de France, Le Journal de Paris*, and even some political and philosophical pamphlets. The abundance of printers, typographers, engravers, and music dealers allowed him to find inexpensive pirated Parisian works without any effort. That was how he acquired the scores of two operas and one symphony concertante by the Chevalier de Saint-George. Since he had a letter of recommendation from Haydn on behalf of George for the Chevalier, it was crucial that he be familiar with the latter's works.

His son hadn't been inactive either. His practice had included playing private concerts organized by bourgeois patrons, lovers of music, who often pretended to be talented instrumentalists, pleased to demonstrate their own playing to visiting artists. In the end George had even given two concerts at the prestigious Théâtre de la Monnaie.

Thus, well before leaving Austria, Frederick de Augustus knew that the mores in Paris were different; in Brussels musicians who'd recently arrived from Paris informed him that instrumentalists showed up on the stage in full dress, that the audience could stroll around the hall while a piece was being played or might even loudly express their opinion during a soloist's performance. He took it all in and truly believed that the city of Paris would hold no surprise for him. And yet, the disconcerting feeling that something had passed him by stayed with him.

✿

Tired of going around in circles, Frederick de Augustus decided to stop ruminating and lie down in bed, hoping that counting sheep would finally let him fall asleep. But just as he put his hands on the armrests to push himself up from the chair, the quarrel between Deshayes and

Giornovichi came back to him and, with it, an epiphany that completely reversed the way he'd read the events of the day until that moment. He instantly dropped back into his seat.

No, Deshayes was not some retrograde old boor nor was Giornovichi an adventurer, they were actually two musicians who were fiercely but genuinely defending their concept of the art they cherished. What he, Frederick de Augustus, had interpreted as lack of discipline and incivility on the part of the audience was rather the manifestation of an uncontainable enthusiasm that expressed itself through these noisy and intrusive raptures. Suddenly he understood that the concert hall was a place where anyone could claim his right to speak. The players were not to be outdone either: the violinists delighted in affirming their uniqueness with iconoclastic bowing, thereby rebelling against the golden rule of the Lully era when an orchestra was judged to be playing 'right' only if there was uniformity of bow movement among all its members. They, too, were participating in the thriving of free expression that henceforth seemed irrepressible.

Mentally he revisited the vast concert hall with its benches, boxes, easy chairs, and what he hadn't noticed before all of a sudden became quite apparent: a space open to anyone where the seats were assigned not according to one's birth but according to the price one was able to pay, a place where the aristocracy encountered the well-to-do bourgeoisie, where ladies of the best families rubbed elbows with well-known actresses and singers, and where ordinary people found their place as if the power of money had neutralized the old social barriers.

Freedom of expression, enhancing individuality and wit, social diversity, it was all new to Frederick de Augustus. Until that moment, as was true for all oppressed people, he knew what it meant not to be free, but he did not know what freedom was. Not being free was something physical you felt inside yourself, in your flesh. The definition of freedom was simple—it consisted exclusively of getting rid of the fetters that subjugated you: the heavy weight of the iron chain that shackled the slave's feet in the steerage of a slave ship, the lashes of the whip that would lacerate the body while doing forced labor on the plantation, the violence of the masters. That was the freedom his grandfather had dreamed of in the hold of the ship that had transported him to Barbados, the freedom his grandmother had won back when she committed suicide, thus depriving the master of the satisfaction of possessing her, the freedom his father had dreamed of when the blood spurted from his back under the blows of the foreman in the island's sugar cane fields. But the kind of freedom Frederick de Augustus was discovering here was very different, a freedom that only men who were already free could conceive of. It was abstract but real, it went beyond the freedom dreamt of by those who were subjugated yet included it as well. It wafted through the Paris air, dispersed, and in his chair, Frederick de Augustus wondered whether that freedom wasn't the early warning sign of even greater transformations.

Finally he relaxed, sensing he'd resolved the mystery of the uneasiness he had felt when reviewing this unforgettable day. All he had to do now was internalize this change to create a new personality for himself, that of a Parisian. Suddenly he felt the need for alcohol, specifically for a small glass of Austrian slivovitz. Reluctantly he made do with the only drink available in the room, a carafe of water. He would discreetly purchase a small flask of brandy the next day. Careful not to drag his babouches and make too much noise, he went to bed and stretched out.

Once again, he couldn't help but think of Giornovichi, but this time with sincere gratitude. Their fortuitous encounter had helped him understand a great many things. And while his mind wandered in that hazy territory between wakefulness and sleep, an anecdote about Giornovichi came back to him. There was a story that one day he'd been invited to the house of a baroness in London to give a concert. As he began to play his concerto, whispering and the tinkle of spoons in teacups had continued. Annoyed, he'd raised his bow and turning to the musicians in the orchestra told them: 'Stop, my friends. These people understand nothing about the arts. I'm going to give them something in keeping with their taste. It will be quite good enough for these hot water drinkers.' And he started to play *J'ai du bon tabac*![1]

This Giornovichi really was a character! Haydn would have never dared to act this way in front of the guests of his master, Prince Esterhazy. Frederick, a smile on his face, slowly drifted off to sleep.

⚜

Soon he began to snore, then his snoring changed into a steady bass.

Unexpectedly, in the middle of this sustained drone, an odd *fortissimo* bass note of a bassoon exploded like a resonant fart right in the face of the irate empress and the furious prince. Maestro Haydn had let this blasphemous sound escape during the fourth movement of his *Seventy-third Symphony*. The prince liked the piece, informally known as *The Hunt*, so much that he had it added to the program at the last minute without any consideration of the musicians' unspoken discontent, infuriated by the frenetic pace of the performances: masked ball, a ballet followed by fireworks in the park, the premiere of an opera for marionettes composed for the occasion, a concerto for baritone, plus this concert in the park open to the general public. All of it to seduce Marie-Thérèse, Empress of Austria, who was visiting the chateau – not the one at Eisenstadt but the one he had built at Esterhaza in Hungary, as if the first one with its two hundred rooms, its chapel, its library, and its galleries modeled on Versailles, weren't enough.

In the dream, Frederick de Augustus didn't see the exact moment when the *Kapellmeister* brought the bassoon to his mouth, but the instrument crudely belched right after the climax of the final *presto*, a prelude to the end of the symphony that would end in a *pianissimo*. Such an insult to the ears of those who knew the work, like the prince!

---

1. *J'ai du bon tabac* is a 17th century French nursery rhyme.

At the barbaric sound, the musicians in the orchestra stopped in surprise, hands and fingers frozen on their instruments. Perplexed, the empress looked at the prince, and in turn, not immediately knowing how to react, the bewildered prince looked at Haydn.

As for him, sitting right behind the prince to be at his disposal at the slightest sign, Frederick de Augustus held his breath in the face of such insolence, unexpected from this musician, normally so poised, and famous although treated like a servant. And there he was now, removing the ceremonial livery of House Esterhazy, which he was wearing for the occasion. He threw it on the floor, grabbed a violin, and started to play a melody from his village in lower Austria, not in any refined or sophisticated manner as he would when he integrated it into his symphonies, but coarsely, like a peasant, like a simple village fiddler.

Then it was the turn of Frederick de Augustus not to contain himself. He leaped across the row of seats where the prince and the empress were and found himself face to face with Haydn on the stage, a drum before him, one of those large drums that could only be played standing up. Suddenly he remembered the music and the beats he'd heard as a young child in Barbados. Drum and violin, Caribbean rhythms and Austrian *landler*. A fantastic duo. A third character appeared beside them: it was little George, his son, holding a four-stringed banjo. The duo then changed into a fiery trio. European rhythms and notes intersecting with those of other places, jolting each other, mixing and fusing, creating sounds never heard before. Enchanted, the other musicians joined the trio of banjo, violin, and drum. The stage changed into a large space of joyful and festive improvisation that soon spilled out of the great concert hall. A grand feast of freedom.

Engulfed by the profusion of sound, Frederick de Augustus was taken back to his distant childhood. He saw himself again alongside his father in Barbados during the *crop-over*, the festivity when slaves were allowed to celebrate the end of the harvest, the festivity when they were allowed to dance and make music with every possible imaginable instrument: balafon, marimba, sanza—an African thumb piano—bead-and glass-covered gourds to shake, bamboo to be beaten, bells worn around the wrists and ankles, spoons to clang together, conchs and jugs to blow.... The one and only day a year when a little humanity and whimsy touched their lives.

Absorbed in these memories, Frederick de Augustus didn't know at what point the prince, abandoned by his servants who had all joined the spontaneous party, also found himself beside them on the stage. He was no longer wearing his magnificent, ornate diamond-set jacket, but had put on the livery of House Esterhazy that Maestro Haydn had just disdainfully flung to the ground. Frederick de Augustus burst out laughing when he saw him in a valet's garb, playing a baryton, that bastardized instrument, half viola da gamba, half cello, of which he was so fond, and for which he had repeatedly treated the *maestro* like a common servant, humiliating him by publicly criticizing him under the pretext that he hadn't composed the weekly piece he demanded for the blasted instrument on time.

The uproarious laughter shaking him awoke him from his dream.

VII

Although he'd fallen asleep very late, when he woke up Frederick de Augustus felt quite well rested. Having gotten up shortly before, George teased him and asked about the nightmare he had in the middle of the night, when he got up to use the chamber pot and saw his father tossing and turning, muttering incomprehensible words that punctuated the monotony of his snoring. Smiling, his father told him he barely remembered his dream, other than that it concerned a huge celebration on a far-away island in the sun, then he announced it was time for breakfast.

One of the advantages of the hotel where they were staying was that breakfast was served in a room on the ground floor. Frederick de Augustus missed his *einspänner*, the typically Viennese coffee served with a generous amount of whipped cream that would perk him up in the morning before embarking on his arduous day, and now had to make do with café au lait and some bread and butter. The hostess told him that for the moment, unfortunately, she couldn't offer any white bread since there was none in Paris and, instead, she suggested some slices of brown bread with quince jam. George, on the other hand, was thrilled to find they did have hot chocolate. A young girl barely older than he brought them their order on a tray. She was wearing a dress with tightly fitted long sleeves under an apron of coarse cloth that went halfway around her waist. She probably worked for the proprietor. After she'd served them, Frederick de Augustus thanked her while George gave her a big smile, which she answered shyly before slipping away.

George's hot chocolate was excellent, just thick enough to be right. Frederick de Augustus watched him enviously as from the flowered porcelain pot he poured the velvety liquid with its exquisite aroma into a large cup before greedily savoring it.

�✖

Back in their room, he began to plan the day's program. Two appointments had to be kept, one with the Chevalier de Saint-George and the other with Legros. The visit to Legros required no preparation, since it was merely a matter of asking for their share of the fee. Would the amount they'd be given really reflect the true total of the evening's receipts? There was no way of knowing. What if he were to ask for Giornovichi's help on this issue?

It was an entirely different story where the Chevalier de Saint-George was concerned. In fact, the two men had already met in Vienna four years earlier when the grandmaster of the *Société Olympique de la Parfaite Estime*, a Parisian Masonic Lodge, had sent Saint-George to see Haydn in the Austrian capital to commission him with a series of six symphonies. Since the Chevalier was not sufficiently versed in the German language to handle such important negotiations with the *maestro* who himself spoke Italian better than French, he had called on Frederick de Augustus to serve as their interpreter. Would he remember him?

Somewhat amused, Frederick de Augustus recalled his surprise when he'd entered the drawing room where he found the two men: the distinguished emissary from Paris was a mulatto! The contrast between the two couldn't have been greater. One white, a brilliant musician but a cartwright's son with a heavy provincial accent that the Viennese ridiculed, isolated from the outside world and kept in semi-servitude by his employer. The other, mulatto, son of an aristocrat and a man of the world, adored in the salons and high places of Paris where he permitted himself all sorts of caprices. One, small, sturdy, solid on his rather short legs, a rounded forehead above an aquiline nose, lively piercing eyes that illuminated a pock-marked face. The other, tall, slender, with an athletic build, lips enhanced with rouge and a powdered face that softened his copper complexion. Lastly, while the one wore ordinary clothing, dark breeches, blue morning coat with a jabot and silver frogs over a vest of the same color, the other reflected opulence and refinement with his silk pants, a delicately embroidered plain satin jacket, and a cape tossed over his shoulders. Nevertheless, their eyes conveyed mutual respect.

Saint-George hadn't been surprised when Haydn introduced Frederick de Augustus to him as an 'officer of the court of Prince Esterhazy'. After all, one could no longer count the number of 'Moors' that were part of the personal guards of European princes. On the other hand, he couldn't hide his surprise—raised eyebrows rapidly dropped—when, after exchanging some words with Haydn in German, Frederick de Augustus had turned to him and welcomed him in French. At a time when skin color was so important and the Blacks who'd managed to integrate into polite society were mostly light-skinned, since most of them were the biological children of white masters, he hadn't at all expected that the interpreter Haydn had mentioned would be such a dark-skinned Negro.

❧

Once the three of them were comfortably seated in cane-backed chairs, Saint-George took the documents he'd brought out of his briefcase, placed them on the table, and handed a letter to Haydn who opened it,

45

then gave it to Frederick de Augustus. It was a missive from Legros, director of the Concert Spirituel, who said he 'was writing on behalf of all French musicians'. He begged Haydn to accept the commission from the Grandmaster of the Olympic Lodge and assured him that, once these works were played and published, they 'would forever guarantee the glory of Europe's greatest musician'. Frederick de Augustus who knew Haydn well also knew that he despised flattery. He gleefully waited for his reaction. Haydn hadn't responded but simply nodded his head as if to indicate to his interlocutor he should stop fawning and get to the point. Accustomed as he was to Parisian salons where no negotiation would take place without bowing and scraping and preliminary wooing, Saint-George was visibly flustered by the maestro's indifference to praise. Without any further ado, the Chevalier disclosed the terms of the commission: six symphonies at twenty-five *louis*[1] each. Both Haydn and Frederick de Augustus were surprised by the amount. No one had ever offered him this much money for a composition. Even though he was holding the contract in his hand, Haydn asked Saint-George to personally confirm the total amount of the fee. Elated, Saint-George repeated the figure and a lively conversation between the two ensued. Frederick de Augustus's head moved back and forth, his face turning from one to the other every time they went from German to French and from French to German. In his excitement Saint-George had added five *louis* more to the total for the publication rights.

As the memory of this long-ago encounter came back to him, Frederick de Augustus decided that Saint-George would certainly not remember him anymore. He didn't realize it then, but now he understood that in all the time they'd been together he never existed in the eyes of the Chevalier. He'd been invisible, transparent, merely a translating voice that could easily have been no more than an automaton. To him he was probably one of those well-trained servants in brocade

---

1. A *louis d'or* was a gold coin of considerable value.

livery, passing platters, filling glasses, setting and clearing the table but always unnoticed by the guests. The next day they might remember the dishes, the wine, tea, coffee, the liqueurs, and even the beauty of the china from which they'd been served, but they wouldn't have the faintest recollection of who had served them.

Under such conditions why would he, Frederick de Augustus, be so eager to meet him again?

First of all, because Saint-George was the director of the Concert des Amateurs, the finest orchestra in Paris, if not in Europe. Meeting him meant seizing the opportunity to book a second concert for his son. Since the seats at the Concert des Amateurs were more expensive than at the Concert Spirituel, he'd make much more money, which, frankly, was one of his objectives. Last but not least, Saint-George was close to Queen Marie-Antoinette, who greatly admired his talent and considered him to be the only French maestro worth listening to. She had even invited him to Versailles to play with her. Well-informed sources claimed that she'd recommended him for the directorship of the Royal Academy of Music, that is to say of the Opera. Thus, there was a possibility that the meeting with the Chevalier might lead to an audience with the queen. Wouldn't that be marvelous? It also turned out that the queen had the reputation of promoting Austrian and German musicians who happened to be in Paris. Everyone still remembered the support she'd given to the Chevalier von Gluck, which had aroused such jealousy among French musicians. Should they be lucky enough to gain this dreamed-of audience, Frederick de Augustus would be sure to introduce his son as coming from Austria, too, which was the absolute truth; and perhaps he would also mention to the queen that he had accompanied her mother when she'd paid Prince Esterhazy a visit at his Esterhaza Palace. In fact, when her Imperial Majesty Maria Theresa had indicated her wish to take a drive through the gardens of the chateau, the prince had ordered Frederick de Augustus to walk in front of his coach, an exotic page preceding the horses. This personal touch might move the queen and, who knows, open the door for his son to a concert at Versailles, just as with young Mozart! At this point in his thinking, Frederick de Augustus smiled and told himself he really shouldn't get too carried away quite yet.

⚜

In Brussels he had created a special 'Saint-George' portfolio consisting of articles clipped from newspapers and journals he'd bought. The time had come for him to read them and quickly skim the ones he'd read before. He wanted to be sure not to overlook some important piece of information about the Chevalier. From his trunk he took the briefcase containing the file, picked up Giornovichi's letter he'd placed on the table beside the bed and went to the living room to sit down. He remembered that Giornovichi's letter wasn't closed, took it out of the envelope, opened it and…couldn't believe what he was reading. It was incredible! This virtuoso on the violin, this braggart, this impudent man, this blowhard was illiterate in French:

> *My deer Saint-George, I rite yew abbut this yungman of rufly 8 yeers old hoo is wissoutanydout a grate violinist, he gaiv a brillyent first consert asnever hurd before…*

⚜

Reading it was far from easy, for it was such a whimsical transcription, obviously written phonetically, and with an Italian ear at that. Frederick de Augustus wondered whether Giornovichi would be a better writer in Italian. He doubted it. He called George, who was busy near the apartment's big window applying rosin on the hairs of his bow, and showed him the letter. Amused upon reading it, he said to his father that the letter was perfectly understandable even if it was written in a very strange way. 'And what does *wissoutanydout* mean,' his father asked. 'Easy,' he answered, 'without any doubt!' Frederick de Augustus marveled at his son's astuteness but, in order not to show it, he went on sententiously: 'I hope you'll never write that way.'

Actually, George had become quite fond of Giornovichi and was just as disconcerted as his father, for he'd never thought that a well-known and recognized artist, a gifted violinist, a brilliant conversationalist and great traveler, could at the same time be illiterate. Noticing his bewilderment, his father said: 'In the world where you are growing up and traveling, you should take nothing for granted. Many things are often not what they appear to be. A stage set always has its other side, don't ever forget that.' He couldn't resist the pleasure of telling him another anecdote about Giornovichi to show him the foibles the man was hiding behind his self-aggrandizement. It had happened in London. After spending an evening with friends, Giornovichi couldn't remember the name of the street where he was living. Not until he began whistling the tune of *Malbrough s'en va-t-en guerre*[1] in despair were his friends finally able to direct the cab to Marlborough Street. Presenting the letter to Saint-George was now completely out of the question. In any case, with a letter of recommendation from *Kapellmeister* Haydn no other one was necessary. He put it back in the envelope intending to destroy it later. When George saw him close the envelope he asked:

'How long does it take for a letter to arrive in Dresden? I didn't get an answer yet to the one I wrote to Mamma and to Friedrich when we were still in Brussels.'

'You've got to be patient. Maybe your brother didn't answer right away. Maybe their letter arrived after we left Brussels.'

'In that case it's lost because I gave them the address of the hotel where we were staying! Do you think they forwarded it to us?'

---

1.   *Malbrough s'en va-t-en guerre* is a traditional eighteenth-century French folksong.

'I'm afraid not. It's not the kind of hotel that goes out of its way to keep a guest happy. Anyway, I didn't leave them our address in Paris because I only chose the Hotel Britannique at the last moment.'

'Well, I'll write them again and give them our new address.'

'If you want. Now let me get ready for our visit to Saint-George.'

❊

He once again focused on the documents he'd taken from his portfolio. Nothing in particular drew his attention while reading until he came across a notice in the *Chronique de Paris* of 1 May 1779, now already ten years old:

> *1 May 1779. M. de Saint George is a mulatto, that is to say the son of a Negress: he is a talented man with a great many natural gifts: he is extremely skilled in all physical exercises, he fires weapons expertly, he plays the violin the same way, he is furthermore an extremely gallant champion in love & sought after by every woman who knows of his marvelous talent, despite his unattractive face. As a great music lover he was given leave to make music with the Queen.*

He didn't recall having read this article; and a good thing it was that he did now, he thought, for it reminded him of something crucial he might exploit: Saint-George was a mulatto like his son George, and perhaps he could use that common point. He couldn't decide. He resolved to wait and see how the meeting would go. On the other hand, what did the author of the article mean with 'his unattractive face' when everyone thought he was extremely handsome? Was it jealousy or was it because he wasn't white? And what was implied by 'his marvelous talent' so sought after by the women who knew about it?

The rest of the reading didn't provide any further information than he already had about Saint-George. Still, he reread the only text written and published by him, a quatrain in the style of the period:

When in the woods I hear the sweet voice
Of the beautiful nightingale as it sings
I think I will enjoy it and listen to
Its sweet voice that enthralls me.

The poem's frivolous banality had disappointed him before when he first read it. Reading it a second time didn't change his mind. He thought the text had no originality whatsoever and revealed nothing about its author: any dandy at the court could have written it.

All that was left for him to do now was take a glimpse at the musician's compositions he'd purchased in Brussels, a symphony concertante for two violins and orchestra, and the librettos of two of his operas, *Ernestine* and *The Hunt*. He didn't want to appear completely ignorant should Saint-George ask him any questions about his music. Even if he knew he was unable to discuss his instrumental work, he could at least hold forth on his librettos. He began with *Ernestine*. When he opened the libretto, an article he'd clipped from the *Correspondance littéraire* fell out. He picked it up and started reading:

Ernestine flopped at the Italiens in the most ridiculous fashion in the world, but flopped in such a way that recovery is no longer possible, something that is becoming rare. Words and music, it was all booed from beginning to end. Saint-George was known for writing pleasant music in a concert; but this experience must have taught him that there's a great gap between an amateur symphony and the music of a drama, and M. de Laclos, who is clever enough to create some pretty little verse lines, must have understood that there's quite a distance to go from there to a play for the theater. What is nice is that the queen, who backed the piece, made more fun of it than anyone else. Nothing put the people in the orchestra seats in a better mood than a certain courier who arrived to reveal the denouement and kept calling ohé, ohé while cracking his whip. Everyone in the orchestra began to yell ohé.

Frederick de Augustus couldn't help laughing out loud. Still at the window, George asked what was so funny. When he told him the episode, George began to laugh as well and tried to imagine Queen Marie-Antoinette shaking her head with its '*a la Belle-Poule*' hairdo, one of those monumental hairstyles that were her secret and were immediately becoming fashionable among the ladies of the court, busily calling '*ohé, ohé*'.

VIII

They were ready to go out, Frederick de Augustus now dressed in the costume he'd rejected the evening before, when it had been his intention to exploit the imagery peddled about the natives of another part of the world beyond Europe. The turban and kaftan were perfectly designed to satisfy this simplistic exoticism. On the other hand, it was now a matter of going to meet a man who'd spent his entire life striving to become integrated into the polite society of Paris. To solicit his patronage, he would thus have to present an image of himself that conformed to the world in which he had so zealously tried to be accepted.

In any event, Frederick de Augustus was impressed with the way in which a 'son of a Negress' had managed to become a distinguished member of the Parisian aristocracy where rank took precedence over everything, even wealth. And yet, in the beginning Saint-George had no social status at all, the Code Noir then in force placing him in the category of slaves because his mother was a slave, even if his white father had recognized him. Indeed, he'd been freed once he set foot on French soil—according to the law 'all people here are free and a slave acquires freedom as soon as he enters here and is baptized'—but nevertheless he could not inherit any title of nobility. However, this didn't take into consideration that the sire, a minor nobleman of the colonies, was extremely attached to his child, an unusual bond for a slave-owning planter. Not only had he done everything to get around the judicial difficulties to obtain a title for his son, but he had also included him in his will.

The father began by buying him the title of 'king's squire'. Convinced that the sword, prerogative of the nobility, was the equivalent of opening the doors to the aristocracy's circles for his son, he'd embarked upon giving him an education in which fencing and horseback riding had an important place, in addition to disciplines like music, math, history, dance, and foreign languages. In the end, when he was sixteen, Saint-George excelled in fencing to such an extent that everyone around him had begun to call him 'chevalier', which gave him the brilliant idea of changing his name from Joseph Bologne de Saint-Georges to 'Chevalier de Saint-George', in the process dropping the final 's' in Georges out of affectation.

From then on, thoroughly exploiting his countless talents, playing on his charm, making himself noticed by incessant histrionics such as swimming across the Seine with one arm tied behind his back one ice-cold day in January, playing violin one evening using his whip as a bow, or firing his pistol at two six-franc coins tossed into the air one by one and hitting them successively with the bullets before they fell down, he'd become the idol of high society. And, the ultimate recognition, he was preparing to take over the direction of the Paris Opéra at the queen's express recommendation!

Yet, despite this apparently successful integration, Saint-George remained hypersensitive about his skin color about which he didn't tolerate any remarks. There were several articles in the file Frederick de Augustus had put together that described his fits of anger. One day, for example, in the Rue du Bac where he lived, someone unknown had called him 'colored boy' and 'poorly washed'. Saint-George got immediately all worked up, jumped at the man, grabbed him by the neck and

54

pushed his head in the gutter: 'Now you're just as poorly washed as I am,' he'd shouted as he dangled him in the ditch.

On the other hand, he didn't object when the young aristocrats in his circle called him 'the American', and with good reason. The time that 'American' was a contemptuous term was long gone, when it conjured up some savage people from the mouth of the Orinoco. Things had changed a great deal since the American colonies had gained their freedom as they victoriously waged war with King George III of England. America was henceforth cited as an example by the philosophers who saw it as the confirmation of the accuracy of their ideas, ideas with which Frederick de Augustus was familiar, having read about them in the papers and brochures he'd bought in Brussels and Paris. They spoke out against arbitrary arrests, they ridiculed the clergy, attacked the authority and greed of the Church, and they denounced the misery of the people who were exploited by an aristocracy that clung to its privileges. In front of the Café du Caveau at the Palais-Royal he'd seen and heard an orator standing on a stool calling loudly for freedom of opinion, abolition of *lettres de cachet*, and suppression of the nobility's privileges. The orator even had the nerve to ask for freedom of religion and the separation of Church and State, an obvious attack against the very foundations of the monarchical order! Frederick de Augustus couldn't imagine such a speech in Vienna, in the Habsburg Empire where the Empress Maria-Theresa reigned and where he'd been living for the past ten years.

In fact, if Saint-George was so flattered to be called 'the American', it was above all because of one man, the Marquis de La Fayette, who had disobeyed his king's orders forbidding him to leave France, and who had secretly embarked for America where he'd actively participated in the American Revolution side by side with General George Washington. His return in France had been a triumph. Welcomed as a hero, lionized, received at the royal court, an object of public admiration, he'd taken advantage of his fame to spread his ideas, some of them as radical as those of the philosophers. For instance, he advocated the suppression of the salt tax and the liberation of all who had been imprisoned for not paying it, as well as the removal of all State prisons. Even more audaciously, he demanded the immediate abolition of the slave trade and the gradual emancipation of the slaves! To drive the point home, he'd joined the Society of the Friends of the Blacks, an association that had just been created for the sole purpose of attaining the abolition of slavery. Finally, to distance himself from the aristocracy, he'd started to sign his name 'Lafayette' rather than the nobiliary 'La Fayette'.

However, Frederick de Augustus, thinking he'd pretty much figured out Saint-George's personality, suspected that the real reason for his fascination with the Marquis didn't lie so much in his ideas as in the success he enjoyed with the feminine sex, for the man's renown was due not merely to his convictions. Several women had fallen in love with him and the young Marquis had shown himself to be a seducer, with the suicide of a count to his name who had discovered that his wife was the mistress of the hero of America. Thus, by letting people call him 'the American' he was reaping double dividends: he added one more jewel to his feat of arms by letting others believe he was a companion of Lafayette, thereby securing a little of the prestige associated with that celebrity.

Sometimes they called him 'Creole' as well, a term referring to Whites born on the islands, to which he had no objection at all. On the other hand, he wouldn't hesitate to unsheathe his sword when someone adventurous labeled him a 'Creole Negro', an expression used to designate slaves and set them apart from 'people of color' who were born on the islands and were free.

That, then, was the man whom Frederick de Augustus and his son were going to meet. That was why he'd put on the fine suit he'd set aside the night before. Furthermore, instead of a sword he was wearing his Turkish saber at his side. He thought that by dressing according to the latest Parisian fashion himself and his son like a little Mozart, Saint-George would believe he was meeting with people sufficiently distinguished to be received in his salon without arousing the disapproval of his entourage.

※

Although he lived on the Rue du Bac, Saint-George had arranged for their appointment to take place at his father's residence, a townhouse on the Rue Richelieu with a full view over the gardens of the Palais-Royal. It wasn't far from the Hotel Britannique where they were staying so that they were able to walk and save themselves the cost of a carriage. Taking advantage of the mild, sunny weather on this Sunday morning in April, it also gave them a chance to wander through the city that they hadn't yet had the time to explore. The Rue Guénégaud, where their hotel was located, came out directly onto the Seine. They walked straight ahead and soon found themselves on the Quai de la Monnaie. Since the Rue Richelieu was on the Right Bank, they had to take the Pont-Neuf to cross the Île de la Cité and, once they reached the other side, go toward the Tuileries.

Many stalls were lining the quay and people were bumping into each other as if the entire population had made plans to meet. They were flocking together in front of cheap eateries where some just stood as they drank while others, sitting wherever they managed to place their bum, were eating as they dipped their fingers in chipped dishes on their laps. They cut meat with their teeth and drank soup straight from the bowl. Closer to the river, burly-armed porters argued about unloading merchandise delivered by the boats docked along the quay. Somewhat farther down, washerwomen beat their laundry on wooden planks next to coachmen who let their horses drink without paying any attention to the dung the animals were dropping. And dogs, dozens of stray dogs were rummaging through piles of trash, roving near the eateries and the

57

fishmongers' stalls with their waft of sickening smells. A mud-covered water spaniel came charging between George's legs so abruptly that he almost fell over.

The place changed into true bedlam when they reached the bridge and began to cross. Onlookers and cars were blocking the street with a ceaseless coming-and-going despite the presence of sidewalks for the pedestrians. Quacks auctioned their ointments and other remedies while, sitting next to his chest full of powders and tinctures, another swindler offered his services. Flower vendors tried to sell roses, enticing the men they approached with lewd allusions, thereby competing with the offers from streetwalkers who weren't exactly subtle about the wares they were peddling. A few steps later they passed some ragpickers with baskets on their back who were protesting the impossible prices the secondhand clothes dealers were asking for shabby old rags, good only for being thrown out, while the women beside them in the process of mending them followed the argument, now and then raising their head from the garments they were patching up. But even more numerous were those who did nothing at all. Slumping against the parapet they were sleeping, playing cards, quarrelling, while they waited for who knows what; in Frederick de Augustus' mind there wasn't any doubt that the brigands and pickpockets originated here.

Here he discovered a wretched humanity, living from day to day, whose indigence contrasted sharply with the luxury, the pleasures, and the activities of those who frequented the Palais-Royal so nearby. All of a sudden, he grasped what the philosophers were criticizing in their pamphlets and the indictment the orator made from his stool whom he'd heard in front of the Café du Caveau. He ended up by conceding that their words, which he'd found much too harsh until then, were not lacking in substance. He suddenly remembered the words of an Austrian baron he'd read in Soliman's library in Vienna when he was preparing for his trip to France: 'The world is a large body of which Paris is the heart.' A very sick body, he thought. He was now certain of one thing, there was a great deal of suffering in this heart of the world that Paris personified in April 1789!

Out of the blue, someone was tugging at Frederick de Augustus' arm. It was an overexcited George, dragging him toward a small group from which drum sounds were coming, and yelling: 'Papa, Papa, come look, come look!' He managed to stay right behind his son as he tried to worm his way to the front row of the circle the crowd had formed. 'Look, look,' he kept yelling, pointing his finger at the scene with the enthusiasm of a nine-year old child: a monkey showman and his animal dressed in a skirt and blouse, wearing a hat with blue and white rosettes. A long rope tied him to the animal. A veritable acrobat, the monkey was dancing and hopping to the sound of the drum and, every time the rhythm changed into drumrolls, he made a somersault, forward, then backward, then stood up again under the applause. Following two or three of these flips he stopped, grabbed his hat with both hands, propped it back on his head uttering sharp little cries and ran back to his master, who petted him and handed him a piece of dried fruit, which he quickly grabbed and greedily stuffed into his mouth, grimacing throughout. Then the man passed his cup around; Frederick de Augustus put two one-sou coins in. George had never seen a monkey. He was intrigued by an animal that was both so human, so clever, and yet so preposterous. He would have stayed another hour had his father not tugged at his arm this time to let him know it was time to go.

They passed the statue of King Henri IV on his horse, erected on the island's central area, and were now on the other side of the bridge, where the crowd was equally large. On one of the half-circles of balconies situated above the bridge's piers, a singer set up next to a book vendor who was selling music scores of popular tunes and ariettas of successful operettas. For a farthing per verse, he'd sing you the melody without your having to make a purchase. Curious, Frederick and George approached. They immediately spotted a sheet with an arietta from *The*

Hunt by Saint-George, an opera that had enjoyed no more success than *Ernestine* but whose aria 'Air de Rosette' had become a true popular craze. Frederick de Augustus, who owned the libretto, had never heard it sung. Here was the opportunity. The 'Air de Rosette' consisted of several verses but he decided two would do. The vendor pocketed the two coins, cleared his throat, took a theatrical pose, and launched into the arietta with many tremolos as was proper for a gallant style:

I

If Mathurin in the grass patch
Plucks the early morning rose
He will bring it to Colette
And place it gently on her breast.
I, who am the youngest one
I don't know if this is love
But in the grass patch I, too,
Would like to welcome such a rose.

II

In the shade of the hazelnut
Should Colette drift off and doze
Mathurin runs to awaken her
With a surreptitious kiss.
I, who am the youngest one
I don't know if this is love
But in the shade of the hazelnut
I, too, would like to be awakened.

To make sure he'd convince the listeners of the passion that consumed the younger one as she tells of the love of her sister and Mathurin, the man ended each verse languorously stretching the sound of 'one' and 'love' across two or three measures, his arms out wide, his head back, and his eyes raised to the sky. The crowd applauded. George and Frederick de Augustus followed suit. The latter thought the lyrics of the arietta were of the same caliber as those of Saint-George's poem with its beautiful nightingale and its sweet voice. He couldn't help but wonder whether those who perpetrated such verses were living in the same world as all those poor folks bustling about on the Pont-Neuf.

Just as they were getting ready to leave the bridge and move onto the quay a throng suddenly burst open in front of them. The people hurriedly cleared the sidewalk to make an opening for five strapping men carrying sacks of charcoal on their shoulders; annoyed, the pedestrians caught in the chaos hurled expletives at them as they moved away from the coal carriers as fast as they could so as not to have their clothes soiled by the black dust coming from their sacks. Knocked around by the crowd, Frederick de Augustus and George only managed to move away at the last minute, almost hit by the first of the coal carriers. Frederick de Augustus couldn't hide his surprise when he realized that two of the men were black. But the latter were even more surprised when they saw the elegant man who stood out in the crowd with his opulent clothing and the superior appearance the saber at his side conferred on him. They motioned a vague greeting in his direction but, uncomfortable without knowing why, Frederick de Augustus turned his head away. These were the first Blacks he had encountered in Paris since they arrived. Were they African Blacks or Creole Negroes? In any event, he didn't want to be confused or associated with them. George, on the other hand, smiled at them, happy to see these men who looked like his father. With a wave of his hand he greeted them cheerfully.

Finally they made it to the Right Bank on the Quai de la Ferraille and began to walk toward the Louvre. The distance was greater than they'd anticipated, and it was hot now. It was neither possible nor desirable to keep walking as they would then arrive at Saint-George's dripping with sweat, which would be most inappropriate. Frederick de Augustus decided to hire a carriage and hailed one.

IX

The coach dropped them off at the address on Rue Richelieu. Because of the great disparity between the passersby, the tranquility of the neighborhood, the elegance of the homes lining the street and the destitution and chaos of the universe at the Pont-Neuf, which they had just left, Frederick de Augustus and George had the feeling that they were in an entirely different city. They went to the gate of the townhouse guarded by a tall man in uniform who observed the two rather unusual visitors approaching him with misgiving. After providing him with their credentials, the guard's suspicion turned to deference as he hastened to assure them that they were expected. He opened the gate and led them to a residence at the rear of a cobblestone courtyard, an attractive building with as its façade a small triumphal arch resting on several marble Doric columns. Following their guide, they took a large staircase and stopped in front of a double door. The guard bowed slightly and vanished. They entered a rather posh living room, its paneling decorated with gilded moldings and a parquet floor covered with an oriental carpet, probably Turkish. With its high windows, the room was well lit. The Chevalier was waiting for them but, to their great surprise, he was not alone.

The other man was as tall as the Chevalier but much younger, around twenty-five Frederick de Augustus estimated. With his broad shoulders and strong, muscular calves he looked like a young Apollo. In contrast to Saint-George he did not wear a wig and his frizzy black hair, its curls clipped short, resembled that of Greco-Roman statues. With great flair, he wore a saber at his side, not a sword.

'Welcome,' Saint-George said as he came toward Frederick de Augustus, hand extended.

To the latter's happy surprise, the Chevalier's tone of voice was warm. They shook hands.

'Pleased to see you,' Frederick de Augustus replied. 'Thank you for receiving us so quickly despite your extremely busy schedule. This is my son George, George Augustus Polgreen Bridgetower.'

'Well then, let me introduce Thomas Alexandre Dumas to you,' Saint-George said as he turned to the man with him.

'Happy to meet you,' Thomas Alexandre Dumas answered.

'Frederick de Augustus is an old acquaintance,' Saint-George went on. 'I met him in Vienna when I was there to offer the commission of a series of symphonies to Haydn, the composer, who is a friend of his.'

Frederick de Augustus had been wrong about Saint-George as it turned out: not only did the Chevalier remember him quite well, but he also remembered the precise circumstances of their encounter. He even provided Thomas Alexandre Dumas, whom he informally called Alex, with details that Frederick de Augustus didn't know, namely that the Chevalier had himself performed the symphonies, intentionally known as *Symphonies parisiennes*, in the presence of Queen Marie-Antoinette. It was an enormous success and the fourth one so delighted the queen that it was quite naturally labeled *The Queen*.

Turning to Frederick de Augustus, he asked:

'That was about three years ago, wasn't it?'

'Oh no, longer than that,' Frederick de Augustus said, 'it was four years ago, in 1785 if I remember correctly. Time flies!'

'Yes, it does,' Saint-George added.

Then, in a paternal gesture putting a hand on George's shoulder, he continued:

'So this is the little chap who caused such a stir at the Tuileries last night! I wasn't there—I was at a private party—but everyone I've met since then is brimming with praise. One of the first among them is my friend Gossec, you know, the one I replaced as head of the Théâtre des Amateurs, whose opinion is extremely important, for he was also the director of the Concert Spirituel for a long time. But the most amazing thing to me was the reaction of the violinist Giornovichi, whom I ran into late last night at a disreputable gaming room at the Palais-Royal. As soon as he saw me come in, he began to extol a young talent he'd just heard at the Cent-Suisses Hall for whom, he said, he'd written a letter of recommendation to be given to me. Apparently, he wasn't aware that you had already contacted me. In any case, to hear this maniac who's always and everywhere claiming to be the best violinist in Paris, launch into a speech so completely contrary to his nature, that is to praise someone else who plays that instrument, compels me to believe that George's playing must be truly exceptional.'

'In fact, we met him right after the concert; we found him to be a bit scatterbrained but most affable.'

'Scatterbrained, that's the word. I've had a few quarrels with him, but we've made peace. We're actually friends.'

Frederick de Augustus knew what he was referring to. It had been rumored that Giornovichi, jealous to see Saint-George succeed Gossec as the head of the prestigious orchestra of the Théâtre des Amateurs, hadn't stopped belittling the 'Negro' at high society suppers. The contemptuous silence Saint-George kept in the face of such ridicule had so irritated Giornovichi that one day, intending to provoke him to a duel, he'd slipped into a reception organized by the Chevalier. He started to take him to task violently and ended up by slapping him in the face. Considered to be one of Europe's most expert swordsman at the time,

Saint-George could have made mincemeat of Giornovichi who was a mediocre fencer, but, aloof, before the dumbfounded guests, all he said disdainfully was: 'I admire your talent too much to fight with you.' Taken aback, the brash violinist left the place in a hurry. One has to believe that he learned his lesson, for it was said that he presented himself a few days later at the Rue du Bac, where the Chevalier then lived, to mumble some apologies.

'He did indeed give us a missive for you,' Frederick de Augustus explained, 'but we didn't think it would be helpful since we already have a recommendation from Haydn. We thought that Haydn was in the best position to be the judge of George's talents. He was his teacher when we were living in Eisenstadt.'

He handed him the closed envelope. Saint-George broke the seal and opened the letter.

'It's in German, I'll read it later. Anyway, the mere fact that it comes from Haydn is enough for me not to doubt the talents of young George, had not the praise coming from every direction after the concert already convinced me of that.'

Noticing that Frederick de Augustus was now looking at Alexandre Dumas who was silently watching them talk, Saint-George exclaimed:

'Oh, excuse me, I realize I didn't properly introduce you to Alex. Alex is a cavalryman in the queen's Regiment of Dragoons. One detachment of this regiment, to which he belongs, had been stationed at Loan until now, but is being transferred to Villers-Cotterêts to secure the region. So he's come to say goodbye. Alex came to France when he was very young and has always considered me his mentor since the day when I managed to persuade his father to register him at the Academy of Texier de la Boëssière.

Realizing that this name meant nothing to Frederick de Augustus, he elaborated a little:

'You see, Texier de la Boëssière is the greatest fencing master of France. You'll understand how important he is when I tell you that he's the one who invented the fencing mask. At first the mask provoked the criticism of so-called purists, but everyone has embraced it since then. His academy is well-known for the quality of its education. I myself was a boarding student there and I did everything to make sure that Alex, too, could take advantage of it. He was eighteen then and now the lad is twenty-seven! One of the queen's most formidable dragoons. I predict a great future for him.'

'I am most honored to make your acquaintance,' Frederick de Augustus said. 'When I first came in and saw you standing beside the Chevalier I thought you were a musician, but I immediately began to doubt that when I noticed you wear your saber like a weapon and not like a ceremonial object.'

'In contrast to me, who chose the sword, Alex had his heart set on the saber and excels in its use,' Saint-George added.

'You, too, have quite a beautiful weapon there,' Alex Dumas said. 'May I see it?'

'But of course!'

Frederick de Augustus drew the weapon from its sheath and handed it to Alex by the handle. He took it and began to examine it with the eye of an expert. He'd never seen anything like it. The very flat blade had a perfect curve, making it extremely efficient for sharp and backhand thrusts. A button incrusted with mother-of-pearl and silver covered the handle whose hilt, meant to protect the hand, was made of bronze. Alex Dumas began to test the saber with brisk cutting motions from low to high and then in reverse, sometimes rounded, sometimes straight, as if he were beheading an enemy or severing a body part. The saber evidently pleased him.

'It's truly beautiful, this weapon. Very well balanced. Where did you buy it?'

'I didn't. It's a Mameluke saber given to me by an Egyptian vizier who was visiting the Ottoman court of Sultan Abdulhamid. Before coming to Europe and attaining my position with Prince Esterhazy in

Austria, I was an officer in this sultan's army, posted not far from the city of Izmir. I much prefer it to the Turkish saber.'

Listening to the adults' conversation, George was shocked to hear his father's words. It couldn't be true. He was present when his father purchased the saber in Vienna with the help and advice of Soliman. Saint-George and Alex Dumas, on the other hand, seemed to believe him. In any case, did they have a choice? Frederick de Augustus ran absolutely no risk that they would check the information with some distant Ottoman sultan.

'Well, if it were up to me, I would gladly recommend this saber to our entire cavalry,' Dumas concluded as he handed it back to him.

Frederick de Augustus put the saber back in its sheath made of thick leather whose long brass snap ended in a steel arrow. It seemed the time had come to broach the reason for their visit, to solicit the Chevalier's influence in procuring another concert in Paris in a different hall, as prestigious as that of the Cents-Suisses where the first concert had taken place, but far more lucrative. He needed money, the room on Rue Guénégaud alone had cost him a *louis* for the month that he had rented it. And there were plenty of halls: there was the concert hall De la Loge Olympique where apparently Queen Marie-Antoinette frequently showed up unexpectedly; there was also the Concert des Amateurs, and the Panthéon on the Rue de Chartres, and why not the Théâtre-Italien where Kreutzer was the solo violinist, the same place where the opera *Ernestine* had suffered its bitter failure. But he wanted to be discreet in his request and wasn't sure if he should make it in front of a third party, Alex Dumas in this case. As he was pondering this, Saint-George, who seemed to have taken a liking to George, asked him:

'Where is George's father?'

He thought it was a preposterous question:

'I thought I already told you, George is my son.'

'I know, but what I mean is his real father, his sire,' Saint-George explained.

'I don't really understand.'

'Aren't you his adoptive father? His tutor?'

Saint-George and Dumas exchanged a look that betrayed the most profound bafflement. Frederick de Augustus caught the look and immediately understood why the two men seemed to be so puzzled. On the French islands where they were born, being a 'man of color' or 'mulatto' was inevitably a matter of having a white father and a black mother. The inverse situation didn't exist, was in fact unimaginable, therefore George's father could only be white. What was more, since the mother was often a slave whose master could do with her as he pleased, behind the word 'mulatto' floated the double infamy of illegitimacy and slave ancestry; hence the desire of those so labeled to hide that part of themselves that they experienced as shameful, not to say tainted. The proportion of white blood that ran through the veins of men of color was of such importance that in the colonies it had produced a hierarchical classification with a suitable nomenclature. Thus, one was *mulatto, quadroon, octoroon, mustefino* or *hexadecaroon*, depending on whether one had half, a quarter, an eighth, or a sixteenth of that blood. Many of these 'half-bloods' claimed a clear separation between themselves and the Negroes and made every effort to live a life identical to that of the white colonists. And not wanting to own slaves, those among them who were free weren't the last to lend the masters their services in pursuing fugitives and putting down their rebellions.

Saint-George and Dumas were certainly not of that ilk, Frederick de Augustus convinced himself. In fact, they'd left the island of their birth quite young, one from Guadeloupe and the other from Santo-Domingo, they'd grown up in the sparkling milieu of Paris where the philosophers, challenging the monarchy and the aristocracy, were demanding freedom and equality and where philosophical associations were defying the powerful circle of colonial planters by demanding the end of both slave trade and slavery. Still, they couldn't imagine that a mulatto child had been conceived by the love of a white woman for a black man.

To Frederick de Augustus, who was born in Barbados, the word 'slave' didn't automatically refer to skin color, but rather to the individual's social condition. The reason was simple: for a very long time most of the slaves on the island had been white, Irish people reduced to slavery by the English. They used to work on the tobacco plantations that were the wealth of the island and it wasn't until the more lucrative cane sugar was cultivated and replaced tobacco, that black slaves began to be imported; they were thought to be better adapted to that sort of labor. But make no mistake, the lot of the Irish was no more enviable than theirs, and often worse. Working on the sugar cane or cotton plantations was hard, to be sure, but it didn't make you sick, which unfortunately was the case with tobacco whose leaves were poisonous.

The effect of that poison was felt when the sun would beat down mercilessly on head and neck and the temperature was above 104 in the shade; they would sweat abundantly and be thirsty. The more they drank the more they felt like vomiting, whereupon dozens of slaves could be seen doubled over the tobacco leaves or collapsing with dizziness. It was at such moments that the foreman proved most cruel, whipping the sick to force them back to work; it was also when most of the accidents occurred, for feeling ill and weak, the cutters would miss their target and cut off their hand or forearm, sometimes cutting their veins.

Frederick de Augustus knew this because of one of his grandfather's friends, an Irish slave, who was so severely poisoned after twenty years of working in the tobacco fields that he had a permanent headache and always kept a flask of rum within hand's reach, a heavy swig of which he claimed prevented him from vomiting every time he felt nauseated. The man was already on the plantation when a Dutch captain dropped

Frederick de Augustus's then still very young grandfather off on the island. When the declining cultivation of tobacco began to make way for sugar cane and a large section of the Irish slaves had been sold or deported to Montserrat and Antigua, this man stayed. He teamed up with his grandfather and grew close to his son, the father of Frederick de Augustus. He, too, used to participate in the *crop-over* feast. And when you heard a violin tune rise above the sounds of the African instruments, he was the fiddler playing. These parties were always a joy: people sang, danced, but most of all they drank. As a boy Frederick de Augustus loved to sit down beside the two cohorts when, after downing several swigs, they used to get involved in sometimes rather confused but always fascinating discussions. Without these conversations where one would tell the other about what he'd suffered, Frederick de Augustus would have never understood that slavery and its cruelty were indifferent to the color of one's skin. It was from the mouth of the Irishman that he learned that the tortures the slaves endured during the Atlantic crossings, whether they came to the Caribbean islands from African or Irish shores, were identical. Even more amazing, however, was the discovery that a black slave was treated better than his Irish counterpart, for he was worth ten times more money and thus the masters would think twice before beating him to death. In addition, the colonists used the African men to sire 'mixed-blood' offspring with often very young female Irish slaves, which produced even more valuable merchandise than either of their parents would. Indeed, Frederick de Augustus had often wondered if he might not have a half-brother among the mulattos who'd grown up on their plantation.

That was the world from which Frederick de Augustus had come. He wasn't about to explain all that to the two others, it would have been too complicated and undoubtedly quite useless. The most important thing for him was to offer a simple and clear response to conclude the topic and move on to the purpose of his visit.

'George Augustus is my child,' he finally said, 'my very own child.

My wife, his mother that is, is Polish. We were married in Biala Pod-laska, a city in Poland in the region of Galicia. We have two children, George is the older one and Friedrich is the younger. My wife is now living in Dresden with Friedrich.'

'Married you say?' Saint-George exclaimed. 'Here in this kingdom it is forbidden by law for any man of color, especially a Black man, to marry a white woman,' he explained.

He was silent for a while, then added:

'You can do whatever you want with a white woman. What? you'll say. Yes, everything! Merely flirt, or make her your mistress, even a jealous mistress, whatever you like! But marry her, absolutely not! Even if you love her and she loves you with a deep, abiding love!'

Frederick de Augustus noticed that Saint-George had uttered the last phrase with such bitterness that it led him to believe it concerned a personal wound. And he wasn't wrong. It was no secret that Saint-George had been madly in love with Louise-Rosalie Dugazon, a remarkable singer of light opera, praised to the skies by public and critics alike for her beauty as well as her reedy voice. Moreover, she had certainly responded to him, for they were both profoundly in love, quite openly and publicly, until the singer gave birth to a son and Saint-George was not allowed to claim paternity, which was then attributed to another man, even if everyone agreed that the child bore a striking resemblance to the Chevalier.

Frederick de Augustus didn't know how to react or respond. Actually, he didn't see the point of this conversation. He'd come to talk about music, about booking concerts and money to be earned, and instead he found himself embroiled in a discussion about the condition of Blacks and people of color in France. He wanted to bring this digression to a close at all costs and get back to the purpose of his visit. So, he ignored what Saint-George had just said and came straight to the point.

'George would like to give a second concert in Paris. We thought that you might be able to help us. That is also the reason why Haydn wrote you.'

'Well, you thought correctly. I can get you another concert at the Tuileries in the Hall of Machines or the Hall of the Pantheon, as a benefit concert. That's what little George should have.'

How much would this 'benefit concert' yield them? He didn't want to give the impression that money was all that mattered to him but, after all, wasn't that the purpose of his trip to Paris? Art was fine, and so was acclaim; but one did need hard cash to eat and drink.

'Will he be paid a percentage of the receipts or at fixed rate as Monsieur Legros obliged us to accept?'

'He paid you a fixed rate? You should have demanded that he pay you according to the system of 'benefit concert' that he invented, which guarantees you a minimum sum regardless of the concert's receipts. It's a way of attracting virtuosos.'

'Thank you for this information.'

'Did you say you're staying at the Hotel Britannique on the Rue Guénégaud?'

'That's correct.'

'A very fine, very popular hotel. So I'll know where to send a courier should I need to get in touch.'

'Thank you. I would also like to congratulate you on your promotion. I heard that you will soon take over the reins at the Opéra de Paris.'

'Thanks to the queen's benevolence. All I need is the letter from His Majesty the King to confirm the nomination and thereby make it official.'

'We do not wish to take up any more of your valuable time. George and I thank you once again and wish you a fine day.'

'Good luck, George Augustus,' said Alex Dumas.

'Thank you, Sir,' he replied, 'I hope you will come to one of my concerts.'

Saint-George reacted immediately when he heard George's last words.

'Ah, I almost forgot. Would you be free this evening? I am giving the premiere of a symphony concertante for two violins that I just finished at the theater of Monsieur—a new hall built by the Duke d'Orléans at the Tuileries Palace. His wife, the Marquise de Montesson, is giving a soiree at her salon for the occasion, after the concert. She is granting me this honor because I'm the director of the private theater she owns. I would like to invite you as well.'

Indeed, in addition to the famous Concert des Amateurs that he directed, Saint-George was also in charge of the private theater owned by the Marquise de Montesson within the Palais-Royal.

The Chevalier opened the drawer of an inlaid chest that held a porcelain inkwell and a goose quill with a sharpened point. He took out two invitation cards and wrote the names of George on one and of his father on the other. Then from a different batch he took another, fancier card of vellum paper and wrote something on it as well. He patted the three cards dry and handed the first two to Frederick de Augustus:

'For the concert, you will each need a ticket to be admitted.'

He gave the third card to George who handed it to his father.

'The soiree at the Marquise,' the Chevalier continued, 'is a private affair. But she has granted me the privilege of inviting a few people of my choosing and I hope you will be among them.'

'Georges Augustus Polgreen Bridgetower, a young violinist prodigy, accompanied by his father, Frederick de Augustus Bridgetower,' Frederick de Augustus read on the invitation, while Saint-George was rummaging through the drawer looking for an envelope. He felt a little shock: the primary guest invited was not he but George. Until that moment he thought he was the one to open the doors of Paris for his son; reading this invitation, he realized that in reality it was his son who was opening them. He suddenly became aware that all the courtesies he was given were due to the talent of his child. Without him, he was nothing but some Negro passing through Paris. The voice of Saint-George, who was still talking, brought him back from his thoughts.

'As I mentioned to you, it's a symphony concertante for two violins. To interpret this work I've managed to engage Rudolph Kreutzer and

Vincent Rode, two of the most gifted young violinists in Paris. They rarely play together for they're jealous of each other, but ultimately they accepted, out of respect for me. It's an occasion not to be missed.'

Frederick de Augustus had recovered from the twinge of envy he'd felt when reading the invitation; quite the contrary, he was touched by the honor the Chevalier de Saint-George bestowed on his son and by extension on himself. As for George, after all the arduous hours spent struggling over the *Études ou Caprices*, it had always been one of his dreams to hear Kreutzer play. He could hardly believe it.

'Monsieur Kreutzer will be playing?' he asked.

'Do you know him?'

'We met him. He even had the kindness to congratulate me,' he added spontaneously.

'We will do everything we can to be there,' Frederick de Augustus affirmed.

X

Frederick de Augustus and George were very happy with their visit, not only for having gotten the promise of a second concert in one of the most prestigious halls of Paris—and that with the backing of the Chevalier de Saint-George—but also for the warmth with which they'd been received. They were equally impressed with the presence of Alex Dumas, and Frederick de Augustus tried to find out more about him: it wasn't his real name. His real name was Thomas Alexandre Davy de La Pailleterie. Up to a point, his life had certain things in common with that of Saint-George. His father, Alexandre Antoine Davy de La Pailleterie, a minor aristocrat who owned a plantation in Santo Domingo, had sold him with an option of repurchase before leaving the island. However, changing his mind a few years later, he bought him back and sent for him to come and live with him in France. He had given him the education of a young nobleman and had spared no expense to please his son, including the most expensive clothes. Unfortunately, Thomas Alexandre's frenzied worldly life ended abruptly when, at age seventy-one, his father was married again, to a woman thirty-three years his junior. People didn't know whether it was under the incentive of his new wife or not, but the fact remains that, out of the blue, the old De La Pailleterie stopped all support of his son and evicted him from the beautiful apartment he occupied near the Louvre. Without any resources, the latter broke with his father, relinquished his name, and in defiance took his mother's name, a black slave called Cessette Dumas. That is how he'd joined the queen's Dragoons Regiment as Alexandre Dumas.

The invitation to the concert had upset their schedule for the day; initially it was quite simple, with a visit to Saint-George, then to Joseph Legros, and then take advantage of the remaining time to stroll around the boulevards before ending the evening once again in the endless galleries, cafés and restaurants of the Palais-Royal. Not only did they now have to cancel their evening at the Palais-Royal, but they had to shorten their walk along the boulevards as well to return to the hotel, rest a little, and freshen up before the concert.

The vehicle they took dropped them on Rue l'Évêque in front of the house of Legros. Obsessed as he was by his model Leopold Mozart, Frederick de Augustus couldn't stop himself from telling his son that during one of his stays in Paris, young Amadeus had lived on the Rue du Sentier, a few streets away. He was trying to convince himself that the coincidence of the paths of his son and Leopold's son crossing bode well for the success of his plan.

He'd only just pounded the weighty iron door knocker attached halfway up on the heavy wooden door, when it turned on its hinges and revealed a valet in tails. He showed them across an interior courtyard before bringing them into a spacious foyer that led to several doors. He knocked on one of them, it opened, and an imposing figure appeared on the threshold. It was Legros. Looking at his rotund body, George had fun thinking that the Director of the Concert Spirituel really deserved his name.[1] As for Frederick de Augustus, he found it difficult to imagine that a man endowed with such a monumental physique could have the voice of a counter-tenor that made—or rather had once made—his

---

1. Legros means 'the fat one'.

reputation. With an affable smile the master of the house asked them to come into a living room where a pianoforte was prominent among the plush armchairs that filled the space. An open score stood on the piano. Was Monsieur Legros busy vocalizing when they interrupted him?

'Welcome to you both,' he said. 'I'm so happy to see you again after that grand concert.'

'We, too, are very glad to be here,' Frederick de Augustus replied.

Legros immediately took out a leather pouch and, without standing on ceremony, handed it to the latter, then added:

'My secretary brought me what we agreed upon. Here are six hundred pounds, please count them.'

Frederick de Augustus took the bag, poured the contents out on a small table placed in front of him, and began to count. The amount was correct, but he wondered on what Legros had based this sum. The price of the most expensive seats—like the one he'd purchased—was twelve pounds, the least expensive seats cost three. A quick mental calculation: if he randomly took six pounds as the average price per seat, the evening would have brought in at least three thousand pounds, for the immense hall at the Tuileries had to hold at least five hundred people, and it was filled. Admittedly, six hundred pounds wasn't to be sneezed at in view of his finances, but it wasn't very much. Even before articulating it, he knew that his question would be out of place, but he asked it anyway:

'How much did last night's concert bring in?'

Legros looked displeased. His voice lost all of its warmth.

'I do not concern myself with the administration, Monsieur Bridgetower. You should know that the halls at the Tuileries do not belong to us, we are merely renters. Consequently, the entire intake of a concert does not come to us. Part of it is set aside for the rent, the fees for the staff, and other things. I calculated your rate after subtracting these fixed expenses. And furthermore, I have been generous!'

Frederick de Augustus decided not to insist. He didn't want to arouse the wrath of Monsieur Legros who, considering his influential position on the musical stage of Paris, had the ability to be an inveterate nuisance.

'I understand your situation and I'm grateful to you. We have other appointments to keep, so please allow us to take our leave.'

Frederick de Augustus stood up and George followed his example. Realizing perhaps that he'd been too curt with them, Legros once again displayed his affable smile.

'You know, the honorarium that a completely unknown musician playing for the first time in Paris receives is always modest. Now that George's talent has been recognized and he has seduced the Parisian public with this first concert, I can guarantee that a second concert will bring in more. I'm prepared to arrange for one as I suggested to you last night. I'm prepared to review the terms of the contract as well.'

Frederick de Augustus heard him out, his face blank. He didn't want to negotiate any further. In any event, he already had Saint-George's more appealing promise. In a polite but cold tone he said:

'Thank you, we will discuss it again when the time comes. George and I are in no hurry. Please permit us to say goodbye for now.'

As they went toward the exit, Frederick de Augustus made sure he caught a glimpse of the score open on the pianoforte; it was the Baron von Gluck's *Orpheus and Eurydice*, the opera that in bygone days, when he was young and handsome, had made Legros' reputation in the role of Orpheus. Gluck had even modified the score to adapt it to the register of his voice. But now that he had aged…

XI

Contrary to what one might have expected, Frederick de Augustus was delighted when he left Legros, because it was the first time he reaped the results of his initiative: George's talent had been proven in hard cash. Feeling the coins inside his jacket made him euphoric. George, who had noticed the contrast between the tone of the conversation with Legros and the happy smile that now fluttered on his father's lips, was intrigued and asked:

'Is that a lot of money, six hundred pounds?'

'Oh yes, it's more than a month's pay at Prince Esterhazy's.'

'But you didn't look very happy when he offered it to you.'

'My dear George, it wouldn't have been very smart to show him that I was satisfied with what he gave me. I had to make him understand that I knew the concert had really brought in more than what he offered me, in other words that we knew he was cheating us. It's a strategy. Next time, if there is a next time, he'll be forced to offer us a great deal more. For a debut, for a young musician who's never given a concert in public before, six hundred pounds is a respectable amount. At the next concert we'll double or triple it. That's good, my boy.'

He grabbed his shoulder and squeezed him against his side as they were walking.

'Great! Then we can take that big walk through Paris that you promised me!'

'Exactly right! It's now or never,'

Since their arrival George had, indeed, not stopped asking to visit the city he'd dreamed of. It was time to please his son. Not only would they visit its monuments, its open-air markets, its boulevards and gardens, but maybe they would expand the visit as far as Versailles to see the original of what Esterhazy had used as a model for his own chateau. Better yet, with six hundred pounds in his pocket he could afford to take an expensive coach that was hired not by the hour but at a minimum of half a day, plus a generous tip for the coachman. The advantage was that they were comfortable, solid, and well harnessed. Also, since they were accepted at the court as well as by nobles and princes, it would make a fine impression on those parading around in front of the concert hall when they saw one of them arrive with an elegant black man and his son, princes from a kingdom left to their imagination. The thought delighted him.

They continued their way to where the coaches were parked. He immediately spotted the coachman wearing the most luxurious livery, and approached him. He explained what they wanted: visit Paris and some of its outskirts, return to the hotel to rest and freshen up, leave an hour later for the Théâtre de Monsieur, and finally after the concert be taken to the home of the Marquise de Montesson. He was careful as well to negotiate the price before they left so there would be no surprises at the end.

It was a beautiful, mild and sunny April day, and the ride was enjoyable.

Reserved and not very talkative at first, the coachman turned into an indulgent guide answering all George's questions, who was intrigued by almost everything he saw. While they were crossing the Pont Royal, he saw a huge balloon rise high above the Tuileries Gardens, a basket suspended from it carrying human silhouettes. It took his breath away. 'A hot-air balloon,' the coachman explained when he realized how astounded the boy was. The latter wanted to know how something that heavy could rise into the air and float around up there. He turned to his father and asked him the question. Frederick de Augustus who always had an answer for everything felt incapable of making up a response and simply said: 'It's marvelous, isn't it?'

They'd seen everything they wanted to see in the center of Paris and, as planned, all that was left now was to go to one of the areas outside the city gates, but George was hungry and since they were near the Palais-Royal they stopped at the Café de la Régence where they ordered an omelet with herbs.

When they were finished, the coachman suggested going to the Faubourg Saint-Antoine, which was relatively close. They merely had to continue straight toward the Place de la Bastille and leave via the Porte Antoine to reach the Faubourg in question.

They arrived at the Place de la Bastille with, in its center, the huge fortress for which the square was named. Frederick de Augustus remembered having heard some of the pamphleteers at the Palais-Royal condemn this prison, for them the very symbol of arbitrary power. He shivered in spite of himself. They continued their route. The streets they were now taking grew narrower and narrower, and some of them were dark, creating the impression they'd never seen a ray of sunlight. It wasn't until they'd passed the Antoine gate that they realized something unusual was happening.

A noisy crowd had put up barricades and several coaches had been stopped. The coachman noticed it too late and, besides, in such a narrow street he couldn't have turned around anyway. Armed with sticks, some demonstrators were carrying gallows with two dangling puppets, which George thought were meant for a puppetry act. He was delighted, thinking it was one of those shows the streets of Paris have to offer, like the ones at the Pont-Neuf or Les Halles, only bigger. He wanted to get out of the coach to watch the puppet play closer, since they couldn't see it very well from the coach. He didn't have time to voice his request.

As if lured by the rugged look of the coach and the opulent livery of the coachman, one group broke away from the crowd and came toward them, shouting like the rest: 'Death to the rich! Death to the aristocrats! Death to the exploiters! Cheaper bread! Down with the clergy! Drown those damned priests!'

Soon the ominous group had surrounded them. The horses grew scared and reared. The coachman barely managed to hold them in place while at the same time trying to calm the demonstrators. George's excitement had turned into fear. He was curled up against his father, not understanding why these people were attacking them. Frederick de Augustus was thoroughly intimidated by the shouting he heard, especially by the cries calling for the death of the aristocrats. They thought they were addressing these to him personally. He wanted to yell: 'You're wrong, I'm no aristocrat, don't misinterpret things because of the coach.' He was glad he wasn't dressed like the previous evening, in his princely Oriental attire with kaftan and turban. But what was so detestable about aristocrats that they wanted them dead? Every patron of the arts he'd known and who had helped him was an aristocrat. If you weren't, isn't that what you aspired to become, as the Chevalier de Saint-George had done?

There was no time for him to dwell on these thoughts, as the crowd's rage was growing. He had to make these ranting folks understand that he was neither rich nor an aristocrat and even less a 'damned' priest. In fact, the 'de'[1] in his last name 'de Augustus' was no reference to any noble or aristocratic origin. He had always introduced himself

---

1. The 'de' in French last names is a sign of aristocratic ancestry.

as 'Frederick Augustus Bridgetower of Bridgetown' to indicate that was his hometown in Barbados. But at the Hungarian and Austrian courts, either intentionally or through ignorance, people called him all sorts of fantasy names—'Frederick Bridgetower of Augustus Bridgetown', 'Of Bridgetown Frederick Augustus Bridgetower' or else 'Bridgetower of Bridgetower of Bridgetown'—so that he decided to settle on a simpler and more familiar form, namely 'Frederick Augustus de Bridgetower'. Indeed, his grandfather's father had been a prince. Like many wealthy and powerful Africans, he had entrusted one of his sons to a Dutch captain to take him to Europe so he could get a European education. However, despite the sum the captain was paid for this mission, the latter had sold the child—his grandfather—to a planter on Barbados. But were they right to also consider him a prince, an aristocrat, two generations later? Then a roar exploded, interrupting his thoughts and redirecting the attention of the group that was about to drag them out of the coach: some of the demonstrators had set fire to the two effigies.

Seeing the burning effigies, the crowd suddenly began to roar 'Long live the Third Estate!' Picked up in chorus, the words sounded like cries of hope and the atmosphere unexpectedly lightened up. The anger arising from the crowd quickly made place for a kind of merriment. Also caught up in this easy-going atmosphere, those who'd been threatening the coach finally just asked its occupants to join them in their shouting. And at the top of their voice George, Frederick de Augustus, and the coachman kept repeating 'Long live the Third Estate! Long live the Third Estate!' to the great amusement of the throng that ultimately let them through. The coachman didn't need to be told twice, afraid the mood might change and become belligerent once more. He rode straight ahead in the direction of the Vincennes racetracks. Having recovered from his enormous fright, George asked his father what the 'Third Estate' was they were paying tribute to, which had saved them. He didn't have a clue. He didn't want to ask the coachman, avoided answering and, instead, congratulated himself to his son for having hired this stable, dependable coach, or else it would undoubtedly have toppled into the ditch, considering the speed at which the coachman was forcing his horses to gallop.

It wasn't until several days later that Frederick de Augustus realized what a narrow escape they'd made. In fact, it was that day that the discontent among the workers of the Réveillon factory in the Faubourg Saint-Antoine, the largest wallpaper factory in Paris, had erupted into a bloody riot.

It lasted three days during which the factory was plundered and wrecked and the intervention by the troops loyal to the king suffered vast numbers of dead, about nine hundred it was said. Incensed by the high cost of bread and the shortage of basic staples brought on by two consecutive severe winters, spurred on by the subtle influence of the pamphlets condemning the suffering of the people, the privileges of clergy and aristocracy, and outraged by their exclusion from the vote for the Estates General under preparation, the workers had reacted aggressively to a speech by their boss. The latter, the previously mentioned Réveillon, had laid out for them his economic theory to make the manufactured products accessible to the largest number of people. According to him, one had to begin by reducing the cost of bread, which would subsequently allow salaries to be lowered. What the workers remembered from the speech was only the prospect of lowered salaries, which would exacerbate their destitute state even more. The boss barely escaped being lynched and only his effigy and that of one of his henchmen were burned.

The coachman delivered them safely home and came back for them in time to take them to the Théâtre de Monsieur for the premiere of a symphony concertante by the Chevalier de Saint-George. As if nothing had happened.

XII

Everything inside the concert hall took George back to the magical universe of his first concert: the orchestra seats and the tiers above them filled with spectators in their finest attire, the stage with the sounds of equally well-dressed musicians tuning their instruments, and especially the lights, those quivering lights of the candles in the countless chandeliers suspended from the ceiling of the amphitheater.

As guests of Saint-George, his father and he had the best seats. Not knowing that he, too, had been invited, they were happily surprised to see Alex Dumas come in. Looking handsome with his great height and the saber still at his side, he sat down near George and they started talking like old friends. When George complained about the tall hairdo of the lady in front of him that kept him from seeing, he offered to change places with him. Two women, obviously friends, arrived, conversing light-heartedly as they settled into their seats. Frederick de Augustus was struck by their appearance. They seemed out of place in a society where the tyranny of form and frivolity ruled. One was wearing a dress with a décolleté exposing her shoulders, which were covered with a light-weight shawl, while the other, dressed just as simply, had a ribbon tied around her waist. Both wore their hair naturally, loose and rather short. Out of courtesy he bowed his head slightly in a subtle greeting. They smiled and the one sitting close to him introduced herself naturally, which was not the norm:

'Good evening, Sir. I am Louise-Félicité de Kéralio and this is my friend Etta Palm.'

For a split-second Frederick de Augustus wondered if they weren't taking these liberties with him because he was the only black man in the audience. He dismissed that thought almost immediately: the way they were, they would have acted the same with anyone who roused their interest.

'Delighted to meet you, ladies. Frederick de Augustus. My son George and a friend, Alex Dumas.'

George recognized something of his mother in Etta but couldn't quite say what. Her dark brown hair? Her eyes? The simplicity of her clothing? He was still looking at her when she turned to him. Their eyes met. In confusion, like a child caught doing something he shouldn't, George quickly turned his gaze to the orchestra. Etta Palm noticed the boy's embarrassment and gently asked him:

'So, George, do you like music?'

'Yes, Madame. I'm a musician myself. I play the violin.'

Hearing this, Frederick de Augustus didn't miss the opportunity:

'He does more than play, Madame. George is a prodigy. He gave a glorious concert a few nights ago in the Hall des Cent-Suisses.'

George was even more embarrassed when he heard his father singing his praises and was a little annoyed with him. And when Etta Palm asked him if he really was a prodigy, he merely nodded his head with a small self-conscious smile.

During the half hour they spent before the concert began, Frederick de Augustus and the two ladies were chatting as if they'd known each other forever. He found out that Louise-Félicité de Kéralio was a translator and an elected member of the Academy of Arras. But she was most proud of her position as director of a newspaper, a paper she had only just created. Nevertheless, of everything she told him Frederick de Augustus remembered above all else that Louise de Kéralio was working actively against the slave trade in an association known as the 'Society of the Friends of Blacks', founded by Pierre Brissot, one of her friends.

As for Etta Palm, whose accent from the Austrian Netherlands was quite familiar to Frederick de Augustus since he'd heard it in Brussels, she was an advocate for gender equality. She managed to tell him very quickly that she had published a booklet, a *Discourse on the Injustice of the Laws in Favor of Men, at the Expense of Women*. When Frederick de Augustus asked her why that title, she launched into a passionate speech explaining that women—in comparison to men—were good for nothing but finding a husband and making babies. Nothing else! And when he asked her if there were others who shared her opinion, she replied they could be counted on one hand. Among these she mentioned the name of a certain Olympe de Gouges who wasn't afraid to express her ideas in pamphlets and even in stage plays.

When she heard that name, Louise de Kéralio couldn't control herself and to the surprise of Frederick de Augustus fired back:

'That woman is crazy. I really don't understand why Etta admires her so much! Do you find it normal that she wants marriage to be abolished, calling it the "tomb of love"? That she shamelessly advocates sexual freedom, asking that the natural proclivities of partners for entering into relationships outside marriage be taken into account? That she demands that the right to divorce become legal? No wonder that she wants children born out of wedlock, bastards I mean, to be given the same rights as legitimate children! Just imagine! A woman who ignores the natural order of things and wants to make policy like a man, that's the Olympe de Gouges our dear Etta admires so much!' she concluded. Frederick de Augustus was somewhat stunned by these words. He wondered how, on the one hand, someone could fight for the freedom of Blacks and, on the other, deny it to one's female counterparts.

As for Etta, Louise's outburst didn't seem to affect her, it was a speech she'd probably heard from her friend before. To Frederick de Augustus she said:

'Where women are concerned, I've always asked Louise to disentangle herself from the influence of Jean-Jacques Rousseau and stop taking *Emile*, her bedside reading, as the gospel truth. Our famous Rousseau claims that women are made expressly to please men, to tolerate his injustices, and that it is the natural order of things for the woman to obey the man. As a faithful apologist, Louise would confine women to the domestic sphere and refuse her any political rights. I never cease to remind her that she wouldn't be directing a paper, if her ideas were to be applied, but to no avail. Despite everything, we're still friends and I haven't given up the hope of changing her mind.'

This exchange left Frederick de Augustus totally perplexed. He was accustomed to the preoccupations of nobles and aristocrats, he was beginning to familiarize himself with the problems of Blacks and people of color in France, he'd taken stock of the poverty, which he'd seen at Les Halles and on the Pont-Neuf, he'd just witnessed the workers and artisans making demands at the Faubourg Saint-Antoine, but it had never crossed his mind that there was a world of women's demands and that, quite like those of men, they were at times confused and contradictory.

※

A small disturbance caused by two gentlemen in search of their seats disrupted the front rows of the orchestra and interrupted the conversation. Recognizing one of them, Alex Dumas whispered into the ear of Frederick de Augustus: 'General Lafayette'. The second one turned out to be Thomas Jefferson, the American ambassador in Paris. A reasonably good amateur violinist, he was a familiar face in the musical world of Paris and one of the subscribers of the Concert Spirituel. He also frequented the high society salons where he was much admired for having written the American Declaration of Independence, which he himself then had translated into French, a text into which he had chiseled these remarkable words:

We hold these truths to be self-evident, that all men are created equal, that they are endowed by their Creator with certain unalienable Rights, that among these are Life, Liberty and the pursuit of Happiness.

They called him an enlightened man. Furthermore, the rumor had it that, inspired by this text, his friend Lafayette was also in the process of developing a Declaration of Human Rights, which he planned to present at the session of the States General.

Seeing these two important figures stirred Frederick de Augustus' curiosity and led him to check what other notables were present. Louise de Kéralio and Etta Palm, who knew several of them, were happy to discreetly point them out. They mentioned names most of which he didn't know, although a few of them did ring a bell. Among these were Choderlos de Laclos, whom he knew as a mediocre librettist but was now a successful writer with *Les Liaisons dangereuses*, the book that the salesman at the bookstore had wanted him to buy; Camille Desmoulins, one of the orators he'd heard at one of the cafés at the Palais-Royal, although Louise de Kéralio said he was a stutterer, sitting next to his wife Lucile; Madame Roland, who ran a much frequented salon, which he found out was on the Rue Guénégaud, next to their hotel; François Joseph Talma, the adored actor of the moment whose posters he'd seen on the walls of the Comédie-Française, seated next to the poet André Chénier—author of the famous verse 'Elle a vécu, Myrto, la belle Tarentine'[1], Louise de Kéralio insisted on specifying—and Fabre

---

1. 'She lived, Myrto, the lovely Tarantine'.

d'Églantine, a failed playwright saved by a song from one of his oper- ettas that everyone in Paris was humming: 'Il pleut, il pleut, bergère, / Rentre tes blancs moutons'.[1] Pierre de Beaumarchais, a watchmaker, arms trafficker, and swindler who'd just come out of the Bastille prison but was deemed respectable once again thanks to the success of his two plays, *The Barber of Seville* and *The Marriage of Figaro.* There was no end to the list. Were one to have any doubt about the popularity of Saint-George and his music, the presence of these personalities and the crowded hall would remove any uncertainty. But Frederick de Augus- tus realized one thing above all else: the importance of music. It didn't exist on the periphery but lay at the very heart of society, indeed of the regime, where all those who claimed to keep things moving in what- ever area it might be in the Kingdom of France interconnected and met each other.

A thunderous applause took over the hall and stopped their conver- sation. It welcomed to the stage Saint-George, preceded by the two soloists, Kreutzer and Rode. As always, Saint-George was elegantly dressed in white silk pants and a brocade jacket.

It was the first time Frederick de Augustus and George heard Saint-George's instrumental music. They found it sparkling and bril- liant, containing everything that created the charm of gallant music. The performance of the two violinists was clean, clear, and precise the way the French loved it, as opposed to the seething but sometimes muddled playing of Italian artists. Nevertheless, used to the music of Haydn that had nurtured them, a music that oscillated between solem- nity and joviality, tempestuousness and passion, Frederick de Augustus and his son thought that Saint-George's work was a little facile, lack- ing depth, with an harmonic development that was too uncomplicated to push the performers to the apex of their talent. On the other hand,

---

1. 'Il pleut…' [It's raining, it's raining, shepherdess/bring home your white sheep]. The song has come down through the years as a children's ditty and is known by every French child.

what pleased Frederick de Augustus was the *adagio* of the second movement where the intermittent use of increased minor seconds expressed a certain melancholy that brought back vague memories of his far-away native island.

While Dumas vanished immediately after the concert, Frederick de Augustus, Louise de Kéralio and Etta Palm continued chatting in the large lobby of the concert hall, despite the disapproving glances from a few elegant ladies who looked them up and down as they passed, hanging onto the arm of their escort in frock coat. The conversation didn't come to an end until George, tired of studying the chandeliers and the setting of the great hall, approached his father and, trying to be discreet, nudged him with his elbow, which didn't escape the two ladies.

As they waited for their coach at the exit door, the image of their vehicle being surrounded by a crowd of people clamoring for the death of the rich and the aristocrats unexpectedly came back to Frederick de Augustus. For a moment he had the bizarre impression of floating between two parallel cities: on the one hand, that of the Pont-Neuf and the working-class areas where people were hungry because there was no bread and where the powerful were cursed; on the other, that of the elite to which the audience in this concert hall of the Tuileries Palace belonged. When these two separate faces of Paris met, the shock could be ferocious, as he had noted earlier!

Their coach arrived and they rushed in. Between a trot and a gallop to make up for their delay, it brought them to the soiree of the Marquise de Montesson, morganatic wife of the Duc d'Orléans, patroness of Saint-George, at her salon at the Palais-Royal.

XIII

Frederick de Augustus commended himself on having spent time in Brussels before coming to Paris to prepare for the worldly life in the French capital. Thus, he knew that the salons were run almost exclusively by women of the nobility or the upper bourgeoisie and that there were two kinds: those where they chattered among themselves, spreading malicious court gossip, displaying their finery, and the salons where writers, artists, politicians, and philosophers gathered, and new ideas were tossed around. The salon of the Marquise de Montesson belonged to the latter.

�֍

Despite their late departure from the concert hall, George and his father arrived on time to hear Saint-George—once again—who, in the role of master-of-ceremonies, announced that the evening would begin with music, with the Marquise on the harp accompanying a singer whose name they didn't remember. Frederick de Augustus wondered if this might not be Louise-Rosalie Dugazon, Saint-George's mistress.

After presenting three songs, a man at the pianoforte followed them.

This instrument was beginning to replace the harpsichord, which had dominated in the salons until then. Musicians undoubtedly found the pianoforte more expressive because, with its strings being struck, it allowed for soft and powerful sounds to be produced at will and thereby moderated their playing, which was impossible with the harpsichord whose notes always had the same intensity, even though its plucked strings delivered a pure, crystalline sound. George immediately recognized the piece the pianist was playing: the *rondo alla turca* by the young Amadeus Mozart, as they called him here, with its rapidly alternating majors and minors, considered to be characteristic of the music of Turkish Janissaries.

※

The evening didn't really become animated until after the musical performances, when the valets and women attendants began to serve drinks and appetizers. That was the moment Saint-George chose to introduce his personal guests to the Marquise de Montesson.

Sitting on a loveseat, she was chatting with three ladies, one of whom instantly drew Frederick de Augustus's attention, not only because she didn't have a sophisticated hairdo like the other women, but also because she was an extremely attractive brunette.

'If I may interrupt, Madame, please allow me to introduce the young virtuoso I was telling you about, George Augustus Polgreen Bridgetower, and his father who travels with him.'

'Delighted,' she said. 'Let me say that I, too, am one of your admirers. I was at the Cent-Suisses Hall yesterday and was captivated by your performance. It was marvelous! If I'm not taking you by surprise, would you play something for us? I'm sure that our guests would appreciate it enormously.'

Before George had time to respond, Frederick de Augustus couldn't prevent himself from intervening, so obsessed was he with the mission he'd assigned himself, to promote the talent of his son at every opportunity.

'George is never taken by surprise, Madame. He is ready to play for you.'

Although everyone had been looking at George until then, all eyes now turned to him.

'Welcome to you as well, Monsieur,' said the Marquise.

'I, too, am delighted to meet you,' the young brunette said. 'You're arriving at a very propitious time.'

Again Frederick de Augustus was struck by her beauty but, judging by the intensity of her eyes and the look of determination on her face, he sensed she was certainly the sort of woman who wouldn't easily be taken in.

'We were just talking with Madame about my play, which will soon be produced at the Comédie-Française. As I was watching you approach, I suddenly had a brilliant idea.'

'What sort of an idea?' Frederick de Augustus asked, intrigued.

'Wait, Olympe, our young virtuoso hasn't answered us yet,' the Marquise de Montesson interrupted. 'Your father tells us that you're prepared to play something for us,' she went on as she turned to George.

'Yes, Madame,' Frederick de Augustus hastened to confirm, eager to win her good graces.

One could never know, her patronage might well be helpful to them. He encouraged his son with a look and a nod. But George was angry with his father who was making him perform without asking his opinion. He didn't feel he was ready at all and he didn't want to play.

'I would like to, Madame, but I don't have my violin,' George said.

'We have plenty of violins here,' said the Marquise.

'I only play well on my own instrument, Madame.'

Frederick de Augustus was floored. How could George contradict him like that in public? How was he going to make up for this faux pas that ran the risk of costing them the consideration of a potential sponsor?

'The artist has spoken,' the Marquise approved with a knowing smile. 'Art has its constraints. I understand you very well. A musician can only summon the muse when he and his instrument are collaborating. So we'll do it another time. Go ahead, don't waste any more time, help yourselves and make the most of this good company.'

Then the Marquise turned to a couple waiting their turn to introduce themselves. Frederick de Augustus felt relieved and was grateful to the Marquise.

'Come, George, I'll introduce you to Baillot, one of our finest violinists,' said Saint-George and grabbed the boy's arm.

Giornovichi, Kreutzer, Rode, Baillot, Saint-George! This country is bursting with excellent violinists, Frederick de Augustus thought while Saint-George moved away with his son. If despite all these talents, his child had managed to make himself noticed and stood out, it was because he truly was a little genius, he convinced himself. In the end, they had no reason to be envious of the Mozarts, father and son.

As Madame de Montesson continued to welcome the guests filing past her, the dark-haired young woman pulled Frederick de Augustus aside.

'I was telling you I had an idea that I'd like to propose to you.'

'Excuse me, but I didn't quite get your name.'

The young woman laughed.

'You're absolutely right, I forgot to introduce myself: Olympe de Gouges.'

'Olympe de Gouges?' Frederick de Augustus said, making no attempt to hide his surprise.

'Yes, indeed. Why the surprise?'

'They told me about you. Etta Palm.'

'Oh yes, we know each other. There aren't many of us, you know, who think that women need to be emancipated from men and lead their own lives. However, that's not what I wanted to talk to you about. It's about theater, my passion, and whether you might not want to be the leading actor in my most recent play.'

She took a copy of the work from a small bag attached to her belt and handed it to him. He read the title: *Zamore and Mirza, or the Fortunate Shipwreck*. What interested him was the reference below the title, 'an Indian drama'. His bafflement increased when he opened the work and saw that the play was preceded by a preface with the title 'Reflections on Negroes'. He raised his eyes with a questioning look.

'Please know, Sir, that the Negro race has always drawn my attention to its wretched lot,' she began to explain. The play dealt with the horrors of slavery and the injustice perpetrated by the white masters. She'd given a private reading of it in the theater owned by the Marquise de Montesson, who found it so interesting that she used her influence to recommend it to the Comédie-Française. However, even before reading it, the group had made it clear to her that they couldn't take on the play unless the title was changed and it was turned into an Indian drama. With the current title it would generate the wrath of owners and captains of the slave ships who were among its greatest patrons. Therefore she had changed the original title *Black Slavery or the Fortunate Shipwreck* to *Zamore and Mirza, or the Fortunate Shipwreck*. But it made no difference. The Comédie-Française found the text too subversive, saw it as an attack on the monarchy and on the interests of the planters who created the wealth of the colonies. Since the theater couldn't immediately refuse a play recommended by a woman like Madame de Montesson, one of their benefactors as well, its administrators invented a pretext they believed to be irrefutable.

'Guess which one?' she abruptly asked Frederick de Augustus.

Caught off guard, he began to stammer:

'Eh, that the play is too long… that creating exotic sets would be too expensive…'

'No, not at all: the difficulty of covering every actor with dirty grease!'

'No!' Frederick de Augustus exclaimed, unable to keep from uttering his surprise and amusement out loud.

'Yes!' Olympe de Gouges went on. 'But wait, there's more. They thought they'd mollified me, but they were wrong. I went back a few days later with a recipe for liquorice juice that produces the most beautiful color of copper! They were cornered.'

'What a woman!' Frederick de Augustus said to himself, admiring the mocking smile that briefly lit up her face, like that of a mischievous child delighted to have played a rotten trick on some smart guys.

'Humankind is the same everywhere,' she stated passionately. 'The color may be different, just as with all animals, with all plants that nature has produced. Everything has variations and therein lies the beauty of nature. And is humankind not its greatest masterpiece?' she concluded as she looked Frederick de Augustus straight in the eye.

Without waiting for his answer, Olympe de Gouges continued:

'In the end, the play was performed without any conviction by a band of made-up actors who had no feeling whatsoever for the text. It was a complete failure. Now, I'm sure of it, if this play, the way I wrote it, had been played by a genuine Black person, it would have truly touched people, it would have made them grasp the injustice of slavery. So I want to give it a second chance, that's why I'm suggesting that you embody Zamore.'

Frederick de Augustus wasn't completely surprised. It wasn't the first time that a Negro was asked inappropriately to play the role of a Black on stage just because he was black. One Sunday in Vienna, when he and George were in Augarten Park with Soliman to attend a *Morgenkonzerte* where he had the opportunity to see the famous son of Leopold perform for the first time, a man had approached them, undoubtedly attracted by Soliman's original attire. Without a glance at Frederick de Augustus and George, the man bluntly addressed Soliman, telling him he was convinced that Providence had urged him to come to this early morning concert, even though he never came here: Soliman was exactly the one he was looking for to play the jealous Moor in the adaptation of a Shakespeare play he'd just finished. He'd given it the title *Othello, the Moor in Vienna* and, according to him, only a genuine Black like Soliman could play the role. Frederick de Augustus didn't refuse Olympe de Gouges' offer straightaway, but he asked her to give him time to read the play before deciding.

They parted company promising to see each other again and Frederick de Augustus went in search of his son.

※

There must have been at least fifty guests in the salon. Some were seated, others were standing and conversing in small groups whose configurations changed as the guests circulated, glass in hand. Even if Alex Dumas, Etta Palm, or Louise de Kéralio weren't present among the invited, he did recognize several people who had been at Saint-George's concert. It was like being inside the *Almanach de Gotha*[1], you only had to turn around to trip over a celebrity. Frederick de Augustus was fascinated by the level of the discussions, which he caught here and there, by the witticisms they tossed around that were immediately picked up by someone else, then launched at a third, possibly to the original source. Verbal fireworks were exploding and bedazzling. Accustomed to the worldly soirees at the Chateau Esterhazy, he noticed a difference. The behavior was certainly courteous but it lacked the weighty protocol. Every individual seemed to be able to express him- or herself with astonishing openness.

He spotted his son at a table where they seemed to be paying him special attention; he didn't seem bored, quite the contrary. It had to be a table of musicians, for hadn't Saint-George mentioned he would take George to meet Baillot?

---

1. The *Almanach de Gotha* was a kind of 'Who's Who' of the nobility and royalty of Europe.

'You see, hot air is lighter than cold air. So when you heat the air in the balloon it will grow lighter and create a thrust upward. It's that simple!' Frederick de Augustus heard as he approached. George's eyes were sparkling with curiosity and wonder.

'My father, Frederick de Augustus,' he said. 'Papa, let me introduce Monsieur Lavoisier. He's explaining the laws of physics and chemistry to me.'

Lavoisier held out his hand. Frederick de Augustus then greeted each guest as presented: Condorcet, Lagrange, Monge, Borda. Visibly impressed, one of them, Condorcet, said:

'You have a brilliant son, Monsieur Bridgetower.'

Frederick de Augustus was stunned. He thought his son was with musicians and here he was at a table of scientists, mathematicians, chemists, and physicists. He was struck by their friendliness. He'd never heard their names before, but if they were guests of the Marquise de Montesson they had to be important. Most astonishing was the fact that they seemed truly pleased to be conversing with a child. He felt out of place and withdrew, leaving them to their explanations of phenomena he deemed too complicated.

One by one, the guests were beginning to say goodbye. Frederick de Augustus, too, thought that it was time to leave. Impatiently, he waited for George who was still at the scientists' table. When he finally joined his father, his eyes still gleaming and a big smile on his lips, Frederick asked his son, as if he'd been in danger:

'Are you all right? Isn't your brain too clogged up? Is your mind still functioning?'

'Of course, it's functioning,' George said amused.

'Did you understand anything of what they were talking about?'

'Oh yes, I learned a lot about Nature. Now I know how a

Montgolfier works. But what fascinated me most was their plan to measure the Earth.'

'Measure the Earth?'

'Yes, measure the Earth for the purpose of inventing a universal measure of length. Taking turns, each one of them explained it to me in a simple way so I would understand. It was Borda who started. He told me there were too many measures of length in the kingdom, between height, cubit, span, inch, palm, foot, fathom, and still more, there's no end to it and it's all very confusing. Then Laplace explained that in order for his measure to be really useful, it would have to be universal, that is to be adopted by all the peoples of the earth. Then Lagrange said that, in order to be accepted by all peoples, the measure had to take the Earth itself as reference, common to all humanity. So, ideally this unity would be a fraction of the Earth's circumference. And when I asked how they were going to measure this circumference, Monge told me they didn't know yet, but they were in the process of figuring that out.'

'Exciting, isn't it?' Frederick de Augustus said, visibly having his doubts about the usefulness of the whole thing.

❧

Basic courtesy required them to thank their hostess before leaving, so they went over to where the Marquise was standing. In her long flowing gown, she was in conversation with a man whom Frederick de Augustus recognized right away from the concert earlier. It was Thomas Jefferson. He had probably broken his right arm, because he was carrying it in a sling. Slightly behind him stood a mulatto woman, holding his briefcase and coat. Frederick de Augustus was impressed to see him there, two steps away, the man who had written his country's Declaration of Independence, an anthem to liberty. When Jefferson finally finished bidding her farewell, he turned to the Mulatto woman who helped him put his good arm into the sleeve of his coat. He looked up at Frederick de Augustus, who gave him a little smile and lightly bowed his head, hoping the great man would return the courtesy and perhaps even shake his hand. Not only did Jefferson ignore him completely but he did so very conspicuously, and thereby instantly dampened Frederick de Augustus' enthusiasm. Jefferson turned on his heels and left, followed by his servant.

The scene hadn't escaped Olympe de Gouges. As soon as Frederick de Augustus and George had said their goodbyes to the Marquise, she approached them and said sarcastically:

'You wanted to exchange pleasantries with that hypocrite Jefferson?'

'Hypocrite?' exclaimed Frederick de Augustus. 'The man is certainly not very affable, but from that to calling him a hypocrite...'

'He came to bid adieu to the Marquise because he's just been called back to his country to take up the post of Secretary of State. I'm sure he'll be happy to return to his slaves.'

'Do you mean to tell me he owns slaves?'

'Oh yes, close to two hundred I've been told.'

'No, no,' Frederick de Augustus protested. 'You must be confusing him with someone else. He is the one who wrote "all men are created equal".'

'Yes. Except for Blacks, Indians, and women. That he owns slaves is one thing, everyone does in America and in our own colonies. What sickens me, however, is that he has become the theoretician of the inferiority of Black people. I can tell you that during a very animated discussion he was having with Condorcet at the Café Procope, I myself heard him confirm that free Blacks were parasites, harmful to society and, like children, incapable of taking care of themselves; that if they were brave it was because their underdeveloped brain was too small to grasp danger before it hits them. Let's not even talk about art, they're incapable of painting or sculpting. That's what your great man professes!'

Frederick de Augustus was dumbfounded. He truly didn't know

whether he should believe Olympe de Gouges or not. But what man doesn't have his contradictions? He tried to reason to lessen the shock he was feeling. Haydn, for instance, was a genius, yet he allowed Prince Esterhazy to treat him as a simple domestic servant. Voltaire, who was said to have invented tolerance, was nevertheless quite intolerant of Jews and Blacks, whom he didn't like at all and would mock to his heart's content. Besides, wasn't it that same Voltaire who had explained the origin of Blacks through the fact that in hot countries monkeys had 'subjugated girls'? In order not to remain standing there speechless and looking stupid, he should say something. So, changing the topic of the conversation, he said:

'You mentioned Condorcet, I know him. George was at his table just now and he thinks George is a brilliant child.'

'Yes, I do know Condorcet as well. I admire him greatly, he supports the same causes I do. I'll never forget the words he wrote in an epistle intended for Black slaves: "My friends, although my skin color is different from yours, I have always regarded you as my brothers." Is that not stronger, more sincere, than that grandiloquent vacuity of "all men are created equal"? And do you know what pseudonym Condorcet used when he published his letter? "*Mr. Schwartz*"! "Black" in German. Just imagine that! In any case, I heartily urge you to read it.'

'I promise. I should spend more time at the salons, one learns so much! I would never have imagined that Jefferson…'

'Just wait, I haven't told you everything about him yet: your Jefferson is against mixed marriages. He has even developed a mathematical formula to determine the fraction of white blood an individual might have. And yet, using his widowerhood as pretext, he brought along the young Mulatto woman you saw, Sally Hemmings, his slave in America, his daughter's governess here. But above all his mistress. All of Paris knows it. Can one be any more hypocritical than that?'

'I don't know,' Frederick de Augustus replied, embarrassed by these revelations, 'but what I can tell you is that we men, even the greatest among us, have a dark side. Well, we must say goodbye now, it has been a very long day for us. As for the play, I'll give you my answer as soon as I've read it. I'm anxious to read Condorcet's piece as well, I mean the piece by Dr. Schwartz.'

They finally left the Marquise's salon, exited the walls of the Palais-Royal, and went to look for a coach, not having retained the one they'd hired earlier to take them back to the hotel. Frederick de Augustus had learned a lot: elements that had been disparate inside his mind until then were beginning to come together to form a more coherent whole.

XIV

They were back at their hotel around midnight. George undressed immediately, while Frederick de Augustus collapsed in the easy chair, sighing loudly as if to say that his tired body needed to relax before going to bed. On the low table next to the chair lay the book he'd bought in one of the bookshops at the Palais-Royal, the title of which he'd already forgotten. He picked it up and, as he carelessly flipped through the pages, he heard some notes on the violin that stopped as quickly as they had started. It was George and his mania for always playing a few moments before going to bed, after putting some rosin on the strings to make sure everything was in good order. In his nightshirt the little boy came to him.

'I'm really tired. I'm going to sleep now.'

'What a day this has been, George! Going from a lovely spring morning to a riot where we were almost hanged like outlaws, then to a glamorous concert, to end the evening at the home of a Marquise where you run into the greatest minds, it's enough to go to your head!'

'I was really scared when I saw that crowd come rushing at our coach. Fortunately, the Third Estate saved us. Actually, what is that famous Third Estate? You still haven't explained it to me.'

Now Frederick de Augustus knew the answer. His conversations at the salon of the Marquise de Montesson hadn't been fruitless.

'It's both easy and hard to understand. French society rests on three orders, the nobility, the clergy, and the Third Estate. Only the Third Estate, which represents ninety-eight percent of the population, works, produces the country's wealth, and pays taxes, but these people have no rights at all, or very few. It happens that right now France is going through difficult times: The State is ruined and up to its ears in debt, there's no bread as you yourself saw, and the Parisians are hungry. Everyone is upset: the poets and philosophers are demanding liberties and writing pamphlets, workers are attacking the managers, in the country the farmers are rebelling against the nobility and clergy who are exploiting them. So, in order to find solutions to this crisis, the king has agreed to a large assembly known as the "States General". It will open next week with delegates arriving from every corner of the kingdom. They'll be bringing lists of grievances that itemize all the things that aren't working in the country. You understand it now?'

'So the workers who threatened us are part of the Third Estate?'

'Yes, just like the boss they wanted to lynch. Most of those managers are middle-class, just like the workers, and the bourgeois are commoners, that is to say, neither nobles nor clergy.'

'And Saint-George, does he belong with the nobles or with the Third Estate?'

''Hard to tell. Inside his head, he surely sees himself as an aristocrat.'

'If we were French, would we belong to the nobility or the Third Estate?'

'I don't know, but one thing I'm sure of: you and I are free men. And I tell you, my son, there is no higher status.'

'We're nothing, no nobility no clergy but we are free men! I'll remember that, Papa. Now I'm going to bed. Are you still going to read? What are you reading?'

Frederick de Augustus read him the title: *Paul et Virginie.*

'It's the book I bought last night at the Palais-Royal, you remember?'

'Of course! The bookseller even told us it's about islands, oceans, and slaves. You think it's as good as *Robinson Crusoe*, which I'm reading right now?'

'I don't know. I'll tell you when I've finished it. In any case, I'm very interested in anything that talks about islands, oceans, and slavery.'

❧

George went away. Frederick de Augustus watched his son go off and started to think about what he'd just told him, that there was no higher status than that of being free. Could he understand that, not knowing what slavery was? Anyhow, he would never broach that topic with him, it might disturb his young mind.

Thinking back, it seemed to Frederick de Augustus that he'd spent the entire soiree at the Marquise de Montesson talking only about slavery. Every conversation had led to it. He wondered why people as intelligent as a Voltaire or a Jefferson, and so many others, thought that Blacks were inferior beings, close to animals, no more than merchandise. Was that idea inherent to European thinking?

He'd barely asked himself the question when he remembered the last conversation he had with Soliman the evening before his departure from Brussels. Soliman had received him in his library. Of all the evenings they'd spent together, this one was the most memorable. For once, fearing perhaps that they might never see each other again, his friend had opened up to him in a surprising way, revealing that part of his past he'd always discreetly covered up each time Frederick de Augustus tried to find out a little more about his life before he arrived in Vienna. Soliman's experience turned out to be entirely different from his own.

Born in Africa on the bank of the Sokoto River, he'd been kidnapped at the age of seven, after his village was raided and his parents slaughtered by Black converts to Islam, henchmen of Arab slave traders who'd come from the North. These Islamized Blacks were even more zealous than the Arabs in their persecution of 'impure' infidels, as if to prove their allegiance to their masters. They came to Soliman's village during the night, surrounded it and, after killing the night watchmen, burned down the houses and captured the villagers who, in their panic over the fire and unable to defend themselves, were trying to flee. Together with the people from the neighboring villages, the traffickers seized about a hundred people that night.

In a forced march, the women with shackled feet, the men kept together by twos with a board that had a neck halter on either end confining their neck, the children chained to one another, the slave hunters brought all of them to Timbuctoo where the traders were waiting. These Arabs came to the great slave market with horses, salt, and man-made products. With the slaves they bought they left either for the Nile basin and the shores of the Red Sea, or went North across the Sahara toward the Mediterranean. Soliman was taken the northern route, walking through the desert for several months. He was as heavily loaded as the dromedary with which he struggled to keep up. He lived through hunger, thirst, the biting cold of the Saharan nights, and the suffocating heat of the day. Many people died. From time to time during their long march he'd notice lots of white bones sticking up from the sand, skeletons of the wretched captives who, unable to keep going, had been abandoned without any qualms over their sad fate.

He finally arrived at his destination somewhere in North Africa.

At this point in his account Soliman stopped, as if recounting the rest was unspeakable. After a silence, which Frederick de Augustus respected, he picked up his story again.

Before selling them, they castrated the boys and men under horrifying conditions. The operation was so barbaric that very few survived: for every survivor about a dozen died. He still couldn't understand how he'd managed to escape it. Perhaps his emaciated body had led others to believe he wouldn't live very long.

Frederick de Augustus was aghast. He knew about the horrors of the trans-Atlantic slave trade, but no one had ever told him about Arab-Muslim slavery, equally horrible, in some respects perhaps worse. He could especially not find any economic logic in the castration that caused the death of so many slaves. He asked Soliman, who replied:

'You see, these slave traders didn't reason the same way those your father knew in the Caribbean did. For them, having slaves reproduce is desirable and even encouraged, for it is essential to their prosperity. It's like having livestock; the more they multiply, the richer the owner becomes. This economic logic doesn't exist among the Arab-Muslim slave traders, obsessed as they are with the fear of seeing these Blacks settling down and having sexual relations with the women in the harems, whose guardians and servants they are. Therefore they had to turn them into eunuchs, castrate them, that is. Worse yet, since they didn't deprive themselves of raping the black slaves, children thus conceived were systematically eliminated!'

Speechless, Frederick de Augustus thus discovered one aspect of the barbarism of slavery that he never would have imagined. Seeing the bewilderment on his face, Soliman resumed his narrative in a calm voice but that grew gradually more intense as the account continued:

'Ask yourself, my dear Frederick, how do you explain the presence today of such a large black population in the Americas while, despite the huge numbers of slaves they imported, this is not true at the sultanates and kalifates? Where did they go, all those Blacks who crossed the Red Sea in the direction of the Arabian Peninsula, packed up in dhows under the most atrocious conditions? Do you think they simply vanished just like that into some immense black hole? It's the result of those despicable practices. Castration and infanticide!'

Soliman had uttered those last words with a vehemence that was rare in this usually so restrained man. As if that evening, when he was saying goodbye to his friend, the long-repressed suffering suddenly broke through uncontrolled. The only friend who could understand it in the city of Vienna, even though he seemed to be perfectly integrated there, was one of its celebrities. He'd stood up and gone over to one of the shelves of his library that held a three-volume work bound in red Moroccan leather. He knew exactly what he was looking for. He took out one of them, came back to Frederick de Augustus, and began to leaf through it.

'Listen to this,' he cried out. '"The only people that tolerate slavery are the Negroes, because of their inferior level of humanity, their place being closer to the animal stage." Those are the words of Ibn Khaldoun in his *Prolegomena to Universal History, Al-Muqaddimah* in Arabic.'

He threw the volume of the *Al-Muqaddimah* down on the little table so forcefully that it rattled under the jolt, causing the bottle of strong alcohol and the liquor-filled glasses to jump.

'You read Arabic?' Frederick de Augustus asked.

Soliman smiled, somewhat more relaxed.

'No, not at all. I read it in the German translation. The only Arabic I know are the Koranic verses they had us drone when they were trying to make us convert by force during our captivity.'

'Who is this Ibn Khardoun?' Frederick de Augustus asked.

'The greatest Muslim historian and philosopher of the fourteenth century.'

'What he says there isn't all that original, I've heard it several times before,' Frederick de Augustus answered. 'Anyway, he's making silly statements. Didn't he see the Slavic slaves of the Arabs? They were white, after all!'

'Doesn't stop his thinking from having had such a great influence that it still persists among today's Arab-Muslims. And since the prophet himself had black slaves... What pains me is that these lines were written four centuries ago and nothing has changed! They still reduce Blacks to slavery. You and I are the exceptions.'

111

On this note of powerlessness their conversation ended.

✦

But after returning from the salon of the Marquise de Montesson, Frederick de Augustus felt less desperate than after his discussion with Soliman. He told himself he'd phrased his final question badly, when he asked how intelligent people could possibly think that the slavery of Black people was in the natural order of things. The better question was really this: what pushed people like Condorcet or Olympe de Gouges to go against the tide of popular belief, even if it meant being blacklisted? He'd had it with turning all this around and around inside his head. He felt he was suffocating. Air, air! … He yearned to be carried off to some other place, to escape from these oppressive thoughts. It would do him good to do some reading.

He took off his shoes, put his feet on the little table and, comfortably wedged into the back of the chair, opened the book he was still holding, and tackled the first sentence. He worshipped first sentences, for him they were the door that gave access to the universe the author suggested. For him, an entry door had to be easy to open: similarly, a book's first sentence had to be simple, clear, and beautiful:

> *On the eastern side of the mountain that rises behind Port*
> *Louis on the Île de France[1], one can see the ruins of two small*
> *huts on a once cultivated piece of land.*

The sweeping sentence breathed. It pleased him no end. So he continued but not for long because his eyelids, heavy with sleep, were closing despite his efforts to stay awake. He gave up the struggle and simply closed them. In his half-slumber, suddenly appearing out of the

---

1. The current name is Mauritius.

semi-darkness, the shiny coins Legros had given him began to dance before his eyes. How much of that was left after what they'd spent this insane day?

Without any warning, a mad desire to go to a gambling house and try his luck at a game of Faro[1] or billiards came over him. His big-time gambling side had suddenly resurfaced. One day in Vienna, at the Hugelman Café, he had bet a month's salary during a billiard game, in small bits at a time of course, but in its totality nevertheless, and he had lost it all. To be able to get back to Eisenstadt, he had to borrow the money from Soliman, to his great embarrassment. He'd sworn to himself he wouldn't make that mistake again, but it hadn't prevented him from doing so a few months later, with the same result.

Until this moment, the presence of his son had curtailed his freedom. Now that he was asleep, he could perhaps go out and come back at dawn before George got up. As a precaution he would take only a third of the money they had left and, if fate smiled upon him, he could win it back doubly, maybe three times over. After all, he wasn't that much of a novice, he, too, knew how to cheat if need be. And should he lose, he wouldn't lose all of it. While he was ruminating, another question came into his mind: how were things done with women in Paris? He knew about Vienna. All you had to do was go to Graben Square, not far from the Plague Column that stood in the center of it, and discreetly slip into one of the alleyways concealed by the opulently decorated houses.

He'd heard that society people in Paris made their amorous appointments at the Théâtre Nicolet on the Boulevard du Temple, where they'd rent half-dark boxes and, during the show—often a little farcical comedy—they would feel as comfortable as if they were in a bedroom. He'd also been told that among true libertines the current crave was for

---

1. Pharaon or Faro is a seventeenth-century French gambling game, played with a deck of cards.

anything exotic and wild. To satisfy their fantasies, they'd begun dreaming of creatures from elsewhere, at first of white Creole women born in the colonies who, once in France, still carried within them, so they claimed, the indolent languor of the tropics. But in the realm of exoticism, many were now in quest of Mulatto women, even Negresses. They had even given him the address of a house where the prices were auctioned. Besides, Frederick de Augustus had noticed that this quest for 'wild love' was also of interest to some of whom he'd never have suspected it: in the *Chronique de Paris* he'd read a short news item reported by a guard of the promenade of the Champs-Elysées. The guard recorded it rather humorously in the following terms: 'Arrested around eight o'clock in the evening, a Negress with an abbot, who said he was her confessor. Discharged, after ordering the abbot not to commit a second offense taking confession from his penitents under the trees, by night.' He'd been quite amused.

Reeling with sleep, he ended up by painfully getting out of the easy chair and undressing without really being aware of it. He collapsed into the bed. He'd barely fallen asleep, when he, too, began to dream of Mulatto women and Negresses, wondering if he shouldn't attempt the adventure as well since, having landed in London as a child and leaving quite young for England's interior, he had never visited any of them. But in what way were these Mulatto women and Negresses different? Did they have something extra to offer?

XV

It took three weeks of planning, of discussions interspersed with many courtesy calls and moments of weariness during which he wondered if he wasn't just wasting his time watching the drivel fly around, when at last Frederick de Augustus attained what he so passionately wanted, a 'concert for the benefit of George Augustus Bridgetower'. It was no mere promise, for the duly signed contract included a firm date as well as the performance location, the Pantheon Hall on the Rue de Chartres. He couldn't have asked for anything more. His goal this time wasn't so much to use his son's talent to dazzle the public as it had at the first concert, but rather to exploit his talent to gain the maximum earnings possible. Thus, in order to be well prepared before the negotiations, he had enquired about the honorarium Viotti had received for his concert, not with the intention of being paid as much as the great master, but to have a base figure upon which to negotiate. It was a good thing, for at the end of the day he had secured a sum of nine hundred pounds, which had surprised even himself.

A lovely sun greeted him when, contract in hand, he left the office and went out into the street. He was in a state of euphoria. At this very moment the world was the way he wanted it to be, the way he'd dreamed it to be. An odd feeling of gratitude toward the city of Paris arose within him; he inhaled its air deeply and wondered if you could make a city feel your love, feel your desire to embrace it. Yes, he loved Paris, its wide arteries bordered with palaces, parks, gardens, and even its winding alleys in which he'd become lost one day while looking for a clandestine house that had been recommended to him; in spite of the beggars who assailed him and a few scoundrels who called out to him, he kept going, his hand on the handle of his saber, through the seedy little streets that, despite everything, he found surprisingly attractive.

Not only was this a beautiful city, it imbued him with a feeling of freedom he'd never felt before, not even in Vienna. In comparison he now found Vienna oppressive, enfolded by its fortifications as if the Ottoman troops were still camping on the banks around the city about to attack, although they'd been defeated more than a century before. But there was something more: where else could he have met some of the world's most brilliant scholars and philosophers who treated him as an equal, who conversed with him and his son as peers? In Eisenstadt he may well have been ranked among the 'officers' of the court in the same way as Haydn, he may well be the indispensable interpreter in German or Hungarian for countless distinguished guests who passed through the chateau speaking French, English, Italian or Polish, but in the eyes of Prince Esterhazy he was still no more than a domestic servant even if he was thought to be superior to lower classes of cart makers, blacksmiths, or the kitchen and stable personnel.

His wanderings led him to a café. He was by himself, George had stayed at the hotel to practice. He went in and sat down, deciding to quench his thirst with a lemonade and rum. When the waiter placed his order on the table, he took the cinnamon stick out of the gold-colored drink, inhaled its aroma, and slowly began to sip. As he was drinking, a newspaper vendor passed by, offering him several options. He picked *La Chronique de Paris*, a title he was already familiar with, which published random announcements of shows, lost and found, miscellaneous news in brief, and other chitchat. He'd barely emptied his glass when the waiter, who must have been watching him, came dashing over to ask if he would like something else. He nodded his head and ordered what he thought looked most like a Viennese *kleine Schwarzer*, a small cup of very strong black coffee. The only advantage Vienna had over Paris was its coffee, he thought. There the waiters wouldn't harass you to place another order. He'd bring you your coffee with a glass of water and a stack of newspapers, and you were free to stay as long as you wanted, while all he would do is refill your water. Unfortunately, this wasn't the case in Paris. But no city was perfect.

He left the café with *La Chronique* under his arm and the contract in his pocket. The alcohol and the coffee had made him frisky. He decided to walk a little more before finding a coach to take him back to the hotel. A few steps later his eyes were drawn to a bookshop across the street: at the sight of it, he thought of Olympe de Gouges and the book she'd recommended. He remembered that he hadn't finished reading the play she'd given him; he had started it but it hadn't really thrilled him, so he'd put it aside and become engrossed in *Paul et Virginie*; he planned to continue reading it later. He crossed the street, pushed open the shop door and went in.

The bookseller was startled to see the tall black man, saber at his side, enter his store. He certainly didn't belong to his usual clientele. More cordial than usual, he graced him with a broad smile:

'Welcome, Monsieur.'

Frederick de Augustus had barely responded when the salesman continued without pausing:

'I am sure that you'll find anything you want here. I have an entire shelf devoted to the islands, Santo Domingo, Martinique, and the Island of Bourbon. I also have books on the Negroes of Africa…'

'I'm looking for a work by the philosopher Condorcet,' Frederick de Augustus interrupted him.

'Ah? Eh…Condorcet?' the salesman was surprised and a bit disconcerted. 'Do you know the title?'

'No, but if you show it to me, I'll recognize it.'

'Let's see, the philosophers are on this shelf… Ah, here it is, Condorcet, *Mémoire sur le calcul des probabilités, Essai sur la théorie des comètes, De l'influence de la révolution d'Amérique sur l'Europe, Sur l'admission des femmes au droit de cité…*'

Frederick de Augustus nodded negatively each time, then finally said:

'It's a text that deals with slavery.'

'I'm afraid I don't have that. But on that topic I can recommend Mirabeau, Voltaire…'

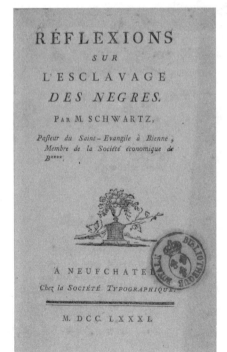

'That's it, it's come back to me!' Frederick de Augustus exclaimed. 'The work was written under a pseudonym, the name Schwarz.'

'Schwartz…,' the bookseller pondered. 'Schwarz… of course! I have a work by a Monsieur Schwarz right here.'

He handed the book to Frederick de Augustus. It was in good shape and hadn't been read yet because the pages weren't cut. He read the title:

REFLEXIONS
Sur
L'ESCLAVAGE
DES NÈGRES
Par M. Schwarz

Pasteur du Saint-Evangile à Bienne
Membre de la Société économique de
B****
A NEUFCHATEL
Chez la SOCIÉTÉ TYPOGRAPHIQUE
M. DCC. L.XXXL

Frederick de Augustus was impressed with the author's audacity: not only did he call himself *Schwartz,* but he also claimed to be a pastor, a Protestant in Catholic France, the same France that not so long ago had murdered them and still barred them from having access to certain important functions! He paid, thanked the bookseller and left. He jumped into the first coach he found to be taken back to the Rue Guénégaud.

George had finished practicing his violin, put it away and, waiting for his father to return, decided to keep reading *Robinson Crusoe,* more than half of which he'd already finished. To take advantage of the daylight, he'd moved one of the chairs over to the window where he'd settled down.

When Frederick de Augustus knocked on the door at last and George leapt from his chair to open it, he saw at first glance that his father was in seventh heaven: a smile lit up his face. How many times lately had he not seen him come back cursing, disgusted with unproductive appointments, with promises without future, and with courtesy visits that in the end were nothing but exercises in hypocrisy. Now he was radiant. He'd barely shut the door when he waved the contract, flapping it around for George to see.

'We did it! We've hit the jackpot! A contract solely for you, all for your benefit!'

George took the document and skimmed it without really understanding it.

'So what am I going to play for this concert?' he asked.

'I discussed the program with the director of the theater. He's leaving us carte blanche under the condition that we put at least one violin concerto on the program—the current fashion in Paris is all about the concerto and the violin—and a Haydn symphony.'

'I'll play a Giornovichi concerto, we promised him we would. For instance, his *Fifth Concerto*, which I like a lot.'

'If you want. But what will be harder is choosing the Haydn piece. Which one to memorize among his hundred or so symphonies?' Frederick de Augustus asked.

'We should choose one the public doesn't know.'

'That will be very difficult. His popularity here is such that every concert has to include one of his symphonies and most often two of them.'

Frederick de Augustus fell silent for a moment and then suddenly his face lit up with a mischievous smile.

'I know what we're going to play, the *Symphony où l'on s'en va*—the Farewell Symphony—!'

George looked at his father in bewilderment.

'It's a work to which I contributed an embellishment,' his father went on.

'How so?'

'It's a long story. You and your brother weren't even born yet. I don't know what came over Prince Nikolaus that summer; but instead of staying in Eisenstadt as usual, he decided to spend the summer at his

120

Esterhaza residence in Hungary. It was a marshy place full of mosquitoes! On top of it all, the construction of the palace wasn't finished, there wasn't enough room, and they prevented us from bringing our wives and children. So Maria, I mean your mother of course, stayed in Eisenstadt. Only Haydn and Luigi Tomasini, the orchestra's first violinist, could bring their families. One month, two months, soon it was autumn, but the Prince stayed on. The musicians became more and more unhappy. Quarrels and fights broke out. Life at the chateau was growing untenable for everyone. Some were talking about resigning. One evening three musicians I knew well because I'd settled a disagreement between them, approached me and asked if I couldn't put in a good word with the prince, since I always accompanied him everywhere. Obviously, I couldn't broach a matter like that with the prince without first seeking advice from someone. I went to see Luigi. He listened, thought for a moment, then told me:

"Parlane con il maestro Haydn, mio caro Moro, troverà di certo una soluzione." He always called me 'the Moor' although I'd told him many times how much I hated that. So I went to see Haydn who listened to me with a harsh look.

"You don't rebel against your prince, young man," he told me. "He's been making me work against all reason for fifteen years, but I comply dutifully, and I don't complain."

"But, Maestro, several of them are at the end of their tether and ready to resign. They miss their wives! What would the prince say if half of the musicians, whose administrator you are, leave tomorrow and you'd be unable to guarantee there'll be a concert that day? That will all come down on you."

He looked at me in dead silence, then he spoke:

"I understand the frustration of all these spirited young men, eager to be back in the arms of their companions. However, there's no point in provoking our prince. We'll have to find a more subtle means of making him understand that it's time to let the musicians go home. Let me think about it, I'll find a way to make him aware of the situation."

He remained silent for another moment, then said:

"Look here, why not by way of music? It's undoubtedly the best method we can find to persuade him. Why not with a symphony, for example?"

"How?" I asked.

"Don't worry about it, I'll find a way."'

'And did he?' George asked more and more curious.

'Yes, and it was a brilliant move. Toward the end of the fall, a concert was scheduled. We didn't suspect anything during the first three movements: it was Haydn's music the way we loved it, inventive and varied, sublime and sometimes theatrical. The surprise came with the final movement: after performing his part, a first musician, a violinist, got up, put his instrument in its case, put it over his shoulder, snuffed the candle by which he read his score and left the stage for all to see, followed by his entire section. Looking puzzled, the prince turned to me. I reassured him and asked him to be patient and wait for the rest, even though I didn't really know what that would be, because neither Haydn nor Tomasini had let me in on the secret. Then a second musician rose, did the same thing, followed by his whole section, then a third, and so on and so forth until in the end, in the now semi-dark hall because the candles had almost all been extinguished, the only ones left were Haydn, Tomasini, and two solitary violinists playing the last notes before falling silent. Surprised at first, the audience had begun to laugh and applauded wildly every time a musician left the stage.

Watching his father mimic the scene George was also convulsed with laughter.

'I understand why you call it the "Farewell Symphony". It must have been very funny! And the prince?'

'He got the message right away. He asked me to call Haydn and when he came and bowed to him respectfully, the prince graciously said: "I've understood you!" He brought his stay to an end the very next day, leaving the Esterhaza Palace for Eisenstadt.'

'That's a really good story,' said George, 'but don't you think it would be too complicated to ask an orchestra to repeat that mime show? We don't have much time left before the concert.'

'Maybe you're right. And besides, the comedic effect might draw the attention away from your performance, while you're the one who should be the only star that day. Well then, we'll choose a different one. I'd like us to propose a program with three pieces, the Haydn symphony and two violin concertos. You picked Giornovichi as the first one, I suggest a concerto by Wolfgang for the second.'

'Ah, no,' George said with a spontaneous cry of revolt. 'I've had enough of your Wolfgang! Wolfgang here, Wolfgang there, it's the only name you have on your lips ever since Eisenstadt. I can't stand hearing that name anymore.'

'Oh, don't take it that way, it was only a suggestion.'

'I'll play a piece by Kreutzer.'

'Excellent idea. A violin concerto by Kreutzer wouldn't be bad at all, especially in Paris. Fine, we'll talk about it some more after dinner. I'm going to take a little rest. In fact, I ended up finding the book by Condorcet. You know, the man who told me you were a brilliant boy. I bought a newspaper as well, *La Chronique de Paris*, to keep us abreast of everything that's going on in this marvelous city.'

Frederick de Augustus who'd remained standing throughout the discussion, collapsed in an armchair while George returned to his corner by the window with the paper.

Once again Frederick de Augustus read the book's title and then cut a few of the pages with a knife, opened it and looked for the introductory sentence:

My friends,

Although my skin color is different from yours, I have always regarded you as my brothers. Nature has formed you with the same spirit, the same reason, the same virtues as the White people. I am speaking here only of those of Europe, for where the Whites of the Colonies are concerned, I will not offend you by comparing them with you, I know how often your loyalty, your integrity, your courage have caused your masters to blush. If one were to seek a man in the Islands of America, it would certainly not be among people with white skin that he would be found.

With an opening sentence like that, the man wasn't double-dealing. But what caught the attention of Frederick de Augustus even more was the last phrase of the page: 'If one were to seek a man in the Islands of America, it would certainly not be among people with white skin that he would be found.' He stopped for a moment, closed his eyes as if to treasure its accuracy when he heard George cry out, all excited. He opened his eyes and saw the boy come rushing toward him, the paper in his hand.

'Hey, Papa, they're talking about Saint-George in the newspaper.'

'Really? Let me see.'

'There,' George said and pointed at a brief article.

Frederick de Augustus read. Three stars of the Opéra—the paper mentioned their names, the singers Sophie Arnould and Rosalie Levasseur, and the prima ballerina Marie-Madeleine Guimard—upon hearing of Saint-George's candidacy for the position, presented the queen with a petition in which they stated that 'their honor and the delicacy of their conscience would never allow them to be subjected to orders from a mulatto'.

Frederick de Augustus received the news like a blow to the stomach. He'd always thought that Saint-George's nomination was a fait accompli, in view of his successes, his connections, his perfect integration into high society, and especially his closeness with Queen Marie-Antoinette. He'd forgotten that, despite all this, there was an invisible barrier he couldn't overcome because of the color of his skin. The Opera, also known as the Royal Academy of Music, was a State institution, created and subsidized by the king. It was so prestigious across all of Europe that they said: Whoever goes to Paris without seeing the Opéra is like the person who goes to Rome without seeing the Pope.'Would the king really allow himself to become the laughing stock of the other European sovereigns and their court by naming a man of color to head this most renowned institution of music? Frederick de Augustus, whose good mood had vanished, wondered how the Chevalier would take it.

Seeing his father's distressed look, George asked:

'What's going on, Papa? Is it serious? You look so very sad.'

'They refused to give Saint-George the position as director of the Opéra.'

'How's that possible? You told me he was the most qualified and that his confirmation was only a formality? Why did they refuse it to him?'

'Eh… what should I tell you… it's difficult to explain… I don't know if you can understand… Be that as it may, I am aghast. I think I'll lie down for a bit before we go out to dinner.'

XVI

Several people had let them know that the issue of *Mercure de France* about to come out would have a review of the concert George had given in the hall of the Pantheon. Frederick de Augustus and George wanted to get their hands on a copy as soon as it appeared at the newsstands. To that end, they decided to have their lunch at one of the cafés at the Palais-Royal where there were several newspaper vendors rather than count on a salesman possibly passing by their hotel. So they sat down at a table at the Café Valois, waiting to be served.

❧

It had been a week since George had given the concert. In addition to the concertos by Giornovichi and Kreutzer, they had selected one of Haydn's *Parisian Symphonies* to complete the program. The audience had been so enthusiastic that George was called back to the stage three times! In contrast to the first concert, not all the spectators were nameless to them anymore: they knew or recognized several personalities.

Olympe de Gouges was there, and Frederick de Augustus had seized the occasion to admit to her that he wasn't keen on acting in her play and that, in any case, he'd never been on stage in his life. Lafayette was there as well, but they were surprised to see Jefferson who had told them he'd attended his last concert in Paris because he was leaving France the following day. Although his arm was no longer in a sling, he was still escorted by the young Mulatto woman. Frederick de Augustus was pleased to see him there. Perhaps George's genius would undermine some of the convictions of the American ambassador who thought that Blacks were incapable of any work of the mind. On the other hand, Saint-George did not attend, which they regretted; moreover, since the rebuff he'd suffered regarding the directorship of the Royal Academy of Music, they hadn't seen him anymore.

❧

They knew the newspapers were at the kiosks when they saw a customer come in holding *Les petites Affiches*. George got up, went out and came back not only with the copy of *Mercure de France* they were waiting for, but also with two other papers, *La Chronique de Paris* and *Le Ménestrel*, which the vendor had made him buy because the latter, he told him, paid particular attention to music and musical shows as well. Frederick de Augustus snatched the *Mercure* from George's hands before he'd even sat down and began to flip through it feverishly. The article was not on the first or the second page. He kept turning the pages, reading the headlines of the various columns, 'Intangible plays in verse and in prose', 'Charades, puzzles, and word games', 'Literary news', 'States General', and so on. He was beginning to think it wasn't there when suddenly in the column 'Concert Spirituel' he saw the review.

'George,' he said, all excited, 'it's here! I found it!'

He started reading out loud:

*A noteworthy debut, & one that is of immense interest
is that of M. Bridgetower, a young Negro of the Colonies, who
played several violin concertos with a clarity, a facility, an
execution & even a sensitivity that is quite rare to find in someone
so young (he is not yet ten years old). His talent, as genuine as it is
precocious, is one of the best responses that can be given to the
Philosophers who want to deprive those of his Nation & his color
of the ability to distinguish themselves in the Arts.*

Frederick de Augustus was thrilled; George, too, was smiling. Suddenly his father burst out laughing.

'Hey George, I didn't know you were a "Negro of the colonies"? And on top of that you're a problem for the philosophers!'

'Where did they get that? My mother is Polish, and you, you're English when you're not being a prince from I don't know what African kingdom!'

'Oh, you know very well I'm not African. I don't even know where Africa is. My father, your grandfather, was born in Barbados and so he didn't know anything about Africa either. The only African I know is Soliman. But it's a handy fable I play with because it makes an impression in Europe's royal courts. I consider myself English because I was born in an English colony, just as the Chevalier de Saint-George considers himself French.'

'So then it's you who are the "Negro of the colonies"?'

'Maybe so. But don't let these questions bother you. What matters is that everyone recognizes your talent. Do the other papers mention it?'

There was nothing in *La Chronique de Paris* while *Le Ménestrel* only had a brief article saying that 'Bridgetower was looked at oddly and liked being applauded'.

'What does "was looked at oddly" mean, Papa?'

'That they looked at you with admiration, that's all,' he replied.

George's face was radiant. He loved playing the violin, he knew he was good—public figures as diverse as Condorcet, Giornovichi, and Kreutzer had told him so—but to see his name and read such laudatory comments in a review as respected as *Le Mercure de France* touched him in a different way. He would have liked to share the article with the entire world.

'I would like you to buy another copy of this review, Papa. I want to send it to Mama,' he said unexpectedly.

'You know perfectly well that your mother doesn't speak or read French; she even has trouble writing Polish.'

'Friedrich can translate the article for her. She'll be so proud of me!'

'All right then.'

'And what about Uncle Soliman, do you think we can send it to him as well?'

'Listen, George, we can't send it to everyone in the world. I'm sure that Soliman can find a copy in Vienna.'

'But then we have to write him to let him know.'

'I promise.'

If George was happy, Frederick de Augustus was even more so. Not only had he gotten the sum agreed upon in the contract, but in addition he'd received a three-hundred-pound bonus from the concert's receipts. Hereafter his son would be a sure source of income.

To celebrate the event he decided to please George, just once wouldn't hurt; he asked him what he'd like to do the rest of the day. Besides music, the boy loved scientific curiosities, machines, and robots. George remembered the optician-physicist who had magically made a flame shoot up from a small sulphurated twig the first time they went to the Palais-Royal, and he wanted to go back there. They went around in circles through the various galleries but couldn't find the magician. Still, it didn't spoil the evening since his father took him instead to the Café Mécanique, where a crowd of people was milling about. He marveled at the service that, without any human intervention, delivered the order that was brought up via a column and appeared through a small iron door, which opened with a loud noise at the level of the marble table. Then they went to the Café des Mille-Colonnes where, under a huge glass dome, a mirror effect multiplied several dozen columns, thus creating the illusion that there were more than a thousand of them. Passing in front of the Café Italien, he was equally thrilled to see the stove in the shape of a hot-air balloon, especially now that he knew why such a balloon could rise into the air. They ended their day with music, after all, by going to the Café des Aveugles to listen to an unusual orchestra consisting entirely of blind musicians.

❦

They finally left the Palais-Royal area and went back to their hotel, having spent a very fine day. Paris had given them everything and they were happy. From time to time, as they were walking to where the coaches were standing, George would make a few little leaps. There were four of them waiting. For fun, George told his father that he wanted them to choose the coachman who'd had the fewest runs that day and so had earned the least money. He was the one they needed to compensate. His father asked him to choose and he picked the most pathetic coach—with an emaciated horse, a badly dressed coachman in a threadbare jacket that was too big and with a felt hat on which he'd stuck a peacock feather. George was delighted and got in first. Just as his father was about to join him, two police officers appeared from nowhere; probably they'd already been watching them for a while. One of them curtly told Frederick de Augustus:

'Show me your identification.'

He knew right away he was dealing with the *Police des Noirs*. It was their duty to prevent Blacks from entering France, for there were allegedly too many of them in the kingdom already. As for those who lived here, this police force was responsible for controlling whether they were in the country legally by checking whether they were carrying their identification, kept in a 'cartouche' that contained a certificate with their name, age, profession, as well as the name of this person's master if the individual was a slave. Those who couldn't produce it would automatically be sent back to the colonies from which they supposedly originated. Alex Dumas and Saint-George carried them. Frederick de Augustus was in a state of shock. By making the people he met believe that he was an African prince, an ambassador plenipotentiary, he'd ended up by convincing himself that everyone accepted this, that he was no ordinary Black man. So it went without saying that carrying the cartouche didn't concern him at all and he'd never bothered with it. And suddenly here was the interrogation that relegated him mercilessly to the category of Black Frenchmen, like the coal carriers they'd run into on the Pont-Neuf, with whom he did not want to be compared under any circumstances. But how to handle this? The thought of being packed off with his son to the cells in Le Havre, Nantes, Rochelle, or Saint-Malo, where they kept the Blacks who were to be deported, and to end up in the hold of a ship bound for the French colonies, filled him with dread.

It was George, terrified, who unintentionally saved them when he asked his father on impulse in German:

'*Was wollen sie von uns, Papa?*'

Frederick de Augustus knew exactly how to manage the situation, he immediately raised his head haughtily, put his hand on the handle of his saber, and began to address the police officers in German, sprinkling his speech with some French words like 'ambassador', 'diplomat', 'prince', to pull the wool over their eyes. He was bluffing and it worked. The two officers didn't understand a word of what he said but they did grasp the fact that they were dealing not with some ordinary 'Negro of the colonies', but perhaps with a foreign dignitary visiting the kingdom and, in their doubt, they gave up.

Throughout the entire ride George and his father spoke not a word; the incident had dampened the enthusiasm they felt when leaving the Palais-Royal. Once at the hotel, they had a light dinner during which neither of them mentioned the episode.

After dinner George got out of his city clothes and went straight to bed without touching his violin, even though he hadn't practiced all day. This was so unusual that Frederick de Augustus knew something wasn't right, that the incident with the *Police des Noirs* had shaken him more than he'd imagined. Was it because of the panic he'd felt when he saw the two agents approach them with their threatening look? Or because of the humiliation they'd caused his father who, until now, he'd believed to be untouchable? To pull the boy out of his gloom and have him go to bed with a smile on his lips, Frederick de Augustus took out a pack of cards and suggested he'd show him some tricks, those magic numbers that always made him marvel, even if he'd seen them many times before. Without even thinking about his father's suggestion George refused, answering he just wanted to go to bed, his voice irritated, on the verge of disrespect, which took Frederick de Augustus by surprise.

Shocked by this unexpected reaction, he felt a little lost. Still fully dressed, he dropped into the chair right beside him and started ruminating. Maybe George's reaction wasn't as discourteous as all that, maybe he was genuinely tired and only very sleepy. All the same, it was the first time he'd ever refused to play cards with him, he'd ever refused to do what he was asked. His son's rebuff and the harsh police probe melded inside his mind, becoming nothing more than two sides of the same coin: he had the feeling he was beginning to lose control of those things that until now he thought he'd been completely in charge of.

Carry the cartouche or not? The question came and went inside his head. He couldn't figure it out. Unable to move, he stayed in the chair for a long time even though he wanted to pick up the book on the little table, become absorbed in it and let it take his mind of things. He didn't know if he'd dozed off but, after a while, in the silence of the night, he heard George breathing regularly, which meant he'd fallen asleep. He then decided to apply for the cartouche for each of them the very next morning, even if it would be costly. He got out of the chair with some effort. He had to go to bed and get some sleep, no matter what.

XVII

George slept straight through the night and woke up in great form as if nothing had happened the evening before. Frederick de Augustus, on the other hand, had slept restlessly, interrupted by many stretches of insomnia. He got up in a rather sullen mood, edgy and unhappy with his son, though he tried as best he could to hide it.

⚜

They went down for breakfast earlier than usual. The small room was crowded but they still found a spot near the large windows that overlooked the garden. Because she'd seen them almost every morning since their arrival at the hotel, the hostess had developed a certain informality with them. She came over to greet them right away, exchanged a few pleasantries, and asked them what they would like. Frederick de Augustus ordered a large black coffee and a small brioche, while George asked for his usual cup of hot chocolate. The hostess told them she didn't know how much longer she would be able to serve them coffee and hot chocolate, and possibly even bread as the supplies were dwindling because of the problems shaking the kingdom, and especially Paris. Nevertheless, she assured them they would always be served first and foremost because they were exceptional guests who'd come from so far away.

They were familiar with the young girl who served them as well. She'd been there from the first day on, taking their orders and bringing their food. Even if Frederick de Augustus still intimidated her, she was quite relaxed with George. A certain childlike camaraderie had developed between them so that, two days after they arrived, George impulsively asked her name: Mathilde. And each morning when he came down for breakfast the first thing he'd do was look for her. As soon as he saw her, he'd give her a big smile, which she shyly returned. On the other hand, Frederick de Augustus never called her by her name. Did he even know it? For him, as for most of the guests, Mathilde didn't really exist as a person onto herself, she was merely 'the little servant with the coarse linen apron'.

The coffee was good but the brioche a little stale. Frederick de Augustus ate in silence, responding absent-mindedly to whatever George was telling him. His mind was obviously somewhere else.

As soon as they were back in their room, George hurried over to his violin as if he'd been deprived of it for days, although he'd only spent one day without it. Taking the instrument from its case, wiping it with a cloth, rubbing rosin, tuning, a small caress, placing it under his chin, raising the bow, and there it was, the first sound surging forth!

Frederick de Augustus, on the other hand, sank down into the wing chair, at loose ends. Not knowing what to do, having negligently skimmed the *Journal de Paris*, which he'd brought up from the reception, he tried to finish the last two chapters of *Paul et Virginie*, but his mind wasn't on it. In fact, he was procrastinating, delaying as long as possible the moment to inform himself where to obtain the famous cartouche that had obsessed him all night long. Maybe he should call on Saint-George.

Finally, he made up his mind.

He told George he was going out without telling him where he was going or what he was going to do; just an errand, he said. George listened to him without actually interrupting his practice but when he saw him open the door, he stopped abruptly, suddenly afraid:

'Papa, be careful with the *Police des Noirs*. Remember what happened to us last night. Actually, don't you think we should be carrying those cartouches, too?'

Already in a bad mood since he'd been awake, Frederick de Augustus took his son's words as a personal insult. All the feelings he'd hidden as best he could were unleashed in an explosion of rage:

'No! Never in my life! You and I will never carry that thing! We are no Saint-George, no Dumas. France did not liberate us, we were born free!'

He slammed the door as he left, leaving George standing there, violin in hand, stunned by his father's tone, the reasons for which he didn't understand.

Frederick de Augustus walked straight ahead. He felt liberated though he didn't know from what. He'd gotten up from his chair to find a cartouche for himself and his son and then his boy's suggestion had suddenly turned him around. He kept walking without really knowing where he was going.

⚜

For a moment George stood looking at the door through which his father had left, then shrugged his shoulders and went back to his exercises. He rehearsed for four hours straight before stopping. While waiting for his father who still hadn't returned, he decided to write his mother and his brother. He'd been wanting to do that for so long! It was a lengthy letter, the first one he'd written them since they'd arrived in

135

Paris. There was so much to tell. There had been no answer to the one he'd sent from Brussels, this time he hoped to get a reply since his father and he now had a fixed address at the Hotel Britannique.

It was already late afternoon when he finished his correspondence. His father still wasn't back. He was beginning to get hungry. Bored to tears in the room, he decided to go down to the garden and get some fresh air.

As he crossed the hallway on the ground floor that led to the little park, he noticed Mathilde through the dining room window; after mopping the kitchen floor with a rag, she wrung it out above a bucket of dirty water. He was surprised to see she was still there and wondered how many hours a day she worked. He was happy to see her without really knowing why. She turned her back to him and had most likely not seen him. Call her? What if she wasn't alone, what if the woman who was her boss was watching her? He hesitated a little longer, then decided to call her anyway. Even if her boss was there, he was only saying hello, there wasn't anything wrong with that.

'Mathilde... Mathilde,' he called softly.

Mathilde jumped, recovered, and turned around. She was standing now, in the same apron she never took off, not seeing who was calling her right away.

'Who is it?'

'George, it's me, George,' he said, appearing in the doorway.

'Oh, George?' she said, utterly surprised. 'You scared me!' she added, using *vous*, the formal *you*.

It was the first time she and George were alone together. She'd never imagined she'd be alone with any of the hotel guests. They were wealthy men, upper middle class or aristocrats, who lived in a world different from hers, with whom any conversation was limited to orders given and received. And certainly not with the son of that Black man who was said to be a prince. She dropped her rag in the bucket, wiped her hands on her apron, and stood there studying him. George was watching her, too, without saying a word. Then he mumbled:

136

'I just wanted to say hello.'

'Hello,' she replied and fell silent.

George told himself that if he didn't come up with anything else to say this would be the end of the conversation.

'Are you alone?' he asked addressing her informally with *tu*.

'Yes, Madame just left for the market at Les Halles to buy provisions for tomorrow. I'm here to do the dishes, wash the table linens, clean the kitchen and the dining room. I'm almost finished. All that's left is to put the tables and chairs in their place.'

George leapt at the opportunity.

'I have nothing to do, I'll help you.'

'Oh no,' she said hastily. 'Out of the question. You shouldn't stay here. Madame will be furious if she sees you,' she went on, now using the informal *you* as well. 'She'll punish me and send me back to my mother. I don't want to go back to be a laundress.'

'Is that what you did before working here?'

'Yes. My mother is a laundress and I used to help her. She's a widow and works at a wash house on the bank of the Seine, near the Pont-Neuf.'

'Near the Pont-Neuf? Maybe I saw her. We saw at least a dozen of them when my father and I crossed that bridge.'

'It's not an easy job: piling up dirty laundry in enormous wooden tubs, covering the top with a piece of cloth on which you spread sifted ashes, then throwing cauldrons of boiling water over it all, then wait for the water to slowly filter through the porous material and saturate the dirty laundry. It takes all day. It's pure hell, I tell you. And the next day, you take the dripping wet laundry out of the tubs, stack it onto a wheelbarrow, and push the heavy load to the wash house. Once there, you soak the dirty laundry in wash tubs, beat it, scrub it vigorously on washboards, put it back and rinse it several times before wringing it out by hand, which is really hard. And all this time you're on your knees or you're squatting. No, really, it kills you! My mother's hands are all swollen and she has chronic back pain. So, you understand, I certainly don't want to go back to working with her at all. That's why Madame shouldn't find you here.'

'But Madame, as you call her, won't be back for another hour or two. Let me help you, it won't even take ten minutes.'

Mathilde looked at him again, hesitated, then shrugged her shoulders as if to say: 'Fine, if you insist.' He helped her take down the chairs she'd put on the tables to clear the floor for cleaning, together they lifted the tables she'd moved, put them back where they belonged, and slid the chairs under each of them. George was right, it took less than ten minutes. Mathilde pulled out one chair and, looking exhausted, sat down near a window that overlooked the alleyway by which Madame would return. George did the same and sat down beside her.

'Now that you've finished your work, are you going home?'

'Oh no,' she said, 'I have to wait for Madame to set the table for tomorrow's breakfast and prepare whatever is needed beforehand.'

'Oh, my! You work a lot!'

'I come in at six o'clock in the morning and go home at seven in the evening, sometimes even eight if there's a lot to do. But I still prefer it to the wash house.'

She looked at George and then, a little coquettish as she showed him her hands, said:

'Look at my fingers, look at my nails. See how chewed up they are from the caustic mixture of hot water and ash in which we'd toss our dirty laundry?'

George took both her hands to examine them. Mathilde pulled them back but, for the first time since he'd come in, smiled at him broadly. She was completely relaxed now, as if Madame's shadow no longer weighed her down.

'Is it true that your father is a prince?'

'Who told you that?'

'Madame did. She told me to be well-behaved when I serve you because "Monsieur is a prince on a mission in Paris". I have to admit that your father intimidated me because it's the first time I've seen a Black man.'

'Really? Were you afraid?'

'Not at all. I just found him a little strange. You, too, by the way. Are you rich?'

'Yes… A little… not too much… I don't know.'

'What do you mean? Rich people know they're rich. They let us know it all the time.'

George said nothing. He only knew they were neither rich nor poor.

'I can't tell how old you are. How old are you?' Mathilde asked.

'Ten, I'll be eleven soon,' he lied blithely, in contrast to his father who liked to make him younger than he was.

'I am thirteen, fourteen soon,' she said.

He didn't know whether she was lying as well.

'Your turn to tell me what kind of work you do.'

'I'm a musician. A violinist.'

And to impress Mathilde even more, he added somewhat proudly:

'I even played at the Concert Spirituel, in the Hall of the Cent-Suisses.'

It didn't have the effect he expected. Mathilde didn't see why that would be anything remarkable. She made a little face.

'The son of one of my mother's friends is a violinist, too. He's amazing! I only heard him play once, at a party of laundresses and washerwomen, to be exact. I'd give anything to hear him again.'

Very interested, George asked:

'What's his name? I'd really like to meet him.'

'Hippolyte. His friends call him Popo the fiddler. He often plays on the Pont-Neuf and is easy to find; he's the musician whose begging bowl overflows more than any other.'

'Ah,' George said, unnerved and not knowing how to react.

'You think you're as good as he is?'

'I don't know, I haven't heard him play yet. Listen, I have an idea. Come up to my room with me, I'll play for you.'

Mathilde looked at him, horrified.

'You want me to get killed? For us who work in the kitchens downstairs it's strictly forbidden to go up to the rooms of the guests.'

'But no one will know! Madame won't be back that soon.'

'No, really. I can't.'

George was quiet. Then he had a better idea:

'Wait here for me. Don't move!'

He scampered out of the kitchen, ran up the stairs four steps at a time to the fourth floor, and arrived out of breath. He was overcome by a nebulous emotion he'd never felt before. It was the first time he'd been talking quite personally with a girl almost his own age. He had a lot of friends at the Palace in Eisenstadt, but they were all boys. It was the rule for boys to be with boys and girls with girls. He took his cherished violin from its case, grabbed the bow, and ran down the stairs as fast as he could.

George found Mathilde sitting on a table swinging her feet as if to revive them after the many hours of standing. She had taken off her eternal apron. It was the first time George saw her without the screen that hid her clothes. She was wearing a linen-cotton camisole and a skirt of coarse linen. The materials weren't of the same quality as the embroidered silk jacket George had on but the outfit looked good on her.

He went over to her, embraced her with his eyes and, raising his instrument, said:

'Mathilde, I'm going to play just for you!'

A bit surprised, not knowing what to expect, she stopped swinging her feet and looked at him. The violin under his chin, George struck up, *adagio*, a gallant romance by the Chevalier de Saint-George, with a profusion of notes with tremolos strewn here and there, which made it even more sentimental. He played without taking his eyes off Mathilde, whom he found lovelier than ever. As for her, she seemed more focused on George's moving fingers than on the melody itself. When George stopped, drawing a last lengthy sob from his instrument, she applauded.

'You like it?' George asked, as anxious as if he were waiting for an appraisal from Kreutzer or Saint-George himself.

'Not too much, but still, a little.'

George was disappointed. It was the first person who didn't tell him that he was excellent, that he was a prodigy. His vanity was hurt. Seeing George's aggrieved look, Mathilde said:

'I don't like the music you played that much, but you do play it very well anyway.'

'You think I play as well as Hippolyte?' George asked mockingly but without malice.

'Yes, almost as well. But Popo plays tunes that make you want to dance. Not only does he mark the beat and move around as he plays, but sometimes he plays in really incredible positions.'

'Anything Hippolyte can do, I can do also,' he bragged, a little jealous.

Mathilde got the message and immediately challenged him:

'Do you know how to play *Il pleut, il pleut bergère...*'

'*... rentre tes blancs moutons*? Of course I do!' he said.

Everyone knew the tune that was most popular in Paris at the time! He'd never played it before but that posed no problem. He began. Before too long Mathilde was swept away and started singing with the music. When the piece ended, George didn't stop but went on to play a sprightly, happy dance melody. Delighted, Mathilde jumped off the table and started to dance. George moved on to a fast-tempo jig. As he was playing, he kept moving around Mathilde, sometimes holding his violin up near his head, sometimes close to his chest, back to front, or vertically like a cello, twisting and turning in wildly acrobatic moves. Enchanted and playful, Mathilde danced and danced her heart out, whirling, clapping her hands to the strong beat of the music. And when, after playing the final sounds on his instrument and taking a purposely exaggerated bow, George stood up and opened his arms wide, Mathilde rushed to him guilelessly, caressing his hair, frizzy like lambswool, finding it strange and attractive. He hugged her back, squeezing her tightly to his chest. A peculiar but pleasant shiver went through him. It was the first time in his life he'd embraced a girl.

A moment later, Mathilde drew back and, her face radiant, told him:

'No one has ever played just for me! I'll never forget this; I'm really grateful to you, George.'

She planted a little kiss on George's lips and moved away. Not expecting this, George didn't react right away but stood frozen, speechless, the violin in his hand and his eyes fixed on Mathilde. She put her apron back on, popped one hand in the bucket where she'd tossed the rag and began to wring it out, twisting it with both hands. Then she glanced out the window at the alleyway that led to the kitchen:

'Now you must go, George. Madame will be back soon, I don't want any trouble.'

She said it so kindly and yet so firmly that George knew he had no other choice but to obey her. He went over to Mathilde, smiled at her, then like a thief put a quick kiss on her cheek. He turned around and left.

Ultimately, he didn't take his walk in the garden, which is why he'd come downstairs. He went straight up to the room and put his violin down. His heart was in a flutter. He couldn't stop thinking about Mathilde's kiss. It was his first one, he was ecstatic. He felt a little like an adult. It was the first time he was experiencing love without his father's supervision. He had his secrets and his father didn't know it: he loved Mathilde and Mathilde loved him, because they had kissed!

It was now very late and still his father had not returned. Never before had he been left alone this long. He was hungry. He couldn't eat at the hotel where they served only breakfast. He wanted to read to make up for his loneliness. He'd finished *Robinson Crusoe*, and because he had no other book, he decided to start on *Paul et Virginie* even if his father hadn't completed it yet. He couldn't find it, he must have taken it with him. So he chose to kill the time with one of his favorite games, cutting paper silhouettes to make a continuous chain of small figurines. But he grew tired. He was still thinking about Mathilde when he fell asleep, exhausted.

⚜

Frederick de Augustus didn't get back to the hotel until dawn, reeking of alcohol. He tiptoed around so as not to wake George who was still sleeping. As he undressed, he made sure once more that George really was asleep before he took off his jacket, putting it down, with the bag that held their assets. He felt its weight, it was quite light: he'd lost two-thirds gambling away the money that the concert had brought in.

In fact, after leaving the hotel, he'd walked for a long time, aimlessly, still tense. It was odd how being stopped like a common freed Black man, even though he'd just come from the salon of one of the kingdom's most powerful personalities, had knocked him off balance, made him lose his superb self-assurance! He was quite pleased he'd finally decided not to carry any identification.

After his prolonged wandering, he'd gone to a café where he spent a good two hours reading various newspapers and consuming many alcoholic beverages. When he left, his composure returned, he settled back into his role as African prince. Sure of himself now, he didn't try to avoid the police, quite the contrary, he passed them without fear. He convinced himself that, since his rotten luck was over, he should even try his luck at gambling. With the money earned, he'd pay a short visit to one of the houses on the Boulevard du Temple before going back to the hotel. So he went to a gambling joint near the Nicolet Theater. He sat down at one of the baccarat tables and ordered a glass of absinth. When he won the first bet, he offered a round to all the other players, like a good prince. Then he began to lose.

When he left the place, the cool night air awakened his still alcohol-infused brain. His first move was to feel his pockets to see if the purse was still there. It was. Then he looked at the time, three-thirty in the morning. He was overcome with remorse when he realized that for the entire day he'd left his son to his own devices and that he must have gone to bed famished. That's when he hurried back.

XVIII

When George woke up Frederick de Augustus was still asleep. He wondered what time his father had returned. After washing up and getting dressed, he went back to the bed and looked at him.

His face relaxed, Frederick de Augustus was sleeping the deep sleep of someone who was pleased with himself, who didn't have a care in the world. Worse yet, he was snoring. George got angry, angry at his father who'd left him alone all day without anything to eat and wouldn't even get up to take his famished son to breakfast and make up for his shameful behavior. He couldn't stop himself and shook him vigorously.

Frederick de Augustus jumped, opened his eyes, his mind wandering for a moment, not knowing where he was. Then it all came back to him.

'Good morning, George, already up?'

'Yes, for a long time and I'm hungry!'

His head clearer now, Frederick de Augustus realized the situation and tried to put things right. He cleaned up quickly, got dressed as fast as he could, and suggested they go downstairs. He tried to justify himself, invented some complicated story, and ended by saying they wouldn't need to carry any identification. Anyway, with the current unrest in

Paris, the police had other priorities before checking up on every Negro who happened to be on French soil.

As they came into the dining room, George gave Mathilde a big smile. She blushed and immediately turned around to her boss to see if she'd noticed. Reassured, she returned George's smile, for whom it was a very different smile from past days; it held something more, an intimate and secret bond he had no intention of sharing with his father.

The hostess welcomed them as usual and they gave her their order. Everything they asked for was available; nevertheless, she told them again that things were going from bad to worse and she was having a very hard time getting supplies. For example, the previous evening she'd spent three hours on an errand that would normally take her not even an hour.

Mathilde brought their dishes. George looked at her differently now and, following her with his eyes after she'd served them, he couldn't help but think of the pointy breasts beneath her apron he'd pressed against his chest the night before.

He was still musing about her when he heard his father say:

'What are you thinking about? I thought that, hungry as a horse, you'd devour your bread and butter and your hot chocolate!'

They ate well and George was ready to start practicing. When they left the table the hostess wished them a good day despite everything that was going on in Paris. George spotted Mathilde in the back of the room, busy clearing tables. He wondered when he'd see her again. He was no longer angry with his father, he wished he could be alone for another whole day.

❁

While George was rehearsing, Frederick read the papers. The unrest in Paris was escalating. In Versailles, things at the States General weren't going well. Challenging royal authority, the Third Estate had first changed itself into a National Assembly, then into a constituent National Assembly that had set itself the task of writing a Constitution for the kingdom of France. And when the king wanted to oust the delegates from their meeting room, one of them had uttered this phrase, quickly picked up by every mouth in Paris: 'We are here by the will of the people and we shall not leave here except by the force of bayonets!'

Hunger threatened the city and the crowd stormed the few bakeries where bread was still being sold. Throngs of people were gathering almost everywhere, depending on the rumors and skirmishes that set the outraged people against the forces of law and order. The unrest reached its peak in the afternoon of Sunday, 12 July, when the rumor came from Versailles that a certain Necker had been dismissed by the king.

Driven by the events and following the movement, Frederick de Augustus and George found themselves back at the Palais-Royal, which had become the kingdom's epicenter. They'd never seen so many people. The place most packed was the Café de Foy where tables and chairs had been put outside and orators were giving passionate speeches. A few individuals in the crowd were wielding a wax portrait of the famous Necker, encircled with black crepe paper as a sign of mourning. Who was this person whose firing provoked such revolt? Frederick found out soon enough.

He came from Switzerland and was the 'Director of the Royal Treasury', in other words the Minister of Finance. Normally, the Minister of Finance had the title of 'Comptroller General of Finance', a title that legally made him a member of the King's Council, in charge of preparing the king's decisions and guiding him. Since Necker was a Protestant and had refused to renounce his faith he, like all Protestants, was denied membership of the Council, as well as many other high functions in the kingdom. The king had been forced to create the title 'Director of the Royal Treasury' for him because he was extremely popular with the people who idolized him and saw him as the only man capable of straightening out France's finances and helping them out of poverty. It granted him the same prerogatives as a 'Comptroller General of Finance' without giving him access to the Council. But now this same king had fired him! It was as if burning tinder had been thrown on a powder keg!

Suddenly, Frederick de Augustus and George saw a man try to climb onto a table right in front of them. It was shaky and almost fell over. He was supported by helpful hands that assisted him and pushed him onto the table, while others propped it up. Frederick recognized the man, he'd seen him with his wife at Saint-George's concert at the Théâtre de Monsieur. His name came back to him now: Camille Desmoulins! The latter took a pistol from his pocket, waved it around, and began to harangue the public in a strong, clear voice:

'Citizens, you know the Nation has asked for Necker to be preserved on its behalf, that a monument be dedicated to him: they have ousted him instead! Can anyone defy you more brazenly? After this blow, they will risk anything and they're considering a Saint Bartholomew's Night for the patriots this evening.'

With a captivated George clutching his arm, Frederick de Augustus was listening closely. The day Etta Palm and Louise de Kéralio had introduced Camille Desmoulins to him at Saint-George's concert, they had mentioned that he stuttered. Well, thought Frederick de Augustus, if every stutterer spoke with the same ease, he'd be happy to be one, too! 'To arms!' Desmoulins shouted as he concluded his speech. 'To arms!' the crowd repeated. Behind him, Frederick de Augustus heard an over-excited woman's voice above all the others: 'To arms... to arms... women, let's arm ourselves!' He turned around and saw a small woman, saber in hand, whose large blue eyes and brown hair bestowed her with a beauty that one couldn't ignore. She was dressed in a fitted red coat that gave her a masculine, soldierly bearing. Fascinated, Frederick de Augustus asked about her and was told her name was Théroigne de Méricourt. She was known for her radical positions, proclaiming everywhere that there would never be any true equality between men and women as long as the latter weren't armed as well, and that she was ready to form and lead such a battalion.

When Frederick de Augustus' attention returned to Camille Desmoulins, he was ending his speech with the following words: 'Let's all wear green rosettes, the color of hope!' He then saw him pull a green ribbon from his pocket that he attached to his hat, after which he came down from the table, took out more ribbons and began to distribute them to those around him. When there weren't any left, people began to tear leaves from the low branches of the trees of the Palais and stick them on their hats, just as Desmoulins had done. Then, galvanized by the orators and armed with axes, sticks, and pistols, the crowd left the Palais gardens and poured out into the neighboring streets and boulevards. Frederick de Augustus spotted Théroigne de Méricourt, easily recognizable by her red coat, at the head of one of the parades, waving high her saber.

Frederick de Augustus and George were afraid to get caught up in a riot like the one that had so terrified them in the Faubourg Saint-Antoine. Despite their curiosity and their desire to find out what all these people were up to, they decided to go back to their hotel. In any case, they were foreigners, even if no one had made the slightest comment to that effect during the various speeches. If they were there, it was purely by chance, driven by the course of events.

In the lounge of the hotel that evening, all the guests were talking about the unrest that was rocking Paris. The news from Versailles wasn't reassuring either, for it was rumored that the king was in the process of gathering foreign troops consisting of Germans and Swiss around Versailles and Paris. Worse yet, apocalyptic scenes were encouraged almost everywhere; it was said that German troops on horseback had trampled and crushed old people, women, and children. But in this batch of bad news items, Frederick de Augustus heard one he thought was encouraging: in the end Lafayette had delivered the preliminary draft of his

Declaration of the Rights of Man and of the Citizen, following his friend Jefferson's example.

They didn't sleep very well because throughout the night they heard shots being fired all over the place. The next day, Frederick de Augustus and George decided not to go out at all except for their midday and evening meals, which they had at a restaurant nearby at the intersection of the Rues Guénégaud and Mazarine. Still, they learned that the city was on the verge of insurrection, that gun stores had been looted, that a convent near Saint-Lazare, famous for its wealth and thus the very symbol of the clergy's exploitation of the people, had been pillaged. Frederick de Augustus began to wonder if it made any sense at all to stay in Paris to boost his son's musical career.

✿

When they went downstairs for breakfast on Tuesday, 14 July, the dining room was practically deserted. When he didn't see Mathilde and it was the proprietor herself who served them, George knew right away that the situation was serious. Despite her willingness, she could only offer them a musty-tasting blackish bread that was hard to chew, and George didn't get the hot chocolate he so loved. The customary warm, cheerful atmosphere was heavy. George couldn't help but ask why the waitress wasn't there; she explained that several of her employees were unable to come, the traffic was difficult or next to impossible, because of the barricades that were being set up almost everywhere.

On second thought, they resolved that the best thing to do was to go out to get information, assess the situation based on what people who were better informed than they could tell them, such as the Chevalier de Saint-George, Legros, or even Olympe de Gouges, if they could find her. They decided to go to Saint-George first, without making an appointment.

As they crossed the Seine, they were caught up in a throng of people

150

in the center of the Pont-Neuf near the equestrian statue of Henri IV. They couldn't extricate themselves anymore and had no other choice but to be carried along. As they soon learned, all these people were heading for the Hotel de Ville to pick up arms and join a newly formed militia to defend the city against looters and foreign troops.

Once at the Hotel de Ville, the demonstrators realized there apparently weren't enough weapons. Angry, those unable to acquire rifles began to shout at the town counselors who were trying to calm them down. In the ruckus and the confusion the people became convinced there were arms stockpiled at the Invalides and abruptly cries swelled up: 'To the Invalides! to the Invalides!'

Hypnotized, as if they no longer had a will of their own, Frederick de Augustus and his son were still being pulled along by the human tide. Among those leading the procession, they recognized Théroigne de Méricourt again, this time wearing a wide-brimmed hat, two pistols at her side and the saber still in her hand.

As they approached the Invalides, they ran into a group coming from the opposite side, almost all armed with rifles, shrieking: 'To the Bastille, to the Bastille!' where the gunpowder was stored, so they said. Thereupon the crowd split in two, the largest heading for the Bastille, Frederick de Augustus and George in their wake. Turning back was no longer an option because of the density of the crowd, both in front and in back, and the more it advanced the more it grew. Some people without rifles had armed themselves with sticks, axes, and spades. Many were wearing rosettes, not green as Camille Desmoulins was wearing at the Café de Foy, but blue and red, the colors of the city of Paris. It was a long, disorderly, noisy march but, paradoxically, there was something warm, something fraternal about it, until the first shots rang out.

Frederick de Augustus and George were terrified. The shots were coming from both the fortress and the demonstrators. They tried to escape via a cross street but couldn't get very far; they threw themselves behind a parapet, hoping that way to avoid stray bullets and cannonballs from the fortress. Suddenly they saw an excited angry group pass by, following a man carrying a bleeding decapitated head on a spike, George screamed out and wanted to flee, but at the last minute his father held him back. They stayed hidden for a long time before going toward the Faubourg Saint-Antoine.

There was no longer any doubt that they had to leave Paris, and fast!

XIX

They decided to leave for London, but three weeks after the Bastille was taken they were still in Paris. George was growing impatient and each time he asked his father why they weren't leaving, he was given a variety of answers, the most recent one telling him the roads weren't safe enough. At times he wondered whether he should always believe what his father told him; hadn't he assured Alex Dumas that his saber had been given to him by an Egyptian vizier?

The truth of the matter was that Frederick de Augustus no longer had enough money. Yes, he could still afford their meals and pay for the room, but they would arrive in London without a penny if he had to pay for the long stagecoach trip from Paris to Calais and for the Channel crossing. Moreover, he thought that by procrastinating he'd end up arranging a last concert that would allow him to raise a bit more money before they left Paris. Thus far his approach had been hopeless, for the majority of the places where he thought he would meet people were closed: gaming rooms, theaters, and even the Opéra. Worse yet, there was more and more talk about making the king return to Paris: this would mean that the halls of the Tuileries Palace would be closed as well and turned into the king's apartments, which would be the end of the Concert Spirituel, on which he was still counting.

A month later they were still in Paris. Scraps of news from Versailles continued to come in, among which—the one that most upset Frederick de Augustus—the announcement that the Constituent Assembly had abolished all privileges. It was hard for him to conceive of a society where farmers would be the equals of nobles and of the valets of princes.

A few weeks later, Lafayette's project, the *Declaration of the Rights of Man and of the Citizen* was adopted. Frederick de Augustus read it, for it had been plastered almost everywhere on the city's walls; he even knew the first article by heart so he could recite it to his son: 'All people shall have equal rights upon birth and ever after. General utility is the only permissible basis for social distinctions.' He found this declaration less grandiloquent and less pompous than Jefferson's. And clearer as well: here men were equal among themselves, for Jefferson they were equal before their Creator but not necessarily among themselves.

※

Frederick de Augustus lost all hope when he found out that Saint-George, whom he'd been trying unsuccessfully to contact until then, had left France and fled to London. He was afraid he'd suffer retaliations because of his close relationship with Queen Marie-Antoinette, who had become extremely unpopular. And he wasn't the only one; others, too, Viotti among them, had left Paris for London for the same reasons. The last person he'd managed to see was Legros but only barely, for the other had dismissed him. He who thought he'd forged himself a place in the heart of Paris' high society, realized that world no longer existed. And then there was George who pestered him with questions that he found increasingly difficult to answer properly. For a moment he even believed his son was beginning to doubt him when, hearing of

Saint-George's departure for London, he'd asked how he could have left if the roads were that unsafe.

Virtually penniless, he decided to stake it all, play part of the little money he still had. He didn't want to think about what would happen if he lost. Luck smiled at him. This time, he didn't tempt fate, managed to control himself, and stopped after winning back double of what he'd bet. They could finally leave Paris as soon as possible.

✵

Stagecoaches were the least expensive way to travel but they held up to sixteen passengers and were uncomfortable. One would lose an enormous amount of time at the relay stations where the changing of the horses had to be negotiated. Massive, and thus very heavy, in bad weather they'd get stuck on the muddy roads, forcing passengers to get out and push. In addition, attacks by highway bandits were common. No, it wasn't appropriate for someone who'd claimed to the Parisian elite that he was a former ambassador plenipotentiary at the Esterhazy court. He thanked his good fortune for letting him win at gambling. They were going to treat themselves to a rented coach, which would be faster and more reliable. Even when poor, one had to maintain one's dignity.

They left Paris one October morning around eleven-thirty, direction Calais. George had hoped to see Mathilde and say goodbye to her but after July 14th she hadn't come back to the hotel, making him very unhappy.

The coach they hired was comfortable. It had glass windows, venetian blinds that protected them from outside looks, and lovely velvet upholstery inside. The coachman loaded their trunk and, making sure they were suitably settled, climbed onto his seat, cracked his whip, and the horses trotted off.

On their way out of Paris George wanted to see the Palais-Royal again, but the coachman told them he was going to avoid that area, for as he went to pick them up at the hotel early that morning, he'd run into a crowd of angry women, some of them with pitchforks, sticks, and pikes, shouting: 'Bread, bread!' They were threatening to go to Versailles to find the king and bring him back to Paris. Frederick de Augustus realized the rumor he'd heard was therefore true. George immediately thought of Mathilde and imagined her in her apron, pitchfork in hand, among the impoverished women from working-class districts, adorned with tricolor ribbons, marching on Versailles.

They left the Rue Guénégaud, crossed the Seine, and took the Rue Saint-Honoré in order to leave the city via the Faubourg of the same name. Forgetting his disappointment in not seeing the Palais-Royal with its gardens, the Tuileries Palace and its dome again, George was watching the city he'd come to know as if he were seeing it for the first time. Frederick de Augustus kept silent. A moment later, he was overcome with nostalgia and closed his eyes. He felt as if he were leaving something he would never in his life find again. The emotion that seized him so unexpectedly had the same intensity as what he'd felt in the balcony of the Hall of the Cent-Suisses at the Tuileries Palace, when he watched his son's triumph at his first concert in Paris. His throat tightened and he couldn't hold back a tear.

XX

The journey from Paris to Calais was pleasant. Thanks to the luxurious coach they'd hired, Frederick de Augustus and George made it in only one day. The weather, exceptionally mild for early autumn, had cooperated as well. Throughout the trip Frederick de Augustus wouldn't stop commending London, the city where he'd landed some thirty years earlier coming from Barbados, and where he'd lived part of his youth before traveling through Europe. He said it was even more densely populated, more industrious, and more prosperous than Paris. More beautiful, too? George had asked. Perhaps, he answered. I'll show you its famous bridge, older than the Pont-Neuf, and the magnificent dome of Saint Paul's Cathedral, that rises high into the sky, overshadowing all the other buildings, not to mention Westminster Abbey where the kings and queens are crowned; I'll take you for walks in the large parks and lovely gardens, I'll show you the docks of the Thames where you'll see the masts of ships from all over the world, swaying like a living forest. It will make you forget Paris!

George was anxious to discover the city where they would seek their fortune now, where his father seemed to know every nook and cranny. He couldn't control his delight anymore when suddenly, as they came around a bend, he saw Calais appear and was exultant when he heard his father say that the coach would take them directly to the boat, which would emerge before too long.

⚜

Things didn't go quite the way they'd hoped. In Calais a storm was brewing, and they had to wait four days in the harbor for the wind to die down and allow the boat to put out to sea. They were forced to rent a room in an inn, whose price the proprietor had increased shamelessly. They couldn't go on board until very late in the evening of their fifth day, but their joy in leaving dry land at last was of short duration because the wind picked up again and began to blow in great bursts, creating gigantic waves that battered the ship, jolting it in every direction like an ordinary tub. Very anxious, they wondered if the boat wasn't likely to sink at any moment. The crossing lasted ten hours during which, to crown it all, George—who'd never sailed, had never even seen the sea before— became so terribly seasick that he did nothing but throw up for most of the journey. Still more bad luck, when they finally reached Dover, the tide wasn't high enough for their ship to enter port; moreover, rather than spending several more hours aboard this luckless vessel waiting for the tide to rise, they resorted to the services of a boatman, a greedy scoundrel who extorted almost as much money from them as the entire crossing had cost just to bring them and their trunk ashore.

⚜

When they disembarked in Dover all the vehicles for London had already left. They departed early in the morning in order to arrive at their destination before sunset, since they weren't equipped to ride at night. Faced with this adversity, Frederick de Augustus decided to live with it, thinking it might be a good thing, in fact; it would give his son some time to rest before starting off on the last leg of the journey. After all, the boy hadn't quite recovered from his seasickness yet and was feeling very weak since he hadn't eaten at all that day because his stomach couldn't hold any food.

The hotel closest to the wharf was the King's Head Hotel. Frederick de Augustus took a room on the second floor. Before they went upstairs to go to bed, he managed to get George to swallow a bowl of oat porridge with warm milk.

He waited for his son to fall asleep before he counted the money they had left. There was far less than he'd hoped, even taking the ups and downs of the trip into account. He had a moment of panic. With what they had left, they would have to take a stagecoach, the cheapest, the most uncomfortable, and the most exhausting means of transportation. It was the only solution to be able to have a few days in London before replenishing their funds. But having said so many negative things about stagecoaches when he was trying to justify hiring a fancy coach for their trip from Paris to Calais, how was he now going to explain this about-face to his son? He didn't know. Constrained and contrite, he recognized he wouldn't be in this situation if he hadn't stupidly squandered their fortune with gambling.

LONDON, 1789

XXI

Not all the carriages waiting in the hotel's courtyard were going to London, but that didn't prevent Frederick de Augustus from instantly spotting a massive double-decker coach, tall on its four wheels and harnessed with six horses. There were a great many people already and he was afraid they'd arrived too late to get what he wanted—two interior seats in the cabin of the central compartment. He knew the best places were in the coupé up front where one had a superb view of the scenery and was sheltered from the swirling dust. He would love to have made his son happy by getting those, but the state of his finances was such that he couldn't afford any luxury seats. On the other hand, despite his disquieting penurious situation, he certainly didn't want to give the impression of insolvency by traveling all the way in the back of the coach where one would be immersed in dust throughout the trip; and he certainly didn't want to be on the upper level, which had the cheapest seats but where the exposure to wind, rain, and flying objects often made one sick. Sometimes, because of an unexpected sharp turn, an absent-minded traveler could even be thrown off his high perch, ending his ride with broken bones on the street. Places inside the central compartment were therefore a good compromise even if it meant being confined with unknown passengers on two facing seats each with room for three. He was lucky to obtain one seat across from the other in the corner of the compartment; at least they would be able to rest their head should they doze off.

They still had a long wait before the driver gave the signal for departure. Facing forward, George tried as best he could to watch the landscape through the window with the raised curtain. He wasn't as talkative as usual, undoubtedly inhibited by the presence of other travelers. In any event, there wasn't much to see of the monotonous countryside that stretched out slowly, at the speed of the heavy six-horse carriage.

An hour later George was asleep. For a long while Frederick de Augustus watched his son's head nod back and forth before suddenly realizing how much of a child he still was. For the first time he wondered whether, in his almost obsessive drive to profit from the boy's exceptional talent, he hadn't pushed him too much, perhaps even mistreated him a little. But no sooner had that idea crossed his mind than he refuted it, using his own unhappy childhood memories that abruptly forced themselves on him as an alibi.

※

He saw himself again thirty years earlier, in London, dressed in scarlet livery, dustpan and brush in hand, running after the horses in the streets of the affluent sections of the West End and the City to pick up their dung and toss it in the large receptacles that stood on the side of the road. The most repellent moments of this task were those right after a rainfall, when the horses' droppings were mixed with mud, creating a soft, nauseating mire in which he'd flounder about. He was barely ten years old, like hundreds of other children bustling about this monstrous city. Worn-out at the end of each day, not having enough to eat with the few pennies the municipality paid him for the labor he performed from dawn to dusk, he quit and at age twelve set himself up as a shoeshine boy, cleaning and polishing shoes. In contrast to the other young boys who'd run from one street to another looking for customers, he found one spot, a piece of sidewalk at Temple Bar, the place where Fleet Street, the City's main road, turned into the Strand, which then led to Westminster. In fact, when he was running around the streets picking up dung, he'd noticed that Temple Bar was the intersection where wealthy businessmen and City merchants were heading for Westminster, while politicians and men of law were going in the opposite direction to meet their City clientele. These elegant gentlemen wanted their shoes brilliantly shined. The most finicky of them were the aristocrats, easily recognizable by their top hats and their dark tailcoats, casually open to show off the silk jacket underneath. Their favorite shoes were the high boots with metallic buckles that required more work from the shoeshine boy; when they felt the latter was dawdling, they had no problem letting him know by ostentatiously taking out their fob watch from one of their jacket pockets and heaping scorn and verbal abuse on the poor kid.

Although his little business did well, Frederick de Augustus gave it up after a few months, tired of constantly having to defend his territory from the ruffians who envied him and would come as a gang to relentlessly bait him.

He'd done other jobs as well: butcher's assistant at Leadenhall Market, porter at Covent Garden helping carters unload bags of fruits and vegetables and sometimes carrying them to the stalls, delivering and selling newspapers to a printer on Fleet Street and, finally, a few years later, dockworker at London's East End, the job that would change his life and launch him into a career as interpreter, thereby opening his way to Central Europe.

So he became a warehouseman at the port. The job paid better than any of those he'd done before, but it was more grueling, too. All day long he hauled cargo from harbors across the world; from ships arriving from the East Indies he'd unload bales of cotton, muslin, silk, as well as sacks of tea, pepper and other spices; from ships coming from the West Indies and America, he'd unload bales of tobacco, cocoa beans, cane sugar, and countless kegs of rum; from those arriving from Africa, he unloaded ivory, coffee, barrels of palm oil, indigo, tropical woods and precious metals.

The sight of these ships with their tall masts originating from every corner of the world filled him with wonder; he would forget his back-breaking work because they made him dream of distant horizons open to the sea. Ships that came from the Caribbean and America often unloaded black passengers of various classes, free sailors, servants accompanying their master—among the nobility it had become fashionable to have a black servant—or slaves of plantation owners. He especially liked to work on those ships as it gave him the feeling of reconnecting with his roots. Moreover, any time he heard that one of them had dropped anchor in Barbados, he'd immediately ask whether that boat hadn't docked in Bridgetown during its coastal navigation, the place where he was born. If so, he'd urge that person to tell him if he'd bought any tobacco or sugar from the plantation of a certain Polgreen, the owner, and if he'd met a worker there, named John Augustus Polgreen, who was his father. Although he lived in London for a dozen years or so, it didn't stop him from occasionally giving in to a moment of nostalgia for his early childhood and his far-away island. It was at those moments that he realized in how many ways his destiny resembled that of his grandfather.

The grandfather whose true name or place of birth he'd never known, other than that he came from the kingdom of Kongo, found himself to be a slave in Barbados, and then had a child with a young slave woman, a baby whom the owner baptized John Augustus Polgreen, his future father.

In turn, John Augustus Polgreen grew up on the plantation, becoming all too familiar with the violence of being enslaved, until the day when the planter died, and his son returned from England with his wife to take over the plantation. He developed a special liking for him and ended up by setting him free. But because he didn't know where else to go John Augustus Polgreen didn't leave the plantation. He hired himself out as a day worker and used his new freedom to learn to read and write.

Thus, he, Frederick de Augustus, was born free of an emancipated father. The planter's kindness had made it possible for him not only to learn to read and write together with his own son, who was his contemporary, but also to attend the French and German lessons the latter was receiving. John Augustus Polgreen followed his son's education with amazement and, when thinking of the young plantation owner, he often wondered how a son could be so different from his father.

But, ironically, Frederick de Augustus's lot would soon correspond to that of his grandfather. The young planter's son had left for England to pursue his education and was clamoring for his companion, so they suggested to John Augustus Polgreen that he send Frederick de Augustus to join him, all expenses paid, so that he, too, could complete his education. John Augustus Polgreen readily approved. A few weeks later, the planter entrusted Frederick de Augustus to the captain of a cargo ship that lay anchored in the port of Bridgetown. And so, even though his passage had been paid in advance, he found himself on board a ship where he was forced to work as a cabin boy without any compensation whatever, simply in exchange for his food. Once in London, the captain got rid of the child before going back to sea, placing him in a home for orphans and abandoned children. Wasn't that a little like what had been done to his grandfather?

Life at the home was so hard that Frederick de Augustus ran away and ended up at Covent Garden, where a group of boys in red jackets drew his attention. The municipality was in the process of recruiting them to clean the streets of the fine Westminster neighborhoods by collecting the excrement of the many horses moving about. He didn't hesitate to join them.

The head of the passenger to his left fell against his shoulder and brought him back to reality. His neighbor had dozed off: he apologized when Frederick de Augustus gently pushed him aside. Lingering in the evocation of his early years, he began to contemplate George again, still asleep in the corner of the compartment, his mouth slightly open. The question he'd avoided before crept back into his mind: was he mistreating him?

No, definitely not, again he justified himself. George would soon be ten years old, ten years of which a solid half had been spent in palaces. He'd always been well fed, he'd always been well dressed, he'd been taught music by the finest teachers.

He'd lacked for nothing and, better still, what child his age could have prided himself on having seen and conquered the most brilliant salons of Paris, except for little Wolfgang Mozart perhaps? At that age I was running around the streets after horse dung, I was hungry, and I was shining shoes, just to eat. Had pure luck not brought me to the East End, where I struggled so hard and met the noble Pole whom I served as interpreter, I would even today still be a wretched drudge perhaps. He was happy with my services and had recruited me to continue working by his side. So it's perfectly normal for me to force him to study and practice his violin; after all, why would it be abusive to wake a child early in the morning and demand that he practice eight hours a day? On the contrary, it's for his own good. If I don't do it, how will we become rich? I've known misery and have no desire to go back to that. And definitely not in London!

He'd barely conjured up London again when a certain unease took hold of him. He'd led George to believe that once they were in this city it would all be easy. And in his childlike naiveté he had apparently believed it. But when all was said and done what did he, Frederick de

Augustus, really know about it? A letter of introduction from Haydn had opened the doors of Paris for them. But what about London? Not only didn't he know anyone worth knowing there, he didn't even know which door to knock on first!

He sank back into the corner of the compartment and, like his son, closed his eyes.

XXII

They entered the London suburbs via Kent Street, a crudely paved street that had changed over from the sand and gravel road they'd been on so far. It was dark and narrow with steep sides between two rows of dilapidated buildings with ash-colored walls, and it stank of horse manure. The first contact of the coach's steel-rimmed wheels with the irregular stones of the pavement was brutal, almost ejecting one of the passengers seated in the center next to George. His hands tightly gripping the bar of his seat, his nostrils and face contracting in the hope of smelling the fetid odor as little as possible, the boy was watching the vista go by, which he found particularly gloomy. Nobody spoke, each preoccupied with the worrisome grinding caused by every jolt of the axles, afraid they might break, the wheels come off, and send the carriage careening.

After what seemed like an eternity to George, the stagecoach left Kent Street and entered a wider street jammed with pedestrians moving about every which way, running the risk of being knocked down. It drove on for almost another fifteen minutes before stopping in front of an inn where other coaches, a few carriages, and many handcarts were parked. George knew they'd arrived when he saw the coachman get down from his horse. Not a minute too soon!

They arrived exhausted, covered with dust, their fine clothes crumpled and grimy, even though they'd been seated inside the compartment. On the way, they had changed horses several times, the coach had repeatedly gotten stuck, and on one occasion they'd even been made to get out of the vehicle to push one of the wheels out of the mud.

Frederick de Augustus hailed a carriage and gave the coachman the name of a hotel on King Street, which he vaguely recalled. The driver asked him which one, for there were more than a dozen King Streets in London. King Street in the East End, Frederick de Augustus replied firmly to give the impression that he knew where he was going. After all these years, the East End was the area he remembered best, it's where he'd lived the entire time he worked on the docks. Again the coachman asked which one, for if there were a dozen King Streets in London there were at least half a dozen in the East End. Frederick de Augustus looked at him, a bit confused. He got tangled up in his explanations, but with the driver's help, finally managed to locate the place where he wanted to be dropped: near the warehouse where they used to store freight from the cargo ships coming from the West Indies. There should be a hotel nearby, one that was considered to be the best in the area at the time.

Not taking his eyes off his father, George was a little disconcerted by his lack of assurance; it was the first time he'd ever seen him like this. And yet, in the coach from Paris to Calais, and even this very morning, he hadn't stopped talking to him about this city as if he knew it like the back of his hand.

They transferred their trunk to the carriage and the hackney coach took off, its metal-rimmed wheels rattling on the street stones. Here and there puddles of stagnating muddy water, which would splash passersby who didn't get out of the way fast enough, were of no concern to the coachman whose only job was to keep moving ahead.

Dumbfounded, George watched the narrow, overcrowded streets go by, the stench that hadn't left them since they'd entered Kent Street

171

permeating the air. Was this really London? He was beginning to have his doubts. He could look for an old bridge as much as he wanted, the dome of a cathedral as high as the sky, an abbey worthy of kings and queens, everything his father had praised so abundantly, but all he saw were tall, round chimneys spewing black smoke, countless church towers whose spires rose up, ghostlike, in a city covered by a grayish fog. All of a sudden, he felt not only tired but deeply disappointed as well.

When they arrived at the specified address there was no hotel. There was indeed a warehouse, but it was decaying and served as both a freight depot and a residence for a mixed population of people of color and whites whose common feature was poverty. The place no longer awakened any memory in Frederick de Augustus at all, but still he could have sworn there had been a hotel here when he left London! Better yet, he even had a very precise memory of it because he and the Polish aristocrat who'd recruited him had spent a night there before they embarked for the Baltic. Like a simpleton he just stood there, contemplating the scene. Anxious to leave, the coachman called at him in a contemptuous tone and demanded to be paid before he'd even taken the trunk down.

In his great disappointment, George was watching his father without understanding what was happening on. They exchanged glances. Frederick de Augustus looked up, desperately searching for an alternative to the situation. In the distance he noticed an enormous sign painted in bright colors and, despite the shadowy evening light, he managed to decipher 'Cobbler. Rooms for rent upstairs'. He jumped at the chance.

He explained to George they'd rent a room. Just for the night, he assured him. The next day, they would go to another hotel he knew; since it was almost night it was too late to go there now. George only partially believed him but said nothing. Laboriously they picked up their heavy trunk and followed the sign.

The first street they crossed was called Pissing Alley; the second was Cutthroat Lane. And when George saw that the street where the shoemaker was located was called Rotten Row, he wondered what kind of place his father had dragged them to.

The landlord showed them to a room on the fourth floor, with all its windows blocked, except for one. It smelled musty and stale and obviously lacked any daylight. Speaking German so the cobbler wouldn't understand, George told his father that he didn't like the room. When Frederick de Augustus asked for a room with better ventilation, he was told there was none, all of them had just one window with some daylight. In fact, the buildings were taxed according to the number of windows, and the more windows there were the higher the taxes. Besides, the cobbler added, it was better for one's health: fresh air caused consumption; by blocking the windows less air could come in and thus there was less chance of getting sick. George understood only half of what the man was saying because of his accent and the odd way in which he pronounced certain words.

Frederick de Augustus had no choice. He rented the room, while the cobbler demanded that he pay the six shillings and sixpence for the night in cash. Trust surely wasn't the rule on Rotten Row, an outraged George told himself.

He was upset, sat down on their large trunk and mutely inspected the room. Locked inside his silence, he was convinced that his father knew nobody here, even if he had actually known anyone before. Then he understood why, during all the time he'd spoken to him so highly of London, he hadn't once mentioned the name of a single musician.

Frederick de Augustus saw his son's unhappy face. He went over and sat down next to him on the trunk, put his arm around his shoulders and said: 'George, Paris is a luminous city, it is instantly seductive. London, on the other hand, shows a stark face at first, depressing even; it's only gradually, by living here and walking the streets of the different neighborhoods, that you end up realizing what opportunities it holds. It will take some time, but, you'll see, my boy, all will be well.'

XXIII

George welcomed the first rays of light filtering into the room as a deliverance, notwithstanding the closed shutters. It had been a bad night, made even more fatiguing because he hadn't been prey to real insomnia but rather to a series of short naps, constantly interrupted just when he felt he was about to fall asleep. What startled him awake the first time were cries of 'Stop thief! Stop thief!' shouted below his window, cries that went to a *decrescendo* and then died out in the distance, suggesting the victim and the perpetrator were involved in a frantic chase. Then he was awakened by some drunks quarreling over a bottle of gin and then, at more or less regular intervals, by a stentorian voice that for some unknown reason barked the hours of the night, each time concluding with: 'May God assure you of a good sleep, my fine masters!' Finally, drifting over this cacophony, the church bells never stopped tormenting him with their disorderly pealing, which depended on the shifting direction of the wind.

But even more unbearable was watching his father sleeping peacefully beside him, indifferent to all the noises of this first London night. He had the peculiar feeling their roles were reversed: since they'd begun their long journey across Europe until now, it was always George who went to bed first and would fall asleep the minute his head hit the pillow, while his father made sure he was comfortable and would sometimes tuck him in before going to bed himself; should George happen to be reading or playing cards too long, or entertain himself with cutting out paper silhouettes as he liked to do to relax after a concert, he'd sternly send him to bed at the first sign of a yawn. But this evening, barely in his nightshirt, Frederick de Augustus had collapsed and begun to snore without even so much as a goodnight. So when George heard new sounds, those of vegetable and fruit vendors loudly praising the quality of their merchandise above the din of the wheels of their carts and the neighing of their horses, when he heard the watchman's booming voice as he drummed on the doors bellowing: 'May God assure you a good day, it is a fine morning', and he saw a ray of light filtering into the room, he was relieved: day had broken, his torture had come to an end. Without waiting another second he woke up his father.

※

The first thing Frederick de Augustus did when he got up was open the room's only window to let the day enter in all its glory. George joined him to breathe the fresh air, too. Frederick de Augustus looked at him and sensed instantly that his son hadn't slept well.

On the other side of the narrow street across from them, a building with its shutters closed was blocking their view. They were studying its façade, black with soot, when suddenly one of the windows opened and a man's head appeared. He looked at them without any surprise or curiosity, bent down, picked up a chamber pot, emptied it on a pile of trash below then, without giving them another glance, he closed the shutter. Amazed at this strange spectacle, George and Frederick de Augustus looked at each other silently for a moment, then their eyes turned toward their pots and, as if they suddenly understood, they each picked up their own and emptied it the same way, out the window. George laughed, thinking of the unlucky one who at that very moment might have been passing beneath their window. But when George asked his father if he could imagine them doing the same thing at the Hotel Britannique in Paris, Frederick de Augustus only had an embarrassed smile. He didn't respond but swore to himself he'd do anything to leave this miserable lair as quickly as possible where chance had forced them to land.

The previous night the owner had told them they couldn't have found a better place to stay in this neighborhood; his building was the only one with a shower room and they could use it for a few pennies more. It was located on the ground floor. George and Frederick de Augustus went down to clean up. The room was small and open to the street. A small bucket and three bowls fitting one inside the other were placed near a tub full with water. One bucket per person only. The used water flowed directly into the street and poured down an open sewer where it stagnated, greenish and foul-smelling. The place was rather congested since there were already three people in it, in the process of noisily performing their ablutions. One of them wouldn't stop spitting as he brushed his teeth, another was blatantly cleaning his private parts while humming a bawdy tune. Frederick de Augustus and George had no intention at all to linger near these uncouth individuals; they washed up quickly and went back up to their room.

As they were getting dressed, Frederick de Augustus informed George of the program he had devised for the day. First they'd look for a place to have a decent meal; they were both hungry as horses, for they hadn't eaten since the evening before, not because they'd been too tired to look for somewhere to eat, but because they didn't want to venture out in this grim neighborhood at night. Once they'd had some food, they would spend the rest of the day looking for a hotel in a less seedy area, consistent with the image he wanted to provide to the connections he planned to make in London. After all, he added in his thoughts, was he not a man of quality, and an African prince at that?

From inside his shoe repair shop, the proprietor, vigilant as a watch-dog, had his eye on the stairs that led to the rooms. As soon as he saw Frederick de Augustus and George come down, he caught them at the bottom of the steps and asked somewhat bitterly whether they were leaving for good. Frederick de Augustus explained they would like to store their trunk in a corner of the shop and pick it up later in the after-noon. However, not very conciliatory, the man replied plainly that they would find their trunk in the street when they returned unless they paid him the equivalent of the price of the room in advance. Take it or leave it. Frederick de Augustus had no choice, he couldn't see them dragging their luggage along all day in search of a hotel. Muttering a most vulgar insult in German, he paid in full. And while he was at it, he insisted that the trunk stay in their room, hoping it would dissuade this crook from renting the room to another customer and thereby double his profit. No, really, George thought again, one couldn't say that trust was the rule in Rotten Row. For an instant he wondered if in their absence the landlord would go rummaging through their things and steal his violin. But he felt quickly reassured: the trunk with its rounded lid was made of strong wood, reinforced with metal at the corners and had a good lock. The only way for him to open it would be to attack it with an axe, and surely, he wouldn't dare do that.

XXIV

In the grayness that covered the city, Rotten Row appeared even more squalid than the night before. George had the impression that new smells had been piled on top of the sulfurous odor of burned charcoal and the stench of garbage and excrement that had grabbed them by the throat when they arrived. Across the street in front of them was a sign they hadn't seen the night before, showing the words '*Crown Coffee and Ale House*' in gaudy gothic letters. It was badly attached and hung lopsided, creating a sense that with the slightest gust of wind it would drop down on the head of the first passerby. It caught Frederick de Augustus' attention who wondered whether, in addition to beer and coffee, the place would have food as well; it was worth finding out, as they were too hungry to let the opportunity go by. They decided to check it out and crossed the street.

George was disappointed as soon as they crossed the threshold. He expected to find a familiar place like the cafés and restaurants in Vienna or Paris where he'd been with his father. Quite the contrary, he found himself inside a semi-dark room where the areas the daylight couldn't reach were lit by lamps with smoking wicks. Worse yet, already packed despite the early morning hour the place reeked of tobacco, beer, and old frying oil. Still more surprisingly, a thin layer of sand covered the floor. George thought it was meant to protect the hardwood but when he looked up and noticed the spittoons standing here and there around the room, he concluded the layer of sand was meant to catch the gobs of spit that didn't reach their target. Indifferent to all of this, Frederick de Augustus took two empty straight-backed chairs with rather narrow seats at a table beside one of the lamps. On the wall a sign said: 'It is forbidden to carry off any sugar or salt'. Who would ever have the idea of stealing sugar or salt from a restaurant? George wondered. Trust most definitely didn't rule around here, he told himself once more.

An innkeeper came over and immediately asked: 'What do these fine gentlemen need?' Put off by this abrupt manner of being addressed, George looked at his father who replied in an equally abrupt manner: 'What do you have to eat here?' 'Anything you want! Make your choice and call me when you're ready', the innkeeper said, handing them a piece of cardboard before going over to a customer who was loudly and insistently demanding a glass of gin.

George watched the man go off without showing them any further interest. The bitter memory of all the disappointments they'd run into since their arrival came back to him: a city that wasn't what his father had promised, where they'd met nothing but unpleasant people, a dreadful night in a miserable room in a sinister neighborhood, and now this greasy spoon! He felt he was in a world where he didn't belong: these men with their accents he found so hard to understand, chattering away at any one at all, the smoke of lamps and pipe smokers, the whiffs of beer, fried food, and tobacco. All he wanted was some breakfast as usual but most of the names on the menu made no sense to him. Mathilde's face cropped up in his mind, a more beautiful Mathilde, sweeter than ever, bringing him his cup of hot chocolate. He broke down.

He began to sniffle, trying to suppress his tears, his body shaking with soundless sobs. Caught off guard, Frederick de Augustus stammered:

'But… what's wrong, my boy?'

179

The words reached George's ears only as incomprehensible muttering. Through his eyes brimming with tears, his father was merely a blurred hovering silhouette whose lips were moving. Frederick de Augustus was deeply embarrassed and could find nothing better to do than ask:

'What are you having, son?'

'I don't want anything! None of it looks good,' George answered between two hiccups.

'Yes, sure there's something! We'll find something you like. You haven't eaten anything since yesterday. If you don't eat, you'll get sick. Let me help you choose.'

Frederick de Augustus picked up the menu and started listing the dishes he thought might please George. After a few moments George calmed down, paying attention to his father's suggestions.

They ended up by ordering a meal that was as much breakfast as lunch. Frederick de Augustus had two glasses of light beer with his food, which he found excellent. To their happy surprise, the establishment also served tea and hot chocolate. Frederick de Augustus would like to have finished with one of those exceptional teas from the Indies that he remembered so well, but the price deterred him. He ordered coffee instead, much less good than what he was used to in Vienna but a great deal less expensive. George wanted a large cup of hot chocolate. Living in permanent fear of running short of money since they'd arrived in London, Frederick de Augustus couldn't help but notice that the chocolate was even more expensive than the tea, but he didn't dare prevent his son from ordering it, hoping it would console him and help him forget his misery.

After finishing their meal they were back in Rotten Row. Frederick de Augustus had only one thing in his head, to find a carriage as quickly as possible to take them far away from this wretched area, to the City where he could make a start with his plans and also show George that London really was as beautiful, and industrious as he had described.

In this area that mixed poor people with quite a lot of Blacks, George and his father didn't stand out because of their skin color, as had so often been the case in the cities on the European continent, but because of their fine clothes purchased in Vienna, Frederick de Augustus suddenly felt that people were looking at him with envy: instinctively he made sure his purse was well hidden inside the buttoned pocket of his vest, as he remembered that London, especially the district of the docks in the East End where they were now, harbored a breed of particularly skillful pickpockets not to be found anywhere else.

As they walked on, he affectionately took George's arm and repeated that they'd landed in this neighborhood only because of their late arrival the evening before, almost at sundown; that he would soon contact renowned musicians and that everything would fall into place. Because George remained obstinately silent, he stopped and looked at him: quiet tears were once again flowing down his cheeks.

'But what is wrong, my boy?'

'How are we going to get the letter that Friedrich and Mama are going to send me now? I gave them the address at the Hotel Britannique. I don't want it to get lost like the one in Brussels.'

Again Frederick de Augustus was caught off guard. He came up with an answer to calm the child:

'Ah, you're thinking about your mother again,' he said somewhat annoyed. 'The Hotel Britannique is a first class establishment. It's accustomed to forwarding the correspondence of their guests. At least, it's what they do for the many English guests that stay there.'

Frederick de Augustus knew he was lying. He had no idea if it was true. Besides, what address would he have given them to forward any mail, since they'd left the hotel without knowing where they'd be staying?

But George insisted:

'Did you leave our address in London with the hotel?'

'Eh... eh... not yet, but I will very soon, as soon as we find a hotel.'

They both fell silent and kept on walking in search of a vehicle. As they continued on their way, Frederick de Augustus thought about his son's tears in the restaurant. And about this sudden reminder of his mother. His own presence alone, which until now seemed to have filled George's life, was no longer enough and he wondered whether the boy was distancing himself from him. He realized for the first time that, in fact, many things separated them.

He, Frederick de Augustus Bridgetower, had been born in an English colony but had come to England at a very young age and always considered himself as English. London was the city of his youth. He had lived there for many years before leaving for the European continent. He knew every one of its nooks and crannies, he knew the accents of the different groups of people. Even if things had changed during his long absence, he would find his bearings in this city again, feel at home again. He only had to reintegrate into a universe that, for better or worse, had always been his.

For his son it was quite a different story. Born in Biala, Poland, of a Polish mother, growing up at a royal court in Austria, then spending time in Parisian salons, there was nothing English about him, he was a pure product of the continent of Europe where he'd come into the world. Although he spoke French, Italian, Hungarian, as well as English, his first languages were German and Polish. England was a foreign land to him. So it was no surprise that he felt lost and unhappy.

He would have to keep that in mind if he wanted to realize his plan, turning the young prodigy into someone who would make them wealthy. Now that he had a guaranteed source of income, he didn't want to squander it by letting George sink into a despondency that might ruin his talent. And toward that goal he saw only one path: erase the boy's entire Central European heritage, and his distant African roots even more so, to turn him into a fine little Englishman. He needed to become as English as the Chevalier de Saint-George had become French in France.

Absorbed in his thoughts, he automatically hailed the first carriage that came in their direction.

XXV

Frederick de Augustus asked the coachman to drop them off at Fleet Street in the center of the City. Even before they were properly seated and the carriage departed, he asked him which way he planned to go, thus letting him know he was familiar with the city and that it wouldn't be in the man's interest to take a roundabout route to cheat him. Surprised by this unusual request, the coachman answered he would take Whitechapel Road to get to the center via Aldgate Street; then Fenchurch to Cheapside, which would take them to St. Paul's Cathedral where he would go left to reach Fleet Street. When the coachman finished, Frederick de Augustus replied in a tone that brooked no opposition: 'Rather than taking Fenchurch Street, take Leadenhall; it's more direct going to Cheapside and St. Paul's Cathedral.'

Indifferent until then, when he heard the name Saint Paul, George emerged from his lethargy: he asked his father if that was the cathedral that he'd told him about, 'the one whose dome towers above all the other buildings in the city?' 'Yes, indeed, that's the one,' he answered, happy to see his son's cheerful spirit finally return, George seemed to have found the enthusiasm again that he displayed every time he discovered something new.

Since the streets weren't too congested yet, the carriage was able to move along at a fast clip. When Frederick de Augustus noticed the entrance to Aldgate and the vestiges of the wall that once formed the boundary of the City, he suddenly had an idea and brusquely told the driver:

'Coachman, I've changed my mind. Rather than going directly to Fleet Street, take the route I'll give you. I'm going to show my son a few important sites.'

'Oh yes, what a good idea, Papa!' George exclaimed.

Thus, on the new route Frederick de Augustus had chosen George discovered what interesting things were to be seen in this part of the city: the great Tower, the large fish market at Billingsgate, the old bridge over the Thames, the monument of the Great Fire—a long time ago, Frederick de Augustus explained, almost all of London had burnt down—, and St. Paul's Cathedral. When they finally got out of the carriage at Fleet Street, George's face was radiant.

The ride had cost Frederick de Augustus a fortune, but he wasn't sorry, for he thought he'd managed to help his child to forget Paris.

Walking toward the Strand, George was struck how it contrasted with the neighborhood where they'd spent the night. It felt like a different country. The houses had nothing to do with the filthy, decrepit buildings of Rotten Row. They were large and beautiful. Some had roofs with gables facing the street, others had façades with strange sculptures, lions painted blue or red, dragons spitting flames, and even flying pigs. Shops, one after another, the watchmakers' and jewelry shops most conspicuous among them with their brilliantly lit windows, the more lackluster printers' shops, and book and magazine vendors with their stalls on the street. But above all else, a profusion of pubs and taverns.

They moved on amid a crowd that advanced in a chaotic way and, a moment later, Frederick de Augustus spotted the Temple Bar monument; carriages were crossing under the great central arch, while pedestrians crossed on either side beneath two small arcades. They took the left one and came out on the Strand, which was wider than Fleet Street and where the carriages could circulate freely in both directions without bothering each other.

Frederick de Augustus thought the place hadn't changed much. When he saw a few kids across the street running after some elegantly dressed men to suggest polishing their shoes, old memories assailed him. Suddenly, he wanted to have his shoes polished! He grabbed George's hand and crossed the street.

Frederick de Augustus showed the shoeshine boy no kindness at all, on the contrary, he behaved with the same arrogance and impatience that he had experienced in the past. And when he tossed the coin he owed the boy for his service, he felt he'd gotten a little bit even.

As they continued, George who upon his father's orders had his shoes shined as well, asked him:

'Why were you so mean to that boy, Papa?'

'Mean? Not at all! By treating him that way, he'll do good work. Do you remember how they treated beggars at Castle Esterhazy?'

'Not very well, that's true. Me, I like music a lot, I love my violin. You think that boy likes to polish shoes?'

'No, of course not! But it's not the same: you, you're lucky, you're a musician. With your violin you'll never be on the street begging or doing that kind of work. Now you understand why I sometimes make you get up at dawn to practice your scales. It's for your own good!'

George nodded, but without any conviction. On they went. Frederick de Augustus wanted to take him to Charing Cross so he could see what made this such a charming city, so different from Paris, as he was still trying to make him forget their arrival and those first disastrous impressions.

Over the brouhaha of pedestrians and vehicles, a diffuse echo of music that floated on the air reached their ears. George stopped, listening carefully, trying to place its source. He recognized a violin.

As if by reflex, without a word, he pushed on toward the place from where the sounds came. Frederick de Augustus could only follow.

The musician was standing at the entrance of a theater, but they didn't see him at first since he was hidden behind a lively crowd, yelling and clapping their hands; some were dancing to the beat of the jig the violinist was playing. They finally found a spot from where they could see him clearly—a one-legged Black man, a cocked hat with multi-colored feathers on his head, wearing a scarlet vest under a blue navy officer's jacket and cotton pants on his good leg. Dancing and whirling on his wooden leg, he was grating his scratchy old violin while he clowned around to the hilarity of the audience. After a while he stopped and, leaning on his good leg, the wooden one raised high, he performed a series of deep bows under the applause of the spectators who encouraged him, crying: 'Bravo, Black Billy...', 'American Billy...', 'You're the king of all the beggars in London, Mr. Waters!' Then, limping, he approached, begging bowl in hand, which was immediately filled with half-pennies.

George was in awe, fascinated with the famous Billy's agility, with the acrobatic and unorthodox way in which he played his violin. It reminded him of Popo the fiddler, Mathilde's favorite violinist, which increased his interest in this Billy Waters even more. He applauded loudly and, in his enthusiasm, insisted that his father toss a coin in the bowl, too. Frederick de Augustus, on the other hand, was uncomfortable; he unwillingly threw his donation in the receptacle. He found the whole scene just too sad.

Of course, he knew who Billy Waters was and why they called him 'the American'. The man came not from the British colonies, not from Africa, but from America. During the War of Independence tens of thousands of Blacks had fought alongside the English because they had promised them their freedom after the conflict was over. When the English were defeated, many sought refuge in Canada, while many others wound up in England, abandoned and without resources. They certainly weren't the largest group of beggars in London, although their visibility would lead one to think so. Billy was one of them. A cannonball had ripped off his leg on the bridge of the ship on which he was fighting for His Majesty. In no way did Frederick de Augustus want to be associated with an individual like this. Besides, this was no model for his son. If only Billy would play some instrument other than the violin, a drum or a trumpet for instance! As for George, he wanted to stay to see the show: he was imagining himself at a concert where Popo the fiddler, Billy Waters, and he would be playing for Mathilde, a happy Mathilde who'd be applauding them. Frederick de Augustus was eager to leave the spectacle as fast as he could. He pulled the boy's arm without brooking any resistance.

The sight of the unfortunate Black, a violinist to boot, had been so disturbing to Frederick de Augustus that he no longer had any desire to continue their walk. He decided it was time to find a hotel and, rather than hoping they'd locate one while wandering around, he told himself he'd better check the classified section of the newspapers. He was sorry he hadn't thought of this when they were still on Fleet Street; he decided to go to a pub, for in the West End pubs periodicals were made available to the customers.

He didn't know which one to pick, but when George noticed the sign of a café called *La Belle Sauvage* and suggested to his father they should go there simply because the French name pleased him, he agreed.

Before he sat down, Frederick de Augustus wanted to make sure they really did have newspapers for the clientele to read. And they did. He knew which papers to check first since he'd sold and distributed them when he was working on Fleet Street, and grabbed the *London Advertiser* and the *Daily Courant*.

The place was cleaner than the restaurant in Rotten Row. People were speaking loudly enough for them to catch some bits and pieces of the conversation. Thus Frederick de Augustus was able to deduce that the majority of the patrons were businessmen having a drink with clients and intellectuals discussing politics, philosophy, and literature. He didn't want to seem pitiful in the eyes of this upper crust, so without looking at the price he didn't hesitate and ordered the tea from India the waiter recommended. George chose a slice of ginger cake.

Frederick de Augustus handed the *Daily Courant* to George while he began to look for the classified page in the *London Advertiser*. The child didn't feel like reading papers at all but flipped through it mechanically nevertheless as he waited for his cake. Suddenly he said to his father:

'Hey, Papa, a boy from Barbados has gone lost. They're looking for him.'

'How's that?'

'Look! Maybe you know him.'

He handed the paper to his father, who read:

A Negro boy, about nine years old, newly arrived from Barbados, wearing a gray serge suit, his head shaved, was lost last Tuesday, 9 August, in Nikolaus Lane. He answers to the name Limbrick. Please contact Mrs. Eades at Ludgate Hill, near Fleet Bridge...

A slight panic seized him. In no case did he want George to be confronted with this story of slavery.

'Did you read the whole piece?'

'No, as soon as I saw "newly arrived from Barbados" I stopped to show it to you.'

Relieved, Frederick de Augustus told him:

'Oh, you know, there are many boys and even adults who get lost in London when they've just arrived. It's perfectly normal. I, too, got lost one day and went around in circles for several hours before I found the place where I was staying again. Well, eat your cake. Is it good? I'll take your paper now, I'll start my search for accommodations with that one.'

He pushed the paper before him aside and ostentatiously started leafing through the one he'd taken out of George's hands. When he came to page three it was his turn to be struck by an article. Printed in bolder letters than the rest and framed by a rectangle in dark ink, it announced a musical program:

Handel Festival. Four morning concerts at Westminster Abbey...

Keenly interested, he reread the announcement several times. He paused for a moment then picked up the paper again. More concerts were announced in different locations: Covent Garden, Drury Lane Theatre, Vauxhall Gardens... so many venues!

Without warning, in a lightning flash, an idea sprang up inside his head. It was so simple that he wondered why he hadn't thought of it before—go to one of these places where music was played and plead with the organizers to have them test his son's talent. Surely one of them would appreciate the young prodigy's true worth: George Augustus Polgreen Bridgetower!

As if to accompany his idea, music in which percussion dominated could be heard from the street, gradually approaching the café. A few customers stood up and rushed out to watch the show.

'Let's go look, Papa,' George said.

They, too, went out to the sidewalk. About a dozen musicians soon arrived where they were standing. Wearing turbans or cocked hats with large multicolored feathers of exotic birds, dressed in long brocade tunics, they proceeded, shifting from one foot to the other rather than walking, without it disturbing the group's harmony. Most dazzling were the drummers and tambourine players; they would beat their instruments, then toss their sticks into the air and catch them just in time for the next drumbeat. Besides small bells, drums, tambourines, cymbals, and triangles, they had other percussion instruments that Frederick de Augustus and George were seeing for the first time.

The excited crowd applauded and, delighted, Frederick de Augustus joined them, clapping his hands to the beat of the band as well, a smile on his face. Seeing him so entranced, the man beside him, equally impressed, said: 'They're extraordinary, aren't they, these Turkish janissaries?' Frederick de Augustus nodded in agreement, but what he specifically noted was that the man referred to the musicians as 'Turks'. But all of them were Black! And these Blacks were successful because the people thought they were playing 'Turkish' music! A new idea occurred to him: turn George into the son of an Oriental prince rather than a good little Englishman as he'd previously been thinking. He himself would be the prince and dress appropriately in flashy outfits. It had worked well in Paris, why not in London?

Frederick de Augustus was well-pleased with himself when they returned to the café to finish what they'd ordered. He asked for a small glass of gin.

XXVI

He had expected things to be simple, that all he'd have to do was present himself, in his exotic Oriental costume, at one of the countless London concerts for the doors of patrons of the arts and music societies to open, as if by magic, for him and his son. But that wasn't how it went. Two weeks after they'd arrived, they hadn't moved from the shabby Rotten Row hotel where they ended up the first day, nor had they found a single opportunity for George to show off his talent. Their financial situation had become alarming and, if Frederick de Augustus didn't correct it quickly, they soon would have no further means by which to feed themselves and pay for their room, no matter how cheap. Still, the two weeks of setbacks weren't completely futile, they allowed Frederick de Augustus to penetrate the mysteries of the relatively closed circle of London's musical life and understand why the strategy he'd adopted so far wasn't the right one.

He discovered that the musical scene was split into two decisively hostile camps, those who extolled early music were on one side and those who defended the modern style on the other. In Paris it was customary to program music of all genres and eras for the same concert, to which no one had any objection. Thus, if George had played a Viotti concerto at his premiere at the Cent-Suisses Hall of the Tuileries Palace, Vivaldi and Rameau would have been on the program as well. Here, where each clan was pushing its own favorite period, it was completely different. Most intransigent were the advocates of early music. No composition found any favor with them unless its composer had been dead at least twenty years. According to them, dissonant modern music went off in every direction and had neither the meticulousness nor the harmonic beauty of the old. Essentially, their repertoire relied on the works of Purcell, Vivaldi, Corelli, Geminiani, and above all Handel, a musician of German origin whom England had adopted so completely that when he died he was buried in Westminster Abbey with full state honors, the only Englishman of foreign origin to have been recognized in this way.

The supporters of early music had an important ally in King George III. Absolutely mad about Handel—he loved *The Messiah*, his grand oratorio—he had slowly but surely transformed the annual celebration of the anniversary of the composer's birth into a political act. He'd turned it into a national and patriotic ritual where, with great pomp, he rallied the nobility, aristocracy, and dignitaries of the Anglican Church around him to attest to the unity and solidity of a kingdom deeply shaken by years of instability following the loss of its American colonies.

However, to his great relief Frederick de Augustus noticed that despite the king's bias for early music, the modern style was continuing to attract more and more partisans, particularly among the growing cohorts of the nouveaux riches who'd made a fortune in business, industry, and commerce. To affirm their status as members of the upper middle class, they opposed the—to their eyes outdated—tastes of the old nobility and aristocracy by defending the new music with such ostentation that their detractors said they were suffering from a 'melomania epidemic'. Nevertheless, the presence of the finest musicians and composers of Europe provided them with a definite advantage when confronting their rivals, stuck in their cramped repertoire of the past. Musicians and composers flocked to London, to that place of high finance, either drawn by the money they could earn from the bourgeoisie so eager for music and with generous wallets, or—in the case of those coming from France—afraid of persecution by the Revolutionaries because of their past intimacy with the royal family. Thus, at one point or another, Mozart, Johann Christian Bach, Viotti, Pleyel, Giornovichi, Saint-George, and other lesser known composers had spent time here. Even Johann Peter Salomon, the greatest concert organizer of London, was born in Bonn. With all of this, what really delighted Frederick de Augustus was that the music of Haydn, not very well known yet, was gradually growing more popular and beginning to rival that of Handel. The rumor was, in fact, that Peter Salomon was going to have Haydn himself come over for the next season. When George heard this, he asked his father if they could go see this Mr. Salomon to let him know they were close with Haydn and ask him to keep them up-to-date on his arrival. Frederick de Augustus vaguely consented, unable to tell his son what he was actually thinking, that it was quite impossible for a totally unknown individual like himself without any references or recommendations, to appear before the city's greatest impresario and bid him to somehow keep them abreast of the schedule of his future guest. But in their current situation he didn't feel like discouraging his son any further. He was sure of only one thing, that the latter would one day be included on the list of illustrious musicians. Hadn't they, too, abruptly left Paris because of the chaos caused by the Revolution, and hadn't they chosen to come to London to seek their fortune?

During his exploration of the London musical milieu, Frederick de Augustus remembered two elements to be exploited when the time came. First was that the split into two antagonistic camps didn't concern the artists but only the concert organizers. The artists would play the music they were paid to play, no matter the era from which it came. The concerts were long, they often lasted more than three hours because of the mania of playing movements the audience liked twice in a row, sometimes even repeating them three times. Knowing this, enterprising soloists would take advantage of it to double their honoraria on the same night. For example, a violinist might begin his evening by playing a contemporary concerto in the first part of a Peter Salomon concert at Hanover Square, then end in a hall at Covent Garden where he'd rush to participate in the second part of a concert organized by the Academy of Ancient Music. He could already see George doing the same thing!

The second element was the infatuation with soloists from abroad. Based merely on being foreign, a newly arrived virtuoso easily filled a hall, while a local musician, even a greatly talented one, would be ignored. This would undoubtedly work in George's favor. After all, didn't he come from elsewhere as well?

※

Frederick de Augustus had it in his head that he would not, under any circumstances, follow the course of the average musician who disembarked, run after the concert organizers, smile obsequiously, to beg hither and yon for a spot on some program for his son. Not only was it unworthy of a prince but it was a long and uncertain road. He needed money right away, consequently his son would have to establish himself as a virtuoso prodigy without any further ado. To this end something grand, something spectacular was needed. A glorious feat! And the sole path he glimpsed for this feat didn't seem at all inappropriate to him: attracting the attention of the king.

The obstacles in his path were countless. How and where could he meet the right people to provide him with access to the king? Despite its increasing popularity these past few years, music here still didn't play the central role in society that it had in Paris. There, being around music and thanks to it, one could easily meet important individuals in prestigious salons: musicians, philosophers, politicians, men of letters, braggarts in search of notoriety and courtesans in search of a fine catch; there they all interacted. In London, on the other hand, people rarely mixed, they'd find each other for their various activities in the closed circles of the clubs. And what club was going to open its door to a Black man, an unfamiliar one at that, whether he be a prince or not? Still, none of these considerations discouraged him.

In fact, by adopting various personalities and ceaselessly navigating between them, the person he was and the one he claimed to be often grew fuzzy in his mind. Over time, without realizing it, he ended up by erasing from his memory his status as servant at Eisenstadt, his life as a domestic, a life that ran to the beat of the prince's demands, where the only enthralling moments were those when he—an exotic star in full dress—would circulate among aristocrats and musicians from all across Europe, switching between German, Hungarian, Polish, Italian, English, and French while serving as their interpreter—and sometimes as a discreet courtier—during the sumptuous receptions the master of the realm would give in their honor.

He introduced himself now only as 'African prince' or, when he felt like it to vary things a little, as 'prince from Abyssinia'. He went out only draped in flamboyant Oriental clothes, supposedly the attire of the country from whence he claimed he came. He had identified to such an extent with this princely character that when George finally gave the much-hoped for concert before Queen Charlotte and King George III at Queens' Lodge, their private residence at Windsor Castle, he quite naturally believed it was a privilege granted him because of his rank rather than the result of a happy combination of circumstances.

XXVII

S eated in the front row of the orchestra, George was waiting for the king and queen to arrive. The violin on his lap, he let his eyes slide across the hall as if he were taking its inventory. In front of him two empty armchairs, one with the stamp of the king on its back. Behind the two royal seats, those of the guests; there were very few, not even a dozen, among whom his father's face stood out distinctly, not because it was the only black face but because of the white silk turban he was wearing. Besides, in his short ruby-colored tunic George, too, looked out of place amidst the musicians around him, all dressed in the uniform of the House of Windsor, a blue livery adorned with gold patterns. His father had insisted he wear the sleeveless tunic with its round collar edged in lace that gave him a vaguely Ottoman look.

As he contemplated the small music room, elegantly decorated but not especially luxurious, and the group of guests among whom the Prince of Wales, the king's son, who had recommended them to the queen, George felt a rush of furtive unease inside. And yet, he had performed many times before in grander, more opulent halls in front of audiences of several hundred without feeling any anxiety. He realized the source of his apprehension: it wasn't because he was going to play before a king and his queen for the first time, but because the circle of invitees made him think of a jury brought together to audition him. This impression was further reinforced when he remembered what his father, with obvious pleasure, had told him: twenty-five years earlier, the then eight-year old Mozart had given a concert before this same royal couple. George, roughly the same age, feared that the monarch would do the same thing Frederick de Augustus was constantly doing and which so exasperated him, compare his talent to that of the young Mozart.

⁕

The king made his entrance. Preceded by two officers of his guard, he did not go directly to the seat meant for him but paused to exchange a few words with his guests, all of whom had risen.

When the king stopped in front of him, Frederick de Augustus saw a large corpulent man with a high forehead above a ruddy face, enhanced with a dimpled chin. He studied Frederick de Augustus, squinting his protruding eyes because of his bad sight, no doubt. The king uttered the conventional words of welcome to him as he'd done with the other guests, which Frederick de Augustus took as a special form of attention; he bowed very deeply as the sovereign moved away. It was the first time he'd shaken a king's hand and he was more than a little proud of it.

Actually, he was surprised and even somewhat disappointed. Accustomed to Prince Esterhazy's lavish clothing, he had expected to see an elegantly attired sovereign, perhaps wearing a crown set with sparkling diamonds. But the man before him was dressed in a rather ordinary fashion. Instead of a crown on his shaven skull he was wearing an outdated wig, which was so small that it barely reached his earlobes. On the other hand, there was no sign at all of the fit of madness he'd suffered the year before, an attack that at times left him so agitated that it was said his doctor had been forced to put him in a straitjacket. Frederick de

Augustus felt embarrassed having dressed so inappropriately, finding the silk costume in which he'd draped himself unsuitable.

While the king passed by each of his handful of guests and Frederick de Augustus was studying him, George hadn't taken his eyes off the queen. He wanted to know whether what his father had told him was really true: they hinted at her ugliness, which stemmed from the fact that she was of African descent, with a mouth that was too large, wide nostrils in a snub nose and, of course, an olive-greenish skin. Intrigued, George had asked his father:

'Must you be black or be of African descent to be ugly?'

'You know perfectly well that's not true, George. There are ugly people everywhere in the world. You've seen them in Vienna, Paris, and right here in London in Rotten Row, in the first café where we had lunch.'

'Why do they say this then?'

'Because they're idiots who will say anything!'

It was all that Frederick de Augustus had told his son in response. Ever since he was born, he'd always wanted to keep him inside a protective bubble. Why upset him by speaking of the everyday life of most Blacks in Europe, of the caricatures of which they were the target, even if occasionally the reality he wanted to obscure would come crashing in, starkly and unexpectedly, as when they'd run into Billy Waters or read that classified newspaper ad about a fugitive slave being sought by his owner?

Apparently satisfied with the answer, George continued:

'But how can a German princess be of African descent?'

'According to the story,' Frederick de Augustus explained, 'she's a descendant of Afonso III, a thirteenth-century king of Portugal, and his Moorish mistress of whom history only knows the first name, a certain Madragana.'

'What exactly is Moorish?'

'A woman who is a Moor, of course!'

199

'And what is a Moor?'

'A Moor is a Black heathen, a non-Christian from Africa.'

'Aha! Is that why Tomasini nicknamed you *il Moro*?'

'Well, yes. It's also, if you recall, why in Vienna a playwright suggested to Soliman that he take on the role of the Moor in a play he'd called *Othello, the Moor in Vienna*.'

Suddenly he fell silent, furrowed his forehead and grabbed his head as if he had a new idea, out of the blue.

'I read the poem composed in honor of the queen for her wedding to the king. The poet wrote that she descended from the "Vandal race" and "still preserves that title in her face", strange, don't you think?'

He recited the two first lines of the praise poem for George:

Descended from the warlike Vandal race,
She still preserves that title in her face.

'What is a Vandal?' his son asked.

Frederick de Augustus wasn't very sure himself, but never wanting to appear ignorant to his son, he concocted an answer he thought was rather clever:

'The Vandals? Warrior tribes who, after occupying Mediterranean Africa, went on to conquer Europe. They settled in Central Europe where they mixed with the local peoples, you know, the Germans, Austrians, Hungarians, and so on.'

'So then, since she's Polish, Mama has Vandal blood. And my brother and I as well, since we're her descendants?'

Frederick de Augustus was totally unprepared for his son's appropriation of the short historic fresco he'd painted of the Vandals. He was afraid that George and his questions would lead him into territories where he'd be totally incapable of inventing plausible answers, so he cut him short:

'Whether Queen Charlotte is a descendant of a Moorish woman or a Vandal is of no importance at all. What I want you to remember is this: when you stand before her, forget any of these rumors. Above all, don't distract yourself by staring at her, that's just not done. And you'll bow the way I taught you, but careful, it's not the same one you use on stage! Once you've bowed, you'll retreat moving backwards with small steps, never turning your back on her until you've reached a reasonable distance. There. Remember it well. They'll judge the Prince of Abyssinia by how his son conducts himself.'

George hadn't taken his eyes off the queen from the moment she'd entered the hall until the moment everyone had sat down after the king was seated. Obviously, he couldn't prevent himself from doing what his father had directed him not to do, stare at the queen's face. She wasn't the hideous creature the rumors had described, quite the contrary. She was small, but that slightness together with her slender body gave her a natural liveliness. Her skin was more olive than swarthy and no matter how hard he looked, he discovered none of the African features they attributed to her. Better yet, her dark brown hair, twisted into a chignon on top of her head, immediately made him think of his mother and when, violin at his shoulder, he gave a slight nod to indicate he was ready to begin the first piece of the evening, the Haydn quartet, and his glance crossed that of the queen, he read maternal kindness and warm encouragement there. Once again, he thought of his mother and the slight unease that had been with him since he was in the room miraculously vanished.

The four instrumentalists played harmoniously as if they'd always played together. The sound coming from their instruments—the nimble grace of the two violins, one of them George's, the steadfastness of the viola, and the solemn depths of the cello—fused perfectly, giving the ensemble an almost orchestral resonance. And when the last note of the fourth movement's final *presto* was played and the musicians rose, George was delighted to see the smile that lit up the queen's face.

However, during the second piece of the evening George surpassed himself. Even if in the quartet he'd just played the violins carried the main melodic lines of the work, he was still only one instrumentalist in a conversation of four. In the second piece, a violin concerto, he was the soloist. Alone, facing the orchestra, facing the audience. He had to give his very best.

In France, and even more so in Italy, what the audience loved in a violinist was the ability to dazzle the listeners with the velocity of the fingers and the working of the chords and upper registers; that way of almost mechanical, all exterior, playing was certainly dazzling but lacked emotion. But here neither technical work nor speed of execution were enough to conquer the listeners; a musician was judged on the way in which he performed the slow movement. That was where his talent was revealed, his sense of music disclosed.

George knew this and had prepared for it. So, when he attacked the *adagio* of the second movement, he focused on one person for whom to play, the queen. It allowed him to concentrate, to find the precision of the *adagio*'s phrasing, and to draw sounds of a clear and vibrant color from his instrument. No excessive ornamentations nor any ostentatious brilliance but a refined melodic *legato* of sustained intensity. He didn't know at what point he was no longer playing for one woman only but for two, as the image of his mother had become superimposed on the queen. When the last note of the third and last movement of the concerto had vanished into the air and, as he raised his eyes before bowing to the king, he saw the queen applauding enthusiastically, a sense of euphoria engulfed him, a sense of having passed a final exam.

While clapping for his son, Frederick de Augustus was watching the reactions of this distinguished audience. They were all applauding. He relished the smile that lit up the face of the Prince of Wales, a smile that was real, the smile of a contented person. The queen's spontaneity made him even happier and when he saw that His Majesty George III himself, a fierce adherent of early music, was applauding with genuine enthusiasm, he was overcome with emotion, as strong as what he'd felt at George's first public concert at the Concert Spirituel in Paris. He was happy and, filled with joy, he only vaguely listened to the Handel piece, chosen by the king, that closed the evening.

❁

Together with his son he attended the first of four concerts organized for the Handel Festival at Westminster Abbey. To make sure they would have the best possible seats, he didn't vacillate but paid the steep price they charged when one had no subscription, twelve shillings for two tickets. The sacrifice was well worth it, for the king was always present at the first concert where he himself would select the final piece on the program. Frederick de Augustus saw it as an opportunity to make his way into the king's entourage, even if he didn't quite know how.

But neither the king nor the queen showed up. The royal box was occupied by the Prince of Wales, to Frederick de Augustus' surprise, for in the quarrel between the partisans of early and modern music, the prince was a fervent partisan of the latter and never ceased goading his father by supporting the most modern music, such as the symphonies of Haydn. Perhaps he was there merely out of duty. The concert ended with the overture to *Esther*, Handel's first oratorio written directly in English.

The prince had only just left the place when, followed by George, Frederick de Augustus headed for the musicians' stage. He still entertained the hope of meeting one who might open the door to what they so desired. He wanted to move faster but the couple in front of them was holding them back. The man and the woman, wearing an English gown with a small train attached at the waist, were walking slowly, too slowly. In German Frederick de Augustus said to George:

'The musicians are already starting to pack up their instruments. We need to hurry!'

The lady stopped suddenly and turned around. Frederick de Augustus almost ran into her.

'*Was höre ich da? Sie sprechen deutsch?*'

Surprised by the remark, Frederick de Augustus looked at her, somewhat annoyed.

'Yes, Madame, as you see, we speak German!' he said in English, impatient to reach the podium where he noticed some musicians were leaving the stage.

He wanted to keep moving but the lady, extremely curious, stopped him with another question:

'Where are you from?'

Frederick de Augustus answered impertinently, trying to make it clear she shouldn't insist but rather let them pass:

'I am Frederick de Augustus, prince of Abyssinia. My son, George Augustus Bridgetower.'

'A pleasure. I am Charlotte Papendieck, in charge of the queen's wardrobe, as well as her personal reader.'

Turning toward the man next to her, whom neither of the two had noticed, she went on:

'My husband, in service to the king and musician at the court.'

Frederick de Augustus was momentarily speechless, trying to make sense out of what he'd just heard. When at last he grasped its profound significance, he had trouble hiding his excitement just as he had trouble believing that luck could be so generous. He glimpsed the advantage he might take of the encounter and began to talk very quickly as if he were afraid the couple was no more than a mirage likely to evaporate from one minute to the next before having heard all he wanted to say, forcing himself to maintain a neutral voice, too, so as not to give the impression of begging. A prince does not beg!

'We come from the court of Prince Esterhazy of Austria, whom I served as plenipotentiary for more than five years. My son was born there. He is only nine years old, but he is a violin prodigy. He has given concerts in Vienna, Brussels, and Paris. In Paris he was so successful that Queen Marie-Antoinette herself was eager to attend one of his concerts. We've been in London for just a few days. I hope that once they've heard him the London audience will welcome him as warmly as it did in Paris.'

When, in conclusion, Frederick de Augustus casually added that George had Haydn himself as a teacher, Mr. Papendieck, silent until then, unexpectedly said: 'Impressive!'

As for her, Charlotte Papendieck observed them with interest. She'd turned around because she heard them speak German but that wasn't what had most aroused her curiosity. London was teeming with German musicians since the taste for instrumental music had superseded vocal music of the Italian tradition, the dominant form until then: they'd been recruited because they were thought to be the finest instrumentalists of Europe. What had sparked her amazement even more was that it was this Black man in a turban and the little mulatto boy who were speaking the language.

As if that weren't enough, she was now finding out the boy was a prodigy. It just so happened that young prodigies were one of the concerts' greatest attractions. Every time the program featured one of them, they wouldn't fail to mention his age, about which they often lied, making him younger by a few months or even a year. The younger they were the more tickets they would sell.

Names began to parade through Mrs. Papendieck's head. Johann Hummel, pianist, twelve years old: his father who accompanied him on his London tour had introduced him as a student of Wolfgang Mozart's who, twenty-five years earlier, had played before the king and queen. Franz Clement, violinist: the concert's poster claimed he was eight and a half, although he was a year older than that. And now, here was this young Bridgetower. In addition to his talent and his age, nine years old, he had something else the others didn't have, he was Black! A Black violin prodigy was so unusual that he'd certainly attract a large audience.

She immediately thought of her queen: she should be the first to listen to this unusual musician and, for several reasons, that should be achieved without any problem.

First, the queen had upheld the tradition established by her late lamented music teacher, Johann Christian Bach, of organizing a concert every Wednesday in her Queen's Lodge pavilion. The king attended it gladly on the condition that the concert would end with a work by Handel, no matter what the program. Furthermore, she had a special fondness for all that was German music, whether early or modern, while her solicitude for German-speaking musicians was legendary. Besides, her private orchestra, the Queen's Band, consisted mainly of Austrian and German musicians, while foreigners were barred from the King's Band. Add to all of this, too, that her son, the Prince of Wales, loved modern music, particularly that of Haydn.

Not in his wildest dreams could Frederick de Augustus have imagined a more felicitous encounter. At the end of their conversation Mrs. Papendieck told him of her plan to approach the queen about organizing a concert at Windsor Castle with the help of the Prince of Wales. She'd done so once before and didn't see why it couldn't happen again. For once, Frederick de Augustus exclaimed with uncommon sincerity and genuine admiration:

'We are so very happy to have met you, Mrs. Papendieck. My son and I thank you from the bottom of our heart.'

Thereafter everything moved incredibly fast. A week after this decisive meeting, Charlotte Papendieck told him that the idea of a concert at Queen's Lodge had charmed the Prince of Wales. However, before having George play before the king and queen, he wanted to hear him first and had therefore decided to hold a private session at his residence.

Mrs. Papendieck was surprised at the importance the prince ascribed to the event. Indeed, he didn't arrange it at Carlton House, his London residence where his private musical soirees usually took place, but at his seashore retreat in Brighton, about twenty miles from London. It was the quiet spot where he had installed his mistress, Maria Fitzherbert, the woman he loved but was forbidden by law from marrying because she was a Catholic. He wanted to be sure she, too, could hear this unusual prodigy, and since she wasn't welcome at Windsor Castle, she wouldn't be able to attend George's concert for the royal couple. Equally surprising, he had invited his uncle, the Duke of Cumberland, and his brother, the Duke of York, to Brighton to hear this still unknown young violinist.

George played three pieces, a short divertissement by Saint-George, followed by a Viotti concerto, and after an intermission of vocal music with piano accompaniment, a string quartet by Haydn. The warm reception the performance received removed any doubt Charlotte Papendieck may have had about the relevance of her initiative. Better yet, George's charm and fine manners had at first so amazed the prince, then captivated him, that in the end, without much thought, he resolved to take the young musician under his wing.

That is how George found himself two weeks later in the elegantly decorated music room, playing for the king and queen.

When the royal couple finally departed and the guests began to leave as well, Frederick went to join his son who was putting away his violin. As they were leaving the podium the Prince of Wales approached, accompanied by one of the guests whom they immediately recognized: he had played the piano at the concert at the Prince's residence in Brighton. He was a renowned composer from Germany who, unfortunately, had stopped his professional musical career to devote himself entirely to astronomy, even if he did occasionally still perform privately for the king at Windsor. A naturalized Englishman his name was William— not Wilhelm anymore—Herschel. The prince again congratulated

George, affectionately patting his cheek, and left. Alone with the two of them, Herschel expressed his admiration for George as well and then advised them to go to Bath, a spa town south of London where in this season the musical life was in full swing. The town had served as a trampoline for many budding musicians and becoming known there would certainly open the way for little George. Although he hadn't lived there in many years, he still knew influential people who could help him. He would write a letter of recommendation to a certain Venanzio Rauzzini, the man who had succeeded him as chapel master.

It wasn't the first time that the journey to Bath had been suggested to Frederick de Augustus. At the concert for the Prince of Wales in Brighton, Charlotte Papendieck, backed by two or three members of the King's Band, had already recommended it to him. If Dr. Herschel, as Charlotte Papendieck called him, advised the same thing it would certainly be worthwhile. Leaving London in order to return more successfully, that was the whole issue.

The evening had been a complete triumph: a concert before the king and queen of the United Kingdom of Great Britain and Ireland, an invitation to Bath and, furthermore, a bonus of twenty-four guineas. He sorely needed that!

As they walked away from the Queen's pavilion, Frederick de Augustus, brimming with satisfaction, began to ponder a coincidence again: his name was Frederick de Augustus and his son was George Augustus. The king himself was George William Frederick and his son, the Prince of Wales, was George Augustus Frederick! He was convinced this was more than a mere coincidence.

XXVIII

L ocated about forty miles south-west of London, the town of Bath was famous for its thermal baths that dated to the Roman period and was highly fashionable among aristocrats and the wealthy bourgeoisie. During the warm season they flocked there for its waters, which presumably cured illnesses from which they suffered, such as gout and rheumatism. Paralytics went there as well, in the hope to regain the use of their limbs, reinforced by their faith in the miracle that had occurred a century earlier, in 1687, when Queen Mary of Modena, the second wife of King James II of England, had been cured from a period of infertility. Having given birth to six children who died instantly, she had no other children for six years, which is when she decided to spend a season taking the waters in Bath and, nine months later, she gave birth to a boy.

However, Frederick de Augustus and George weren't going to Bath for its thermal waters, but for its concerts. During this season they were in abundance and in the most varied of places, cafés, public halls, churches, private homes of wealthy sponsors. That is where George needed to be, to bring him out of the idleness that London had forced upon him.

Bath was known for another reason as well, its social life. It was the elegant meeting point of the aristocracy and members of the gentry, a literary and artistic crossroads where illustrious men could forget their dignity and take advantage of its happy, slightly playful atmosphere. Fostered by games and speculators, money was easy.

In addition to wanting to promote George and having the opportunity to fatten his purse, Frederick de Augustus was careful not to reveal to his son that this second aspect of Bath attracted him, the games especially. There were a myriad of them: games of dice, of money and cards, while the most popular ones were faro, piquet, whist, lansquenet, and basset; then there were the gambling games, where you could bet on everything and nothing! Often these activities were conducted under the same roof in what was known as assembly rooms. The assembly rooms of Bath contained a large hall that could hold several hundred people, where ballroom dancing took place as well as masked balls, concerts, with several adjoining smaller halls reserved for gaming. In contrast to the pubs and clubs, the place was open to both married and single women, which added to its charm and simplified meeting people. Imagination and levity had truly found shelter in Bath. Besides, it was said that Bath was the place in England where husbands were least jealous and wives most accessible. And that wasn't all: having made careful inquiries, Frederick de Augustus also knew that on Avon Street you could find inconspicuous well-kept houses where he could go. Bath was equally well-known for providing that sort of attraction. So the town offered everything to make him happy!

✿

Dr. Herschel's letter of recommendation to Venanzio Rauzzini had greatly expedited their introduction into Bath's high society and its musical circles. If he still had some doubts about William Herschel's reputation in Bath, the warm reception Rauzzini gave them upon reading the letter removed any uncertainty. After all, for sixteen years he'd been the city's most celebrated man. A wide-ranging musician – oboist, organist, harpsichordist, pianist, and composer, he had concurrently filled the functions of music teacher, chapel master, and orchestra conductor of the city's assembly rooms. However, ever more preoccupied with his passion for astronomy, he'd abandoned his musical profession. One of his students reported that one January night the sky, which had been overcast until then, happened to clear up. 'At last, there it is!' he'd cried out in front of the astonished student and, dropping his violin, rushed over to his telescope.

In March 1781, when he discovered what he thought was a new comet and it turned out to be a new planet he named 'Georgius Sidus' in honor of King George, the planet that would later be known as Uranus, he became as famous as Newton who had discovered the principles of universal gravity. Since Antiquity, since the era of Ptolemy, only six planets were known, Mercury, Venus, Earth, Mars, Jupiter, and Saturn. And here he'd just discovered a new one! He, an amateur astronomer! All of Europe's scientists corresponded with him, and visited him. That's when he abandoned music and left Bath definitively to settle in a London suburb, near the king. Enthusiastic over the work and discoveries of the brilliant amateur, whose origins were from Hanover like his own, the king made him his 'personal astronomer', providing him with vast subsidies so that he could continue to explore the celestial universe.

Furthermore, Rauzzini fell for Frederick de Augustus' charm: clever as always, the latter had spoken Italian as soon as he identified his host's background. At the time, when the hegemony of German musicians was dominant, what more flattering praise than to speak his own language with a musician who did not come from Germany?

The first concert was scheduled for December 5th, less than a week after their arrival, a true honor since seeking a concert and seeing it booked almost immediately was highly unusual. Better yet, the concert was going to be held in the large renovated hall of the assembly rooms, where Herschel had been the orchestra conductor for so long.

Since they arrived, they hadn't had a chance to visit the city and it wasn't until just two days before the concert that they did so. They liked it right away. They liked its streets without sidewalks, so wide that they were called 'parades', aptly named because, following the whims of fashion, it was there that the ladies in all their finery and the gentlemen dressed to the nines would parade. The houses that lined these avenues, most often attached, were built of a stone whose color tended toward the pale while the façades were decorated with pretty Corinthian columns.

From Duke Street, where they were staying, they went up South Parade to New King Street to see what was once Herschel's apartment. George had insisted on going there to look at the music salon they'd heard so much about. It was a veritable shamble: there was, indeed, a piano, but to see it you had to closely examine the room, for it was hidden under globes, maps, telescopes of different sizes, and reflectors, while a cello stood deserted in a corner. George wanted to stay longer to see everything, but Frederick de Augustus urged him on because he was eager to visit the Roman baths. They were impressed with the building of the Pump Room, the large room adjacent to the baths, which had a fountain from which flowed the famous medicinal water that was sold by the glass. Frederick de Augustus bought two. He emptied his in one gulp, but George only managed to swallow half since he thought the water was too salty and smelled of sulfur.

They went home, George exhausted but happy, while his father, who was happy, too, wasn't tired in the least. He mentioned he wanted to go right back out again, by himself, and did.

The next morning Frederick de Augustus woke up in a very good mood. It was the evening before the concert. During his outing the previous evening, he had won a nice sum of money at whist; he was so proud of it that he told George—a rather unusual fact, for he never spoke to him about his gaming winnings or losses. Obviously, he didn't mention where on Avon Street he ended his night.

He suggested to George they'd go to the baths, but the boy flatly refused. Frederick de Augustus insisted, explaining that it would relax him and be a good way to prepare for the next day's concert. A little irritated, George answered that he didn't like the smell of the baths and would rather stay alone to practice. Truthfully, he was actually relieved to see his father go. For a while now, ever since his father's all-day absence had provided him with the opportunity to talk with Mathilde and get his first kiss, he was beginning to find his constant presence progressively more burdensome.

Once he was alone, he removed the violin and bow from the case and meticulously rubbed the strings with rosin. When he was done, he caressed the violin the way you caress someone you love, brought it up and wedged it somewhere halfway between his heart and his head, between emotion and technique, the two poles of his music. He raised the bow and, gliding it across the strings, drew sounds from it, light sounds that flew off, as if the horsehair didn't really rub the strings but only barely grazed them. A violin should be an instrument whose strings you caress, he thought, an instrument with 'caressed' strings rather than 'rubbed' ones. Don't you love what you caress? Though a pianist, an organist, or a percussionist could change his instrument with every performance, depending on what the performance hall put at his disposal, a violinist, on the other hand, gave his very best self only with *his own* violin. He carried it with him everywhere. It was his counterpart.

He rehearsed for four hours straight. His father came back, two newspapers under his arm and a small bottle in his hand. Obviously very cheerful, he launched into an enthusiastic, effusive account of his morning:

'A pity you didn't want to come, George. There were very few people at the baths. And guess what? I almost witnessed a miracle! Yes, a miracle! A man both of whose legs were paralyzed came out of the baths walking! I didn't see what he was like before but when he came out of the waters, I watched him throw his crutches away. He didn't need them anymore! Look, I brought you a small bottle of water from the Pump Room. I know you don't like it very much but have a little of it anyway. It will cleanse you, even rid you of illnesses you don't have and, again, I tell you it will do you good for tomorrow's concert.'

'No, thank you,' George said. "I don't want any, it smells too awful. I've rehearsed well and feel fine, I don't need any miracle water.'

'Well, as for the concert, even the Bristol press has announced it.'

'Where is Bristol? And why is that a surprise?'

'Bristol is the city that competes with Bath when it comes to music. It's not far from here. Herschel gave some concerts there when he lived in Bath. Maybe we should go there, too.'

He handed the papers to George who opened the *Bristol Journal* first and began to read the announcement.

Frederick de Augustus was pleased because not only did it mention George's age, as usual, but it also stated that he'd been a student of Haydn's. The second paper, the *Bath Chronicle*, gave the same information as the Bristol one, but provided the program's details and the places where tickets could be purchased.

AT THE NEW ASSEMBLY ROOMS.
For the benefit of
Master GEORGE FREDERICK BRIDGTOWER,
a youth of Ten Years old, Pupil of the celebrated HAYDN,
On Saturday morning next, the 5th of December, will
be a GRAND CONCERT of Vocal and Instrumental MUSICK;
when Master BRIDGTOWER will develop his talents on the
Violin.
Act I. Overture. Haydn.—Song, Miss Cantelo.—

Quartetto, Pleyel.—Song, Mr. Harrison.—Concerto Violin,
Master Bridgtower, Viotti.
    Act II. Concerto Piano Forte, Mrs. Miles (late Miss
Guest). Song, Mr. Harrison.—Concerto Violin, Master
Bridgtower, Giornowich.—Song, Miss Cantelo.—Full Piece.
    To begin precisely at Twelve o'Clock.
    Tickets 5s. each, to be had at the New Assembly-Rooms,
Pump Room, Lintern's Musick Shop, at the Libraries, and
of Mr. Bridgtower, at Mr. Phillips's, No. 10, Duke Street.

※

As planned, the concert took place Saturday morning at noon. It was
a triumph. The following day, Frederick de Augustus hurriedly bought
papers to relish the comments that would be laudatory, he was sure of it.
He was right, they were all ecstatic.

Since the article in the *Mercure de France* about his first concert in
Paris, George had not enjoyed as much gratifying praise as what the *Bath
Chronicle* had written. Frederick de Augustus began to read out loud:

*Saturday in the hall of the Assembly Rooms, this city's music lovers
witnessed the most marvelous show one could attend, thanks to Master Bridgetower. His touch on the violin and his performance were
equal to, if not surpassing, those of the finest professors current and
past. Those who were lucky enough to be present were enchanted by the
astonishing abilities of this wonderful barely ten-year old child. He is
a mulatto, grandson of an African prince...*

Amused, Frederick de Augustus stopped: 'Now they're making you
my grandson. Fine, if that can make you even younger in their eyes, so
much the better!' he said. He went back to his reading then stopped
again, his face radiant this time:

215

'Ah George, they're talking about me, too. Listen to what this paper says:

His father's natural nobility and elegance were the object of everyone's attention. He is one of the most accomplished men of Europe, able to converse easily and with charm in several languages.

'You see, Papa, you are a true prince,' George said poking fun at his father a little.

Frederick de Augustus didn't catch the irony and went on:

'And you, the grandson of a prince!' still enjoying himself.

The second paper, the *Bath Morning Post*, wrote about George:

On Saturday the young African prince, whose musical talents have been so highly praised, gave the most popular concert this city has ever seen.

There were more than five hundred and fifty people in attendance! Everyone was thrilled with a performance that aroused enthusiasm and astonishment. Walking on air, Mr. Rauzzini himself declared he had never attended a performance of this kind. While he played, intense joy spread across the child's face. His father, who was present in the hall, was so deeply moved by the applause for his son that tears of happiness and gratitude flowed down his cheeks.

⁂

Never before had a concert earned them as much. The money was given to Frederick de Augustus. George gave three more concerts in Bath and two more in Bristol, adding Haydn, Corelli, Saint-George, and Pleyel to the program. The latter was a student of Haydn whose music the

London public was beginning to appreciate. The path to a career in London was now open.

Before leaving Bath, Frederick de Augustus picked up his finest pen and produced a letter of gratitude that he sent to the *Bath Journal*. He signed it 'The African Prince'. In this flowery letter where he spoke of himself in the third person, he made sure that between the lines 'the nobles, members of the gentry, visitors and residents of this marvelous city of Bath' would understand they were not the first to discover and applaud the talents of the 'son of the African Prince'. This honor was reserved for Their Majesties the King and Queen, and for His Royal Highness the Prince of Wales. They had inundated the young prodigy with praises when he performed for them at Windsor Castle, his first performance in Great Britain.

XXIX

Their stay in Bath was brief but very beneficial. Arriving in November as anonymous visitors lost among the masses, they returned to London in January, now famous, one for George's musical prowess, the other for his 'urbanity, his exotic elegance, and his mastery of every European language spoken in the city', as the *Bath Chronicle* had so rightly stated. Thanks to the money they'd made, they were finally able to leave the squalid hotel in Rotten Row and move to lodgings on the Strand in the City.

The celebrated tour in Bath was a jewel in his crown that added to his renown and hereafter was always mentioned on the posters by his father. This, plus the additional information of his age and his attribute as a student of Haydn, soon became an ordeal for George. Frederick de Augustus had turned it into a source of revenue to be exploited to the maximum. A squanderer, always short of money, he scheduled several concerts a week for George. Sometimes he even made him perform two concerts on the same day in places that were far apart from each other. George knew that these always packed private concerts, no matter what the size of the room, brought in a great deal of money, but he didn't know how much nor what his father did with it, other than buy them fine clothing.

He never left George alone, dragged him along everywhere he went, whether it was to the affluent bourgeois with whom he sought contracts or to high society receptions where he hoped to draw some advantage. He was managing every facet of his son's life. And George was suffocating! The only times he was able to breathe were when Frederick de Augustus left him alone, disappearing for part of the night and not returning until early dawn. Without any friends his own age and not knowing where to go, he'd lock himself in the room and tried to fill his isolation by playing solitaire or composing little melodies on his violin. He hardly read anymore, not because he didn't like to, but because he had no one to guide him or recommend any interesting books. And, of course, in those moments of solitude he missed his little brother Friedrich enormously and, above all, he thought a lot about his mother, transforming bygone times with her, even the most unpleasant ones, into wistful memories. He would like to have been with her then, rather than with that father who was simultaneously intrusive and faltering. He'd also think about Mathilde, but a Mathilde who gradually began to lose her reality.

One event, however, his first public appearance in London marked a decisive turn in his life.

Since they'd come back from Bath, George had only played in private salons of wealthy music lovers. Through his persistence, Frederick de Augustus succeeded in getting him scheduled for a performance at the Drury Lane Theatre. Given his skill at this, he carefully orchestrated George's entrance on the stage: during the intermission of a performance of *The Messiah*—following a tradition that Handel himself had established, who used to play small pieces on the organ between the acts of his oratorios—the audience had the surprise of seeing him dressed in a scarlet tunic. He played a solo violin piece and it was brilliant. The

Prince of Wales was in the audience. It was the first time he'd seen George play since he'd organized the soiree for the king and queen at Windsor Castle with the help of Mrs. Papendieck. He was just as impressed as he'd been the night the boy had played for his mistress and himself in Brighton. At that time he'd considered taking the young musician under his wing. Now he decided to do it.

✵

Under the prince's protection, George felt liberated. The prince had recruited him into his private orchestra and made it clear to his employees that, as an exceptional musician, George would have privileges such as rehearsing in the prince's music room and having access to his private library. In addition, he put a bedroom at his disposal where he could spend the night any time he wanted. Thus, beyond mere sponsorship, the Prince of Wales was showing the young musician great benevolence. In return, George very quickly grew attached to him and began to spend much of his time at Carlton House.

Frederick de Augustus, until then champing at the bit, let his resentment of the Prince of Wales explode for the first time when one afternoon George gave him to understand that, ever since the prince had taken him under his wing, his career had acquired a whole new dimension. And he began to list: he'd played at Westminster Abbey in the king's presence with Johann Hummel, a young prodigy of Mozart's, to celebrate Handel's birthday; with Franz Clement, another Viennese prodigy who was his age, he'd performed a series of concerts in the very fashionable halls of the Hanover Square assembly rooms; they had heard him at the Salomon concerts, the Professional Concerts, the Barthelemon concerts, at King's Theatre.... And when His Highness decided to come to the aid of the weavers of Spitalfields, a dilapidated district of East London, ruined by the import of silk from India and China, he'd called on him, George, to give a concert for the benefit of the descendants of the Huguenot silk workers whose ancestors had fled Lyon when the Edict of Nantes was revoked…. The press hadn't been idle either: the *Gazette*, the *Public Advertiser*, the *London Chronicle*, the *London Times*, the *Gentlemen's Magazine…* they were all full of laudatory reviews.

Frederick de Augustus was deeply hurt when George ended his conversation with the news that his father need no longer run around to beg for performances, that the prince was now in charge of everything. And if, despite it all, Frederick de Augustus wouldn't heed this directive, George wasn't going to honor the engagements he'd make.

Frederick de Augustus took the intrusions of the Prince of Wales into their lives very badly. They were still living together but the relationship with his son had changed. George showed an ever increasing independence: he now refused to wear the 'Oriental style' tunics he'd had tailored for him, he no longer automatically invited him to his performances, especially when held at the prince's residence, the concert receipts no longer came into his hands but went directly to George…. Even his tastes and manners were changing. All he'd wear now were the English-style clothes the prince gave him, who was very generous with his money—he was known for his colossal debts—, and during his leisure hours he was reading novels from the library at Carlton House, as well as books on the history of England, her kings and queens, and her great men.

Of all the changes the one that bothered his father most was the way in which George now expressed himself. He had lost his accent completely and was now speaking a refined English with that aristocratic intonation that Frederick de Augustus couldn't help but find condescending. It upset him all the more because there might now be some doubt that George was his son, that he'd raised him, since their behavior led people to believe they belonged to two very different milieus.

As the months passed, he became increasingly aware that George was getting away from him; it seemed that he was turning against him more and more. Never in his wildest dreams had he imagined such a thing could happen. George was *the* son, the one of his two boys he'd chosen to help make his dream come true, the one whose talents were supposed to help him escape from the troubles to which destiny had wanted to condemn him and finally let him make a fortune and become a brilliant member of society. He had lugged him around all over Europe, from Biala Podlanska to London, via Eisenstadt, Vienna, Brussels, and Paris. He had taught him everything: how to behave, how to dress, what to do and what to say. Even if he'd been strict sometimes, forcing him to tirelessly practice his violin to improve, it was for his own benefit, for both their benefit! He'd made him into the Wolfgang Mozart of his generation, the best-known and most famous of all Europe's young prodigies. And now this same son was turning on him! By entrusting George to the prince's guidance he had lost him. He'd allowed his son to be stolen from him, the Prince of Wales had stolen his son! And what could he do against such a powerful man, against a prince?

He felt duped and full of bitterness. A void opened inside him. The man, until now celebrated for his civility and charm, changed to such a degree that, barely eight months after their triumphant return from Bath, he was declared *persona non grata* in Great Britain and ousted from the kingdom with a formal prohibition to ever set foot on English soil again.

XXX

What led to their break-up was the letter George received from his mother and brother, the first one since they'd left them behind two, almost three years earlier. He'd written them from Brussels and then again from Paris without receiving any answer. In his most recent missive, written in London, he was able to provide them with a return address at Carlton House and, to his great joy, he finally got a response. He opened the letter feverishly. Friedrich had written it in German, but his mother had added a few lines in Polish, in a handwriting almost as awkward as that of her nine-year old son.

Friedrich told him they were doing well. He added that he'd made great progress with his cello and that, once the time was ripe, he hoped to join the Dresden Staatskapelle, the famous orchestra of the city of Dresden, and to become as famous as his big brother. He concluded by saying that the roof of their house needed repair but that, for now, they were still waiting for the money their father had promised before his departure.

In the few lines she'd written, his mother told him she was very proud of his successes, that she'd especially liked the article in the

Mercure de France and counseled him to be worthy of the confidence of His Highness, the Prince of Wales. In the meantime, she was longing to see her big boy again.

He came back to their apartment at the Strand, pleased but also a little sad because of the financial problems Friedrich had mentioned.

His father was there, sitting at the table, a pack of cards spread out before him, studying the possible combinations for his next poker game. Still very excited, George exclaimed:

'Papa, I finally got a letter from Mama and Friedrich!'

A bit surprised, Frederick de Augustus raised his head.

'Where did you get it? I didn't see anything when I came home.'

'It came to Carlton House, the address I gave them in my last letter…'

'Carlton House is not your address! Your address is here! This is where we live!'

'I just wanted to be sure the answer would reach us this time. At the residence of the prince…'

'Stop with that prince of yours! Did you forget that I am your father, not he?'

Taken aback by the reaction of Frederick de Augustus, who was angry about a mere address instead of being glad to have news of his family, he replied, his enthusiasm brusquely dampened:

'You don't care about this, I see!'

'Yes, I do! But I'm busy right now.'

'Busy playing cards? You really don't want to read it?'

'Yes, of course I do! Put it on the table, I'll read it later.'

For a moment George hesitated, then putting the letter down, he asked tersely:

'Why don't you ever write them?'

'Am I supposed to inform you every time I write them?'

'I know you never write them. You also promised me you'd write to Uncle Soliman, but you never did.'

Frederick de Augustus didn't answer and kept shifting his cards around.

George continued:

'We have to send them some money for the roof of the house in Dresden. Friedrich says it's completely ruined.'

Frustration seeping through his tone, Frederick de Augustus raised his eyes from his cards, looked at his son, and spat:

'Your mother doesn't need any money. I gave her the whole payment I received from Prince Esterhazy before we left. She has enough to live off for at least another year.'

'That's not true! Friedrich made it very clear they're living quite modestly. Read the letter if you don't believe it. We must send them some money.'

'You've no right to tell me what to do. You're becoming more and more insolent with each passing day! I'll read the letter when I'm done preparing for my game. So, for now, just leave me alone.'

He immersed himself in his cards again. For a moment George observed him without saying a word, then he went to his room and slammed the door.

He avoided his father for several days, then their relationship became a little more relaxed as if they'd both forgotten the incident. He understood that any allusion to the prince disturbed Frederick de Augustus, so he did his best to circumvent it, but the problem kept cropping up, despite his best efforts. Anyway, how could he keep himself from bringing up what had become the essence of his life?

On the other hand, despite his resentment Frederick de Augustus hadn't lost the hope of bringing his son back under his wing. It was a matter of pride and dignity for him. Constantly thinking about a strategy to make it work, one day he thought he'd found it. But the idea he believed to be so marvelous resulted instead in the open rebellion that initiated their break-up and ended with his expulsion from the kingdom.

That particular afternoon he'd come home beaming, happy to have managed the kind of maneuver he treasured, selling a performance by George for a steep price to one of those nouveaux riches for whom it was a point of honor to offer private concerts in their salon. Despite George's prohibition that he book engagements for him, Frederick de Augustus thought the affair was so lucrative that George couldn't refuse. In fact, he hadn't done very much. As soon as the lady to whom he'd been introduced realized he was George Bridgetower's father, she'd asked him immediately whether the boy might not give a performance at her house. She loved modern music, she said to justify her interest, mentioning that Pleyel, the young Franz Clement, and Viotti, yes, Viotti himself, had played in her salon.

Frederick de Augustus had sensed instantly this was a good deal. Skillfully manipulating, asserting that George's calendar was extremely filled, mentioning the names of well-known personalities whose invitations he'd declined for lack of time, he succeeded in raising the bid. Convinced that Frederick de Augustus had done her an exceptional favor—he'd let her know that in order to play at her place he'd be obliged to cancel a previously scheduled concert—she offered him a price that was close to double what he was usually paid. Better yet, he'd managed to have the lady give him a significant down payment.

Thus, Frederick de Augustus was very jovial and pleased with himself when he came home. This time around he would take control of his son again.

George was lying on the big sofa near the living room window, reading a book he'd borrowed from the prince's library. Thrilled to tell him the news, Frederick de Augustus called to him as soon as the door was closed:

'Ah, I'm so glad you're here, George! I have some very good news! You're going to play at Mrs. Schwellenberg's Thursday evening...'

'Where?' George said, straightening up. 'You know perfectly well you needn't bother about me anymore. Maybe you forgot but it's the prince...'

'No, no, this time it's something exceptional. You cannot refuse. She is a great patron of modern music. Viotti, Pleyel, and your friend Franz Clement have all played at her salon.'

'Patron or not, I already told you not to get involved with my schedule anymore. And besides, I don't feel like playing for this Mrs. Schwe… Schwel whom I've never even heard of.'

'Excuse me? You think you can say no, just like that? I've committed myself and already accepted a sizeable advance…'

'All you have to do is give it back.'

'Don't talk nonsense! Anyway, I've already spent half of it. Fine, so Thursday it is, we'll go to Mrs. Schwel…'

'No, I can't. Even if I wanted to, I couldn't.'

'And why not? I know your schedule very well and I know you're free this Thursday…'

'In principle I'm free but, Papa, Viotti is giving a concert at the Royal Pavilion in Brighton on Thursday. I've asked the prince if I could attend. He told me that both Carlton House and the Royal Pavilion are always open to me and that I can attend any concert that takes place there. I might even be playing with Viotti Thursday! That's more important to me than a soiree at this lady's place.'

Yet, Frederick de Augustus wouldn't let up. In an almost affectionate voice he tried to appeal to George's emotions by playing on his family feelings:

'Perhaps I took you off-guard, my boy, but try to understand. This concert is very important to me. It's all about my word, my honor, my credibility. You would make your father very happy if…'

'If you knew it was that important, you should've asked my opinion first, before committing yourself. You're not to make decisions for me on your own anymore!'

George stood up, picked up his book and locked himself into his room, while a stunned Frederick de Augustus watched him, aghast.

Saying that Frederick de Augustus was shocked by George's response is an understatement. He was completely bewildered! Before the Prince of Wales came into the picture, things had always been done this way: he would arrange the concerts, George would play; he decided, George performed. And now he was supposed to check with him first?

The episode hurt him deeply and forever. This time he no longer doubted it, he had lost his son. His resentment of the prince intensified and gradually extended to the entire English society, at least to that part of it that he'd been courting until then, and that he thought had accepted him thanks to his eccentricities as prince of Abyssinia.

※

With his brooding his behavior changed. The once so charming, civilized, seductive man was transformed into a touchy individual, sometimes withdrawn, sometimes quarrelsome. The first incident happened as if by chance during a concert at Covent Garden in the presence of the Prince of Wales. The *Chronicle* of 11 March 1790 reported it as follows:

> *At the end of the Second Act, the Hallelujah chorus was encored; and here a scene ensued that had nearly thrown the audience and band into confusion. The African Prince, from one of the slip, insisted, in the most insolent manner, that the chorus should be repeated. Much as it was desired, yet John Bull was not to be dictated to by a sable son of the torrid zone [NB]. The principals and chorus in course left the orchestra. "Turn him out," was the general cry. After a violent struggle, this mighty Prince was turned out of the house. When order was restored, the principals and part of the choir returned, and the chorus was repeated!!!*

As if this article had opened the floodgates, rumors began to circulate. True or invented, his escapades and drinking sprees became the object of brief newspaper articles. They implied he was squandering the money his son had earned to pay his gambling debts. It seemed that the press, unanimous in its praise of him up until then, had suddenly decided to discredit him.

A great reader of newspapers, Frederick de Augustus at first didn't become overly dismayed over what he considered to be pettiness: he told himself he no longer wanted to bow and scrape to anyone from now on. However, it all fell apart when he read a particularly venomous article in the *Gazette* of 9 April 1790:

The African Prince, as he is styled, appears as an advocate for the abolition of slavery; his character something of the Mungo stamp. The Black Prince would do well, before he dare to disturb the peace of the English audiences—to study the old ballad—of "There's a difference I sing, Twixt a Beggar and a King."

He knew where the allegation came from. Two days before, when he was in a pub near the port, he'd seen two men come in, one of whom was wearing a captain's outfit. Without any reason he assumed it was the captain of a slave ship and his quartermaster, in charge of supplies. He was seized by a fierce dislike of them and when their eyes met he felt they'd sized him up contemptuously. To provoke them, he ordered a glass of gin, which he downed in one gulp and then, in a loud bright voice, sang "Amazing Grace," the hymn that slave traffickers despised because it was written by a former repentant slave trader who, having become a pastor and abolitionist, condemned them resolutely. An argument followed and Frederick de Augustus was unceremoniously thrown out of the pub.

The article affronted him painfully, almost physically; he experienced it like the sting of the whip on the slave's back. For the first time since he was in England, a newspaper reminded him of his origins, of what he'd wanted to forget. Intense rage surfaced in him and, with it, a cry: 'Yes, indeed, I know I'm Black! So what?' Suddenly it came to him that, among the bourgeois and aristocrats he so liked to frequent, many had made a fortune in the slave trade or, at least, had Black servants whom they didn't treat much better. Yet, these Blacks were everywhere: porters, errand boys, walking behind their mistresses, holding their umbrella, perched on the back of carriages.... He'd always ignored them, he'd always avoided being associated with them. Even when the reality of their presence imposed itself on his everyday life, he tried to deny it: he hadn't wanted his son to listen to the beggar violinist Billy Waters, he'd roughly ripped the paper publishing a classified ad looking for a fugitive slave out of his hands. And how many times had he not tried to avoid participating in the debate on the abolition of slavery being raised in English society, echoed by the newspapers, whether for or against, because he considered it none of his business? And yet, throughout his life, in the background, the question had accompanied him: in Barbados on the plantation where he was born; in Vienna where Soliman had described the plunders of the Arab-Moslem pro slavers who rode across Black Africa, Koran in one hand and saber in the other; in Paris where he had endured the outrage of the cartouche, rubbed elbows with mem-

bers of the Society of Friends of the Blacks, read Condorcet. None of it had ever driven him to action. But here it was, a malicious piece had just transformed the 'African prince' into a rebel who was going to swing over to the side of the abolitionists, this time for good!

He decided to take an active part in the movement. A few days later, he joined the Society for Effecting the Abolition of the Slave Trade, attracted by the graphic image of the association, a medallion representing an African on his knees, beneath which are inscribed the words: 'AM I NOT A MAN AND A BROTHER?'

Reproductions of it could be found everywhere, engraved on stamps and wax seals, printed in newspapers and pamphlets, drawn on snuff-boxes and cufflinks.

Two days after he became a member, as he opened the *Public Advertiser*, he found an impassioned call against the trade addressed to the members of Parliament. The letter was signed Olaudah Equiano on behalf of the association Sons of Africa. The name intrigued him. He made inquiries and discovered that it was an association composed of a dozen Blacks, directed by this Olaudah Equiano. He wondered why until now he hadn't heard of this man who surely was the most distinguished Black living in England.

Captured in the Bay of Biafra at the age of eleven, initially a slave in the Caribbean, notably on Frederick de Augustus' native island, Barbados, Equiano then found himself on the plantations of South Carolina where, after ten years of servitude, he succeeded in buying his freedom. Next he roamed here and there and everywhere, sailor, merchant, explorer—to his credit he'd even made an abortive attempt to reach the North Pole—and, above all, he'd become famous from one day to the next when his autobiography appeared, with the title *The Interesting Narrative of the Life of Olaudah Equiano*. The work was a resounding success, rivaling in popularity and sales figures with *Robinson Crusoe*, the book by Daniel Defoe that George had liked so much. Together with a few friends he'd created the association Sons of Africa, whose task it was to make the horrors of the slave trade known, and fight for its suppression through lectures, letters and articles in newspapers, and speeches in Parliament.

Frederick de Augustus immediately left the Society for Effecting the Abolition of the Slave Trade to join Sons of Africa. The Society for Effecting the Abolition of the Slave Trade was fine, it did its work effectively with talented lawyers such as Granville Sharp as director, but all its members—Methodists, Quakers, and Anglicans—were white.

Admittedly, the organization Sons of Africa was affiliated with the Society for the Effective Abolition of the Slave Trade because the latter was larger, better known, and had greater means but, as an autonomous group within it, its members remained in control of their agenda.

All his life he'd fled onwards, but the article in the *Gazetter* had taken him back dramatically to his alleged origins; he'd drawn the conclusion that European society would gladly admit you, open its doors to you, as long as you didn't question what was essential, that is, in this case the profits it made from the slave trade. With Sons of Africa he was for the first time associated with a group in which Blacks took their own destiny in hand. Being among themselves like this gave him a feeling of liberty and authenticity. With these companions, there was no need whatever to take on postures as an 'African prince'.

He had eagerly read Olaudah Equiano's book, and others as well, such as that by Ottobah Cugoano—himself ripped away from the shores of the Gold Coast when he was thirteen—with the long title, *Thoughts and Sentiments on the Evil and Wicked Traffic of the Slavery and Commerce of the Human Species*, and also the *Letters of the Late Ignatius Sancho, an African*. The author, Ignatius Sancho, who was known as 'the extraordinary Negro' at the time, the first Black man to vote in a British election, had his portrait painted by Thomas Gainsborough, which hung on a wall at the office of the association.

The reading Frederick de Augustus did had so transformed him that he now considered futile everything he had aspired to before. The memory of the Chevalier de Saint-George and Alex Dumas, two men he had admired and even envied, came back to him. Then he understood why such literature, a resolutely anti-slavery literature of combat, consisting of testimonies, protests, and demands, didn't exist in France. It couldn't originate with people of their kind whose entire endeavor consisted of becoming as French as the French of France, of forgetting and making others forget their roots, trying in the end to blend, colorless, into a society where there wasn't any place for their uniqueness.

XXXI

The sudden, unanticipated break-up with his son occurred the night that his association, supported by countless others committed to the anti-slavery struggle, lost the court case that was supposed to, once and for all, settle the question whether slaves were human beings or merchandise.

A few years earlier, finding they were running short of potable water because of navigational mistakes that had greatly extended the length of the voyage, the captain of the slave ship *Zong* had a hundred and forty-two slaves thrown overboard to salvage what water remained and thereby save the life of the crew, at least according to his statements. Upon his return to Liverpool, the ship's owners sued, not for murder but to get the insurers to compensate them for the lost cargo of slaves. Appalled, Olaudah Equiano got hold of the lawyer Granville Sharp, who decided to lodge a complaint of *massacre*! The trial was the object of great publicity and it was in front of a huge public that the judge dismissed the case of Granville Sharp and his associates.

Frederick de Augustus went back home that night bitter and depressed.

What is this claim that human people have been thrown overboard?

This is a case of chattels or goods. Blacks are goods and property; it is madness to accuse these well-serving honourable men of murder.... The case is the same as if wood had been thrown overboard.

The phrases the judge pronounced during the verdict were still turning around in his head when he opened the door and saw George there, reading. Apparently, he liked the book since he was smiling, his face aglow.

'What are you reading?' Frederick de Augustus asked him.

'A very funny book! *Life and Opinions of Tristram Shandy, Gentleman.* An autobiography, or rather an imaginary autobiography, very funny!'

'Instead of reading an imaginary autobiography, you ought to read a true story, the one I recommended several days ago already.'

'Which one?'

'This one, here!'

Grabbing the book and waving it in front of the boy, he raised his voice:

'*The Interesting Narrative of the Life of Olaudah Equiano*, written by himself!'

'You know, Father, that doesn't interest me all that much. I'll read it when I finish *Tristram Shandy*, if I have time. This book has had a lot of success. The prince himself recommended it to me.'

Here was the person he shouldn't have mentioned! Frederick de Augustus immediately erupted into a frenzy.

'The prince, the prince! I've had it with your prince! It's the only name on your lips, you no longer think except via him! Don't you have any other references? You think you're his son? Perhaps you think you're an Englishman now?'

'Yes, why not?' George replied impertinently, in that tone his father so disliked. 'You yourself always suggested I become a true Englishman!'

His words hit home. Frederick de Augustus was to blame: hadn't he himself instructed George to do everything to become a true little Englishman? He'd succeeded all too well!

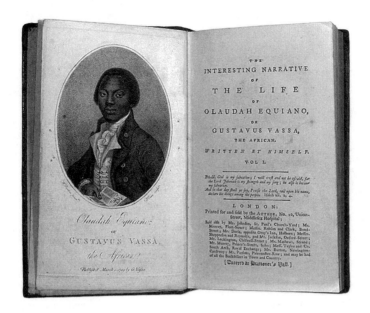

'Even the prince thinks that I...' George wanted to continue.

'Stop your nonsense. Don't forget where you come from. Your grandfather and your father come from the plantations. After all, you are black, just as I am! Your prince is nothing but a hypocrite and he's pro-slavery, among other things.'

Surprised, frightened by his father's face, distorted with resentment, George had risen. The latter went on:

'Don't have any illusions about what you are. A piece of merchandise, a movable goods. You'd do well to read this book, so you understand!'

In a movement of uncontrolled anger he tossed the work in the direction of George who had no time to duck; the book hit him full in the face and his nose began to bleed. Dazed, all he could do was cry. As if by coincidence, the book fell open to the frontispiece and the first page:

Through his tears the black face of Olaudah Equiano became confused with his father's and he found himself hating them both.

Frederick de Augustus immediately regretted his impulsive move. He made a vague gesture toward George to apologize and console him but, furious, the boy shouted:

'Don't touch me! I don't want to see you anymore, I hate you!' He quickly grabbed his violin and *Tristram Shandy*, ran out the door and slammed it behind him. Sheepish and deeply embarrassed, Frederick de Augustus yelled: 'Come back, George, come back…', but he had already vanished in the night, in the direction of Carlton House.

⚜

A regular of Carlton House, George had no trouble being welcomed by its servants. When he presented himself to the prince in the morning with his swollen face and told him what had happened, the latter fell into a royal rage. For him, it merely confirmed the rumors going around about this unworthy father. He promptly summoned him and as soon as Frederick de Augustus showed up he ordered him out of the kingdom as speedily as possible. All the same, being a good prince, he gave him the sum of twenty-five pounds to cover the costs of his journey and meet his needs until he would find an 'honest' job in whatever country he wished to go—Austria? Hungary? Poland? —far away from England.

⚜

Frederick de Augustus left London on 5 January 1791. No one knew where he had gone. He disappeared from George's life and was never seen again. George Augustus Polgreen Bridgetower was now under the exclusive tutelage of the Prince of Wales. He was eleven years old.

236

XXXII

For weeks George was very unhappy. Strangely enough, despite all the comfort he enjoyed at Carlton House where the prince had given him a home, he missed the father he'd rejected. He was overcome with nostalgia for the adventurous life they'd led together and, thinking he might recapture a few of those moments, he'd leave the palace to return to some of the places where they'd spent time. Once, when thinking about him, the memory of Billy Waters, the one-legged violinist, came back to him. He felt a sudden urge to see him again. Frederick de Augustus, he recalled, had tossed a half-penny in his bowl; this time around, George was going to give him a whole pound. Finding the route he and his father had taken, he found himself in front of the theater where they'd watched Billy with his scratchy old violin perform his acrobatic show. No Old Billy! Not only was the place completely silent, it was deserted. What had become of him? An immense sorrow swooped down upon him.

Another time he decided to visit the East End, specifically the area of Rotten Row. When he passed by the cobbler, above whom they'd rented a room for several weeks, he wondered whether it had been this decrepit and unhealthy when they were staying there. Or else, was it because he now looked at it with the eyes of a gentleman accustomed to the luxury of Carlton House? He had the impression everything was now dirtier and the people more destitute. A gathering in a small park at Cutthroat Lane drew his attention. A crowd of animated men was waving coins and bills. They were betting on two boxers, one a rather short Black man and the other a tall white with a craggy face, mercilessly thrashing each other with their bare fists. The white man shot out with an uppercut and hit his adversary. He fell as the excited crowd shouted loudly, but got back up immediately and, nimble as a cat, his lips bloody, leapt and crashed his head into the white man's solar plexus. The two adversaries rolled on the ground and continued beating each other up. It was a battle without rules, any kind of blow was acceptable. George couldn't bear the carnage and rushed off. The spectacle cured him of the melancholy that made him alter those places where his memories reconnected him with his father into enchanted domains. He went out less often and could finally write the letter he'd always wanted to write to his mother, a letter he'd begun several times but never finished, for he didn't know how to explain to her what had happened to his father.

Little by little, the feeling of abandonment wore off, thanks to the warmhearted protection of the prince, who offered him the best of what a young musician growing up in a royal court could hope for.

First, they threw all the Ottoman style clothing George still owned in the trash and replaced it with what an English gentleman was expected to wear. The prince also recruited tutors in various disciplines to initiate him into the culture that any reasonably well-educated young man should possess, classical literature and philosophy, the sciences and mathematics. As for music, he made sure that his protégé studied with the finest masters. Thus, the composer and organist Thomas Atwood, a former student of Mozart's, was hired to teach him music theory and composition; the conductor of the Royal Opera orchestra, the French violinist François-Hippolyte Barthélémon for the violin; and lastly, the

238

pianist Muzio Clementi for the keyboard. In addition to these lessons he was given countless work sessions with the Italian Felice Giardini, with the impresario and violinist Peter Salomon, as well as with Viotti and Giornovichi, who were both in London then; in short, with the musical elite of London. The only one missing was Saint-George who was too preoccupied with his demonstrations as swordsman.

George's repertoire, which until then rested basically on two composers, Viotti, Giornovichi, and a few pieces by Haydn, became considerably more wide-ranging. It now included Corelli, Handel, Mozart, Pleyel, and the chamber music of one of Handel's contemporaries, underrated until then but with a constantly growing reputation, Johann Sebastian Bach.

At the same time, his public appearances became less frequent and, above all more selective. His prestige grew among his peers as well: at age thirteen he was already permanent violinist at the highly respected Italian Opera of Haymarket; at fourteen, one of the regularly invited musicians at Covent Garden for the concerts of the Lent period; and at sixteen, he became first violinist of the orchestra of the Prince of Wales! For his eighteenth birthday the prince presented him with a gift of inestimable value, a violin made in the workshops of the Guarneri family in Cremona.

George Augustus Bridgetower was no longer the object of curiosity as he'd been at the beginning; he had become an accomplished musician, absolute master of his instrument.

His relationship with the prince had changed as well. From protégé he'd practically turned into an adopted son. And when during a hunting trip George's horse abruptly reared, and he fell off and was seriously injured, the prince had him brought to the royal Pavilion in Brighton to be taken care of, under the maternal eye of Maria Fitzherbert.

XXXIII

George heard the news through a rumor making the rounds among the members of the private orchestra of the Prince of Wales: Haydn was in London!

At first, he didn't believe it. It was, in fact, a rumor that periodically circulated at the beginning of each musical season. As early as November 1789, when he and his father arrived, Peter Salomon had spread the same story, undoubtedly hoping it would boost the number of subscriptions. But George remembered Haydn. He didn't see how that man from the hinterlands, who'd never seen the sea, loyal to his prince despite the aggravations he sometimes had to suffer at his hands, now at age fifty-eight he was going to abandon his native Bohemia to undertake a long and perilous journey to London.

And yet, there he was, Haydn himself! It was no rumor. For three long days the newspapers wouldn't stop relaying information, specifying he had arrived the day after New Year's Day and had received an enthusiastic reception; everyone wanted to see him, everyone wanted to invite him. The *Gazetter* reported that Charles Burney, the author, well-known for his three-volume *General History of Music*, had written a long poem with the title *Verses on the Arrival in England of the Great Musician Haydn*, which could be purchased for one shilling. But what truly convinced George was Peter Salomon's declaration, published in one of the papers. The happy impresario recounted that it had all happened because of the death of Prince Nikolaus Esterhazy, carried off by a sudden illness, which had released Haydn from his obligations. The news of this demise had spread very quickly, and every European court was willing to pay a fortune to acquire the famous musician. Salomon who, by a stroke of luck, happened to be on the continent, was the first to meet Haydn in Vienna where he had settled.

'I am Peter Salomon from London, I have come to find you. Pack your bags. We will sign an agreement and we'll be in London in two weeks!' George had the feeling that Salomon was embellishing his story just a little. Convincing Haydn to leave Vienna certainly could not have been that simple. There must have been a financial arrangement involved he wasn't mentioning.

So, Haydn was in London! George was completely overwhelmed: this was his teacher, underrated for so long, but today the most celebrated composer alive. No concert of modern music was performed without one of his symphonies or overtures on the program. The *Morning Chronicle* clearly articulated the general reaction:

A series of concerts is planned under the auspices of Haydn whose name is a powerful monument while lovers of instrumental music consider him a god of erudition.

And when Haydn finally gave his first concert, the same newspaper wrote:

The First Concert under the auspices of HAYDN was last night, and never, perhaps, was there a richer musical treat. It is not wonderful

that to souls capable of being touched by music, HAYDN should be an
object of homage, and even of idolatry; for like our own SHAK-
SPEARE [sic], he moves and governs the passions at his will.

His new Grand Overture was pronounced by every scientific ear to
be a most wonderful composition; but the first movement in particular
rises in grandeur of subject, and in the rich variety of air and passion,
beyond any even of his own productions. The Overture has four move-
ments—An Allegro, Andante, Minuet, and Rondo. They are all beau-
tiful, but the first is pre-eminent in every charm, and the Band per-
formed it with admirable correctness. The audience was so delighted
that at general request the second movement was encored; there was an
insistent demand that the third be repeated as well, which only man-
aged to thwart the composer's modesty.

However, George kept wondering whether the now famous and
adored Haydn would remember the six- or seven-year old boy who,
hanging onto his father's coattails, used to haunt the halls of the Castle
of Eisenstadt, that boy whom he would teach between two concerts?
What to do to make the master remember him, knowing that dozens of
other now surely forgotten students had also passed through his hands
since then?

Once again, the passion of the Prince of Wales for modern music
provided an unforeseen blessing.

♋︎

A few days after his arrival, even before he gave his first concert,
Haydn was invited by the Prince of Wales to a musical soiree in his honor.

He presented himself at the agreed-upon time, tastefully and elegantly dressed, which impressed George, who remembered him as a
man always in Esterhazy's livery. How London had transformed him,
and in such a short time! Haydn came in and approached the prince

who was awaiting him standing among his guests. He didn't have to go far, for the prince left the group and came toward him, and to George's great amazement was the first to bow before the musician. Somewhat surprised by this gesture, a proof of his legendary modesty, Haydn in turn paid his respects as he bowed down very low.

George was not in the circle of guests surrounding the prince, which included Salomon and Giornovichi. Standing in a corner of the room, he had no intention of introducing himself to the celebrated musician without being called. He would wait until the end of the official program to approach him, for the moment when protocol would relax and guests were free to circulate.

The musical part of the evening was both solemn and full of joy. Not only had the forewarned instrumentalists brilliantly interpreted extracts of the most exquisite modern music, but it had also been enlivened with catches and glees, those popular songs, full of humor and bawdy innuendo.

It wasn't George who approached Haydn, but the reverse. From the distance, while congratulating the orchestra musicians on their brilliant performance, Haydn saw a face that looked familiar to him and then he knew: he recognized George. He went over to him without any hesitation. George, as if paralyzed, saw him approach:

'George, isn't it?'

'Yes, it really is I, Papa Haydn,' George replied, intimidated by the presence of the great man facing him.

He'd used the term 'Papa' spontaneously. He wasn't the only one to address him this way; in Vienna many people called him by that name.

'I am delighted to see you again!' Haydn said, opening his arms widely.

Gratified, George nestled against him. Then, holding him at arm's length to take a better look, Haydn continued:

'How you have grown! Not only are you a man now, but Salomon tells me that you've become a first rate violinist, one of the best around.'

The naturalness with which Haydn had approached him made him briefly forget that he was standing before the most important musician of his time. That pockmarked face, those vivacious eyes that sometimes gleamed with the same mischief as could be found in his music, that provincial accent so often ridiculed, George relived it all with deep emotion.

'Thank you,' he said. 'I thought you had forgotten me.'

'Ah,' Haydn laughed, 'how could I forget the son of *il Moro*, as Tomasini liked to tease your father. How is he?'

'He's no longer in London. He left the country for new adventures.'

'That doesn't surprise me from him. As for me, it would make me very happy to hear you play.'

'You could hear me in May during the great annual Handel festival, under the patronage of Their Majesties.'

Peter Salomon who'd just joined them heard the last sentence of the conversation and immediately objected.

'You won't have to wait that long,' he said. 'I have scheduled him for your concert on April 15. He will play in your new Grand Overture, which we have put back on the schedule because it is in such high demand, and also as the soloist of a violin concerto.'

'*Wunderbar!*' Haydn said, delighted. 'I can't wait to hear him.'

Three major events, the third of which was not of a musical nature, marked the eighteen months Haydn spent in London: his first public concert side by side with the maestro, the moment he learned of Mozart's death, and finally, the visit he made together with the maestro to Dr. Herschel.

The concert was unforgettable not because it was the first time he shared the poster with the illustrious musician; this was true for several others, too, who had not drawn any special benefit from it as he had.

Nor was it the feeling of having excelled during the concert, he was accustomed to that. No, what made the first concert stand out indelibly in his mind was that every newspaper review linked his name with that of Haydn. He was especially pleased with what the *Gazette* had written in its April 18th chronicle:

> *We heard Haydn's Grand Overture for the third time, which had aroused such admiration; each time we hear it with new pleasure again. The violin concerto by young Bridgetower was masterfully interpreted.*

From his point of view, this was truly a recognition, an appreciation more fulfilling than the inscription 'student of Haydn' at the top of a small publicity poster.

The second event he was to remember was also the saddest. It happened in the month of December. Haydn had retired to his dressing room after a concert he himself had just conducted. Once again, the evening had proven the public's enthusiasm, which had remained unchanged for the year he'd been in London. Transported by his music, the very large audience had compelled the orchestra to encore several movements so that in the end only his compositions were played, to the detriment of the concertos by Giornovichi and Clementi, which had also been scheduled. Extremely happy, Haydn had invited a few musicians he particularly respected to join him. George was one of them.

The atmosphere was joyful. The maestro abandoned his requisite earnestness and, eyes sparkling with merriment, made his guests laugh while he entertained them when pronouncing his heavily accented English vocabulary. That's when Peter Salomon entered with the announcement of Wolfgang Mozart's death, of which he had just heard.

George saw Haydn crumble, his face changing instantly from joy to extreme sorrow. His eyes were glistening with tears. Salomon asked everyone to leave, except George with whom Haydn had a special relationship.

'Do you remember, Peter, our last dinner with him? When we were about to leave, he told me weeping: "We are undoubtedly saying our last farewells in this life." I cannot believe that Providence has called a man who is so irreplaceable to the other world.'

The two musical geniuses had a close bond. Haydn felt admiration and friendship for Mozart, who was younger and called him Papa Haydn as well. They were both freemasons, members of the *Zur wahren Eintracht*, the lodge of True Harmony, of which Angelo Soliman was the grandmaster. When Mozart dedicated six string quartets written especially for him, Haydn wrote the following to Leopold: 'I must tell you before God and as an honest man that your son is the greatest composer I know, in person and in name.'

A grief-laden silence drifted over the small gathering. George thought it was time to leave the two men alone with their memories of the last hours they'd spent with the lamented musician and asked permission to withdraw.

It wasn't until he was in the coach that took him to Carlton House that he felt the full significance of this death. Ultimately, he, too, had a special connection with Wolfgang Amadeus. He had never met him, he'd only once caught a glimpse of him when Soliman had taken him and his father to see Mozart play at a *Morgenkonzerte* in Vienna. Yet, he had been his life's companion, both as a model and a foil. Without Mozart he might not have been the famous musician he was today: it was on his father Leopold that Frederick de Augustus, his own father, had patterned his behavior. George couldn't do anything without his mentioning the name Mozart. Mozart this, Mozart that! His father had so harped on him about Mozart that he'd ended up by disliking the man. And here was Mozart, no longer with them, nor was his father, Frederick de Augustus. He, too, felt horribly alone and began to weep.

When he arrived and crossed the esplanade leading to Carlton House, he was no longer crying. Grief had been replaced by a strange feeling. In some way he felt liberated now: Mozart and Frederick de Augustus, two tutelary figures who had managed his childhood, were no longer around. He was free of them.

※

Just before Mozart's death, during one of their conversations, Haydn mentioned to George that he'd been invited to give a few concerts in Bath by an Italian castrato named Rauzzini, an important musical personality of the town. As a little self-promotion, George answered that it was in Bath where his musical career in England had truly begun and that he knew Venanzio Rauzzini quite well. It was to him that Dr. Herschel had addressed the letter of recommendation, which had facilitated their introduction into the city's musical circle.

'Herschel?' Haydn said, amazed. 'Do you know him?'

'Yes, of course,' George said, surprised himself. 'Why?'

'I'd heard of him when he was in the service of the King of Prussia because he interpreted several of my works at the court of Hanover. Then I learned that he deserted during the Seven Years War and had taken refuge in England where he was living off his music. I completely forgot about him after that. But these past few years his name had become more famous than ever because of his discoveries in astronomy. For a long time the great work of the Creation has fascinated me. I read a book that made a great impression on me, *Universal Natural History and Theory of the Heavens* by Immanuel Kant. Also, when the small book by Herschel *On the Construction of the Heavens* was published, I started reading it right away and it filled me with wonder, even though a few pages were too technical for me. I would really like to meet him, if possible.'

They didn't discuss Herschel again and George had completely forgotten this conversation until the day when a messenger came to tell him in person that he was invited by Haydn to accompany him to Dr. Herschel's house the following day. George was elated, all the more so because he thought he wouldn't see the maestro again who, his season having come to an end, was getting ready to return to his beloved Vienna, in spite of the fabulous offers by King George III to convince him to remain in England with a suite at Windsor Castle as his residence.

Seeing Herschel again filled George with equal enthusiasm. His stay in Paris and his conversation in the salon of the Marquise de Montesson with the chemist Lavoisier, the mathematicians and physicists Monge, Lagrange, Borda, and Condorcet, the scientists who wanted to measure the circumference of the Earth, had bestowed on him an enduring fondness for sciences and technical methods.

Dr. Herschel was not in London proper but in the small town of Slough, at about a dozen miles' distance. When George arrived at Haydn's place early in the morning, the carriage they were supposed to take was already there, but he had to wait for the maestro who wasn't yet ready. Half an hour later Haydn finally came out and started by thanking him for his willingness to come along. George couldn't help but notice the new attire the maestro was wearing with such great poise. Despite all the years spent in Paris and London, George had always retained in his mind the image of the original Haydn, the chapel master of the Esterhazy family. However, of that no trace was left. He was sitting next to a rich and satisfied man, exuding calm assurance, the only musician alive accepted in the programs of the Academy of Ancient Music. A week earlier, the University of Oxford had made him a doctor honoris causa in music and when George had greeted him with 'Papa' Haydn, he'd corrected him, mischievously referring to himself as 'Doctor' Haydn!

XXXIV

They arrived in Slough in the afternoon. The property was large and consisted of two buildings, one a residence and the other an observatory. A very happy Herschel welcomed them as they descended from the carriage. After his compliments to Haydn, he congratulated George on the marvelous career he'd achieved since he'd heard him play as a young boy of nine at the Brighton residence of the Prince of Wales. In turn, George expressed his sincere gratitude for having encouraged them, his father and himself, to go to Bath. Before showing them his telescopes, Herschel invited them to a light meal.

As they moved toward the house, a relatively young woman came out to meet them:

'My sister Caroline,' Herschel said as he introduced her, 'my indispensable collaborator.'

Before Herschel introduced her, George's first impression of her was wrong. Seeing her approach, he thought she was the astronomer's wife, or maybe his servant and that, either way, she was coming to let them know the meal was indeed ready, and she'd come to invite them in. As he was to find out later, he was far from imagining that Caroline was no mere collaborator of her brother—that is to say, an assistant to help him merely by collecting data—but that in her own right she was an astronomer herself, very talented as well, the first woman in the history of astronomy to discover nebulae and new comets.

'I'll wait for you at the observatory,' she said after greeting them. 'I'm taking notes that can't be interrupted at the moment.'

She left and Herschel asked his two guests to follow him. They entered the living room. After serving them and exchanging some small talk, Herschel, curious and admiring, posed the question that undoubtedly must have tormented him for a long time:

'Tell me, Dr. Haydn, how do you manage to sustain that capability for always creating such rich, new, and original music?'

'I was cut off from the rest of the world, you see,' Haydn responded after some thought, 'no one in my entourage was able to make me doubt myself, so I had to be original.'

'Ah, if it were only that simple!' Herschel cried out. 'In spite of what I wanted, I felt that my music was stagnating, oscillating endlessly between that of Johann Sebastian Bach and yours, without arriving at the richness and grandeur of either one.'

'I liked what you did very much,' Haydn interceded.

'You're very kind, Doctor Haydn, but I know that my music was leaning toward the ordinary. So, in order to be creative I had to look elsewhere.'

'Which is to say?'

'When I read about all the marvelous things one could discover with a telescope, I became so excited that I wanted to see the heavens and the planets through one of those instruments with my own eyes and, why not, discover something new. Knowing how to look is an art as well, an art to be cultivated, just like music, you know.'

'And how did you manage to get ahead of all those professional astronomers?' Haydn asked.

'Very simply,' Herschel replied. "My originality stemmed from my ignorance. Professional astronomers, as you call them, whether they be in London or Paris, are all obsessed with applying mathematics to the movement of the planets in the solar system. For that they need precise measurements. Therefore, in the realm of instruments, they favor precision rather than power. As a result, they've forgotten to observe the universe of stars beyond our solar system. I, on the other hand, have worked to augment the power of my telescopes and started to systematically explore the celestial vault in order provide a coherent description of it. Thus I have gradually come to know the great tome of the Creator and arrived at the page of the seventh planet.'

Sitting in his chair, George was drinking in the words of the two doctors who were speaking German, their mother tongue. He was the first to get up when Dr. Herschel finally indicated that they were to leave for the observatory.

At the observatory, Haydn rushed over to the gigantic forty-foot instrument pointing toward the heavens, the largest telescope in the world. Caroline joined them. George, however, went over to the small seven-foot telescope, small but historic, for it was the instrument with which Herschel had discovered Uranus, thereby doubling the size of the solar system that, since Antiquity, had stopped at Saturn. It was also the first time a planet was detected by telescope. He admired his ingenious set-up, a tube inside a frame linked to pulleys activated by a handle, the whole thing mounted on casters, thereby allowing a single person to work it. Seeing the young man in front of the instrument that seemed to mesmerize him, Caroline left her brother and Dr. Haydn and went over to him. George immediately flooded her with questions, which she answered graciously and with patience. To his great delight, he saw her open a drawer and take out one of the registers on which Dr. Herschel recorded his observations. She opened it, turned the pages and showed him a note written on Saturday, 17 March 1781, at eleven o'clock:

Saturday 17th March 1781. 11 h
I looked for the Comet or Nebulous Star
and found that it is a comet, for it
has changed its place.

George couldn't get over it. It was the crucial note, the eureka moment! He read it again: 'I looked for the Comet or Nebulous Star and found that it is a comet, for it has changed its place.'

He put his hand on the page reverently as if he were touching a sacred papyrus; it made Caroline smile. His questions continued, however; and so he learned that Caroline and her brother had also discovered two moons of Uranus they had named Titania and Oberon. Hearing these names, George exclaimed:

'Shakespeare!'

'Yes,' Caroline said amused.

'Midsummer Night's Dream!'

'Yes, indeed, bravo! That is exactly where these names come from. These two moons were like fairy tale characters to us.'

✻

Haydn and Herschel left the large telescope and joined them as they continued their discussion. The astronomer was explaining what he called the 'construction of the heavens', how, thanks to patiently counting the stars night after night for several years, he had, with his sister's collaboration, succeeded in drawing the shape of our galaxy, the Milky

Way. He went over to the same closet from which Caroline had taken a register for George a few minutes before and pulled out another one, opened it and unfolded a large page.

'This is the shape of the Milky Way, Dr. Haydn.'

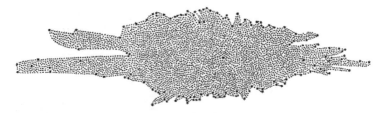

Breathless, George and Haydn looked at the diagram in silence, enthralled. Haydn thought that the drawing had the contour of an island and immediately thought of Kant's Universe Islands, which he suggested in his famous book on the theory of heaven. He asked:

'Do you, like Kant, believe that in the infinite space of the universe other Milky Ways have developed, each one forming a kind of "universe island" among countless others, located at distances that are beyond our imagination?'

'No,' Herschel said categorically. 'I did believe that for a long time, but by scrupulously observing the stars I haven't seen any beyond them. The Milky Way, our galaxy, covers the universe in its entirety, there are no others.'

※

It was deep in the night when George and Dr. Haydn left their hosts. Still under the charm of the celestial universe to which Herschel and his sister had introduced them, they spoke little, listening to the silence and watching with new eyes the myriad of stars shimmering in the sky. The so familiar starry vault seemed even more grandiose and more unfathomable than ever before. Faced with the firmament's infinity, an idea lightly stroked Haydn: what if, despite the great admiration he felt for him, Dr. Herschel was wrong in thinking that the Milky Way, our galaxy, encompassed the entire universe all by itself? For, if he with his large telescope had discovered things no one had seen before, who could be sure that with an even more powerful telescope other galaxies beyond ours might not be discovered? Perhaps Kant was close to the truth with his myriad of island universes. When he finally emerged from his thoughts and his silence, he leaned over to George, addressing him absentmindedly as if he were really talking to himself:

'When I looked through that gigantic telescope and saw all those stars whose existence I never suspected, I was overwhelmed. For several minutes I was unable to say a word. I had the strange impression I was hearing a grand oratorio, the oratorio of the Creation!'

XXXV

Since Haydn's departure no major event had come into George's quiet and comfortable life as an English gentleman, an existence essentially devoted to music and the small pleasures of life at court.

He practiced horseback riding and had become quite skilled but after his fall he'd begun to dread equestrian sports. In contrast to his father, he was not a gambler and rarely frequented horse shows, although the dexterity with which the jockeys drove their horses fascinated him.

On the other hand, he was an excellent dancer and especially fond of a new dance, the waltz. This dance at three-quarter time that originated in Austria, after surpassing the traditional dances at the court in Vienna, then Paris after the Revolution, was now busy conquering London. George liked it because it lacked the solemnity of the minuet and other contradances where, squeezed into their court attire, prim dancers of both genders lined up in two rows, moved around hopping in ridiculous baby steps, from time to time, with bent knees. The only contact these dancers had with their partners was with their hands, which they would momentarily grasp only to immediately let go again. Instead, with the waltz you could wrap your arm around the woman and form a couple, circling around closely together. And when the couple began to whirl around and around, nothing else existed in the world for the young man besides the creature he was carrying off in his enthusiasm, that woman he had to seduce at any cost. The grace with which George waltzed and his special kind of beauty had made him very popular at the balls the prince organized. Every young woman wanted to dance with him; he knew it and had no qualms taking advantage of it. Thus, to those who particularly pleased him he'd suggest he'd give them private lessons, free of charge, which allowed him to engage in many flirtations and even a few affairs.

※

George also continued to be an assiduous reader of newspapers, a habit he'd acquired at a very young age from his father. Of course, he was interested in the news from Austria, Hungary, and Poland, but what really fascinated him were the twists and turns of the French Revolution, the Revolution that had made them flee Paris earlier than planned. Since the columns in the English papers focused chiefly on the commentaries rather than on actual information, George would avidly look for French reviews and each time he located one read it carefully to find out what had happened to the people he'd met in the French capital. In truth, it was difficult for him to follow, for he got his hands on the periodicals in a jumbled way, not in the order of their publication but with a delay of several months and sometimes even of a year or more.

This was how he learned that the Chevalier de Saint-George had ended his stay in London and joined an army corps of men of color created by the Convention, the authority then governing France. He was the leader of a brigade with the rank of colonel. Alexandre Dumas, too, was a member of the same corps but as a company leader. This spectacular reversal stunned George. In fact, he remembered that it was because of this same revolution that Saint-George had fled France, fearing persecution because of his contacts with Queen Marie-Antoinette and the aristocracy. What had disturbed George, too, was that the legion of Saint-George and Dumas was fighting at the Austrian front, in the corner of Europe where he'd spent his childhood and to which he was still quite attached.

As he kept reading, he noted that this revolution, one of whose earliest witnesses he'd been, was getting out of control and with each of its jolts grew even more incomprehensible. Thus, in 1793, the king and especially the queen whom he remembered with such affection had been guillotined within a few months of each other. Although it saddened him, he could understand these executions, since he'd been well aware of the hatred the people of Paris felt for the monarch and his wife when, carried along by the human tide, his father and he had marched on the Bastille despite themselves. What he didn't understand, however, and what pained him deeply, was the execution of Lavoisier, that amiable man who had discovered that the air contained a gas, which he'd named 'oxygen'—even if his English tutor in science and math, with his small town mentality, attributed its earlier discovery to one of his compatriots, Joseph Priestley. It was the same Lavoisier who in the salon of the Marquise de Montesson hadn't hesitated to converse with the little boy he then was, patiently explaining to him that without this gas nothing could burn in air. He was accused of being a 'traitor to the Nation' for reasons that remained obscure to George. And after his sentencing, when he asked for a deferment of his execution so he could finish an experiment he was involved with, the inflexible and narrow-minded President of the Revolutionary Tribunal rejected his request, proclaiming that 'The Republic has no need for scholars or chemists!'

Hearing of the execution, the mathematician Lagrange who, as George recalled. was present at the table of scholars speaking with him during that unforgettable evening, had cried out: 'It took them no more than a moment to cause that head to fall and, perhaps, a hundred years won't be enough to reproduce a man such as he.' George fully agreed with that statement.

He'd only barely gotten over the shock of Lavoisier's execution when he heard of the death of Condorcet, in the prison cell where they'd locked him up. At first, George had trouble grasping the whys and wherefores of these struggles between revolutionaries that were the cause of so many deaths. He truly didn't understand until he managed to unravel the tangle of the hostile factions: two irreconcilable camps confronting each other to the death, one the Girondins and the other the Jacobins, with their allies, the Montagnards. The Girondins were for a constitutional monarchy and a federal, decentralized France. The Jacobins, on the other hand, being more radical, were for a centralized republic, one and indivisible, directed from Paris.

Thus, Condorcet sat at the National Convention as a Girondin deputy. Instigated by a Jacobin deputy, an order for his arrest was declared, but for several months he succeeded in hiding in Paris. Unfortunately, the moment he fled the capital to find refuge in the provinces, he was recognized, arrested, and incarcerated. Two days later, they found him dead in his cell. The year was 1794.

George was profoundly distraught over the death of this courageous man whose book had made such an impression on Frederick de Augustus. How could he forget this scholar's words, which his father had uttered in an emotional voice: 'My friends, although my skin color is different from yours, I have always regarded you as my brothers'?

Taking stock, George realized that 1793 and 1794 had been two years of slaughter: Lavoisier and Condorcet, of course, but also Théroigne de Méricourt and Olympe de Gouges.

In May 1793, Théroigne de Méricourt presented herself at the door to the Convention to attend a session of the Assembly but was prevented by a band of Jacobin women who grabbed her physically, accusing her of being a friend of the Girondins. They ripped off her clothes and, as she stood naked, whipped her savagely in public. She owed her rescue to a Jacobin deputy who was passing by, a certain Marat, but she was so shaken by the event that she went mad. She was locked up at the Salpêtrière Hospital to which her brother had her admitted.

Olympe de Gouges had an even more tragic fate. She was executed one sad morning in November 1793. Before offering her head to the executioner, courageous and rebellious to the end, she cried: 'Children of the Fatherland, you shall avenge my death!'

George was grateful to the editor of the column that reported the execution for having provided numerous details of her life that he hadn't known. So, in reaction to the *Declaration of the Rights of Man and of the Citizen*, written by Lafayette and adopted by the Constituent Assembly, Olympe had written a pastiche she'd entitled *Declaration of the Rights of Woman and the female Citizen*. One of the arguments, oh how prophetic, she'd put forward to demand the rights of women was: 'Woman has the right to step onto the scaffold; she should have an equal right to step onto the tribunal!' But here she was, having failed to step onto the tribunal, she had stepped onto the scaffold.

Closing the periodical, George recalled that wisp of a woman, a dark-haired beauty, sworn opponent of hypocrisy, supporter of the freedom for Blacks and women, formidable pamphleteer fighting every injustice. She'd been condemned to death because she swam against the current of the majority opinion. Challenging the Terror, she'd offered to defend the king and had written a pamphlet in favor of her Girondin friends. Faithful to herself, all the way to the scaffold!

Of the entire group of women he remembered, only Louise-Félicité de Kéralio had come out unscathed: she had voted for the death of the king. On the other hand, he found no news at all of Etta Palm. Nor of Mathilde! Ah, Mathilde, his first kiss, his first love! The last image he had of her was the one his imagination had created while he and his

259

father were fleeing Paris, that of a woman of the people armed with a pitchfork, a tricolored ribbon pinned to her apron, marching intrepidly on Versailles. Yet, he knew that he would never see the name Mathilde in the papers, she was one of the thousands of anonymous women who had also left their mark on the events but whose identities history hadn't retained.

🙦🙤

In February 1800, the day he turned twenty, he was looking for a book in the prince's library and, lost among a pile of English magazines, found a French publication called *Le Moniteur universel*. He was surprised he hadn't found it earlier since he often passed by that shelf. He picked it up gingerly, its yellowed pages indicating it was an old copy and, indeed, it was dated 1794, already six years old. George discovered something he didn't know: The Revolution had put forward a remarkable act, it had proclaimed the liberation of slaves! In fact, on February 4th of that year the Convention had passed a decree stipulating that 'The National Convention declares the abolition of Negro slavery in all the colonies; in consequence it decrees that all men, without distinction of color, residing in the colonies are French citizens and will enjoy all the rights assured by the constitution.' George immediately thought of Olympe de Gouges and Condorcet and bitterly consoled himself with the idea that this decree was their posthumous victory. But he thought of his father above all, for when all was said and done it was his passionate fight against slavery that had been the reason for his expulsion from England. This decree led George to conclude that, despite everything, in some way the French Revolution had remained loyal to the ideals that had engendered it, liberty and equality.

In the last issue of the *Mercure de France* he laid his hands on, George read a piece that made him very happy. Still in their quest to

260

define a unit of universal measure, Lagrange, Monge, Borda, and Condorcet—the article was certainly written before the death of the latter—had finally agreed on a protocol to measure a quarter of the meridian of the earth.

When they were talking with him in the salon of the Marquise, they didn't know yet how they were going to proceed to actually calculate the circumference of the Earth. Apparently, they had found the right answer. The news made him happy because he'd ended up by believing that the Revolution had killed off all the scientific activity he so admired. However, such was not the case, it seemed that it had provided it with a new boost, even if some of the scholars had been decapitated.

Nevertheless, these few encouraging pieces of news were not enough to lessen George's resentment against those who had executed all these people. In any event, he had to such an extent internalized the values and prejudices of the aristocratic milieu in which he lived that the turbulence of this revolution upset him. Every paper he read promoted the idea that it was a threat to the kingdom of England and, reading *Reflections on the Revolution in France*, the highly popular and extremely critical book by Edmund Burke, of which the prince's library had no fewer than four copies, only reinforced his hostility.

In any case, France was currently no longer a kingdom nor a republic, but a country under the direction of someone named Bonaparte, who had proclaimed himself Consul for life and wanted to extend his domination across all of Europe.

XXXVI

G eorge could never have imagined that one soiree, moreover a soiree devoted to hearing songs, was going to irrevocably unleash a
series of fortuitous events that would force him to break out of the
cocoon of conventional ideas in which he was evolving, make him see
things differently, and understand the reasons that had led his father to
change.

Always looking for originality, the Prince of Wales had organized a
soiree specifically for vocal music, a kind of diversion where texts skillfully put to music would alternate with catches and glees. During the
evening, two songs drew his attention, one on a poem of Shakespeare
and the other on a poem by Anacreon. They were composed by a certain
Ignatius Sancho, a name his father had often mentioned when he
embraced the abolitionist cause. George knew that the posthumously
published correspondence of this Ignatius Sancho had enjoyed great
success, but he didn't know the man was also a composer. Apart from
the Chevalier de Saint-George, he knew of no other black composer.
His curiosity peaked, he wanted to find out more about this 'African'
composer who'd put poems by Shakespeare and by a Greek poet of

Antiquity to music. So he decided to acquire his famous correspondence. It was a shock: he discovered that one of the friends of Ignatius Sancho was a writer by the name of Laurence Sterne whom he warmly thanked in his novel for his fierce condemnation of slavery. The novel? *Tristram Shandy!* The book that had triggered the definitive break with his father! By unexpected paths the ghost of Frederick de Augustus was forcefully coming back into his life.

Then an idea began to make its way: perhaps he'd been unfair with his father. He no longer had any doubt that his father had certainly loved him. Suddenly George realized that he'd not understood that all that rage, that violence which had consumed Frederick de Augustus during their final months together was merely the reverse of the feelings he was incapable of expressing. But how, at age eleven, could he have understood all that? If men as well-known as Laurence Sterne were against slavery, perhaps defending the abolitionist cause didn't mean one was disloyal to the United Kingdom of Great Britain and Ireland, as his education at the court of the prince had taught him. Perhaps his father was not the ingrate, much less the traitor, he had thought.

In one of those moments of uncertainty when his thinking was balancing between, on the one hand, loyalty to the monarchy and the defense of privileges— a part of which was owning slaves—and, on the other, sympathy with the abolitionist ideas of his father, an article in the *Morning Chronicle* unnerved him: in Santo Domingo rebelling black slaves had taken complete control of the island under the leadership of a certain Toussaint-Louverture and were preparing to proclaim their independence from France as the English colonies in North America had done. For the first time he didn't agree with the opinion the paper expressed, which urged England to reinforce the security on the plantations in order to prevent any further spread of such revolts. Without being able to explain it, his heart was leaning toward the insurgents. Obviously, he was very careful not to discuss this with anyone else.

One evening, the dance lesson George was giving to a young lady went on longer than expected, and with good reason! It expanded, making room for an exhaustive flirtation. So he came home very late. Thrilled with his evening but at the same time remorseful about the thought of his concert the next day, he decided to work on his score despite the late hour. In the music room he noticed an unfamiliar newspaper on the sofa, probably left behind by one of the musicians passing through, whom the prince loved to invite. He read its title: *Zeitung für die Elegante Welt*. An issue that already dated back several years. He flipped through it, found it was of no interest to him whatsoever, all it talked about was trivialities and gossip about Viennese society personalities whose names meant absolutely nothing to him. He was about to close it when the name Angelo Soliman jumped out at him. Intrigued, he read:

The Negro Angelo Soliman was found dead on 21 November of an apoplectic fit on a street near St. Stephen's Cathedral.

That was all. One line. Stunned, he collapsed on the sofa. The offhand way in which the paper announced this death shocked him profoundly. Dead in the street like a dog! It didn't even say where he was buried. And yet, Soliman was not just anyone in Viennese high society! His 'Uncle' Soliman, his father's friend, a man who had meant so much to him in his childhood. An enormous, deep sadness pervaded him so that it took away any desire to rehearse and he went to his room instead. A feeling of loneliness and isolation, not unlike what he had felt after his father's departure, came over him.

XXXVII

1802! He'd been in England for already thirteen years, eleven of them under the wing of the Prince of Wales. He heard about his mother's illness one day in February. His mother! He had left her when he was nine, now he was twenty-two. Thirteen years since he'd seen her. His brother's letter was alarming: if he waited too long, he might not see her alive again. But, strange as it may seem, the news brought him a kind of solace in the sense that it would give him the opportunity to move away from the prince's court and entourage for a while, a place where he felt his position was becoming increasingly awkward.

The Prince of Wales was more than magnanimous when George asked him for an extended leave. Not only did he offer to pay for his journey, but he also gave him a generous purse to be given to his mother. At the end of their conversation, just as George was about to go out the door, the prince called him back:

'When would you like to leave?' he asked.

'Tomorrow, if possible.'

'Come and see me again before your departure.'

'I would like to, Your Highness, but I'm afraid I won't have time. As you know, the carriages for Calais leave very early in the morning.'

Visibly annoyed the prince was silent for a moment. Then he said in an imperious tone:

'So, do not leave tomorrow! Leave in two days. Come and see me tomorrow afternoon. I will be in Brighton, I will await you there.'

'Yes, Your Highness.'

George was unhappy, but how could he say no to a command?

※

The next day, the Prince of Wales seemed delighted to see him appear. He was waiting for George with Maria Fitzherbert, which was rather unusual. George knew that she was also very fond of him. She had watched over him after his accident with the horse when they'd brought him to the Brighton pavilion to recuperate. She carefully supervised the care he was given and he realized she truly loved him, to the point that she'd remind him at every opportunity, half in jest, half seriously, that she was his second Mama, because just like George's mother, her name was Maria, too.

Still, George was unable to guess what was hiding behind the complicit smiles of Maria Fitzherbert and the prince. They soon brought him to the room where he normally practiced. He was afraid the prince would ask him to play them a last violin piece before his departure, something he really didn't feel up to.

They entered the room. Straightaway George saw an easel on which stood a painting covered with a sheet. In a rather mischievous tone, the prince said:

'Go ahead, lift up the sheet.'

George lifted the fabric and looked at the image he'd uncovered, thunderstruck.

It was his portrait! Yes indeed, the painter Henry Edridge, famous for his painting of Prime Minister William Pitt and of the legendary explorer of West Africa, Mungo Park, had been at the Royal Pavilion several times to do the portrait of the prince's mistress and, taken with George's 'exotic' face, had asked him once or twice to pose for him. However, it had never crossed his mind that those few quick pencil lines on a white sheet of paper would lead to this magnificent portrait. He wanted to speak, to say something, but he was too dumbfounded and nothing came out of his mouth. Maria Fitzherbert said:

'A handsome man, don't you think?'

'I don't know what to say, Your Highnesses. I don't know how to thank you,' George replied, flattered and embarrassed at the same time.

He couldn't take his eyes off the painting. The secret had certainly been well kept. Fascinated, inscribed by the painter at the bottom of the work, he read the words 'Master Bridgetower'. Finally he relaxed and half-smiled. In fact, he was ecstatic.

'I'll take it with me wherever I go.'

'Oh no,' the prince responded in a tone he meant to be solemn but that couldn't conceal a true affection. 'This portrait is staying here, in this room. I won't give it to you until you return.'

'That will induce you to come back soon,' Maria Fitzherbert said.

'Oh, rest assured, Your Highnesses, I will certainly come back.'

'Don't forget to give your mother our wishes for a speedy recovery,' Maria concluded before they let him go.

VIENNA, 1803

XXXVIII

'*Jak wspaniale znowu ciebie zobaczyć, mój chłopcze!*' his mother exclaimed, hugging him tightly as his brother Friedrich watched, bemused.

'Me, too, Mama, I'm so happy to see you again!' George answered in the same language.

He hadn't spoken Polish in more than a decade, but the words were coming back effortlessly.

'*Jak Ty urosłeś!*' she said, holding him at arm's length to get a better look at him after first clasping him very closely against her chest, smiling and weeping at the same time.

'Mother is right,' Friedrich interrupted, repeating his mother's words in German as if George hadn't understood. 'I hardly recognize you! Remember, I was only seven when you and Father left.'

'You, you've grown a lot, too,' George answered, although he was half a head taller than his brother.

Turning to his mother, consciously ignoring her hollow features and her boniness, he said:

'You've hardly changed at all, Mama. Friedrich's letter really frightened me!'

'We wanted you to come as quickly as possible,' Friedrich explained.

'You know, George,' the mother began again, 'sometimes I'm in so much pain that I have trouble standing. When those attacks occur, I can barely walk.'

It had been a long journey, but George had finally arrived. Less than a week after receiving his brother's letter and without taking time to respond, he'd left London in a hurry. When he knocked on their door it was Maria herself, his mother, who opened it, since they had no servants. She uttered a cry of surprise when she realized that this tall, elegantly dressed boy with the mass of curly hair was her son. Hearing his mother cry out, Friedrich, who was practicing his cello, dropped his instrument, came rushing out, and guessed right away that this handsome young man was his brother.

Before his arrival, George had never suspected that his mother and brother's living conditions were so grim. For someone who had spent the better part of his life in princely courts, he discovered they were not eating well, often having just barely enough. In addition to the fact that his mother's dresses were outdated, some were mended and, as he saw it, all of them sufficiently threadbare to be tossed in the garbage. Friedrich's clothes were made of poor quality fabric. Yet, in their letters they'd never complained, except the one time that Friedrich indicated they needed money to have the roof repaired. And it still wasn't fixed. Where it was damaged it was covered with a tarpaulin to keep the rain from coming in. His father had clearly not sent any money and that made George angry with him. He also held it against him that after his banishment from England he'd never gone to Dresden. No one really knew where he was despite the rumors his mother imparted to him, which had been reported to her by one of their acquaintances, a master mariner who traded with the Caribbean. Each year he'd drop anchor in Grande-Saline, a port in Santo Domingo where he'd stock up on sugar, rum, and tobacco. This captain thought he'd heard that Frederick de Augustus had joined the army of Toussaint-Louverture who was linked with the Black forces on the island. He'd even implied that Frederick de Augustus was a lieutenant-general in this army and had changed his name. His mother refused to believe it. She claimed she knew the man she'd married very well: sure, he was a foreigner, he came from far away, was different from most of the people around him, but he was sociable and well-educated. He wanted to be accepted by society and worked so that his sons would be taught to become well-known musicians. That's why he'd left for Paris and London with George, their older boy. Why would he have thrown himself into such a foolish adventure?

George had silently concurred, not wanting to upset his mother. But deep inside he made a far harsher assessment. He knew his father was a gambler, a charmer, a boaster, and unstable, ready to do anything that came into his head. After all, hadn't he abandoned his wife to seek fame and fortune on the roads of Europe? So, all in all it was quite plausible that, once his dreams of recognition and integration had been thwarted, he would have signed up with Toussaint-Louverture, the embodiment of the ideas he'd embraced in London.

In Dresden George focused on the task of improving his family's daily life. Four months later when he accompanied his mother to take the waters, the roof was repaired, Maria had a new wardrobe, as did Friedrich, thanks to the money the Prince of Wales had sent along. They were eating better. They went out as well, to take advantage of the diversions the city offered, which they'd never done before.

※◊※

George had taken his mother to the spa not only because he remembered the virtues of the waters in Bath, but also because he was hoping to give some concerts there to make some money.

Together with Friedrich, they left for Karlsbad. After a short while there, they moved on to Teplitz, a small town halfway between Dresden and Prague where, as George had learned in the interim, the waters were more effective than those in Karlsbad. They spent three weeks there. Their stay was extremely beneficial, not only to Maria's health, but to their finances as well. Both places had wealthy spa visitors. George and Friedrich gave several concerts and these performances yielded enough money for them to stay in the best hotels without having to worry.

※

George was happy to be with his brother again. He discovered he was a fine cellist and playing together brought them so close that a true relationship developed between them, both on stage and in everyday life.

During one of their conversations he asked Friedrich what his dream was. While he expected him to say that he, too, aspired to leaving Dresden and making a name for himself on the great musical stages of London, Paris, and Vienna, his brother's ambition did not go beyond the local area; he wanted to become a member of the Dresden Staatskapelle, the oldest orchestra in Dresden—founded in the sixteenth century—but, above all, the most respected in the entire free State of Saxony. Friedrich even confided to George that he'd be perfectly happy if he could play with them just once in his life. He'd already auditioned one time but had failed the test. But they'd given him to understand that he could try again after working hard for a few years, which is what he was doing. Impressed with his younger brother's determination, George vowed that before his departure he'd do anything to make sure Friedrich's dream would come true.

Still, despite the joy of being back with his mother and brother again, the monotonous life in this city began to weigh upon him rather quickly, its not insignificant musical activity notwithstanding. Not only did he miss the splendor to which he was accustomed in London, but he also felt his musical career wasn't making any headway. He was feeling the call of Vienna more and more. 'In Vienna, everything is music, and music is everywhere, on the throne and under the thatch': these words of Soliman were constantly going through his mind. The more he thought about it, the more he wanted to return to the capital of the Germanic Holy Roman Empire, and as quickly as possible.

London was rich and cosmopolitan, George was lecturing himself; it welcomed the greatest variety of musicians from all over Europe with open arms, but the musical genres there were compartmentalized, coexisting but never truly coming together. Early music on the one hand, modern music on the other. Purcell and Handel face to face with Haydn and Mozart. In Vienna, on the other hand, all these kinds of music and the musicians crossed paths and nurtured one another, as they belonged to the same historical continuity. Haydn and Mozart were the heirs of Bach, Handel, and of all those who had preceded them. They, in turn, could only engender a new generation of musicians that would also invent its own music. What could be more exhilarating than to be enrolled in that process? A musician like George could not resist.

XXXIX

F inally, in the spring of 1803, after a year with his mother and brother, George decided to leave Dresden for Vienna. But first, as he'd promised himself, he insisted on helping Friedrich realize his dream of playing with the Dresden Staatskapelle.

George approached the *Konzertmeister* of the orchestra, whom he knew well and with whom he'd developed a certain friendship. He'd been one of the first public figures to contact George as soon as he heard he was in Dresden—he already knew him by reputation—and immediately invited him to play with the orchestra, which George wholeheartedly accepted.

Therefore George approached the *Konzertmeister* and suggested that, before his departure, they give a special concert. He used some flattery, too—'this orchestra is one of the finest in the world and, believe me, I know what I'm talking about'—as if his fame alone were not enough. Without any hesitation the conductor enthusiastically accepted the idea: a concert featuring the one who, for a decade, had been first violinist of the future king of England, who had played with Haydn in London, the child prodigy who at age nine had made his triumphant debut in Paris, could only enhance the prestige of the Staatskapelle. All that remained to be done was agree on a program.

During the discussions, George managed to have the *Konzertmeister* acknowledge that the Staatskapelle was a little behind where the newest music was concerned, and that it would be good to offer an original program. Not only would it enrich the orchestra, but it would also extend its brilliance beyond Saxony and, why not, turn Dresden into a renowned musical center that would be placed just behind Vienna. After several meetings, they agreed on a completely new program. No Viotti, no Mozart, not even any Haydn. The first part that George suggested would be an homage to the city with works by two of its local musicians, a violin concerto by George and a cello concerto by Friedrich, the two composers also being the soloists, of course. The second part was suggested by the *Konzertmeister*: he wanted to present the very first symphony by a composer never played in Dresden before, but about whom they were talking more and more in Vienna, a certain Ludwig von Beethoven. George knew neither the name nor the work but consented, all too happy that he'd managed to get Friedrich, his little brother, to play with the orchestra of his dreams.

⁂

The concert was a success. The audience's enthusiasm for the Beethoven symphony overshadowed their reaction to the concertos by the Bridgetower brothers, but this didn't offend them. Quite the contrary, they were thrilled to have captivated the public with a previously unknown work, one they'd never played before, which showed a clear recognition of their talent.

When the concert ended, a distinguished-looking gentleman came toward George, visibly delighted.

'Allow me to introduce myself—Joseph Gelinek—and congratulate you. Since its premiere I have never heard this symphony played so beautifully. I am overwhelmed.'

'You attended the premiere?'

'Yes, three years ago, in Vienna. Beethoven conducted it himself.'

'Ah, you're not from Dresden?'

'No, I live and work in Vienna. I'm a pianist and I'm just passing through on my way to Teplitz.'

'I'm planning to leave for Vienna at the end of the month myself.'

'A very good idea. You really must go. I have many friends there. Wait I'll give you a letter of recommendation for one of them, Prince Lichnowsky. He is one of the local patrons, a generous man who'll be able to help you. In fact, he had Beethoven stay with him for a while.'

'So you know Beethoven?'

'Yes, of course. A young composer in his thirties whose reputation is really growing. Prince Lichnowsky had him come from Germany a few years ago to study composition with Haydn and Salieri.'

'Ah, he studied with Haydn? So did I, I was his student, too, and am very proud of that.'

'Not Beethoven! He claims that Haydn didn't teach him anything. What's more, when the maestro suggested he mention "student of Haydn" next to his own name at the bottom of one of his compositions, he refused! An insolent man, I tell you. But a musician who cannot be ignored, alas.'

George didn't understand the meaning of the 'alas' but didn't press Gelinek on this point. After his 'alas' the latter was briefly silent, then began again in a voice where admiration and aversion mingled:

'An incredible pianist. He seems possessed by a demon when he plays.'

'I hope to have the opportunity to hear him when I'm in Vienna. I'm really much obliged to you for your recommendation,' George told him when at the end of their conversation Gelinek wrote a note to the prince and took his leave.

A few days after the memorable concert that had made Friedrich so happy, George said goodbye. Performing with the Staatskapelle seemed to have liberated Friedrich as if by magic. He told George that staying in Dresden was no longer quite so important to him and that he'd be happy to join him in England as soon as circumstances permitted. Indeed, for the two brothers it was a matter of a simple goodbye. But, with a lump in her throat to see her oldest son leave again, Maria made him promise he'd come back to see her before returning to London, and George complied. Thus, on 31 March 1803, leaving his mother with a large part of the money he possessed, he went to Vienna, the city he'd left fourteen years before.

XL

After crossing the Danube and driving for a while, when the carriage was close enough to the city to distinguish its outline George felt a strange sensation of familiarity. The prodigal son was returning home. Surrounded by a wall called the Bastion that, in turn, was surrounded by a vast piece of overgrown land known as the Glacis, from the distance Vienna looked like an island in the middle of an ocean whose waves were made of tall windswept grass.

While the carriage crossed the Glacis, memories of his childhood came back to him. He recalled that large processions and celebrations used to be held on this terrain. Soliman would sometimes take him there and that was a very special treat! He especially liked the military parades, the fairs, and the local dances: the parades because of the panache of the cavalrymen, their brightly colored uniforms, and the military music whose simple lively cadence made him irresistibly want to march as well; the fairs for the sleight of hand the magicians performed, conjuring tricks that both entertained and intrigued him; the local dances because they were so different from the masked balls and well-orchestrated soirees held at Prince Esterhazy's palace. Soliman, who knew everything, had mentioned to him that very long ago, before it became an area for games, celebrations, and parades, the Glacis had served as a bivouac for the Ottoman armies who had besieged and occupied the city in the sixteenth and seventeenth centuries, while the Bastion was built as a defense from their attacks.

The carriage entered the city walls via a gate on the north-east and came into a tangle of narrow streets where tall houses huddled one next to the other; at times the streets curved abruptly, which in the winter resulted in cutting the windy drafts sweeping through them. After a quarter of an hour at a slow trot, the carriage soon left the maze of little streets and took a large avenue. The city's appearance rapidly changed. George now saw wide spaces roll by filled with baroque edifices whose façades looked like theater sets, splendid monuments, luxurious residences, countless churches, all of which gave Vienna its special character.

The journey ended on the large square of St. Stephen's Cathedral. It suited him fine, for the room he'd reserved was on Kärtner Street, quite nearby. He could have gone there on foot were it not for his large trunk, so he was forced to hire the services of a porter.

✼

A few days after his arrival he presented himself at Prince Karl Lichnowsky's. He brought the letter from Gelinek with him as well as a note the Prince of Wales had written on his behalf, which he'd been advised to produce any time he deemed it necessary, a kind of declaration by His Royal Highness recommending him in the most laudatory terms.

When the valet announced him, the prince didn't keep him waiting but asked his servant to bring him in immediately. When George was led into the salon, the prince was there, standing in the doorway. With benign curiosity he watched the unusual visitor draw near, whose face was the color of amber framed by a mass of tight curly hair.

'Mr. George Bridgetower, what a divine surprise!' he said warmly as he extended his hand.

He had him sit across from him in a fine upholstered chair. George was touched by the spontaneity and friendliness with which the prince received him.

'I am deeply honored, my Prince.'

'I was aware that His Royal Highness the Prince of Wales had granted you a leave, but I didn't know it included a visit to Vienna.'

While George looked astonished the prince added:

'You know Johann Hummel, do you not?'

'Yes, of course, we gave several concerts together in London.'

'Hummel has been recruited by the new Prince Esterhazy to assume the post made available by the death of our dear maestro Haydn. On his way to Eisenstadt he spent several days here and gave two concerts under my patronage. He's the one who spoke to me of you.'

'Indeed,' George said, as if to confirm the prince's words, 'I asked for a leave to visit my mother in Dresden. Once there, I couldn't resist the temptation of Vienna.'

'That's good, you did well to come,' Prince Lichnowsky said.

George was flattered that the prince had heard about him and that his name, and maybe even his reputation, had preceded him. He decided not to make too much of it and not to produce the note from His Royal Highness, and so he only took out Gelinek's letter, which he handed to the prince.

'Gelinek!' the prince exclaimed when he saw the signature. 'So he is in Dresden?'

'Merely passing through. He was on his way to Teplitz and strongly counseled me to go to Vienna.'

'Once again, you did well to come here. Paris discovered you, London consecrated you, Vienna will bring you glory if you handle things well.'

He was silent for a moment and watched George whose face was beaming with pleasure. He continued:

'I will help you. I'll start by having you meet Schuppanzigh,' he said as if it was self-evident that everyone knew this man.

George had never heard of him. Prince Lichnowsky noticed and began to provide more details. He explained that Ignaz Schuppanzigh conducted a string quartet in his service. The quartet was well-known for its hitherto unrivaled interpretations of the chamber music of Haydn and Mozart but, most of all, because it gave the first recitals, in stages as they were composed, of the quartets by Ludwig van Beethoven, the prince's protégé.

George reacted promptly when he heard the name.

'I am familiar with Beethoven, I played his *First Symphony* with the Dresden Staatskapelle. Your indebted Gelinek was there. He told me that he's an extraordinary pianist!'

'That dear Gelinek must surely have spoken to you about Steibelt as well?'

'No, not that I remember.'

'Didn't he tell you that Beethoven was as if wholly possessed by the devil when he played the piano?'

'Yes, he did.'

'Well, he keeps repeating that far and wide ever since he attended the musical joust between Beethoven and Steibelt, which left the latter quite humiliated.'

George knew what they were, these jousts: a contest in improvisation between two pianists, each of them supported by an aristocrat. He'd never attended one, but had heard that one of his London instructors, Muzio Clementi, had faced Wolfgang Mozart in such a duel. Mozart had been the victor. In the present case, the prince had of course supported Beethoven, his protégé, so George was interested to hear his account.

'Ah, you should have experienced that moment!' the prince began again. 'Daniel Steibelt was very famous in Paris. He made the public quiver and the ladies swoon with new and almost magical effects,

283

tremolos he created as he prolonged the sounds of the piano by using the two pedals. He was so in demand that in the end he thought of himself as the greatest pianist in the world. Very full of himself, he landed in Vienna one morning with the clear intention of proving that he was the best of all and wouldn't rest until he could measure himself against Beethoven, whom he saw as his only true rival. He wound up challenging him. The duel consisted of improvising on a composition by the opponent that he would see for the first time. Steibelt being the one who'd made the challenge, was the first to begin with a sonata Beethoven had just written. He launched into an affected improvisation, using and abusing the pedals that had become his trademark. The audience gave him thunderous applause. When he stood up after the last note was played, he condescendingly signaled to his adversary he was giving him his place.

Stung to the quick, his eyes darkened, his hair a mess, Beethoven leapt from his chair, grabbed Steibelt's composition in passing, glanced at it disdainfully, and ostentatiously putting it upside down on the music rest, sat down at the piano and began to sight-read it backwards without any difficulty. Then he took one of the composition's themes and, without taking his eyes off Steibelt, launched into a dazzling improvisation that continued for about thirty minutes. Steibelt didn't wait for the end: offended, ridiculed, humiliated, he left the hall despite the repeated calls from Prince Lobkowitz, who was his patron, not to depart. He left Vienna the next day and swore he'd never come back as long as Beethoven was there.

My friend Gelinek, himself an excellent pianist, was there. He came to see me afterwards and, trembling all over, told me: "I've never heard anyone play like that. He improvised in a way I never even heard Mozart himself do it. He performs feats on the piano I would never have dared dream of. It's making me ill. This man is inhabited by Satan." What I forgot to tell you is that a year earlier Gelinek himself, a renowned pianist, had been defeated by Beethoven in a similar duel. Shaken by his unfortunate experience, he decided to stop playing, at least for a while. Thus, he was feeding the secret hope to be present at Beethoven's downfall. The latter's latest victory unnerved him so that he decided to go to the waters to regain his strength and start again.'

While the prince took an obvious pleasure in telling the whole story, George's anxiety was mounting. For the first time he had his doubts: would he succeed in Vienna as Prince Lichnowsky had wished for him? There were so many talented musicians that the competition was rough, and people wouldn't do each other any favors. What he'd just heard was both enlightening and intimidating. Listening to the prince, this Beethoven with his quick temper didn't seem a particularly kind person. He was the type of rival one wouldn't like to find on one's path, apt to ruin the career of a young musician. He was going to have to avoid him.

'Let's get back to Schuppanzigh,' the prince continued, interrupting George's ruminations. 'His quartet will be playing at the palace of one of my good friends, Prince Lobkowitz, next Friday. He's going to interpret a piano sonata by Beethoven, arranged for string quartet. I invite you to come. It will give you a chance to meet Schuppanzigh and possibly play with his quartet and have people get to know you. You will also meet Lobkowitz. That can only be useful, for one cannot succeed in Vienna, or at least begin an artistic career, without a sponsor. Look, since we're talking about him, Beethoven, for example, was barely known when I took him under my wing about ten years ago! And look where he is now! So, come and meet me at Lobkowitz' next Friday, without fail.'

XLI

Standing in front of the tall mirror in the modest room he'd rented upon his arrival so he wouldn't fritter away his money, George slipped on the last piece of his suit, a deep blue morning coat with lapels whose lengthy lapels fell on his hips as they opened. He smoothed it down with his long fingers, more befitting a pianist than a violinist. The morning coat was more relaxed than tails, which is what he wanted. He looked at himself: wide tie loosely knotted, short straight vest, pants tucked into high leather boots, his elegance was completely English. He had carefully retained the precept implanted in him by his father, Frederick de Augustus, that the least he could do was dress with care and make a good impression when invited to a person of quality.

Should he bring his violin or not? He hesitated for a moment, then decided to bring it. As a general rule at this kind of musical soiree, a newcomer was asked to play something, and his subsequent reputation would depend heavily on this first performance. He didn't want to be caught off guard. If he had to play, it would be with his own violin, the instrument the Prince of Wales had given him, which had now been his companion for years.

He was pleased that the Lobkowitz residence wasn't very far from where he was staying, it would save him a ride. After a last glance in the mirror, he went down the three stories separating him from the ground floor and out to Kärtner Street, which led to Augustinestrasse where he turned left. At the intersection of this street with Siegelsgasse he saw the palace of Prince Lobkowitz, a sumptuous building that came at him like the prow of a ship. He stopped for a moment to admire its baroque façade, then looked for the entrance. Prince Lichnowsky happened to be in the vestibule when the servant ushered him in. George was surprised by the absence of Prince Lobkowitz, their host, who should have been welcoming his guests.

Lichnowsky showed him to the concert hall on the second floor; together they went up the red velvet-covered stairs, which opened onto a large room whose splendor rendered George speechless. The guests were already there but the session hadn't yet begun. There weren't many invitees, about twenty or so, ladies in evening gown among them. Very few were in their seats, most of them still standing around in small groups chatting and drinking. Scanning the room, Lichnowsky spotted a man in an armchair, a crutch placed beside his seat. He went over to him, beckoning George to follow him.

'Franz,' Prince Lichnowsky said, 'this is the young man I spoke to you about. George Bridgetower.'

'Ah, it's you. I'm happy to bid you welcome.'

Smiling broadly, the man extended his hand. Lichnowsky continued:

'Mr. Bridgetower, Prince Franz Joseph Maximilian von Lobkowitz.'

'I am deeply honored, Your Highness,' George said.

George now understood why Prince Lobkowitz hadn't awaited his guests in the vestibule: he was disabled.

'I hope we'll have the pleasure of hearing you play this evening,' Prince Lobkowitz said.

George looked at Lichnowsky, who interceded:

'That will depend on Schuppanzigh. Come, I'll introduce him to you before the concert begins,' he said to George.

They went over to the area reserved for the orchestra. One of the musicians was already there, seated with his violin. The man seemed to suffer from a worrisome obesity.

'Ignaz, this is George Bridgetower. He's come to us straight from London where for a very long time he was first violinist with the royal orchestra. I was anxious for you to meet him.'

Then, turning to George:

'Ignaz Schuppanzigh, founder and first violinist of my quartet.'

George bowed:

'Delighted, maestro. I was very anxious to meet you as well.'

Without getting up, Schuppanzigh held out a hand with bulging fingers, bestowing a benevolent smile on him.

'Welcome to you, Mr. Bridgetower. I really hope we shall have time to get to know each other better after the concert.'

'Prince Lobkowitz wants him to perform something for us tonight, doesn't he, Mr. Bridgetower?' Lichnowsky said.

'I would like to, but I did not prepare anything, I'm somewhat taken by surprise…'

'Don't worry about it,' Schuppanzigh reassured him, 'it's a completely informal soiree. We're not at a gala concert, this is simply entertainment among friends.'

'When do we get started?' Lichnowsky asked.

'Very soon,' Schuppanzigh responded. 'Everyone is here, we're only waiting for Ludwig now.'

Lichnowsky repeated the evening's program to George: a transcription of Beethoven's *Seventh Sonata in D Major*, arranged for string quartet by Ferdinand Ries, one of his young pupils.

'While we wait, let's go back to my friend Lobkowitz,' Lichnowsky suggested.

As they were conversing with the still seated Lobkowitz, a man came flying in and without standing on ceremony came right over to them. Short in stature, a determined face, an olive complexion, without a wig, his hair a mess, plainly dressed, he was out of place and yet he seemed completely at ease. George knew right away it was Ludwig van Beethoven.

Lichnowsky allowed the new arrival some time to greet his host, then introduced George.

Among the comments made in Dresden, which George hadn't reported to Lichnowsky so as not to hurt his feelings, Gelinek had described Beethoven as 'a small, ugly, swarthy and gruff man' whom the prince had presumably sent for from Germany. But George found him not to be like the man they had described. Yes, he was short, his face bore scars of smallpox, but there was nothing gruff about him; on the contrary, he had very affectionately shaken Bridgetower's hand and told him with true cordiality how happy he was to meet him. George was relieved and felt an almost spontaneous liking for him. The attraction between them seemed to be reciprocal.

✺

The quartet's performance of the transcribed sonata was remarkable. Even Count Razumovsky, the Russian ambassador at the court of the Holy Empire and the group's sole amateur who played second violin, was excellent. Beethoven himself seemed satisfied. Once again, George wondered if he could hold his own in this city where the musicians were all so excellent. He didn't have much time to think about it as Lichnowsky loudly asked him to play something, with Schuppanzigh's consent, obviously. George graciously agreed, certainly not wanting to make a bad impression by having them beg or, worse, by refusing.

He played a capriccio by Giornovichi that he knew well and he played it brilliantly. When the applause stopped, Beethoven came over to congratulate him, telling him spontaneously how impressed he was. Not expecting such a compliment from this person who they said was poorly behaved and conceited, George was both surprised and intimidated. Something in George seemed to please Beethoven and simultaneously amuse him. Was it because he thought George and he were a special breed, forthright among this fauna of aristocrats who were all so alike? With a gleam of mischief in his eyes, the composer told him: 'Now I'm going to play for you!' using the informal *you* instead of the formal one when addressing George. He went over to the piano, sat down, and after a few arpeggio notes to draw the guests' attention, he enthusiastically began to play a variation in G Major, a classical rondo where the left hand played repeated chords and the right hand an almost staccato melody, all of it *allegro vivace*. He played with his whole body, raised his hands up high while banging the chords, thereby reinforcing the playful side of the piece, which was called *Rage Over a Lost Penny*.

The evening ended pleasantly. Before leaving, Beethoven mentioned to George that he would really like to see him again so they could get to know each other better.

XLII

George woke up in a good mood, still under the spell of the evening spent at Prince Lobkowitz's palace. With the unanticipated ease and cordiality with which he'd been admitted into the inner circle of those who made music come alive and prosper in Vienna, he almost thought he was living a fairy tale. What had most touched him and made him happiest was his meeting with Ludwig van Beethoven. Their spontaneous mutual affinity was least expected of all. He fervently hoped the composer would keep his promise and try to see him again.

By a happy coincidence, the window of his room overlooked a large park sparkling beneath a fine springtime sun. Everything was coming together for the morning to bring him luck.

Not knowing yet what he was going to do with his day, he decided to have breakfast at a café he'd noticed near Stephansplatz. A short walk would do him good. As he went down the stairs, he started to think about the kind of coffee he'd like with his breakfast for, ever since he'd traded hot chocolate for the famous beverage the Turks had introduced, he didn't yet have any preference among the different options the restaurants offered.

After a copious breakfast—he finally decided on a *Schwarzer*, a large black coffee without cream—he spent some time reading the newspapers. He started with the *Wiener Zeitung*, which always devoted many columns to the international news. Thus he learned that the Treaty of Lunéville, which was signed two years earlier and had established a fragile peace between France and Austria after the latter's armies were vanquished, was threatened by Bonaparte in his desperate thirst for conquest. Vienna was no longer safe from attack.

However, the even more distressing news was that Bonaparte had restored slavery, although the Convention of 1794 had abolished it. How could he go back on that achievement, which for George was one of the Revolution's greatest accomplishments? The English, he reflected, were right after all, this Bonaparte was a monster. He thought not only about his father, possibly still fighting in Santo-Domingo, but also about the Chevalier de Saint-George and Alexandre Dumas. He wondered whether those two, men of color like himself, with their black legion, would continue to serve a regime that was explicitly refusing freedom for Blacks.

He finished his reading with the *Zeitung für die Elegante Welt*—in which he'd read of Soliman's death—a paper made up primarily of miscellaneous bits and lightweight articles, more in accord with the spirit of the city where people felt the need to escape in search of pleasure, indubitably so they wouldn't have to think about the upheavals shaking up Europe. It was a good thing he did, for his eye fell on an already old, completely unexpected obituary of Etta Palm, more precisely of 'Etta Palm the spy of the French' as the article labeled her. Calling her a spy intrigued George but, as he continued reading, he understood what was involved. The paper had devoted more space to the death of Etta Palm than to that of Soliman, providing countless details, which he eagerly read. She'd left Paris and returned to the Netherlands, her country, in 1792. However, in 1795, when the Dutch patriots rose up and created the Batavian Republic and the French Revolutionary troops subsequently invaded the country to place the new republic under its supervision, Etta Palm sided with the invaders. She was arrested, accused of being paid by the French, and incarcerated in a fortress in The Hague. She died only a few months after she was set free, her health having seriously deteriorated under the harsh conditions of her years in prison.

George folded the newspaper again. For a moment he closed his eyes, remembering the easy-going, attractive woman, candidly engaging his father and himself in a conversation during the premiere of a symphony by the Chevalier de Saint-George at the Monsieur Theater. He recalled how proud she'd been to tell them she'd written a small work, *Discourse on the Injustice of the Laws in Favor of Men, at the Expense of Women.*

George concluded bitterly that the women of the Revolution he'd met in Paris, at least those who'd stood tall to loudly and clearly demand their equality with men, had suffered tragic fates. Why? he wondered. He couldn't find an acceptable answer. He got up, put the papers back on the rack, and left.

Since it was a beautiful day, he decided not to return to his room right away. He wandered around Stephansplatz in the center of which stood Saint-Stephen's Cathedral, whose Gothic style differed remarkably from the area's baroque buildings. When his gaze fell on the tall tower dominating the church, old memories came flooding into his mind: when his father and he had newly arrived in Vienna, Soliman had urged them to climb up it, for, he told them, there was no more magnificent view of the city than from the top of the famous tower. He had taken them there and, after a tough ascent of three hundred steps, a glorious panorama lay before their eyes. Once they were back down and moving away, Frederick de Augustus had turned around to admire the cathedral again and, incapable of abandoning his obsession, had exclaimed: 'George, just think, this is the church where Wolfgang Amadeus married his beautiful Constance!' Soliman had been careful not to mention what George would find out later, that he, too, had married his wife Magdalena in the same cathedral but that a clause had been added to their marriage contract: 'At the Archbishop's request, it is forbidden to disclose this marriage.' Was it out of fear of irritating Vienna's upper classes, which wouldn't look favorably upon this lady from the Strasbourg nobility being wed to a 'Moor', a lady who, furthermore, was the sister of General François Kellerman, very famous since he'd brought revolutionary France its first great victory by crushing the Prussian army at Valmy?

He finally left Stephansplatz and took Kärtnerstrasse back home.

He'd only just closed the door when someone knocked. Not expecting anyone, he wondered who it might be. The landlord perhaps? But he'd paid the room's rent in advance.

He opened the door. Saying he was surprised was an understatement. The person before him was none other than Ferdinand Ries, Beethoven's student, the author of the quartet arrangement of the sonata played the previous evening. He'd spoken with him a little, of course, but not to the extent that would spur him on to a visit the next day. Intrigued, George held out his hand and warmly invited him in. Ries seemed even younger than his nineteen years, maybe because of the timid smile that lit up his face:

'I have a letter for you from *Herr* Beethoven.'

'A… a letter for me? From Beethoven?' George stammered.

'Yes. Please, here it is.'

He handed George the letter and added:

'Please excuse me, but I must leave. I'm expected somewhere and I'm already late.'

George thanked him and saw him to the door. Once he was alone, he stared at the letter for a moment then opened it excitedly. He read:

To George Polgreen Brischdauer
May 1803
Please be so kind as to meet me at half past one at the Café Taroni

in Graben. We shall then go to the home of Countess Guicciardi where
you have been invited to dinner.
Beethoven

George was amazed and at the same time extremely flattered. He
hadn't expected Beethoven to contact him so quickly. Not only had he
kept his promise, but he must have spoken about him to his acquaintances in sufficiently favorable terms for a countess, who had never met
him, to invite him to dinner. How could they describe such a generous
man as irascible and misanthropic? As he folded the letter again, he
noticed a small detail that amused him: Beethoven had spelled his name
'Brischdauer', the way he pronounced it in his Rhineland accent.

❧

The large square in Graben was familiar to him. When they were living
in Vienna, his father would sometimes take him along to have something to eat in one of the many taverns, just to please him. George loved
the two fountains at each end of the square but hated the Plague Column that had been erected in the center to celebrate the end of the
epidemic that quite a long time ago had ravaged the city. When he was
a child the statue of the witch who symbolized the Plague used to ter-
rify him. The Café Taroni wasn't unknown to him either—he had a
memory of enjoying a delicious hot chocolate there—and he recognized it as soon as the carriage stopped.

Beethoven wasn't there. George realized he was early and waited for
him. As he was looking for a place to sit, the young man at the counter
came toward him and, without even asking whether he was indeed
George Brischdauer, said he had a message for him. For the waiter, the
first dark-skinned customer to enter his establishment could only be the
Brischdauer they had described to him and for whom he was waiting.

Beethoven had changed their meeting place at the last moment. He was now waiting at the *Weissen Schwan*, the White Swan. The irony of the situation was that the new address was on Kärtnerstrasse, his street. He was not put out by having made the long trek to Graben for nothing and hurried to find a carriage. Throughout the ride he was cursing the traffic congestion, which was slowing them down.

When they reached Neuer Markt, the district of the new market, the congestion was so bad that he preferred going the rest of the way on foot. He wasn't very far now, anyway. He walked to the Donnerbrunnen Fountain, in passing noticing the statues around it, allegories of the Danube's tributaries. Soliman had told them that the sculptor had originally created them as nudes but since the empress found them indecent, she had them removed and replaced. He continued on his way and, soon after passing the Capuchin Church where the Habsburgs were buried, a few more steps brought him to 42 Kärtnerstrasse, where he was expected.

He spotted Beethoven as soon as he came in. Two bottles of red wine, one already empty, stood on the table. Another man whom George didn't know was with him. The composer noticed him as he approached and said in a cheerful voice:

'Look, here's the young man we're waiting for!'

He was wearing the same clothes as the night before. From his thick black hair, which didn't seem to have been touched by a comb recently, escaped a few locks falling onto a bumpy forehead in a fringe like that of Titus.[1] The raw daylight displayed a detail that George hadn't noticed in the soft sheen of the chandeliers, a dimple on the right side of his chin. Turning to his companion, Beethoven said:

'This is the remarkable Brischdauer I told you about.'

The man, small and rigid, had white hair and was visibly much older. Apparently myopic, he placed thick spectacles on his nose before extending his hand to George.

---

1.   Titus is the son of Rembrandt. (Tr.'s note)

'Nikolaus Zmeskall von Domanovecs, counsellor of Hungary in Vienna and an excellent cellist. He is my indispensable friend, my 'utility' friend as I jokingly like to call him,' Beethoven continued. 'Without him I cannot write a single note!'

George wasn't sure what Beethoven meant. Was he making fun of Zmeskall? Seeing his confused look, the composer smiled and said:

'Look what he brought me.'

He took a pencil box from his pocket and opened it. Several well sharpened goose quills were neatly arranged inside.

'You see, I'm too clumsy to sharpen my quills, so he does it for me,' he explained. 'You see why I'm fond of him? But have a seat!'

George sat down. Nikolaus Zmeskall who until then had watched him in silence suddenly addressed him in Hungarian, as if memories were coming back to him and he wanted to test a hypothesis:

'Ön Maure fia, aki az eisenstadt Eszterházy palotában dolgozott?'

'Igen, miért,' George replied.

Not knowing one word of this language, Beethoven seemed at first surprised. But when Zmeskall wanted to continue the conversation in Magyar, he interrupted him, annoyed:

'Just speak German, for God's sake!' he exclaimed.

Zmeskall apologized, like a child caught red-handed. George sensed he was very careful not to upset the composer and was ready to accept anything from him.

'I was asking him if he wasn't the son of the Moor who used to work for Prince Nikolaus Esterhazy. I remember that when I was on a mission in Eisenstadt, the prince had a black page who was present at every ceremony.'

'And so?'

'He told me that, yes, that Moor was indeed his father.'

'Ah,' Beethoven said, looking at Zmeskall with an ironic smile. 'Do you know what they called me in Bonn when I was young? "The little black Spaniard". Do you know why, Baron Zmeskall? Because of my brown-black skin. For those people I had to have a Moorish ancestor. Someone, somewhere in my ancestry had black blood!'

He watched the face Zmeskall was making, not knowing how to react, and with a malicious smile he retorted:

'You see, Zmeskall, I, too, am black! Don't you think I look a little like George?'

To hide his embarrassment Zmeskall took off his spectacles and began to clean the thick lenses, almost like magnifying glasses. As for George, he was amused to see that the Hungarian diplomat didn't realize Beethoven was pulling his leg, although George himself had briefly wondered whether there wasn't some truth in what the composer was saying, since he'd said it with such conviction. George explained Zmeskall's embarrassment to himself as coming from the obsessive fear that nobles at European courts felt of having any black blood in their genealogy. He remembered Queen Charlotte whom they found ugly because of her Vandal and Moorish ancestors. He was very happy that Beethoven had so wittily turned this prejudice into mockery. Without any transition, pointing at the glass he'd poured for him, Beethoven told George:

'Go on, join us and taste this robust wine from the Vienna hillsides! It's an authentic *heuriger*!'

Beethoven raised his crystal glass. Zmeskall and George followed suit. George wasn't a wine lover and grimaced as he swallowed the first sip. He thought the beverage was harsh and slightly acid. His expression amused Beethoven:

'The *heuriger* here is always a bit green. To appreciate it better you should add some lead salt to sweeten it.'

He hadn't finished speaking yet when he glanced toward the door and exclaimed:

'Look, a surprise, there's *milord* Falstaff!'

George followed his gaze and saw Schuppanzigh's massive

silhouette. His extreme corpulence was, indeed, reminiscent of Shakespeare's buffoon. He joined them and sat down breathing heavily, delivered from the torture of having to move about. Beethoven seemed in a really good mood, perhaps helped a little by the *heuriger* of which he rapidly emptied another glass:

'I had an idea when I saw you come in,' he told Schuppanzigh. 'I'm going to write a piece I will call *In Praise of the Fat One*! Just for you!'

He was dominating the conversation and, despite the cutting remarks he kept making in their direction, Zmeskall and Schuppanzigh listened without any protest.

When Zmeskall said he had to leave because of an urgent obligation at the chancellery, Beethoven told him he'd let him know when he was about to use his last goose quill and would be running out. As he watched him put on his coat and adjust his glasses, the composer, suddenly inspired, said:

'You know that sometimes I, too, use glasses? I'm going to write a little piece for viola and cello, *Duet with 2 Obligato Eyeglasses!*'

Zmeskall thought it was a very comical idea:

'Yes, that would be really funny. We'll play it together with *In Praise of the Fat One!*'

This time George couldn't help laughing out loud. Watching Zmeskall leave, he wondered what other services the diplomat-baron could be performing for Beethoven in their ostensibly strange relationship.

Schuppanzigh had brought some pages of the score of a new Beethoven quartet that he was rehearsing for the next concert. He wasn't expected, but he needed to see Beethoven right away to discuss a few passages in the piece. He'd gone to his house first but not finding him there went looking for him in the places they were inclined to frequent. Before coming here, he'd started at the *Schwarzen Kamel*, a restaurant and wine bar close to the Graben, then to the Café Taroni. Had he not found him here he would have continued his search at the Restaurant Jahn. He pulled out one of the pages of the first movement and showed Beethoven an annotated passage: 'Look,' he said, 'there are some insurmountable difficulties here that can't be played. This needs to be rewritten or at least simplified...'

Never did George expect the scene that followed. Without warning, the composer's good mood vanished. Furious, with a darkened look, he shouted: 'Do you think I worry about your catguts when inspiration calls on me? No one touches my music! You will play it the way I wrote it!' He grabbed the sheets and threw them at Schuppanzigh. 'Don't bother me with this again!' 'I thought that...,' Schuppanzigh began. 'No, don't. You're not to think!' Beethoven cut him off. Schuppanzigh got up laboriously, picked up his bundle of pages, turned around, and went away without another word.

Schuppanzigh was barely gone when Beethoven was overcome with regret.

'I was hateful, wasn't I? Make no mistake, Schuppanzigh is an extraordinary musician. Not only do I regard him very highly, but he is indispensable to me as well. No one interprets my quartets the way he does. I'm going to have to apologize to him.'

There was plenty to be confused about in this behavior. Schuppanzigh and Zmeskall were not merely very fine musicians who appreciated and defended Beethoven's music, but they were also friends, whose company he loved and with whom he shared meals and good wine. Close friends in a way. And yet, Beethoven didn't always treat them properly. How hard it must be to be the composer's friend, George thought.

They were now alone, having an amiable conversation. Beethoven found George's career quite interesting; he was different and talented, his company was unlike that of the Viennese whom he considered superficial, people who could only think about drinking, laughing, and dancing. He promised to introduce and recommend him to the art patrons in the city and, to suit his action to his word, he took a letter from his pocket and handed it to George:

'For Baron Wetzlar, an extremely wealthy man and a patron of musicians. Meeting him will be well worth your while.'

George thanked him:

'I am truly touched by the friendship you are showing me.'

Beethoven looked at him, rummaged through one of his pockets, took out a pair of glasses he rarely wore, put them on his nose, and looked at George again:

'Do you know why I like you? Because we are both Black, but in addition you are handsome!'

He put the glasses back in his pocket and stood up.

It was time to go to the Countess Guicciardi.

※

As he went home after dinner, George's curiosity got the better of him; he wanted to know what was in the letter Beethoven had given him. He opened the unsealed envelope. The length of the missive, whose handwriting wasn't always easy to decipher, surprised him. He began to read:

To Baron Alexander Wetzlar von Plankenstern
Vienna, from my home, 18 May 1803
Although we have never spoken, I am nevertheless taking the liberty of recommending to you the bearer of this missive, Mr. Brischdauer, as a very skillful virtuoso and a complete master of his instrument—besides his concertos he also plays remarkable quartets. I heartily bid you to provide him with many other connections. He has already had the benefit of being noticed by Lobkowitz, Fries, and all the other distinguished music lovers.

I believe it wouldn't be bad at all if you brought him to Thérèse

Schönfeld's, where, if I am not mistaken, many friends come together, or else at your place. I know that you will be grateful to me for having introduced him to you.

My very best wishes to you, my dear Baron.

Your most devoted Beethoven.

George refolded the letter. He no longer had any doubt, Beethoven was a good and generous man.

XLIII

The evening at the home of Countess Guicciardi had further deepened their relationship. Beyond a mutual liking, it soon turned into a true friendship that comprised an affection that didn't appear in the bond Beethoven had with all the others, even with Zmeskall or Schuppanzigh. Beethoven had imposed George on his circle of friends. During the months of April and May of 1803 they became inseparable. Not a day went by that they weren't together, either at a musical soiree at the home of an aristocrat, in one of the cafés or taverns Beethoven was accustomed to frequent, or else simply on a long walk in Vienna and its surroundings. George had joined the circle that gravitated around the composer and whose diversity impressed him: musicians from all walks of life, princes and patrons ready to munificently open their purses for him. At first, afraid he'd forget their names, he amused himself by making a list. In the column 'Musicians and other chums', he noted: Ignaz Schuppanzigh, Ferdinand Ries, Karl Czerny, Anton Schindler, Domenico Dragonetti, Wenzel Krumpholz; under 'Princes, counts, and barons' he wrote: Nikolaus von Zmeskall, Karl von Lichnowsky, Joseph Franz von Lobkowitz, Andreï Razoumovsky... Then, as new faces appeared and others quickly disappeared, he quit.

One thing astonished him, however, which was the unfailing loyalty of a small circle of friends regardless of the contemptuous way in which Beethoven sometimes treated them. At times he would call them his 'utility friends' and heap sarcastic remarks on them. For instance, not only did Zmeskall sharpen his quills for him, but he also performed a myriad of everyday tasks that Beethoven couldn't handle. Ries often played the role of errand boy, and, even though he was always the first to play his quartets, Schuppanzigh was a persistent target of the composer's ridicule. George was a little taken aback to hear Beethoven ask Zmeskall to find him a domestic servant, and then have Ludwig confide to him somewhat cynically: 'A friend is valuable only by what he can do for me.' So, what role am I performing for him? George thought, not without some apprehension.

Cheerful, jovial, and full of life one moment, then suddenly enraged about a word that displeased him or that he felt was inappropriate, with angry explosions immediately followed by remorse, which then drove him to write letters of apology—that was Beethoven. George had also noticed that, in contrast to the musicians of Haydn's generation who saw themselves as indebted to the princes who employed them, Beethoven brazenly displayed his independence. In his eyes, talent prevailed over the rank one held in society. He'd told George that in music school one didn't learn, one fought! And Ries had even reported to him that once, during one of his famous rages, Beethoven had addressed Prince Lichnowsky, who had after all welcomed him to Vienna, lodged, fed, and subsidized him, with these words: 'Prince, what you are, you are by the chance of your birth. What I am, I am by my own doing. There are, and there will always be, thousands of princes. There is only one Beethoven!'

Until now, however, things couldn't be going any better with George. Beyond the amiable companionship they had, an almost fraternal relationship of older to younger brother had developed, between a composer and confirmed musician and a younger one, gifted and already quite brilliant, but still finding his way. It seemed that Beethoven had found something intangible in George that he himself couldn't define, but that was assuredly lacking in his other human relationships.

✠

Coming back from breakfast, which he usually had in one of the cafés on Stephansplatz, George found a letter slipped under his door. Checking the envelope he knew right away that it came from Beethoven, for who else would write his name as 'Brischdauer'? He read:

> *To George Polgreen Brischdauer*
> *Come today at noon, my dear B., to the residence of Count Deym,*
> *which is where we were together the day before yesterday. They may*
> *want to hear you play one of your own pieces. You decide. I cannot be*
> *there before half past one and, as I wait, I'll simply enjoy the thought*
> *of seeing you today.*
> *Your friend,*
> *Beethoven.*

George smiled. Count Deym was none other than the husband of Susanna Guicciardi, the countess who had invited them to dinner shortly after they'd met. He was smiling because at that dinner he'd discovered something: Beethoven looked as if he was in love. Not with the countess but with her daughter Giulietta. He'd guessed it immediately when he saw how Beethoven was looking at the young girl with the dark blue eyes and the pretty little face surrounded by a halo of dark brown curls. Any doubt he may have had disappeared when, simpering, she asked Beethoven to do her a favor and play *her* sonata for her— which is how George learned he had written her a sonata—and Beethoven, who could be so rebellious, went meekly to the piano although all the guests had already stood up to bid farewell, some even putting on their coats, others their gloves or their hats. Nobody dared move when the first notes sounded, so that everyone listened in silence while they stood. The meditative melancholy tinged with sadness of the first movement's *adagio sostenuto*, the ethereal grace of the *allegretto* of the second, and the furious restlessness of the final *presto agitato* balanced each other in a perfect ensemble that moved George profoundly.

As the days went by, their intimacy grew to the point where Beethoven allowed George to become his confidant. Thus, during one of their conversations, when George came back to the sonata dedicated to Giulietta to praise its excellence once again, Beethoven couldn't hold back and said:

'I am in love with her!'

George had noticed how the composer had looked at her lovingly that first evening at Countess Guicciardi's home. For the first time Beethoven was talking like a smitten adolescent.

'How long have you been in love with her?' George inquired.

'For two years already. Ever since the first piano lesson I gave her.'

'Ah, she was your pupil?'

'Yes. When I entered the music room where she was waiting for me at the piano, I was instantly struck by her beauty, so different from most women here: a true Mediterranean beauty! You know, she's from Trieste. When I took her hand to help her place her fingers on the keyboard correctly, I couldn't stop myself from trembling. And when she raised her head and looked at me with those big eyes, it was the coup de grace, I was lost.'

'Do you know at least if she loves you as well?'

'Oh yes, I'm almost sure of it. When I dedicated this sonata to her, the *Sonata no. 14*, which is my Opus 27, No. 2, she gave me a miniature.'

He had it on him. He opened the small case. George held the ivory miniature and studied it. The portrait resembled Giulietta, pretty with her dark brown curls and her plunging neckline but, a remarkable fact, the artist had also caught what he, George, had observed as well when he met the young woman, that look that, without quite knowing why, he'd found slightly shifty, and distrusted.

'She's beautiful, isn't she?' Beethoven said.

'Eh, yes,' George replied. 'But you know, Ludwig, beauty isn't everything and...'

'Yes,' Beethoven interrupted, 'she also has the grace that goes hand in hand with beauty. Just as in music where...'

He kept on talking. He was idealizing her, attributing virtues and feelings to her that George didn't see. He felt as if, at thirty-three and nine years his senior, such a greatly admired musician as Ludwig was, in matters of the heart, his junior. With the experience of his love affairs in London, George placed Giulietta in the category of flirts who played with, and exploited, their charms. However, he said nothing about what he was thinking and when Beethoven finished extolling Giulietta's virtues he simply asked:

'Do you think she'd be prepared to marry you?'

For the first time George sensed his friend was somewhat hesitant: 'I know she loves me.'

After some silence, he added in a toneless voice:

'But will her parents let their daughter become the wife of a *van*?'

George didn't immediately understand. Only later did he discover that Beethoven, madly in love, had put aside his contempt for titles of nobility and tried to have Giulietta's parents believe that the *van* of his Batavian ancestors was the equivalent of the Germanic aristocratic article *von*. Yes, indeed, when it was in his interest Ludwig could forego his principles and make compromises. The love life of his friend and mentor was complex and paradoxical. There were countless, attractive young women who admired his musical genius and he was constantly infatuated with this one or that one. However, not one of them had really fallen for him, not so far at least. And it was even said that one of them, a certain Magdalena Willmann, had viciously sent him packing by snarling at him that he was 'ugly and half crazy'. George wondered if Giulietta, the current beloved, would prove to be any different.

Be that as it may, he was happy with the thought of being invited again to Countess Deym and find his friend there.

✺

As planned, his hosts asked him to play, and he gladly complied with their wishes. They applauded when he suggested he play two pieces rather than just one as they had requested. The first was a piece for solo violin, the same one he'd played in London at his first public appearance during the intermission of the *Messiah*. The second was a rondo he had composed, which ended with a dizzying *prestissimo*. It was warmly received. Beethoven, who arrived just in time to hear him play, was full of praise. After all, in a way wasn't George his protégé? In an excellent mood, following upon George's last notes, he sat down at the piano and improvised a capriccio, full of humor, which he announced as a 'musical portrait of a scatterbrained friend, George Brischdauer'. Then, quite spontaneously, George joined him with his violin and under general rejoicing the two agreed to improvise on a theme by Haydn. At the end of the performance, neither of them knowing who had come up with the idea first, they agreed that Beethoven would write a sonata for violin and piano for George, which they would perform together!

XLIV

The idea of giving a concert with Beethoven stayed with George, it was all he could think about. He had played with Haydn, he was going to play with Beethoven! It wouldn't be a piece that already belonged to the existing repertory, but they would perform music composed for the occasion, a sonata written specifically for him! It was its consecration. In order to highlight the exceptional character of the event, he would rather that the concert be held at a public venue instead of a private salon as was customary with a new piece.

To his great disappointment he discovered that, despite its rich musical life, Vienna, strictly speaking, had no concert halls, contrary to London and Paris. The only possibility, he was told, was to rent a theater on a day that the house was dark, or else a restaurant with a large room such as the Restaurant Jahn, with which he was quite familiar. It had a ballroom that was also used for concerts. Furthermore, Mozart had played there in his time, as had Beethoven. The problem was that it was too small for the event he envisioned and the ceiling not high enough for a violin to create all its effects.

Not knowing quite what to do, George confided in Schuppanzigh, unaware that in addition to Prince Lichnowsky's quartet he also conducted the public concerts held in Augarten Park. Schuppanzigh quite naturally offered to add it to one of the already scheduled programs of a *Morgenkonzerte* given in the park's great pavilion. George clearly remembered those: once, when he was a child, his father and Soliman had taken him there to hear Wolfgang play.

✠

As many others in the composer's entourage, George had discovered that Beethoven tended to procrastinate and had the habit of working simultaneously on several pieces as well. For these reasons he tried to raise the topic every time he could. Finally, convinced they needed to set a deadline if Beethoven was to finish, he managed to get him to agree to a firm commitment for Sunday, 22 May 1803. He immediately notified Schuppanzigh of this.

Yet the days went by. Two weeks before the agreed upon date George was seriously worried. If he didn't receive the score very soon, he wouldn't have the time needed to rehearse and bring himself up to the level of the pianist against whom he was going to be measured, Beethoven himself. Hence he absolutely had to find a way to make him finish his composition.

The occasion presented itself about ten days before the date set. Beethoven had invited him on one of his daily walks. In fact, the composer was used to walking every day, no matter what the weather. When he felt like it, he would go around the city not once but twice. He would often walk alone, dressed in an ill-fitting frock coat or a large black overcoat, the pocket bulging with a newspaper or a thick notebook. He'd walk at a brisk pace, his head forward, determined, deeply absorbed in his thoughts. He'd stop suddenly, take the notebook from his pocket, start scribbling feverishly, then go off again at the same pace.

Still, sometimes he'd invite a friend to accompany him and his behavior would radically change; instead of the solitary walker deep in thought, he would become an eloquent man, discussing his reading, his philosophical convictions. And sharing his reflections on life and the world around him.

Since it was public knowledge that Beethoven very frequently changed his address, sometimes living between two apartments, George made sure that he hadn't moved yet to the new place Ries had found for him in the Pasqualati house inside the Bastion, but was still living at the Theater an der Wien where the director had offered him gratis accommodations, in return for which he would compose an opera.

The newly constructed Theater an der Wien stood outside the city walls, on the banks of the small Wien River. Since George wasn't entirely sure of its location, he left his place on Kärtnerstreet early to be sure he'd be on time for his appointment.

In fact, he found it easily. A guard pointed out the composer's apartment to him. He knocked on the door and was surprised to see it opened by Beethoven himself, in dressing gown and bare feet. He obviously wasn't ready. He invited George into the living room and asked him to wait while he changed.

George was stunned by the disorder that reigned in the room: manuscripts and books piled up everywhere, the leftovers of a cold meal on the table together with two half-empty bottles of wine, dirty clothes tossed on a sofa. Near the window stood two pianos, one of which had no legs. On a small stool in the center of the room was a coffeepot, which reminded George that Zmeskall had told him Beethoven liked to make his own coffee with precisely sixty grains. He wondered how the composer could concentrate and write in such a mess.

Beethoven suggested an unusual route for their walk. They went along the small stream for which the theater was named, then crossed the Glacis in the direction of the big wooded park of the Prater. Needless to say, they were chatting the entire time. Beethoven tended to speak loudly as if George didn't hear him very well and, conversely, quite often asked him to repeat a sentence he hadn't really caught, or requested that he articulate more carefully.

They began their conversation with small talk but gradually, without noticing, slipped into more personal things. They discovered their childhood had in some ways been similar: fathers who, suspecting their talent, had forced them to practice furiously at ungodly hours, had passed them off as younger than they really were the better to exploit them, and had squandered the family's money, one on gambling, the other on alcohol. Then they spoke of what they loved outside of music, their reading in particular. Beethoven was surprised to hear George say that Shakespeare was one of his favorite authors, unaware he'd been given an English education and that characters such as Othello, Hamlet, Falstaff, and Macbeth were part of his intellectual universe. Beethoven loved Shakespeare, too, and told George that one day he might write music for one of the playwright's themes. George was not familiar with the three German writers Beethoven mentioned— Goethe, Schiller, and Kant—except for the last one on account of his theory on the 'universe-islands' that Haydn had discussed with the astronomer Herschel.

When they reached the Prater they were surrounded by nature and, although not far from the city, without a trace of any other humans. The twittering of birds overshadowed every other sound around. After a few steps, Beethoven stopped. For a moment he stood motionless, deeply engrossed. Then he raised his eyes to the treetops, lowered his head and, sweeping the nearby vegetation with his glance, began to walk again. George thought the maestro had stopped to savor the birds' song more carefully and, to show he was in tune with him, said:

'It is magnificent, isn't it, the singing of these birds? Although I don't know much about them, I recognized the song of a tree finch among all that twittering.'

Beethoven looked at him as if he didn't really understand what he was talking about.

'What singing of birds? What finch?' he asked.

George realized his companion hadn't heard a thing. Embarrassed, he tried to make amends.

'Eh, I meant that what nature offers us is magnificent, birdsong, the sound of the wind, trees, flowers...'

'Ah,' Beethoven said, 'you have no idea how happy it makes me to wander around among trees, grass, and rocks.'

He noticed a large flat rock on the side of the path, went over to it, sat down, and took out his notebook. He scribbled some signs that looked like music notes and a few words next to them. Sitting beside him, not wanting to be indiscreet, George was careful not to look at what the composer was writing.

The latter raised his head and looked at his young friend.

'I promise you, I prefer a tree to a man!'

He was quiet for a moment, then said confidentially:

'I'm going to confess something to you, George. Exactly a year ago I was in the worst possible state: my ears were buzzing, my stomach was causing me terrible pain. Worse yet, I was disgusted with people's treachery. I was utterly depressed. Living no longer made any sense to me, I was ready to leave this world. What saved me was that I left Vienna and settled in a little village, Heiligenstadt, in the middle of nowhere. I was alone with the trees, brooks, vineyards, rocks, and when the weather was good, I could see the Carpathian Mountains in the distance. Suddenly I came alive again! How could I've been thinking, even for a moment, of leaving this world before giving it everything I felt budding inside me? I came back reinvigorated, ready to take destiny by the throat. Since that time my music is more than music. It's a message I transmit to the world, a message of peace, brotherhood, and liberty. It must make the fire of the human spirit surge forth. That's what nature brought me.'

He put the notebook back in his pocket and got up. As for George, he had never really appreciated nature. Yes, in England he'd gone hunting a few times, but for him it had been more of an athletic and social endeavor than an opportunity to contemplate the landscape. He'd spent his entire life in cities and palaces. All he'd retained from his father's stories about nature in Barbados was the hostile end: the mind-numbing sun coming down on the plantation workers, the lethal traps the forest held for fugitives, the tropical tornados that would sweep away everything in their passing. He'd never thought nature had soothing qualities, or even any healing power.

They continued their stroll, now heading toward the city. In half an hour they would reach the Bastion walls and their walk would come to an end. It was time for George to broach his concern without, however, giving Beethoven the impression he was badgering him. Tactfully he asked:

'If I may be so bold, the notes you wrote in your notebook just now, were they on nature or on music?'

'Music, of course!' Beethoven answered. 'Everything we feel ends up in music: love, joy, sadness, beauty. Music is a higher revelation than any wisdom or philosophy.'

George felt that at last he'd reached the moment when he could introduce his topic:

'That's how I feel, too. When I play, the violin possesses me and my entire being becomes music. Our concert of 22 May already fills me with happiness.'

'Ah, our concert?' he said as if he no longer remembered it. 'May 22nd, you said?'

'Yes, and that is soon, less than two weeks…'

'I haven't started it yet, not even an outline. After finishing my *Second Symphony* I immediately began on a third, a symphony to celebrate Bonaparte.'

George stopped in his tracks as if struck by a bullet. Stunned, he looked at his companion:

'Bonaparte? A symphony for Bonaparte?'

It was Beethoven's turn to be astonished at Bridgetower's reaction. 'You don't know Bonaparte?' he exclaimed.

Enthusiastically he began to explain. A long story.

From his early youth on, he'd been nurtured by the ideas of the *Aufklärung*, the German Age of Enlightenment. At the university in Bonn, where he was briefly registered in 1789, pamphlets and poems glorifying the French Revolution used to circulate. One of his professors had even translated *La Marseillaise* into German. This drove him to embrace the republican idea with fervor. Once in Vienna, he'd started attending the musical soirees organized at the French Embassy where he would have an important encounter: he met Rodolphe Kreutzer, the greatest and most prominent violinist in Europe, who introduced him to the ambassador, a general by the name of Bernadotte. During their conversation, the latter couldn't stop talking about Bonaparte, his exploits, his victories over feudal monarchs, his dazzling conquest of power. Thus, in his mind Bonaparte had become the savior of the Revolution, the incarnation of his ideals, the visionary man at the head of a fraternal humanity, equal to the great Roman consuls, a secular god come down from Mount Olympus! How else could he celebrate him except by composing a symphony to his glory?

George couldn't get over it. Raised in the innermost circle of English aristocracy, he saw Bonaparte as a usurper, an individual thirsting for dominion, the 'ogre of Europe' as they called him across the Channel. Even worse, and this touched him in a wholly personal way, the man had reestablished slavery, even though the Revolution had abolished it. How could such a person embody liberty?

He listened, said nothing about what he was thinking, not wanting to embark upon a subject that would divert them from his goal. Rather, he preferred going back to a name Beethoven had uttered: Kreutzer!

'I know Kreutzer,' he said. 'I met him in Paris. A great violinist. He was present at my opening performance at the Concert Spirituel and even congratulated me. So he was in Vienna?'

315

'Yes. We played together and I thought he was very good.'

'After Kreutzer, I will be playing with you,' George said. 'I hope you'll find me very good as well,' he added jokingly.

'I don't doubt it for a moment. I tell you this in all sincerity, you are the only violinist I know on Kreutzer's level.'

George was touched by this spontaneous praise. He didn't react to the compliment and said:

'Since you haven't started writing our sonata yet, perhaps if we postpone the concert by one or two days that will give you time to finish it.'

'Good idea. Let's postpone the concert by two days. That will give me enough time.'

'Good. So May 24th then. Let's hope it won't pose a problem for Schuppanzigh's programming.'

George was pleased. He'd gotten what he wanted, a firm date.

XLV

The day after his walk with George, Beethoven put aside his work on the 'Bonaparte' symphony to finally tackle the sonata for violin and piano he'd promised his young friend. Time was of the essence, there were only ten days left before the event was to take place. He would have to write it very rapidly, which was not his custom. While Mozart was well-known for his ability to conceive of an entire work in his head, even while playing pool, and to write scores in one sitting almost without deletions, this was not the case for Beethoven. Composing was a never-ending battle for him: first he'd jot down outlines based on the notes he'd taken on a pad here and there, which he'd subsequently copy and correct, then—once the piece was completed—he would still make one revision after another before he reached the form he considered acceptable.

The sonata he planned to compose had the unique trait of being intended for a specific individual: *George*. He had previously dedicated pieces to benefactors and musician friends, but he'd never had them in mind while he was writing. The music he composed was created for itself, for its intrinsic beauty, not for any recipient. Thus, for example, the three first trios for piano, violin, and cello that he had dedicated to Lichnowsky might just as well have been dedicated to Lobkowitz without changing a single note. Two of his friends, Wenzel Krumpholz and Johann Punto, had already asked him to write sonatas for them, one for mandolin and the other for horn. But when he composed them, it was their instruments he had in mind rather than the sponsors.

This time it was different, he was writing *for* George, the unparalleled violinist. The sonata would have to be on a par with his talent, with technical demands that only he was able to achieve. Consequently, his piano part had to comply with the same demands. Unlike the classical sonatas that favored one instrument over another, here he had to establish a vigorous dialogue between two equal virtuosi, almost like a concerto where the pianist would take the place of the orchestra.

Suddenly he remembered that, at the time, he had found the final *allegro* of his *Sonata in A Major*, Opus 30, No. 1, dedicated to Alexander I of Russia a year earlier, had been too brilliant for the piece, enough to unbalance it. He then thought of replacing it with an *allegretto* more in the sonata's spirit. He could readily see that finale, a jubilant and exuberant tarantella, as the one for the new sonata. There was his third movement. Now all he needed to do was compose the first two.

He'd always believed that the finale of a work should reflect the density and intensity of the first movement. This time he would have to work backwards, so that the first movement would match the third.

A few months before, he'd drafted a few notes for a projected sonata that he hadn't finished. He'd put them aside and forgotten about them. He picked them up and, driven by the same energy and passion that animated him for his 'Bonaparte' symphony, he worked very quickly. He finished the first movement in four days and was happy with it: a brief solemn a*dagio sostenuto* introduction in which the violin and the piano played one after the other, preparing the listener for the joust of the two musicians who would then mercilessly confront each other in a dazzling *presto*, as if to snatch away each other's right to speak.

On 22 May, two days before the concert, George had received nothing from Beethoven. Nervous at the thought of appearing at the concert without any rehearsal, a concert he considered the most important one of his life, which the musical elite of Vienna would attend, he decided to go to the Theater an der Wien to try and put some pressure on the composer; George knew very well that he could be extremely unpleasant when someone disturbed him during his work, but he had no other choice.

All went well. Beethoven was in a nightshirt busy counting his grains of coffee. To George's great disappointment, he was told after a brief conversation that only two movements were ready, the first and the third, but that he was still working on the second one. He promised to hand him the complete score a little later in the day, or else have Ferdinand Ries deliver it to him early the next morning, the day before the concert.

✺

After George left, Beethoven went to work in a frenzy. Truth be told, having finished the first movement, he'd stopped thinking about the sonata completely and had put it aside. New ideas for his third symphony, the 'Bonaparte', had taken possession of him. But now that there were less than forty-eight hours left before the concert, he couldn't procrastinate any longer, he had to get to it and finish this sonata.

Still in his nightshirt, he sat down at the legless piano, which he'd placed directly on a table; this, he claimed, allowed him to feel the vibrations, one way of 'hearing' the music. It was no secret anymore that gradually the composer was, indeed, growing hard of hearing.

He began to compose. He wanted the second movement to be in complete contrast with the incandescent energy of the first, a calm and meditative moment before plummeting into the mad whirlwind of the third. He decided on a lyrical, soothing *andante con variazoni*.

The day before the concert he still hadn't finished, but that didn't stop him from taking his daily walk and meeting Zmeskall at the *Weissen Schwan*. Late in the afternoon he went home and back to work. It took him more time than he'd expected, and he finished very late, around midnight. The concert was supposed to begin at eight-thirty in the morning.

At four-thirty in the morning he sent for Ferdinand Ries. Thinking something serious had happened to the maestro—his health occasionally left something to be desired—the latter arrived in all haste. Without even greeting him, Beethoven said:

'Quickly, copy the violin part of the first *allegro*.'

Ries looked at him, bewildered. Beethoven realized he needed to explain:

'It's for the concert with Brischdauer in a few hours at the Augarten. My copyist is already occupied elsewhere.'

He cleared a table that was collapsing under a pile of manuscripts and had Ries sit down. He picked up the score the composer handed to him and, at five o'clock in the morning, began to copy music that had to be premiered in public three and a half hours later!

XLVI

George arrived at the Augarten-Halle, the large pavilion in the park, half an hour before the publicized time. Beethoven wasn't there yet and, alone in the room that was reserved for the musicians, he used the time to look at the score again, which he'd received only shortly before. He'd almost ripped it out of the hands of poor Ries when, a little before six in the morning, he'd showed up at his door, completely out of breath.

Before noticing anything else, George saw that both the piano and the violin parts of the third movement's *presto* were copied perfectly; no surprise there, for they had been written long before. On the other hand, only the violin part of the first movement was copied, while the piano part was merely indicated here and there. As for the second movement, there simply had been no time at all to have it copied. Beethoven had only just finished it as Ries was copying the violin part of the first movement. The composer sent George the very manuscript on which he'd been working and where he'd noted only the violin part with barely any indications for the piano. In short, an altogether rudimentary score.

At last Beethoven arrived. He seemed in a good mood. Scratches on his face were evidence of his having shaved a bit too fast. He took off his old morning coat and greeted George warmly. Noticing the score in his hand he said:

'I see that Ries brought you the manuscript on time.'

'Yes,' George replied. 'I've only had two hours to study it, but I am ready.'

'I knew you'd be ready. You'll see, we are going to astonish them! Well then, my friend, let's go.'

As he entered the hall, George was at first disappointed that it wasn't completely filled, but this didn't last long when he saw that, in addition to the familiar faces of Ries, Czerny, Lobkowitz, Lichnowsky, and Zmeskall, there were notables in the audience to whom he'd never been introduced before, or only very briefly, who were honoring him with their presence. Among them, besides Count Razoumovsky, the Russian ambassador, were Count Wezlar to whom Beethoven had recommended him and whom he'd met only once, the British ambassador and, more surprisingly, young Prince Nikolaus II, the grandson and successor of Nikolaus I Esterhazy, whom George had known when he was living at the Eisenstadt chateau. In any event, a distinguished audience.

✿

Beethoven sat down at the piano. George handed him the only copy of the second movement. After putting it down on the music rest, he turned to George. Their eyes met and for several moments remained fixed on each other, incapable of pulling away, as if held by a force of intense, quasi-erotic attraction. Two partners sharing a secret and preparing to reveal it to the world. George, who now knew him well, recognized Beethoven the provocateur in the light that gleamed in his eyes, the man who had once said to him: 'I do not write for the masses but for cultivated people'. Suddenly he understood what the composer had in mind when he told him, just before entering the hall: 'We are going to astonish them': they were going to present something new to this 'cultivated' audience, something off the beaten track, something that would shatter previous ideas and cause the formal tonal framework of the sonata to explode, the sonata such as Haydn and Mozart had bequeathed it to them.

Finally, Beethoven nodded to him; they could attack.

First George, alone, as special guest, in magnanimous homage from the composer to his friend: a slow introduction, *adagio sostenuto*, solemn and dramatic at the same time. He had never done this for any other of his sonatas. 'Here I am and I'm waiting for you,' the violinist seemed to say. The pianist responded, with equal solemnity. The violin began again, the pianist responded, and so on, two lovers, two rivals, two protagonists seeking each other, feinting, contemplating, hesitant. Then, suddenly, no longer able to contain themselves, came the attack: they threw them-selves into a furious *presto* in which their energy, too long restrained, exploded. With each thrust of the bow it seemed a spray of sparks burst forth from the strings of George's violin. When the first part of the *presto* was repeated, George improvised a cadenza in imitation of that of the piano in the eighteenth measure:

Beethoven looked at him, surprised. Briefly George felt anxious; had he offended the composer, who didn't tolerate that the spirit of his music be distorted and often even wrote the cadenzas he then imposed on the soloists? No, he was wrong. Ecstatic, forgetting he was perform-ing for an audience, Beethoven leapt from his seat, kissed him as he cried out: '*Noch einmal, mein Lieber Bursch!*' 'One more time, my dear boy!' He sat down again, and they repeated the passage. At the end of the movement George had the feeling that the audience, thunderstruck and dazed, was awaiting the continuation with some apprehension.

Still under the effect of the mad stampede of the first movement, the listeners were surprised by the serenity of the second, with its calm soothing *andante con variazoni*. George had placed himself behind Beethoven so he could read the violin part on the single manuscript over his shoulder. Most of the time, Beethoven was improvising as he played and yet they played without any difficulty as if they'd repeatedly rehearsed the piece together. When they finished the movement, part of the audience was so enthusiastic that they asked for it to be encored.

At last, the two instruments attacked the finale. The dialogue started up again just as enthusiastically, an echo of the first movement, but less dramatically and brighter, to the great delight of the public, transported by the irresistible beat of the tarantella.

The two musicians were jubilant. They kissed each other. For them it was a complete success. But to see some of the spectators, upset by the novelty of this sonata, rush to the door to leave the place without a word, it could be said that not everyone had enjoyed the concert. Nevertheless, several of the aristocrats in attendance suggested that they perform the new work at their abode.

The two musicians went to the dressing room to find morning coat and violin case. Beethoven saw the desk near the window and, inspired, suddenly went to it and wrote something on the first page of his manuscript. He had that mischievous smile he displayed when he made puns or teased his friends. Intrigued, George was watching him. Beethoven asked him to come closer:

'Look,' he said. 'I've dedicated it to you.'

George hadn't expected such a sign of esteem at all. So, in Beethoven's eyes he had the same importance as the princes and patrons to whom he had dedicated his works! Deeply moved, he approached and looked at the sheet:

He tried to decipher what was written at the top of the page:

'Sonata mulattica composta per il mulatto Brischdauer, gran pazzo e compositore mulattico', *'Sonata mulattica* composed for the mulatto

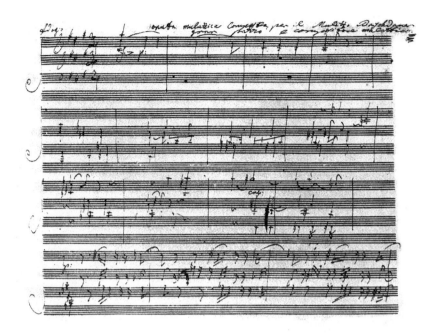

Brischdauer, that crazy man and mulatto composer'! George smiled. He understood now why Beethoven had made that impish face while he was writing the dedication.

'Thank you so much,' George said, extremely moved. 'I am very touched.' He wanted to take the score.

'No, I'm keeping it for now. I'll give it to you after I make some changes.'

'Well, then I won't give you back the tuning fork you lent me until you give me the manuscript.'

'I have many of them. You can keep that one, it's a present.'

'So then I have no bargaining chips left?' George said, pretending to be annoyed.

'Don't worry, I'll give it to you. It's your sonata.'

It was only eleven o'clock when they were ready to leave the Augarten-Halle.

Having gotten up very early without taking time to have breakfast because he was so preoccupied with the concert, George was hungry. He suggested to Beethoven they have a drink before parting. There were plenty of small cafés in the park. Beethoven accepted but proposed they go to Jahn's, known for its cuisine and its wines, rather than some tavern in the park. There was no better place to celebrate their success and their friendship, more solid than ever now. After all, Franz Jahn had been the chef at the Schönbrunn Palace, at the Hapsburgs. George immediately agreed with the plan and they decided to meet up again two hours later at the Restaurant Jahn.

XLVII

The cuisine at Jahn's was equal to its reputation. They were having their second bottle of wine, a vintage from the banks of the Rhine that Beethoven, as connoisseur, had chosen. They were a very happy pair. George was elated about having managed to interpret such a difficult piece so masterfully without any rehearsal and being congratulated for it by Beethoven in public—and what a public!—and also because the sonata had been dedicated to him. He was on cloud nine. He adored Vienna!

'Vienna, what a city!' he couldn't help exclaiming.

'Ah really, you like the Viennese?' Beethoven asked.

'Yes, very much. I would never have dreamed of such a reception.'

'Don't have any illusions about the Viennese. They're a superficial people. As long as you give them beer and sausage, they'll keep quiet.'

George found it a harsh judgment but said nothing, blaming these excessive words on the alcohol.

'In any event, I shall always be grateful to Vienna for having met you and being your friend. Such a warm-hearted friendship!'

He looked at Beethoven with emotion, perhaps intensified a little by the wine. He admired, he loved this man. Beethoven looked at him. George's sincerity moved him. He said:

'I really like you, George. You are handsome and gifted. As I've told you before, since Kreutzer I've never come across a violinist as outstanding as you. Today I will add this: You have a panache in your playing that I've never seen anywhere, not even in Kreutzer! Well now, that deserves a fine champagne!'

He ordered a bottle right away, popped the cork noisily, filled George's glass, then served himself.

'To you, George, to our friendship, to the *Sonata mulattica,* the *Sonata for Brischdauer!*'

Carried away by his enthusiasm, George raised his glass and cried:

'To our enduring friendship, to all our friends!'

'To all our friends,' Beethoven repeated, 'to our patrons, and,' he added mockingly, 'to all those princes who, in truth, are our servants!'

They emptied their glasses and refilled them. Then George went on:

'To our loves, too!'

Then, looking at Beethoven tenderly, he said:

'To Giulietta!'

'Ah, yes, to Giulietta!' Beethoven reiterated, as delighted as George.

'You still love her as much as before?' George asked.

'Of course! Look, I always carry the locket she gave me.'

He took the case from his jacket, opened it and, keeping it in his hand as if he were afraid that George might touch it, he showed him the portrait, then immediately put it back in his pocket. Beethoven had displayed the portrait for only a split second, but that split second was enough for George to feel confirmed in the severe judgment he had already formed of the young woman: everything in that pretty little face attested to affectation, the teasing look, the bewitching smile, the halo of dark little curls framing the face. Inebriated as he was, he neither knew nor was able to control himself and said:

'I'm not sure this little flirt deserves such great love from you.'

Abruptly Beethoven lifted his head, as if emerging pugnaciously from his intoxicated state.

'Who gives you the right to call her a "little flirt"?' he sneered in a sudden fury.

He'd changed radically. The line in the middle of his forehead was deeper, his eyes were flashing. George barely recognized the cheerful companion with whom he'd just been having such a good time.

'I was told...' George mumbled, equally and suddenly sobered up, '...eh... the Count von Gallenberg was seen...'

'That mediocre musician! Do you think Giulietta would leave me for that... for that...'

He was trembling with such rage that he couldn't find the word he was looking for.

'But...,' George wanted to interrupt.

'But what?... Who gives you permission to speak about her this way? You have no right to insinuate anything of any kind where Giulietta is concerned. No one has the right to interfere with our love, not even you!'

'Ludwig, I...'

'That's enough. I never want to see you again! Never!'

He pushed his chair back with such ferocity that it almost fell over. He stood up, knocking the table in such a frenzy that his champagne glass fell and crashed to the floor. He snatched his morning coat off the hook, shouted that everything should be put on his bill, and with his head thrust forward like a bull, stomped out.

XLVIII

At first, George thought Beethoven would soon come around from his anger as happened so often with him. But this was not the case. For the entire week after the break-up, George tried in vain to find an opportunity to reconcile with him. He certainly didn't want to be found unexpectedly in one of the places he knew Beethoven frequented, for fear he'd be the target of a humiliating public rejection. Still, one day he gathered all his courage together and decided to present himself at the Theater an der Wien. Unfortunately, once there, he learned that Beethoven had just moved to Pasqualati's. But he didn't dare venture there.

Waiting for the moment when he could explain himself to Beethoven and put their quarrel behind them, George was spending a great deal of time at his favorite cafés on Stephansplatz. Sometimes he'd buy reviews to take with him when he felt like reading something other than the local press.

That morning he had bought a copy of the *Mercure de France*, already a few years old. He was extremely fond of that journal because of the variety of sections it contained. Here he discovered that the project of the scientists he'd met in Paris had been finished. They had finally realized the universal measurement system of which they had dreamed. They'd called it the 'meter' and established it as equal to one ten-millionth of the length of the earth's meridian along a quadrant. So they had found the means by which to measure the circumference of the Earth! George was thrilled, as if he, too, had completed the project from beginning to end. 'A *unit* which in *its determination* was neither *arbitrary nor* related to *any particular* nation on the *globe*': the commentary accompanying the article clearly reflected what the French scientists of the French Revolution with their love of universality, had wanted. For George, this unity, which also started from the principal of equality of all the world's peoples, attested to human brotherhood as well. Together with the abolition of slavery, he thought, it was one of the most beautiful legacies the Revolution had added to the patrimony of humanity.

After finishing the periodical, he got up to look for his daily *Wiener Zeitung* but then saw a copy of the most recent *Allgemeine Musikalische Zeitung* in the newspaper rack. He took it out at once. Leafing through it, he was pleased to find a review of the new sonata they'd played the previous week at Augarten. He threw himself upon it. What a shock! The critic wrote that Beethoven had 'pushed his concern with originality to the point of the grotesque' and was thereby committing an act of 'musical terrorism'! No less! He continued by saying it was yet another confirmation of a composer's curious whim to always want to be different from the others.

Once his bafflement had lessened, George began to think that this report might serve as a pretext to meet with Beethoven. To that end, he was counting on Ries whom he liked and with whom he'd always felt comfortable, but when he made the suggestion the latter gave him no hope at all. Not only had the composer read the article but through a strange combination of circumstances, he had run into the critic one evening at the *Schwarzen Kamel*. Highly incensed, he'd gone over to him and lashed out with the most insulting thing he could find to say: '*Was ich scheiss eist besser als du je gedacht,*' 'What I shit is a great deal better than anything that will ever come from your pen'! No, he shouldn't nurture any hope to discuss the article with him. Nevertheless, George wasn't ready to give up, he begged Ries to intercede for him with the composer anyway, so that he might receive him or, at least, give him the first page of the sonata with the dedication meant for him, as he had promised.

The response Ries brought him a few days later was devastating. Beethoven wanted to leave Vienna for Paris where he planned to play the premiere of his 'Bonaparte' symphony. He had confided to Ries that, in order to attract the good graces from the Parisian musical circles, he now intended to dedicate the sonata to Kreutzer. George was deeply hurt when he heard this. Thus, the *Sonata mulattica*, which had been composed for him, was going to become the *Kreutzer Sonata*! That is when he realized the break was final, that he had nothing further to expect.

XLIX

E ver since he'd been in Vienna his social life had been confined to the milieu around Beethoven. Now that the composer had put an end to their friendship, George couldn't keep seeing these people as if nothing had happened. He dreaded an unfortunate encounter with Beethoven and his capacity for causing harm. He felt alone, very much alone.

Was there even one person in Vienna whom he'd met through someone other than Beethoven or his circle of friends? He thought of Haydn, of course. But Haydn was old and sick, and after conducting *The Creation* one final time, the last oratorio he'd written right after his return from London and the memorable visit to Herschel, he had retired from musical life and was no longer receiving anyone.

A few years earlier, in London, when he'd learned of Soliman's death in the *Zeitung für die Elegante Welt*, he'd promised himself he would pay his respects at his tomb once he was in Vienna. But until this moment not only had his very full schedule not allowed him to do so, but the promise had faded from his mind. Now that he was at loose ends, he thought of it again and Soliman's memory came back to him acutely.

Angelo Soliman! His father's friend, the masonic brother of Mozart and Haydn! The man whom they said had been the inspiration for the creation of Selim Bassa, the Pasha in *The Abduction from the Seraglio*! The confidant and friend of Emperor Joseph II with whom one could often see him taking a walk in the city! Where in Vienna was he buried?

No one among the people he questioned knew the answer or had even heard of Soliman. The city had left no trace of the man who had been its most famous Negro. Then George remembered that Soliman had not only been a member of *Zur wahren Eintracht*, the Grand Harmony Lodge, but that he'd been its grandmaster. The lodge no longer existed, it had been dissolved, but the guard of the former temple told him that Soliman's body was in the Imperial Natural History Museum. This astonished him. Had they consecrated a special crypt to him because of his fame, his friendship with the emperor? He wanted to go to the tomb of the man who had been such an important part of his childhood.

At the museum they directed him to the 'room of curios'. He couldn't believe his eyes! Angelo Soliman had been stuffed. His skin, stretched over a wooden mold, was embellished with feathers and cowry shells. Two other Blacks surrounded him, a little girl of six and a fully dressed gardener, all of them amid exotic animals that were stuffed as well. Here he was, that distinguished man who, throughout his life, had for these Europeans incarnated the 'perfectibility' of the African as advanced by their philosophers, the 'savage' who, because of education, work, and devotion, had become 'civilized' and so perfectly well integrated that society's elite considered him a peer, that man was now displayed like a typical 'savage', half naked with feathers and shells! George couldn't bear it, it turned his stomach, and he rushed out of the room. He was sorry he had come. He would like to have kept the image of Soliman as the benevolent man who had taken him for walks through the streets of

Vienna, who had brought him to the fairs at the Glacis, who had enchanted him with the fantastic stories he invented for him. The destiny of his father and that of Soliman became superimposed, two Black men repudiated by the society that had lionized them. But then, he himself, what was going to become of him, who was half Black?

In a state of extreme despondency he returned to his apartment on Kärtner Street. He collapsed in his armchair where he remained for a long time, eyes closed, meditating, filled with anxiety and very lonely. When at long last he opened his eyes, his gaze fell on his violin. The sight of the instrument drew him out of his stupor. He rose, picked it up, took it out of its case and caressed it. He felt less alone with this violin that had been with him always and everywhere, and thanks to which he'd become what he was. The great affair of his life, music, recaptured him and made him think of Beethoven again, with whom he'd shared so many intense emotions. With some bitterness he told himself that one ought not to rupture such a friendship on a whim and for such a futile reason. During their walks Beethoven would often proclaim his love for humanity, but by loving humanity too much, had he not ended up by forgetting people?

With his violin in hand, George went over to the window that faced the park. For a moment he looked at the flowers, the trees and their leaves. Summer was approaching. Suddenly a bird entered his field of vision. Rather than alighting, it stopped in its course, flapping its wings in place several times, then whirled around and vanished. George gave a hint of a smile. He would like to have been as light and carefree as that bird, like a musical melody floating in the air. Separations, upheavals, ordeals, in his life he'd known them all. One more adversity wasn't going to stop him.

He raised his violin, wedged it against his chin and began to improvise in minor mode on the themes and variations of the *Sonata mulattica*, the *Sonata à Brischdauer*.

EPILOGUE

Beethoven was indeed planning to settle in Paris during the year 1804 and give the premiere of his 'Bonaparte' symphony. Although already famous in Germany and Austria, he wasn't known in France yet. To win over Kreutzer, professor at the Conservatory, one of the founders of the new French violin school, renowned across Europe, he decided to dedicate the sonata written for Bridgetower to him instead. In a correspondence with his publisher, he speaks in laudatory terms of Kreutzer, a 'fine and charming man', whose simplicity and unaffectedness he praises, as well as his qualities as a virtuoso, while making a barely veiled allusion to George for whom the piece had been composed: 'The sonata having been written for an expert violinist, the dedication suits him all the more.'

However, Rodolphe Kreutzer never played it. Berlioz, who didn't like it, wrote that Kreutzer decided never to play the composition because he found it to be 'outrageously unintelligible'. More technical explanations have been offered, however, by several music critics: presumably Kreutzer had a very *legato* and melodic concept of the violin, somewhat in the Italian style, while this sonata accumulates staccato notes, especially in its finale.

In Paris Beethoven didn't present his 'Bonaparte' symphony either. Ries recounts that when he told Beethoven that Bonaparte had declared himself emperor, the composer loudly vented with disappointment: 'So he is nothing but an ordinary man! Now he's going to trample every human right, he will merely follow his ambition, he will want to rise above everyone else, he'll become a tyrant!' Irately, he tore off the title page that bore Bonaparte's name, ripped it to shreds and threw it away. He rebaptized the work *Sinfonia Eroica, composta per festiggiare il sovenire di un grand'uomo.*

A few years after Beethoven's death, the *Sonata no. 14*, dedicated to Giulietta, became known as the *Moonlight Sonata*.

Angelo Soliman's stuffed body was displayed for fifty-two years in the Imperial Natural History Museum. His daughter Josephine, whose mother Magdalena was the sister of general Kellermann to whom Napoleon gave the title of Duke de Valmy in 1808, pleaded unsuccessfully for her father to be given a sepulcher worthy of him. During the Austrian Revolution of 1848, at the time of the battles taking place in Vienna on 31 October, an incendiary bomb destroyed the museum and the bodies of Soliman and his two companions were reduced to ashes.

The character of Soliman appears in the novel by Robert Musil, *The Man without Qualities.*

As for George, he briefly returned to Eisenstadt, the place of his childhood, then, after a visit to Dresden to say goodbye to his mother and brother, he left Austria. After a short visit to Italy, he returned to England where he lived for the rest of his life. He had a lifelong musical career as violinist, professor of music, and composer. After his mother's death, his brother Friedrich joined him in England where they gave several concerts together. George, who had married and had one daughter, died in London on 20 February 1860 at the age of eighty-one. He is buried at Kensal Green Cemetery.

His portrait by Henry Edridge, reproduced in this book, is at the British Museum.

The *Kreutzer Sonata* inspired Leo Tolstoy, who wrote a short novel by the same name, which in turn inspired the *String Quartet No. 1* by the Czech composer Leoš Janáček, with the same title.

The meeting of Beethoven and Bridgetower also inspired the American poet Rita Dove who published a volume of poetry with the title *Sonata Mulattica: A Life in Five Movements and a Short Play.*

ACKNOWLEDGMENTS

This is a book of historical fiction. The work has taken me several years during which I took courses in music history, and consulted countless texts, documents, and articles. I also visited the important sites where the story takes place, Vienna, Heiligenstadt, the Eisenstadt chateau, Paris, and London.

Needless to say, such an undertaking would have never been accomplished without the help of several individuals. Among these, I should mention Pierre and Evelyne Millet who let me listen to the *Kreutzer Sonata* for the first time and gave me my first CD of the sonata; Barbara and Wolfgang Helbig who presented me with my very first boxed set of the complete symphonies of Beethoven and translated texts for me into and from German; Krisztina Keresztély, Marcel Garbos, José Hoyet, who did the translations into Hungarian, Polish, and Italian, not forgetting Francine and Alain Guida. I will also mention Professor Larry Wallach of *Bard College at Simon's Rock* who welcomed me into his courses on Baroque, Classical, and Romantic Music; I am equally thankful to him for the many conversations we had at his house, and in the cafés and restaurants in Great Barrington, Massachusetts.

My great gratitude goes to Etienne Pfender, violinist with the

Philharmonie de Paris, for his willingness to read and comment on the manuscript, which prevented the non-musician that I am from making countless technical blunders where the art of the violin is concerned; his great knowledge also led me to correct several historical errors. Of course, my gratitude goes to Marie Desmeures of the Éditions Actes Sud, whose remarks as a rigorous publisher constantly pushed me to get back to work to improve the manuscript.

Finally, my thanks go to Christine Salomon who accompanied me in this work by re-reading the manuscript as it progressed, catching clichés and anachronisms.

And I cannot forget the pleasant atmosphere of mornings spent writing in the café *Royal Custine* in Montmartre.

ABOUT THE AUTHOR

 **Emmanuel Dongala**, born 1941, is a Congolese chemist and novelist. He fled to the United States during the civil war in his native country in 1997, and was offered a professorship at Bard College at Simon's Rock where he taught until 2014. He is the author of the novels, *Little Boys Come from The Stars*, and *Johnny Mad Dog*, that has been adapted for film. He lives in Massachusetts.

ABOUT THE TRANSLATOR

Marjolijn de Jager is a translator of both French and Dutch. She has translated three titles for Schaffner Press. Her translation of *Congo, Inc: Bismarck's Testament* (Indiana University Press) was shortlisted for the Best Translated Book Awards in 2019. She lives in Connecticut.